THIS is me...

Sarah Ann Walker

Copyright © Oct 8 2013 Sarah Ann Walker (1)

All rights reserved.

ISBN: 0991723112
ISBN-13: 978-0-9917231-1-9

DEDICATION

To Jakkob

You are the most beautiful soul I have ever known,
And I couldn't love you more if I tried.

You have been the greatest blessing I have ever received
in this crazy little life of mine.

XO
Mommy

CONTENTS

Acknowledgments   i

PROLOGUE   9

TIRED   Pg 11

ASLEEP   Pg 55

NIGHTMARES   Pg 133

AWAKE   Pg 305

ACKNOWLEDGMENTS

To my Husband…
Again, with the perfect book cover. Thank you.
And thank you for helping me disappear into my scary writing world again.

To my Parents
Thank you for your excitement and support once again.
I love that you love me doing this- It helps when I'm totally freaked out.
And a special thanks to my father for buying my first 50 copies *or so…*

To Paola
Once again, you remain my longest, dearest friend, and I adore you.

To Brenda Belanger, my Boston Bruins Beauty,
I thank you for meeting me exactly when my first book came out and for holding my hand this past year with patience and kindness.

To Chris Carmilia of 'Chris' Book Blog Emporium'
Your encouragement with my last book helped me through the dark, dark days of bad reviews. So I thank you, always.

Thank you
Deniro, Rosanna, Jen, Suzy, Sleepy, Carla, BEE, Peggy, Hayley, Julia, Crysti, Jettie, Ada, Drh, Dena, Katica, Gladys, Shanyn, Sam, Tracy, Briana, Jodie, Marg, Tara, Lisa, Deborah, Suzanne, Joan, Shelley, Cori, Megan, Triple M books, and many, many others.

And finally… To **MY** Kaylas
Christina-Hawaii Kayla, Jennifer-New York Kayla, Kimberly-New Jersey Kayla, Monica-Florida Kayla & Stephanie-California Kayla.
You were the first 5 who loved my first novel, and you were the first 5 to tell me I had some talent. And for that encouragement and support I've included a little piece of each of you in this novel so you always know how much I have appreciated your love and support, right from my beginning.
Christina and Kimberly… I thank you, forever.

This journey has been hard, and I've taken some wildly creative criticisms over the past year. But I've also been told I have written an amazing story with so much depth of emotion from some Readers, it allowed me to swallow the handful of negatives for the multitude of positives.
So I thank you, sincerely.
Sarah xo

Sarah Ann Walker

PROLOGUE

"Yes, this is Marcus Anderson. Yes, Suzanne Anderson is my wife. Um, yes, that's right; I'm her next of kin..." Marcus holds his breath as his new reality sets in.

"Oh, god... When?" Marcus whispers.

Walking slowly back into his study, the shaking is so great and walking so hard; Marcus sits down at his desk.

In a moan, he asks, "Where is she?"

Clutching the phone, Marcus stops as the pain sets in. With great restraint and gentle tears, Marcus cries for all that is lost.

"Hi baby, what's up?" Mack sits in his living room, smiling for his Kayla.

"Oh, god... When?" Mack whispers.

Standing slowly, the shaking is so great and standing so hard; Mack drops back down on the couch.

In a moan, he begs, "Where is she?"

Clutching the phone, Mack stops as the anguish sets in. With a pause in breathing, Mack weeps for all that is lost.

"What the *fuck* are you TALKING about?? *WHAT?!*" Stopping, Z can't breathe as his new reality sets in.

"Oh, *god*... When?" Z whispers.

Walking slowly back toward his bedroom, the shaking is so great and walking so hard; Z collapses where he stands in the hall.

In a moan, he cries, "Where is she?"

Laying down on the floor, Z clutches the phone and cries out as his agony sets in. With great sobs and coughing gasps to the unknown, Z screams for all that is lost.

THIS is me...

TIRED

CHAPTER 1

MAY 3

Oh my god, I'm so tired but I'm pretty sure I'm sleeping. How is it even possible to be tired while sleeping? Huh. That's a new one. What's happening to me?

I'm pretty sure I must be asleep. Nothing is moving, and everything is so dark. I can't hear or see, and I can't move or breathe. This has to be a dreamless sleep, and yet I feel kind of awake. What the hell do I do now?

I swear I'm here, but I'm not. I swear I can feel, but I don't. I swear I hear people, but I'm all alone.

Where am I? What have I done?

I hate sleeping. I have *always* hated sleeping which is kind of weird, I think. I mean really, who hates sleeping? Nobody. But I do. I really hate it.

I don't know why, but for as long as I can remember I have hated the lack of control I feel when sleeping. It's like I'm nervous when I sleep, or I'm scared something will happen to me when I'm asleep. Actually, I can't really explain it because I think I just hate sleeping.

Maybe I'm one of those people who can live on very little sleep. Yeah, that's probably it. I'm not weird, or scared, or nervous, I just don't need much sleep when I'm sleeping.

When did that happen? I wonder if I was a bad baby who never slept. I wonder if I was a toddler who never napped. I wonder if I was a teen who never slept till noon on week-ends. Huh. I can almost guarantee that one. As if my parents would have ever let me sleep till noon on a weekend.

Time was much too valuable to waste. Time was almost a commodity in my home. Time is when everything happened. My parents didn't waste a moment of time, so I know they wouldn't have allowed me to waste any of my own time, especially by sleeping.

Maybe I should ask them one day if I ever liked sleeping. Maybe? Ah, maybe I shouldn't. God knows, if I was a colicky baby, my mother would probably still be pissed at me for it. Yeah, I would just remind her that I sucked as a baby, and then she'd treat me like crap until I apologized for *being* a baby. And really, is it worth it to know if I actually ever liked sleeping? Ah, no... Totally not worth it.

Christ! I wish I could wake up though, I'm kind of tired of all this sleep-thinking.

*****

"*Suzanne? Suzanne, I know you can hear me. I know you're here. Please, Suzanne. I need you to wake up now. I need you to open your eyes. Please, Suzanne. It's Mack.*"

I don't think I know that name but I think I know that voice... I think.

"*Suzanne, please. I'm looking at your EEG results, and I can see that you're on your way back. I see it. Suzanne, I'm here and I'm helping you, but I need you to help me too. I need you to wake up now, Suzanne...*"

Do I know this man? Am I still sleeping or am I awake? Ugh... this is so confusing.

"*Suzanne, Chicago Kayla will be here soon. Don't you want to see Kayla? I know your Chicago Kayla wants to see you awake very badly. She's been here every evening to see you. I'm staying with

Chicago Kayla, and I need your help. Chicago Kayla is torturing me just like your New York Kayla does and it's too much for me. Remember you always told me two Kaylas were too much? Well, you were right. I can't handle being alone with two Kaylas anymore. Can you wake up for me now, Suzanne? Can you help me?"

I remember a Kayla, I think.

"Suzanne, I need you to wake up now. It's Mack, and my throat is killing me. I swear I have never spoken so much in my life as I have in these last 2 days. You're killing me here. Could you please wake up now, so I can give my voice a rest? Come on, Suzanne. It's time now. I need you to wake up and I need you to talk to me."

Who the hell is this? God, he seems so familiar to me. But who IS he?

"Suzanne, its Mack. YOUR Mack. Can you hear me, Suzanne? If you can hear me, please just give me a little movement. Just move your fingers a little while I'm watching you. Or, could you open your eyes for me? I would really like you to open your eyes for me- for just a second if you can. You have such beautiful eyes Suzanne, and everyone wants to see them open again. Suzanne, please... I just need a little movement, so I know you're here with me, and then I'll stop talking, I promise."

"Suzanne, Kayla will be here soon, and she'll be all pushy and Kayla-like if you're not awake yet. I KNOW you don't want that. God, I don't want that. So why don't you just wake up for me, and I'll tell Kayla you're awake, and then she'll leave you alone. How does that sound? If you wake up for me now, I'll protect you from your treacherous Chicago Kayla when she gets here. Does that sound good?"

"Please, Suzanne. I need you to wake up now. I miss you, and I really need to talk to you. I'm your person, remember? You can tell me anything, remember? Come on Suzanne, I need you to wake up now. I need you back with me. I miss you very much, and I love you very much, Suzanne."

He loves me? Who the hell IS he? He sounds so nice. But seriously, who the hell is he? Think. Think, dammit.

Shit, I'm so tired; I kinda want him to stop talking for a bit now. I need to sleep quietly, I think. And I hate this dream. It's all weird and depressing and exhausting really. It's like I can't get out of this asleep. I feel trapped in my awake, which is just exhausting in my asleep.

"Please, Suzanne. You have so many things to wake up for. You have so many people who want to see you awake. You have a whole life just waiting for you. But you need to come back now so you can live it."

Oh. This guy sounds so sad now. Ugh. He's making me feel sad now. Well, that's not really fair, is it? It's not like I can tell him to shut-up, because I'm asleep over here. Forget it. I'm done. I'm not listening anymore. Good night...

CHAPTER 2

Suddenly I remember my grandma. Why now? *Why?* I try to never think about her, and I don't want to think about her now. God, I loved her. God, I *miss* her.

My grandma was so sweet and kind. My grandma was such a wonderful, beautiful woman. She wasn't old or creepy when I was little- my grandma was just beautiful. I remember clearly how beautiful she was. I think everyone who ever met her remembers how beautiful she was. I remember always wanting to be beautiful like my grandma, but I *never* was.

Sometimes when I would visit her, I hated my grandfather so much. Well, maybe not hated him so much as *feared* him. My grandfather was stern and cold, and truthfully, just grouchy all the time. He never smiled and he never really spoke to me. He just always seemed so mean and distant, or like he didn't like me or something.

But my grandma was never mean; she was always sweet and kind to me. Whenever my grandfather started on one of his angry fits, my grandma would just 'shush' him, take my hand, and lead me out of the room. She always did that. I forgot about that, but now I remember. My grandma always kept me away from my mean grandfather when he was in his grouchy moods. My grandma always kept me safe from my grouchy grandpa Edward.

My grandma was always nice to me, and my grandma always loved my hair. Oh! She did. I forgot! My grandma *always* loved my hair. She loved my light blonde hair when I was a little girl, and she loved my strawberry blonde hair when I was a bit older. It's funny how I forgot that, but now I remember. My grandma loved my hair.

After my baths my grandma would sit me in front of her gold and mahogany vanity and she would brush my hair dry. It seemed like hours would pass while she told me stories about when she was a little girl. She told me funny, amazing stories while brushing my pretty blonde hair for hours, until it was dry.

Maybe that's why I insist on keeping it long? I don't know, but I can't believe I forgot that. I can't believe I forgot my grandma loved my hair and I can't believe I forgot how many hours she put into brushing my hair dry when I was little.

Most days I wondered why she liked me.

I loved everything about my grandma- I really did. And I especially loved her name. Strangely, my grandma's first name was Thomas. There is some long, funny family story about her father losing a bet the night she was born, and so he had to honor the bet by naming his first child Thomas, regardless if it was a boy or girl. Apparently, my great-grandfather was a man of his word, so when my beautiful grandma was born, she became Thomas Montgomery, to the humor of everyone, grandma Tommy included.

And when my mother had me, my grandfather forced my mother to stick with the family tradition of naming their girls 'boy' names. Not that it was much of a tradition seeing as my mother is Elizabeth, but whatever, maybe it just skipped a generation.

My grandfather made my mother name me after my grandma, Thomas Montgomery-Hampton, and so I was named Thomas Suzanne Beaumont, which I love because of my beautiful grandma Tommy.

I always wanted to be beautiful like my grandma, and I ALWAYS wanted to be called Tommy like my grandma was, but I was never beautiful like her, and I was NEVER called Tommy. God, my mother hated my name even though it was her mother's name.

Of course, my mother wouldn't hear of me being called Tommy. Actually, I don't recall my mother ever calling me by my full name- stopping only at Suzanne Beaumont, even when she was angry at me.

When other kids had their full three, sometimes four names

yelled, or spoken harshly to them by an angry parent, I always felt strange when I heard it- almost sad or something. Just once I wanted my mother to yell 'Thomas Suzanne Beaumont get back here', or 'shut your mouth Thomas Suzanne Beaumont' or whatever it was she yelled at me at the time, but she never did. Never, ever, did I get to hear my full three names yelled at me.

I realize now as an adult it's such a stupid thing to remember or to have cared about. But at the time, I was sad that I couldn't be Thomas or Tommy like my grandma was.

God, I wanted to be just like her when I grew up. I wanted to be beautiful, strong, Tommy, who everybody loved. I wanted to be exactly like my grandma, but I never was. I was always just Suzanne.

I remember when my beautiful, charming, elegant grandma Tommy died, I actually felt heartbroken. I know everyone is sad and maybe even a little desperate when someone they love dies. Maybe a young girl feels extra sad when her grandma dies, but with me, it hurt so bad I couldn't breathe right for months.

I remember crying incessantly. I remember I couldn't stop crying, no matter how many dirty looks I received from my mother. My mother told me I was embarrassing her with all the drama and hysterics. My mother even threatened to have a doctor give me medication to calm me down at the funeral if I didn't stop acting so 'inappropriately'. But I just couldn't stop.

I remember how much I hated my mother during the initial days after my grandma suddenly died. She was just so cold about HER OWN MOTHER! It was shocking to me that she never cried or even looked sad at all about grandma Tommy dying.

I couldn't stop crying from one moment to the next, but my mother didn't even cry once. At least not that I saw. Actually, I'm sure of it because I don't think my mother *can* cry.

Oh! I remember a conversation between my mother and grandfather- that's right! My grandfather asked my mother 'if she was even *bothered* by her mother's death?' I remember my mother laughed and asked, 'why would I be?' I remember my grandfather's pale face and I remember my mother's vicious smile. And that's when I knew my mother could care less that her very own mother was dead.

My beautiful, charming, elegant grandma Tommy was dead, and my mother laughed. Wow! How could I forget that?

Anyway, I was thirteen when she died, and everything seemed to change for me then.

I remember my grandfather wanting me to sit beside him in the front row at the funeral, but my mother refused to let me. And when I tried to protest I received 'the look' from her, and that was it. I didn't say another word.

So I sat beside my mother while hundreds of people talked to her, and sometimes even to my father about the wonderful, charming, stunning Tommy Montgomery-Hampton. My mother smiled and nodded, and even indulged in light laughter about some wonderful thing my grandma did over the years, but NEVER did she cry.

I did though.

Actually once the tears began, I couldn't stop them, no matter what I did, or thought of. I pictured good things and even yummy things, but nothing worked. No matter how hard I tried to stop, I just sat there and cried and cried.

I know I looked ugly, and I KNOW my mother was totally embarrassed by me, but I couldn't stop. I even remember my father leaning over tenderly with a tissue and telling me to 'knock it off' in my ear while smiling at me gently in front of the large crowd of people who attended the funeral. But I just couldn't stop sobbing.

Finally, midway through the ceremony my mother gently placed her hand on my knee to comfort me *I thought*, until slowly I felt her fingernails dig into my skin. Harder and harder she dug her nails into my leg until I could barely breathe from the pain and from the need to cry out.

God, it was such a strange thing to do- hurt someone badly so they cry harder while whispering in their ear, 'stop fucking crying, you fat fucking baby.'

Holy *shit!* I forgot that! My mother swore at me, and squeezed harder and harder into my skin until I gasped out loud, and then she glared at me kind of sideways and removed her hand from my leg. Wow. *That* was messed up.

Anyway, after the ceremony my parents had a huge party, or I guess a 'wake' at my grandparent's house. I remember being so sad in my grandma's house because I didn't know what to do with myself or my tears without her there to comfort me. So I just wandered around until I stopped in my grandma's little solarium at the back of the main floor.

We always loved that room. Well, she loved it first, but then as I got older I loved the solarium too.

My grandma bought and discretely hid a TV for us in a chest near the glass doors, and she and I would sneak inside and watch movies together when my grandfather was out, or otherwise occupied in his study.

It was our little secret, and I cherished it. I loved the fear I felt knowing we could be caught with something as 'common' as a television, but I always knew my grandma would protect me even if my grandfather found out or caught us. But we were never caught and I don't think he ever found out.

God, I loved my grandma Tommy in our solarium during our special secret time together, hidden in the room under big comfy blankets watching funny movies alone.

After a while, I remember the guests began leaving, and I made my way back to the main dining room where food had been laid out. With shaking hands, I picked up a little sandwich, just as I spotted my mother in the corner talking to some of her friends. When we made eye contact she subtly shook her head no at me, and I dropped the sandwich at once.

Seconds later, my grandfather was beside me putting the same sandwich on a small plate for me with his back turned to my mother.

Oh god, I was so scared. My grandfather didn't know about my mother saying no to me I don't think. Or maybe he did know and that's why he turned his back to her. Actually, I'm not sure if he knew, but I DO know I absolutely panicked at the thought of disobeying my mother and having her punish me for it later. I knew my grandfather wouldn't be with me at our house when we returned, when my mother could be really, *really* angry at me. And so I shook my head at my grandfather, refused the little sandwich, and just froze.

Eventually, the room started to spin a little for me, and I remember my grandfather pulling me to his side as I started to breathe all funny.

Within seconds my *concerned* mother was at my side pulling me from his grasp, while telling everyone within hearing distance that I hadn't been feeling well earlier, and that the day had taken its toll on me.

Leading me from the dining room, my mother continued to coddle me until we entered a guest room upstairs. And as soon as we were alone I tried to apologize for the sandwich, but my mother shook her head no again, effectively shutting me up instantly. And then she slapped me across the face. Wham! I was absolutely stunned.

She hit me so hard, I actually fell sideways and backward onto the floor, landing hard on my butt. I couldn't believe how much that slap hurt. And as I grabbed my cheek in my hand, completely shocked, my mother said calmly, 'that's for embarrassing me at the funeral. Expect much, *much* more punishment when we get home for that little near-*fainting* episode.'

And that was it. After she sneered her awful threat she left the room, and I burst into tears again, alone, at my beautiful, charming, elegant grandma Tommy's wake, in her huge, awesome home, which I always loved.

I remember I cried for my grandma that day, but I realize now I cried for me too, because somehow I knew my young life was over when my grandma Tommy left me.

And now I know. I was never beautiful like Tommy, and no one ever thought of me as Tommy, but I wanted to be. I wanted to be just like my grandma. I wanted to be beautiful, strong, lovely Tommy, but I'm not. I'm still just Suzanne.

I wonder why I'm remembering all these things now. What a strange way to dream, or to reminisce, or to feel nostalgic, especially now when I'm sleeping but kind of awake. Weird.

CHAPTER 3

MAY 4

"Suzanne! Wake up right now! Seriously. I don't want to sit here just staring at you anymore 'cause I'm tired of it! Everyone is so fucking tired of it. It's ENOUGH!" What?!
 "Kayla, stop!" What the hell is happening?
 "No, Mack! Suzanne needs to wake up now!"
 "Kayla, Suzanne will come back soon. You need to just-"
 "Fuck that, Mack! Suzanne! I've had it with you! Wake the fuck up! NOW!"
 "Kayla! If you yell at Suzanne one more time, I'll bounce you from this room!"
 "Piss off, Mack! You wouldn't dare."
 "Try me!"
 "Oh, fuck you... I'll call Kayla tonight and see *if* she *lets you bounce me from the room. How'd you like that?"*
 "Kayla, I don't think you want to go there with me- Not right now. Listen, I know you're stressed out, and I know you want Suzanne to wake up, but-"
 "Mack. Don't you dare try to shrink *me right now. I don't need a Shrink. I need Suzanne to Wake. The. Fuck. UP!"*
 Jesus Christ! Why is she so mad at me? What the hell did I do wrong? Honestly. I mean, I'm sleeping here, kind of, and this woman just keeps yelling at me. Yeah, like I'm really gonna wake up for YOU. What a bitch!

"Suzanne, I'm just going to give you a manicure, alright? Yeah, I'm sure you'll like that. You just lie there all relaxed, and I'll paint your nails for you. How does that sound?"

What the hell? Is this woman bi-polar or something? I can't keep up with her words or her moods.
"Kayla, DON'T!"
"It's fine. Shut up, Mack."
"Kayla, I mean it. You're acting very irrationally right now. Can you please talk to me? I would really like to know what's bothering you, besides the obvious of course. Kayla, please- just talk to me."
"I'm fine Mack, honestly. But Suzanne isn't, is she? You're not fine, are you Suzanne? What's the matter SWEETIE, cat got your tongue?" What?! I don't know what the hell this woman is talking about.
"Kayla-"
"Hey, SWEETIE, I'm just going to paint your nails now, okay? Would you like that?"
"Kayla, THAT'S ENOUGH! I know what you're doing, and it's not working. STOP. Now!"
"Suzanne, I'm painting your fingernails now, blood RED! Do you like that?! Awful, bloody, dark RED! Did you hear me? I said your nails are RED, like Whore's RED!" What?!
Oh god, I swear my heart is pounding through my chest. And I feel kind of funny, like scared or desperate or something. What's happening?
"Kayla, stop this. Kayla, look at me. Now, Kayla. Look at me, right now. Look what you're doing to-"
"No, Mack."
"Kayla, NOW! I want you to turn and I want you to look at me, right now."
"No, Mack..."
Oh, now *she* sounds all sad or something. What a Psycho this bitch is.
"Kayla, turn and look at me, right now."
"Mack, I can't."
"Kayla, look at me..."

Oh, now he sounds all sad too. What the hell is going on?
"*I'm so tired, Mack.*"
"*I know. Come here and sit with me.*"
Yeah, take a load off, ya Psycho!

"*Mack... I can't really deal with all this shit anymore.*"
"*Kayla, I'm leaving your apartment in the morning. I'll be out of your apartment, and you can have all your space back. You can have some time to yourself again. My stay was supposed to be only temporary back then.*"
"*That's not it. You're fine. I kinda like torturing you for Kayla. It's just, I'm tired of all the Suzanne* Shit *all the time, you know?*"
"*I understand. And you've been a very kind and generous host, but I'll be settled tomorrow morning into my rental, and you'll have your own space again, and you can take a break from all this for a while. Maybe take a few days for yourself. Maybe you should stay away for a few days. I know how tired you are, and its okay, Kayla. It really is okay to be tired of all this Suzanne shit.*"
What Suzanne shit? What did I do? Who the *hell* is this woman? And why *the hell* is she so mad at me?

In the silence that follows I just try to breathe. I'm not sure what the problem is, but I feel like I should know. I wish to god I could wake up, but I'm just so tired from all this sleeping.

It's like I'm trapped in my body somehow. I feel so awake, but so damn tired. I feel too awake to keep sleeping, but way too tired to wake up.

"*All we do is wait. That's it. We wait and wait. We've spent almost 3 months just waiting, and I can't stop wondering what we're all waiting for? What if it's bad? What if nothing is the same again? What if she really is gone this time?*"
"*Kayla, I honestly don't believe that to be true. I believe she's here just taking her time so she can come back to us fully recovered.*"

"But will she ever be fully recovered? I mean really- look at her."
"I hope so. I believe so Kayla. I think she's going to come back again stronger than ever."
What am I recovering from? What happened to me? God, I wish someone would say one friggin' thing that makes sense for once.

"Do you think I'm a terrible person, Mack? Am I a bitch for being tired of all this- this Suzanne drama all the time?"
"No, I don't think you're a bitch. You're a mean, sadistic, nasty, man-eating woman, but you're definitely not a bitch."
Wow. I think she's laughing. Laughing?! What the hell? Who makes someone laugh by saying such awful things to them? This is just so twisted.
"Thanks, Mack. You're always so nice to me. When you dump the other Kayla, make sure you give me a call, okay?"
"Give me a hug, and go home. You're totally exhausted. But I'll see you later, and I'll be out of your hair in the morning. And by the way, if I ever dump Kayla, another Kayla is the last person I'll be hooking up with. Just an FYI." Is he smiling? He kind of sounds like it.
"Fair enough, Mack."

When there's nothing but silence, I think I kind of exhale. It's weird to be here, but not here. I feel like I'm intruding on these people, though they're here in *my* dream. I don't know them and I don't understand what's happening, but I feel kind of desperate to get away from them.
I wish I could just wake up because I'm really tired of all this shit, too.

"Mack, I really have enjoyed you being around. You're a great guy to live with. Actually, you hold the title of being the only *man I've ever lived with. And though it's only been 2 and a half months, I'm gonna miss your Mackness around my apartment."*

"Kayla, please don't get all soft on me. Crashing at your place for the last 10 weeks has been absolute hell," he laughs. "Go home and relax. I'll see you later."

"I'm sorry about earlier, Mack. I just thought I could scare her awake or something."

"I know exactly what you were trying to do, and it was a good thought. But I don't think scaring Suzanne is the way to get to her. Increasing her heart rate won't bring her back, but at least it IS proof that there's more going on now than there was before. We'll figure this out, and we'll have her back soon. I know it. You have to be patient, Kayla."

"I'm trying... But time is running out."

Times running out for what?

"I know, but I won't stop fighting for her. Just be a little more patient and she'll be back with us soon, okay?"

Where am I?

"Okay. See you later, Mack. Did you want to have Chinese at midnight? You know, our last hurrah or something?"

"Sounds good. I'll call it in and pick it up on my way back to your place. Just go home and relax. I need you to relax, and I need you to stay healthy for me."

"You know Mack... Suzanne was right about you. You really are the most amazing man, certainly, that I've ever known. I'll see you at home. And thanks."

"No problem."

"Um, Suzanne... I'm really sorry. I didn't mean to scare you, or to be mean to you. I just want you to wake up so badly, I sometimes forget to be nice. But I'll see you soon- maybe in a few days. I just need a little break now, and I hope you understand. I've got to go for a few days, but I'll be back soon. I miss you, Suzanne."

When there is only silence I wait for more, and then...

"Jesus, Suzanne. You just couldn't wake up and stop all THAT insanity, could you?"

Ooops, sorry.

CHAPTER 4

MAY 5

Am I awake? Honest to god, I can't figure out what's happening to me. I can hear people talking all the time. I hear that guy talking nonstop, but I'm just so cold and dark and alone.

I can't understand what's happening here. I can't even figure out what I'm doing here. But I feel completely trapped.

It's like I'm in a little crawl space, or maybe in a cave somewhere. It's like I'm a little girl hiding in the dark again, in the little hidden broom closet past the guest bedrooms.

Oh! I remember my hiding spot. I remember staying in there when I was young when my mother would be calling out my name for my punishments.

Ugh, I remember the smell of the closet where I hid. It was so gross in my little girl memory. It was like I was surrounded by lemons AND alcohol or bleach, or something chemical like that. It always smelled so potent and strong in the space where I hid. God, the smell used to burn my eyes and nose when I was little.

The smell would sometimes even stick to my clothes and hair. Sometimes, after leaving my hidden closet I could smell that awful closet stench in my nose for a while, even after I changed my clothes and sprayed perfume on my hair. I know I didn't *actually* smell like lemons and alcohol anymore, but I still smelled it in my nose afterward when I was finally free. It was such a gross smell for me. It used to make me gag, even hours after I left the closet.

God, I remember the little hidden broom closet where I hid. My mother would always pass the little closet on her way to our side of the upstairs; the side with our bedrooms. But sometimes she'd wait there in front of the door, maybe just thinking or waiting for me to surface. I don't actually know why she would just wait there, but she always did.

Maybe she would wait in the hallway for me to show up suddenly because I stupidly thought she'd stopped looking for me... But I never thought that. I *always* knew she was still looking for me, and I never came out. I was never as stupid as she said I was.

I remember sometimes hearing her talk to herself. I remember holding my breath while waiting, almost crying with my fear because I didn't want her to find me. I remember the bad things she would say about me when she didn't know I was in the little closet listening. I remember all her bad words about me, all the time.

And I remember learning what some of those bad words meant afterwards. I used to try to remember what she called me when she was angry, so I could find out later what the words actually meant. I remember so many bad words from my mother, all the time.

It was so sad for me to finally understand the words she called me, especially when I knew they weren't true. I knew I wasn't what she called me, and I knew I didn't do what she said I did. But she would still mumble the bad words about me to herself while I waited in silence, desperate to get free of the stinky, hidden, little broom closet on the guest side of the upstairs.

For years, I remember desperately trying to wait her out. I remember counting for so long, sometimes even counting all the way to five thousand until she stopped waiting for me. I remember once even counting to ten thousand until I stopped hearing her call my name- I was really scared that day. *That* day she was extra angry at me for hiding, and she said lots and lots of bad words about me that weren't true.

And sometimes even my father would call for me when my mother was very angry at me. But again, I just held my breath and waited for him to stop calling for me as well. I never came out of the closet for my father. And I NEVER came out for my mother when she was angry with me.

After a long time, they usually gave up looking for me. Usually, they went away. Usually, I could wait them both out. Usually, if I was real quiet, counting silently in my head, crying silently in the dark, my parents would go away eventually.

Usually, if I was really quiet they would stop looking for me, and I would be safe for a while. Safe from the punishments and safe from all the bad words.

It's funny that I was so afraid of her back then because my mother was just so *small*. She was so skinny all the time; it's like she stopped growing at 12 years old or something. Actually, I remember my mother was always sickly skinny.

Why was I so afraid of her when I was little? Huh. It's kind of weird now, because I think I probably out-weighed her adult body when I was 12 years old myself.

Why did she like looking like that? Who wants to be shaped like a little girl?

My mother was just so skinny and small, and she always wore dark clothes to make herself look even skinnier. She told me I should always wear dark clothes to look skinny because she looked good and she was skinny. She told me we had to be skinny so men liked touching us.

So my mother was super skinny like a little girl, but she had awful wrinkly hands like an old lady. God, my mother's hands and arms were so skinny and bony when I was little, she always looked like a little girl skeleton to me. I didn't know why she wanted to be that skinny. I didn't know why she wanted her bones to push out of her skin, but that's what she wanted, so that's what they did.

I remember when she bushed my hair when I was young I hated seeing her hands touch me through the mirror. My mother would hum quietly while staring at my eyes through the mirror, just as *I* watched through the mirror her lovely face while she hummed and brushed my hair.

I remember always closing my eyes during this quiet time with her, and I remember my mother always kissing the back of my head once my eyes were finally closed.

I think she thought I liked her brushing my hair when I was little, but I really didn't. My mother's skinny skeleton hands scared me so badly I used to have to try very hard not to shake from my fear of them.

I remember always waiting for my mother to put the brush down and wrap her tiny, bony hands around my throat. I remember thinking her gross, bony hands would slowly work their way around my throat, gently closing, tighter and tighter, until I stopped breathing altogether.

Sometimes, I just *hoped* I would stop breathing, so I wasn't afraid anymore. But I never stopped breathing, and I've *never* stopped being afraid of her.

I don't know why I remember my mother always liked brushing my hair. It's so strange to remember now but after our baths together she would dress me quickly so she could begin brushing my hair dry. I think that was the only time my mother seemed kind of nice to me. Well, as long as I didn't look at her awful skeleton hands, she seemed kind of nice to me.

But the rest of the time my mother was just a mean little girl-sized skeleton, whose hands looked like they wanted to wrap slowly around my throat, gently closing, tighter and tighter until I stopped breathing finally.

I wonder why I don't hear her in my dream. Has she finally stopped looking for me?

*****

"Suzanne, its Z. Can you hear me, love? Can you open your eyes for me, please? I'm so desperate to see your eyes on me. God, Suzanne, I miss you so much. Can you please wake up for me now? I know you're here and I know you're coming back to me, but could you please try to come back now, Suzanne? Could you please try to wake up for me?"

I don't know this man. And he's not the same man as before- the Mack. I know I don't know this man. How does he know me? Oh, shit! Am I *still* sleeping?

"Suzanne, New York Kayla is going to be here any minute now and she's feisty as hell today. Do you really want to piss off your New York Kayla? Come on Suzanne. It's time."

Time for what? Who are these people? Where's Marcus?

"Suzanne, I can't stay here much longer today but I'd really like you to wake up for me now. We have so much to talk about. We have so many things to discuss, and I can't do anything if you don't wake up for me. Open your eyes, love. Mack is here with you and New York Kayla is coming soon, and we all just want you to wake up so we can talk to you. Please, love? Please wake up for me."

I don't know you, and I don't think I can wake up. Where's Marcus?

"Suzanne, its Z. I'm still here with you. I've been here every day, waiting for you to come back to me. I've left New York and I'm waiting here for you. We're all waiting for you, love. Could you please wake up now?"

Who's waiting? Where's Marcus?

"Suzanne, I love you so much and I'm so sad without you. Everything just hurts so badly without you, and I'm so tired of living like this. I'll wait forever if I have to, but I'm begging you, Suzanne- I need you to wake up for me. I know you're coming back, Mack told me, but could you please hurry up, love? Please, Suzanne... I'm so lost," he moans.

Wow. This is so weird. I have NO idea who this guy is, but his sadness is like, on my skin and inside me or something. It's like I can feel his words when he speaks them. His words wash all over my skin, and they make me feel sad for him. His voice is so dark, and his words are so sad, and I feel terrible for him.

"Z, I'll stay with her, but you really have to go now."
"I know, Mack. I'll just stay a few more minutes with her."
"Z. You have to go now. If you're caught here, it may be another setback for me."
"Mack, please. I just need a few more minutes with her."
"Z- I know you're desperate to stay with her but this is going to only hurt the situation. Please leave for now. Go back to your apartment and call me from there."
"Mack, I can't leave her today. I just can't. Today feels... different."

Oh, wow. Is this guy crying?

"Listen to me Z. Z! Look at me. I'll care for her, but you have to leave now. You have to. I'll care for Suzanne and I won't leave her today, I promise. But please, for Suzanne's sake, get out of here now. If Marcus sees you I don't know if I can change his mind."

Marcus?!

"Okay. I'm sorry."
"Z, you never have to be sorry. I know how much you love her, and I know how desperate you are to care for her. If I could, I would place her in your care, believe me I would. But I can't. So I'm asking you to leave FOR Suzanne, just for now. Just for today."

He loves *me*? Am I HER? Who the hell IS he?

"I know... I'm leaving. It just hurts so bad some days, and there's never any time. I never have the time-"
"Z, I want you to call my cell the minute you leave here. I'll place my cell on speakerphone beside Suzanne, okay? You can talk to her when we're in the clear, okay? Please leave now, but call me soon. I'll be waiting for your call."
"Okay. Bye, Suzanne. I'll be back as soon as I can. I love you, sweetheart. Please wake up soon. Please, love."

When there is only silence, I feel myself falling again. I can't stand this feeling. I think I'm awake, but I'm totally asleep too. This is such a strange, like, suspended feeling. My body doesn't really feel anything at all, and my head kind of hears these people, but I don't know what I'm listening to. I can't actually understand them at all.

I feel like I'm watching a movie with the sound down low, but with my eyes wide open. When these people talk I hear bits of what they're saying, but I can't make out the whole conversation so I can't understand them.

Maybe if I could see them, I would know what they're saying. Maybe if I could see their faces, I would know who they are and what they want from me. Maybe... But I just don't know how to wake up.

CHAPTER 5

"Hi Marcus. Have you been here long?"
Marcus! Marcus is here?
"Hey, Kayla. No, I've only been here a few minutes. Mack just left to give me a little privacy with her. How was your flight?"
"Good. My flight was good, Marcus."
"That's good."
This is kind of weird. Marcus sounds the same but different. I wish I could ask him what the hell is going on. Where are my parents? I don't think I've heard my mother at all.

"Kayla, please don't look at me like that. I know you hate me. I know everyone hates me. I know Mack hates me, and the other Kayla hates me. And I know HE hates me. I know it, but I can't change that. I WON'T change that."
Marcus? Why would anyone hate Marcus? He's *Marcus*.
"I actually don't hate you, Marcus. I just hate what you've done, though sadly, I can almost understand it. I know you love Suzanne, but what you're doing is wrong. You're lying to everyone Marcus, and you're lying to yourself the most."
Holy shit! What's he done?
"It's NOT a lie, Kayla. Suzanne loves me, she told me. I know she loves me. She told me she loves me, and I know she does."
"Marcus, Suzanne DOES love you, but not like that. Not anymore."
"Yes, she does. You don't know Suzanne..."
"Actually, I-"
"NO YOU DON'T! I know Suzanne, and I know what she wants and needs. You have only known her a couple months, but I've known her forever. And she's my wife!"

"I've known Suzanne at her worst, which translates into years, Marcus."

Who the hell are you? Why are you talking to my husband like that? I wish I could yell at this woman because she doesn't know me, but Marcus does! He's right. He knows me more than anyone does.

"Kayla, I have known and loved Suzanne for 2 lifetimes. I know when she's messed up, and I know when she's happy. Suzanne has been the only person I've ever truly known and loved my whole life, and I know she would want this. I know she would want me to do this. She told me once."

"Marcus, you're wrong. Please... please *just listen to me for a minute."*

"I can't."

"Marcus, I'm *begging you to just hear me out."*

"It's all the same, Kayla. Every one of you say the same things over and over again. It never changes, but I want it to change. I know what she wants; she told me a long time ago what she wanted. I know Suzanne. And I know what I have to do."

Wow! I think Marcus is crying.

"Please, Marcus. Please, listen to me."

Holy SHIT! I think this woman is crying too. What the hell is going on? Why does everyone cry all the time?

"Talk Kayla. Go ahead. Get it off your chest."

"Marcus, please don't kill Suzanne." WHAT?!

"Wow. That was a low blow, Kayla. Even for you."

"It's not a low blow. That's what you're doing. You're killing her."

"I am NOT killing her. She's gone. She's not here anymore. This is not HER! You KNOW that!"

"I don't know that and neither do you. Mack showed you the MRI results and the head Neurologist showed you the latest scans and the latest test results. And Dr. Carmilia showed you the newest assessment of her changes. Everyone sees the change but you. Suzanne has more brain function and she's been reacting to some stimuli. She even had a physical reaction when Kayla was *trying to provoke her yesterday. Suzanne is here. She's just not here fully. YET."*

"Suzanne is gone..." Marcus moans.

No, I'm not! I'm here, Marcus! I'm right here, SLEEPING!

"She is NOT gone- I know it. Please Marcus. It doesn't cost you anything to keep her here. There is no burden to you financially, or otherwise-"

"Fuck YOU, Kayla! You think it's the money? It's not even MY money. I have my own money."

"No. I don't think it's the money. I'm just trying to say, that there's no cost to you to wait-"

"No cost? Are you fucking blind? This whole thing is a cost to me. I have to stare at my dead wife, waiting every day for her to finally die. I have to wait and wait. There is no forward and there is NO back. I have to wait, but she just won't die! She's gone, but she just won't LEAVE!"

NO! I'm not gone. I'm here! I'm totally here! Shit! Oh god, I need to wake up from this sleep.

"Marcus, you can walk away and I'll take care of her. I'll care for her and I'll wait for her to wake up."

"She's not going to wake up. Are you delusional or something?! Look at her, Kayla. Look hard. She's all fucked up, and awful, and DEAD!"

I'm not! I'm NOT dead! SHIT! Oh, *god*... What do I do?!

"She IS all fucked up, and awful- But she's NOT dead. She's NOT! Look at her right now! Look at the increase in her heart rate, even in this moment as we speak. She is here. LOOK!"

Awful? Fucked up? What are they talking about? I'm just asleep. That's all. Why am I awful and fucked up? Why would Marcus say that? That's so mean, and Marcus isn't usually mean. Marcus didn't think I was awful and fucked up before. What The Hell Is Happening?!

"Kayla, I don't want to talk about this anymore. It is going to happen. It's decided. I won and next Friday it's going to happen.

Suzanne is gone, and I'm really tired of talking about this with everyone."

"Marcus, you can walk away. You can leave and pretend she's dead. You CAN move on. I promise I'll take good care of her, and I will. I'll keep her away from Mack, or anyone else *you choose, but please,* please *let me care for her. Please, let me keep Suzanne."*
Silence.

Oh my god. I can't even understand what's happening here. What do they mean? Who is this lady, and why doesn't Marcus want me anymore? Why is he going to kill me? *How* is he going to kill me? Oh my god. What the hell is happening?

"Marcus, Suzanne's grandfather is starting the second round of appeals. This isn't over yet. I know you want it over, but I can't really understand you anymore. I don't know why you want to rush this. Why are you rushing this when you can walk away? You can wash your hands of all this and walk away. I've given you your out, so why won't you take it? Why won't you just walk away?"
"I... can't."
Yes, Marcus! Just walk away. Leave me alone!
"Marcus, why can't you?"
"I can't... because... I still love her. Even after everything she's done to me, I, ah, still love her."
What did I do? What the hell did I do? How is he going to *kill* me?
"Suzanne never meant to hurt you, she-"
"But she did."
"I know she did. But Marcus, you know she tried. You know she tried to be your wife again. She tried so hard, but she couldn't try anymore. She didn't want that for herself but more importantly, she didn't want that for you."
"That's a lie, Kayla. It wasn't about me; it was about Suzanne wanting someone else." What?!
"Marcus, THAT'S not true. Suzanne didn't want someone else-

she wanted a different life. But she DID try. She tried so hard to be with you. She tried to fulfill the fantasy for you. Suzanne was heartbroken over hurting you. She NEVER wanted to hurt you. She didn't want to hurt anyone, but especially you."
"But she did."
How? What did I do?
"Yes, she did hurt you. Is that why you want her dead now?"
WHAT?!
"Oh, god... How could you think that?"
"I don't know you Marcus, so I have to ask. Are you sure you really want to just let Suzanne go, or do you want to maybe hurt her? Even just a little? Um, maybe you want your revenge this way?"
What revenge? Oh my god. What did I do to Marcus?
"I don't want revenge anymore. I WAS angry before. God, I was so pissed off at her for so long. I felt betrayed and embarrassed by what she did. I stood by her for so long, for so many years, I can't even count them. I was her first boyfriend, her husband, and then her first lover. I tried so hard for so long to love her like she needed, but it was always so hard with her. Everything with Suzanne is just so hard all the time. Being with Suzanne is just exhausting."
"I know. Loving Suzanne is awful- I DO know that. I'm exhausted by her- by loving her, and I haven't had even a tenth of the time you have with her. But you can let go now. You can be free of Suzanne. I'm giving you the choice Suzanne doesn't have."
"That's what I'm doing."
"Are you?"
"No! Not like that- That's not what I meant. I just mean, she's gone now so I'm going to let her go. I'm going to let her body go, like she wants. She told me."
"But I want to keep her for a little while longer. I'll take care of her, I promise. Can I have her, Marcus?"
"No. Suzanne is mine. She's MY wife. Suzanne is still mine for now, and I'll take care of her to the end."

"Marcus, please... Suzanne isn't yours anymore. You KNOW that. We have the letter. We know she left you. YOU know she left you. Marcus, just let her go so you can be free of all this, and I'll take good care of her. I love her, and I'm a nurse, so I'll take good care of her until she wakes up, I promise."
"She's not going to wake up this time, she's-"
"Yes, she is."
"I don't want to talk about this anymore. I would really like you to leave now. Please leave, um, before I ask Security to make you leave."
"Marcus-"
"No. It's done, Kayla. Please get out of this room. Please leave now."
"Marcus, I just want to talk with you a little-"
"Mack has already spoken with me and I know how the rest of you feel, but it's my decision. It's my choice because I'm her husband, and it's done."
"Marcus, you may legally be her husband, but you're not-"
"I AM her husband. Even the Judge said I was. So please leave."
"Can I just talk to Suzanne a little?"
"NOW, Kayla. Get out of here NOW! You aren't going to stop this. So get the fuck away from me, right now! I want to spend a little time with my wife. Alone."
"Okay, I'll leave but please calm down. I'm going to go but I'll talk to you later?"
"It doesn't matter anymore Kayla. I don't care if I ever see any of you people again. Nothing would have ever happened if Suzanne hadn't met any of you people. Nothing would have changed for us. Nothing!"
"Marcus, I-"
"Get out Kayla. Now."
"Okay..."

As my dream is bathed in silence, I feel like I can finally exhale. What did I do? I can't think of anything I did to make Marcus want to hurt me. I did everything right, or at least I tried really hard to do everything right. I always tried so hard to be good for Marcus. What the hell did I do wrong? How is he going to let me go?

"Suzanne, I love you. I really do love you, you know? Please don't listen to them. And please don't listen to their lies. I'm not doing this to hurt you; I'm doing this FOR you."

When there is silence again, I think Marcus has left. God, I desperately want to talk to him, because everything around me is so confusing all the time.

"I know what you did, and I know what you've done, but I'm not angry anymore. I'm really not. I love you Suzanne, so I'm doing this for you. They don't know you, but I do. I know what you want because we talked about it before. We talked about all the things we would and wouldn't do for each other. We talked about when you wanted me to help you and when you wanted me to let you go. So that's what I'm going to do. I'm letting you go now."

When I hear Marcus start crying, I feel devastated for him. Marcus doesn't cry, and Marcus isn't mean. He's a bit of an ass, but he's never really mean. I wish I could wake up and tell him it's going to be alright. I wish I could tell him I trust him. I know he's doing the right thing, because I know he isn't mean. I *know* it.

"Suzanne, loving you has been the greatest burden of my life." What?! *"Loving you has been hell. I have loved you and hated you from the moment I met you, but I've always loved you more. I loved you even when it hurt to just look at you. I've loved you even when you hurt me so badly, I cried from the pain...*

"But I always believed in the dream, you know? Even when things were really bad. Even when you were really bad, I always believed you and I would be okay. I believed in you, even when I

should have stopped believing in you a long time ago. And now look what you've done."

Oh, god. I've never heard Marcus say words like this. He NEVER says words like this. Marcus thinks people are too dramatic and sappy, so he never says words like these. He hates shows of emotion, and yet here he is. God, he sounds so *sad*.

"Suzanne, it's only ever going to be you, you know? I'm going to love you always. Especially after."

Oh, Marcus.
I think my heart is breaking for him. I wish I knew what was happening so I could apologize and make it all better for him.
If I could just speak to him, I would promise to try harder. I would promise to *be* better. I would promise to be good... If only I could speak to him.

CHAPTER 6

MAY 6

How the hell do I wake up? This guy keeps asking me to wake up, but I'm not even sure if I'm asleep, or like dead or something. I'm not really sure if I'm even alive, so how the hell do I wake up? My body is all floaty and painful and warm. And I'm kind of gaggy or something. Even my brain feels floaty. I'm not sure where I am or if I'm even here, so how do I wake up?

*****

"Suzanne, its Kayla. You know me- I'm Kayla Rinaldi from New York. You know my voice. You know my charming New York accent." Charming? *"I know you remember me. I'm unforgettable, remember? I'm gorgeous, and funny, and smartasstic, and sexy as hell, and good in bed, and really, really freakin' tall... Remember?"*

I am so tired of these strangers talking to me all the time. I'm so tired of trying to figure out who they are. God, what can I do to shut them up?
And why does she want me to know she's so tall? Why the *hell* do I care if she's tall? Why do I need to know that? Who gives a shit?!

Why do all tall people feel the need to tower over us vertically challenged individuals? Why do they always lean over us and talk down to us?

Why do all tall men treat us shorter people like we're less than they are- demanding and taking from us because we couldn't possibly fight their power and height?

Why do tall women always wear high-heels? It's not like they even need them. Why do they do that? They already know they're tall. They already know they have an advantage. They know they can succeed where we shorter people can't. And yet they wear their heels and flaunt their longer, leaner bodies, and all the success they attain because they had a height advantage to start them off. They even flaunt their tallness to men in a way we shorter women could never do.

I really think I hate tall people. Is that weird? I wonder why I actually hate them. I don't know but I'm pretty sure it's hate, or maybe it's fear. I'm not sure. But I don't like tall people.

Tall women are mean and catty because they know they're better than me. And tall men are mean and well, just *mean* because they know I can't fight them. Huh. I never thought of that before. Why would I fight a tall man?

Marcus is tall. He's over 6 feet tall, and he's long and fit and athletic looking, and *way* taller than me. He always makes fun of me for being short- not that 5'3 is excessively short or anything, but it's short enough to need help with the high cupboards and the high closets.

5'3 is short enough to be annoying, though not short enough to seem really, really short. Why does Marcus always make fun of me for being short? It's not like I can change my height.

I don't think I really thought about it before but Marcus does say comments about me being too 'thick' for my short stature. Marcus has suggested things I should do to erase the extra curves around my middle so I wouldn't look so pear-like. Marcus has told me to lose 30 pounds around my hips and ass to straighten me out a little, just so I wouldn't seem so short.

Marcus even said that it was too bad I had a big ass because without it I might look like a cute, petite little doll, but sadly, with my huge ass and hips... oh! *And* my big thighs, I just look more like a short woman carrying around 30 extra pounds on her middle that she couldn't be bothered to lose. Shit! I forgot that too.

"*... Suzanne, please. I miss you and really need to talk to you. Mack is going crazy over you, and I'm going crazy over Mack, and Z is so lost, he's breaking all our hearts, even Kayla's... We're all just so trapped now...*"
Trapped? *You're* trapped? Jesus Christ lady! I'm the one whose trapped listening to all you people go on and on while I'm trying to sleep, or wake up, or whatever the hell I'm trying to do. As if *YOU'RE* trapped.

Oh my god! I wish this lady would just shut the hell up. Her accent is brutal and annoying as hell. What self-respecting *New Yawker* would ever keep that accent? It's awful!

Christ! I bet they have speech therapists for that on every street corner in New York. I've even heard there are like 12-step programs for that accent. Maybe I could get her a gift certificate or something...

"*Z's new apartment is waiting for you. He's selling his New York apartment in case, and bought this one in Chicago for you. Don't you want to see it? Wouldn't you like to help Z decorate your new apartment together? Z has left it completely bare for you. I think he bought a couch to sleep on and a coffee maker, but that's it. He's waiting for you, and I know he's dying to have your help and input...*"

My apartment? What the hell is she *talking* about?! As if Marcus would ever sell our home for an apartment. No matter how nice, or expensive, or upper class, Marcus would still find an apartment beneath us. Marcus would *never* buy an apartment. This lady is horribly confused.

"*Z is waiting for you...*"
Oh My God! Just shut up already! Who the hell is Z? Where the

hell is Marcus? And how do I get this annoying woman to Shut The Hell Up?!

I think I need more sleep, or better sleep, or to wake up, or, or *something*. I need to get out of this nightmare. This feels like a never-ending dream through hell.
It's like every single thing I hate in life is all in my dream to torture me. Ugh... Brooklyn accents, tall people, angry women, strangers, people talking, darkness, and feeling completely trapped. Shit...
Why don't I just start dreaming about my mother and really get this party started. Um... actually no.
I'll take this weird, annoying dream without adding my mother to the mix. Christ! Anything has got to be better than dreaming about my mother.
Now that I think about it, this lady's Brooklyn accent isn't *so* bad. I guess it's kind of charming. *Kind of.*

Suddenly, I'm jolted by the sensation of being touched. What is that? Oh god. Who's touching me? I hate that. I hate being touched. Why is this happening? I'm still dreaming right?

CHAPTER 7

May 10

Why can't I move or change, or like, be normal or something? I keep hearing people talk. All these strangers come in and out, but nothing changes for me. I see nothing and I barely hear them, but they're always here. It's like this constant buzzing in my head- constant noise but rarely a clear sound.

Sometimes I hear actual words but I don't understand what they mean, or what they're trying to tell me.

I hear all these people but I don't know any of them, well, except for Marcus. I know him and I hear him. He seems so sad or maybe tired- I'm not sure which. I know Marcus, but I don't really know *this* Marcus. Even he seems so strange to me.

I wish I could just wake up. I wish I could move out of this darkness. I wish I wasn't trapped in this darkness all the time because it makes me kind of tired, even though I think I'm still sleeping. I don't know what to do.

I don't know how to open this closet door anymore.

*****

"Hi, Marcus. How are you?"

"I'm fine, Kayla. But I really don't want to see you or any of her friends anymore. I'm going to talk to security and have you all banned from her room from now on."

"Marcus, you can't ban Mack."
"Oh, we'll see. I bet I can."
"And her grandfather?"
"Screw him. Where the hell has he been all these years? I've met the man 4 times in all the years Suzanne and I have been together. He means nothing to us. Suzanne and I know what's what. We know he doesn't love us. We know he's irrelevant. Don't we, Suzanne?"
"Marcus, tomorrow isn't going to happen- I guarantee it. There's a new reason to stop this. There's a new medical reason for this to stop. We have some strange news about Suzanne that we've been waiting to share with you."
What?! What about me?
"It doesn't matter..."
"Actually Marcus, it DOES matter. Would you like to know what has happened? Maybe you'll feel better about leaving Suzanne alone. Maybe you'll even change your mind about her. Would you like to hear about it?"
"No, Kayla, I wouldn't. I'll still win no matter what you think you have against me. I'm her husband, and I've already won. Even my lawyer says an appeal by her grandfather and Mack won't help because there's no basis for it. There's no new information from her grandfather or from her 'best friend' Mack that can make a difference."
"But we have-"
"You have nothing other than false hope on your side. But I have Suzanne on my side. I know she wants this because she told me. Suzanne doesn't want to be like this anymore."
Ha! You're right Marcus. I don't want to be like this anymore.
"Marcus, I have to show you something."
"I'm not interested."
"Marcus please. Just look at me for a minute. Just look at what I have here. I'm begging you."
"Listen, Kayla, it doesn't matter. There is nothing-"
"Look Marcus."
"What is...? Oh my god... THAT'S NOT TRUE!"

What?! What's not true?
"It IS true. This is real, and this is Suzanne."
"No, it isn't. It isn't even possible! She wasn't like that."
Like what?!
"Suzanne was like that, and she would be happy about this."
"Actually, she really wouldn't..."
Holy shit! Marcus is sobbing. What did I do?
"Marcus-"
"Get out of here Kayla. NOW! I want to be alone with my wife now. I want to be alone with her. She needs me. Suzanne needs me to stop all this for her. She doesn't want this. She never wanted this."
"Marcus, please listen to me. This isn't about you anymore. This is about Suzanne now."
"I KNOW THAT! It was always about Suzanne. It's ALWAYS been about Suzanne. Christ! Every minute of every single day with Suzanne has been about Suzanne. But it's too much now. It's too much for us, so I'm helping her. I'm going to make this all go away for her. I'm going to end this now."
Make what go away? What did I do? Shit! I thought I was being good here. I thought I was being a good girl, all quiet and still. Being quiet and still is what everyone wants from me. It's what I always do. No one gets mad at me when I'm quiet and still. So what did I do wrong?

"*...Suzanne takes your hand, and she leads you down the river...*"
Oh god, Marcus sounds like he's moaning.
"What are you talking about Marcus? What are you singing?"
"*... and you know that she's half crazy, but that's why you want to be there...*"
"Marcus what are you doing?"

THIS is me...

Oh my god... I love this song. Why is Marcus singing it to me? Why is he singing? Marcus only sang this song once to me. One time on our honeymoon, Marcus sang 'Suzanne' and I wept and asked him to stop.
   Marcus knows he can't sing this song to me. Marcus knows I can't hear this song.
   This song is too much for me. This song is too *beautiful* to me. This song is too beautiful FOR me. I have always known I wasn't enough for him. I have always known THIS Suzanne wasn't great enough for Mr. Cohen's Suzanne.
   Why is he doing this to me?!

"Marcus, you're talking a little strangely right now. Would you like to go get a coffee with me? Why don't we just go grab something from the cafeteria for a few minutes? We can come right back if you'd like."
   "No, I'm fine. But you're not going to be. You have exactly 10 seconds to get the hell out of my face Kayla before I make your life a living hell! Do you understand what I'm saying to you? Do you HEAR ME, Kayla?"
   "Are you threatening me, Marcus?"
   Holy SHIT! What the hell is happening here?
   "Yes I am, Kayla. So get out now, before I fucking hurt you like I'm going to hurt Suzanne." WHAT?!
   "Okay Marcus, I'll leave. And thank you."
   "Thank you for WHAT?! You think I'm just an asshole and a monster."
   "Yes I do. But you just gave me the ammunition I needed to stop you, so thanks for that! You fucking dickhead!" WHAT?!
   "Kayla, what are you talking about? It's too late!"
   "No, it isn't! HELP! Security!! HELP ME!!!"
   Holy SHIT! Why is she SCREAMING?! Oh god...

I'm so tired from trying to pay attention, and listening to her screaming is deafening. Listening to Marcus yelling is exhausting.

What's he going to do to me? Did he hire someone to kill me? Why would he talk so casually about killing me? I'm a good wife and a good person. I do everything right. And Marcus is proud of me for being good. So what's HAPPENING?

OH! My mother IS here- I can feel her. She's brushing my hair, and she's smiling at me through the mirror again. Ugh, I can see her bony skeleton hands again. There they are- so white and so thin.
Dammit, my mother's hands are around my throat again. My mother's hands are choking me again.
Slowly, I feel the pressure as her smile widens. Slowly, I feel her thin fingers pushing into my skin again. Slowly, I feel her fingers tightening around my throat again. Slowly, I feel the panic...
Again.
Why does she always do this to me? I mean she always stops, so why even do it? It makes no sense to me.
I know she knows I'm scared. I know she knows she scares me. I know she knows I'm afraid of her every time she does this to me. But she always stops. When my eyes close and I push out a hard breath, she *always* stops strangling me.
Oh god, why does she stop? I don't get it. Just do it already!
Still squeezing, my breath is getting harder and harder. Oh! Maybe this time she won't stop. Huh.
This time she seems like she really wants to keep going. This time I'm really, truly panicked. Maybe this is finally the time she doesn't stop.
Wait! This time I don't want to close my eyes and stop fighting. This time I want to see her smiling at me. This time I want to watch my mother kill me.

With a gasp, I open my eyes.

And staring at Marcus' twisted face, I'm stunned back into my darkness as chaos explodes around me.

Sarah Ann Walker

THIS is me...

ASLEEP

Sarah Ann Walker

CHAPTER 8

MAY 11

"Suzanne, its Kayla. Wake up for me again, okay? I want to talk to you for a minute. I just need a minute and then I'll let you go back to sleep. Please talk to me so I know you're really awake, and then you can go back to sleep, I promise."
Wow, how strange is that? Who wakes someone up just to let them go back to sleep? Why would I even bother?
"Suzanne, I've been waiting a long time for you. We all have. Can you try to wake up again and look at me for a minute? Marcus is gone, so you're safe now. And Mack is on his way. Mack should be here with Kayla in a few minutes."
Opening my eyes, I try to see through the haze, but everything is really bright. It's like I'm blinded by sunlight. I feel like my face is toward the sun on a hot day. I feel like I can close my eyes and still see the dark shape of the round sun shining behind my eyelids.
"Suzanne..." she whispers.
Trying to blink away all the bright, I look closely at the blurry face in front of me. Who is she? And why the hell is she crying AND smiling?
"God, Suzanne... welcome back. You scared the shit out of me, and I'm trying not to yell at you here. Well, not yet anyway. I'll yell at you a little later, okay?" Huh?
Staring at this woman, I'm at a complete loss. I don't know her, but she seems to know me. What the hell is she talking about? Why would she yell at me? I haven't done anything wrong yet.

"Suzanne, its Kayla. Can you see me alright? Can you try to speak to me? The feeding tube was just removed, and the

doctors are waiting outside to talk to you, but I wanted to talk to you first so you weren't scared."
What doctors? Crap! Am I in a hospital? Shit. I hate hospitals. Trying to turn my head takes forever, but eventually I see. Yup, I'm definitely in a hospital, though it looks quite nice. This room doesn't seem like a hospital room much, well, except for all the hospitally-type stuff everywhere.
"Suzanne, can you please say something. Just say hi if you can, and I'll leave you alone."
God, my throat is killing me and I haven't even spoken yet. I know it's going to hurt more as soon as I try to speak, but she looks so happy to see me; I really should try to speak to her.
Clearing my throat, which just *kills,* I whisper, "hello..."
"Oh GOD Suzanne, Hi! Jesus *Christ!* I never that I'd be so glad to hear your voice again. How do you feel? We only have a minute here because the doctors have to talk to you and examine you, but I'm so glad to see you awake."
Bursting into tears, the woman is just beaming at me. Jeez... Who is she? And holy annoying accent.
"Are you a nurse?" I whisper.
"Suzanne, it's me Kayla. Can't you see me?"
"Yes, I see you."
"Suzanne, its New York Kayla. Remember me?"
When she looks at me so expectantly, I kind of feel bad for her but I don't think I know her though. Looking hard, I'm sure I don't know her at all actually.
"Suzanne, we're friends. I'm your very good friend Kayla Rinaldi, and I love you very much. We've known each other for a while now, and we're very close friends. Do you remember me? Do you remember Mack, and Chicago Kayla, and Z? Do you remember Marcus?" Oh!
"Where's my husband?" I kind of groan. God, my throat really is on fire.

"Marcus? Um, he's tied up at the moment. He'll be here shortly though, I'm sure. Ah, do you remember me and Mack, and Kayla? Do you remember Z?"

Isn't she Kayla? I swear she said her name was Kayla. What the hell is going on here? But before I can ask her the door pushes open and interrupts us. Turning my head slowly, I see 2 men walk into my room. Holy shit! 2 men!

"Suzanne..."

I can't help my flinch. Why am I so scared suddenly? What's happening?

"Suzanne you're safe, I promise. No one will hurt you here. These doctors just need to examine you and talk to you. You've been asleep for a long time, and they have to check you out a little."

Panicking, I quietly beg, "Please don't leave me with them. *Please...*"

Oh god, I can't be alone with 2 men. Why am I so scared? Shaking, I hear my teeth chatter as nausea overwhelms me. Suddenly throwing up all over myself, I can't help it. I wasn't able to move my body very well. But as I start panicking again at my slow movement the woman reaches for me in a tight hug.

"Suzanne, look at me. You're okay. You're safe, I promise. I'll stay here with you if you want, and Mack will be here soon. These doctors won't hurt you. They just need to run some tests, and they need to talk to you a little. I'll stay right here though if you want, I promise. Suzanne, you're okay."

When the woman takes my hand and rubs my back with her other hand things suddenly feel a little better. Breathing slowly, my chest isn't as tight as it was. Closing my eyes, I even *feel* a little better as she holds my hand.

When I open my eyes 2 women have joined the men. Oh, thank god.

"Suzanne, please stay with us. This is Dr. Cobb and Dr. Robinson, and they've been watching over you while you slept. They won't hurt you, I promise. No one will."

Opening my eyes, one man is leaning close to me with something in his hand. Oh god! Flinching, I close my eyes again. I can't do this! They can't do this! Why is this happening?

There's something wrong but I don't know what it is. I don't know what's wrong, but I hate it! I can *feel* something is wrong and I can't do this!

Please fall asleep. *Please...* I just need to sleep again. I don't want to know this. I don't want to feel this. I don't want any of this anymore.

"Suzanne!"

I can't stop this. I can't talk to her and I can't talk to them. My body is shaking, and I hear the voices all around me, but I can't do this. There is so much noise and movement all around me. Oh, god... I think people are touching me.

I swear I hear my name again through the noise. I know she's yelling to get my attention, but I can't do this. I won't do this!

"NO!" I shriek as loud as I can even as my throat screams in agony. I think I must have torn my throat wide open. Maybe they cut my throat open. Maybe they squeezed my throat for the last time.

I don't know what to do anymore. Shaking and gasping, I try to ignore them. I don't want to hear this. I don't want to feel this. Oh my god!! They're going to kill me again.

After a last thought of death, I feel myself falling.

I know I'm falling far away. I just need to sleep away this death. I need to sleep through this fear, and then it will finally be over. I need to sleep away this life again.

CHAPTER 9

"Suzanne, its Mack. I'm here, Suzanne. I'm here with you in the hospital. You can open your eyes now. I know you're awake and I know you woke up a few minutes ago. Come on, Suzanne, wake back up for me."

I really don't want to. Waking up was so loud. There was all that noise and yelling and struggling, and just stuff going on around me. I don't want to wake up again. I think I prefer the never-ending dream I was in.

"Suzanne, I know you're awake and just faking sleep. I can tell- I've watched you sleep far too many times to not know when you're faking it." Wow. That sounds creepy. "Why don't you want to wake up now? You are completely safe with me and I need to talk to you. We're alone, and I really, really want to talk to you for a minute. Please, Suzanne."

Ugh. This is so annoying. Nobody shuts up around here. They all just talk and talk. Shit. Hasn't anyone heard of, like, meditation or something? Just sit quietly and shut the hell up for a minute. It's like they can't deal with quiet. Well I can. I love quiet. Quiet lets me know I'm safe. *What?!*

Opening my eyes, I'm nearly blinded by the light again. Everything is just so bright and blurry suddenly. I don't remember this from last time I woke up. Hey! Where's Marcus?

"Marcus?"

"Ah, no. Marcus had to leave for a little while. I'm sure he'll be back soon though. I know he really wants to see you, so I'm sure he'll be back soon."

Turning, I'm curious about the voice I keep hearing.

Oh! He doesn't look like I thought he would. This man's voice is so nice sounding. His voice is very calm and soothing, almost soft-like. I thought he would be short and round with glasses maybe. I don't know. He doesn't sound at all like he looks though.

Smiling at me, the man takes my hand into his own, but I really want out of his grasp. Trying to pull away, I try until I see his frown. This guy is very good looking. He's very attractive, and I feel *very* uncomfortable holding his hand. Why won't he let go?

Pulling away from him again, the man finally let's me free. Slowly sliding my hand across the bed feels like it takes me a lifetime, but finally, my hand is just mine. Finally, I'm not being touched.

"Welcome back, Suzanne. It's so good to see you awake. I've been waiting for-freakin-ever for you to wake up," he grins.

"Oh, okay. Sorry, sir." When he frowns again, I realize I've said something wrong. "Um, sorry to make you wait, sir."

"Mack."

"Oh, okay. Are you a doctor?"

Dammit, now he looks all he all stressed again. I'm not sure what I'm doing wrong but I'm really trying here, and he looks like everything I say is the wrong thing. I should probably stop talking now because silence is always safer for me anyway.

"Suzanne, do you remember me? I'm Mack. Do you remember me as your doctor, Mack?"

"No, I'm sorry sir. How long have you been my doctor?"

As he lets out a hard exhale, I feel like I'm in trouble. Ugh, what do I say now?

"You're safe, Suzanne. I'm not mad at you, and you're doing nothing wrong. I'm just a little surprised that you don't remember me. We're very close friends, you and I."

"I thought you were the doctor?"

"I am YOUR doctor, but I'm also a close personal friend of yours. I've been waiting for you to wake up, and I thought you would remember me."

Looking hard at him, I try to remember. He is very handsome. He's dark haired with lovely eyes, hazel greenish-brown I think. He has a warm smile and he doesn't look mean at all. I wish I could remember him because he looks like a nice person to know.

"I'm sorry..." I mumble shaking my head.

"That's alright, Suzanne. There's no need to apologize. You've just woken up, so you probably need a little time for the memories to come back to you."

"Um, okay. Sorry that I don't remember you."

"Please, Suzanne, don't apologize. Everything is going to be alright, and you're going to get better. I'm sure your memory will return to you shortly. We'll just talk a little, and see what you do remember. Is that okay with you?"

"Sure. But where's Marcus? Is he here?"

When the doctor looks all confused again and kind of mad at me, I'm scared that I'm making him angry with me. Shaking his head slightly, he puts on a horribly fake smile, and lies to me. Somehow, I can tell. I'm not sure how I can tell, but I totally can.

"Marcus was here earlier, but he had to leave for a little while. I'm sure he'll be back as soon as he can though. Do you remember seeing him when you woke up?"

"No. He was here? Why did he leave me when I woke up?"

Smiling, the doctor says, "Marcus was overwhelmed when you finally woke up, so he just needed some time to collect himself. Everything's fine though. I'm sure he'll be back as soon as he can."

I don't know what's happening here. Why would Marcus want me awake, but then leave when I wake up? That doesn't make any sense.

"Was he mad at me?" I whisper.

"No. Not at all, Suzanne. Marcus was just emotional when you woke up. You've been asleep for quite a while now, and I'm sure he didn't think you would wake up today, so he was a little shocked, that's all."

"Why was I sleeping? I remember dreaming forever. It was the longest night of my life, I think. Oh! Where am I?"

"You're in a hospital in Chicago, where you've been asleep for some time. Everything's going to be fine though. You're well, and you should recover fully."

"Recover from what? Why was I asleep?"

Okay, that totally sounded like I was slurring my words or something. I heard that. I was all slurry and sleepy sounding. It's like I'm drunk but not really. Weird. Maybe I'm just hearing myself oddly, like you do on an answering machine or something. You know, you hear your voice but it doesn't sound like your voice, or... oh!

This is very strange for me. I know there's more going on- I *know* it. I don't feel like I was asleep but I DO remember dreaming, which means I must have been asleep, right? God, this is so confusing, and I already feel really exhausted again.

"Are you feeling tired? You seem to be having a hard time speaking at the moment. Would you like to have a little rest? I could come back in an hour or so, and we could talk more then, if you'd like."

"Okay, thank you, um, Doctor." Shit! What was his name?

"I'm Mack. Your doctor and *friend* Mack. Remember what I told you, Suzanne? Do you remember me telling you my name a few minutes ago? Do you remember me telling you I'm Mack?"

"Yes, of course. Um, do I call you Mack? Or Dr. Mack? Is that your last name? I'm sorry; I don't want to be rude to you. What would you like me to call you?"

Looking at me for a few intense seconds, the doctor seems to be thinking of what to say to me. This is so weird. I mean really, it's just a name. What the hell is the problem here? Is it because I'm talking weird and my voice is extra deep and sleepy sounding, and just totally weird in my head?

"My name is Dr. Michael MacDonald, but you've always called me Mack."

When? When did I call him Mack? Shit. I think this guy is crazy. I've never met him before in my life. And, as if I'd ever call a doctor by a nick-name. That's just so tacky and disrespectful and juvenile. I would NEVER do that.

"Well, it's been a pleasure to meet you Dr. MacDonald." When he suddenly flinches, I think I'm in trouble for something. Shit! "Um, I'm sorry. What do you want me to call you?"

"Dr. MacDonald is fine, Suzanne. Just relax. I'll come back soon and check on you. Is that alright?"

"Sure, I guess. Dr. MacDonald?" Ugh, he flinched again. "Um, do you know where my mother is? I thought she'd be here by now."

"She isn't here right now- she's out of town. So don't worry about her for now. Just rest, and I'll come back soon to speak with you."

He totally looked like he was lying to me again. This is so weird. Dr. MacDonald got all red, and he gulped hard when he told me about my mother. What the hell is going on?

"Is everything alright with my mother? You seem to be hiding something about her. Did my mother say something mean to you? If she did, I'm really sorry. My mother can be mean sometimes. Sorry if she was mean to you."

"Your mother wasn't mean to me Suzanne, so please don't worry about her. She just isn't available right now- that's all. I'll see you soon," he smiles.

When he stands to leave my room I am totally relieved to be alone.

Okay, Dr. MacDonald just left my room super quick. It's like he wants to do something quickly, or report something quickly, or tell on me quickly about something. Shit. What did I do wrong? Is he going to tell my mother on me? I thought I was very respectful to him. Dammit. I'm totally scared that she's going to be mad at me when I see her.

Trying to exhale again, I realize I'm holding my breath. Why can't I just relax? I'm really exhausted now and I'm more than ready to have a sleep, but I feel too nervous and tense. I NEED to sleep, but I hate the feeling of my mother being mad at me. It's even worse with her than when Marcus is mad at me.

Okay, time to sleep. My brain is all fuzzy, and I feel like crap. My stomach is all nauseous, and my hands are shaky, though I really haven't moved them much at all. Actually, I've barely moved my body at all. What the hell? *CAN* I move my body?

Okay, focus. Move body, *move.* Oh, my arms are moving a little. Come on legs. Move! Oh good, they can move too, I feel it. I can't really see it because my head hurts too much, and my eyes are getting super blurry from being tired, but I feel my legs moving, so that's good. Ugh, I really do feel pretty shaky and nauseous, and kind of like I want to cry, which is strange as well because that's something I never do either. I never, ever cry.

Okay, enough. Closing my eyes tightly, I'm just going to rest for a while, and then try to get up and out of this bed a little later.

Good. That's a plan. Maybe when I wake up Marcus will be here and he can tell me why I'm even in the hospital. I would really like to know what I did to end up in a hospital again.

CHAPTER 10

MAY 12

Waking again I am absolutely exhausted because the people just won't stop around here. The noise won't stop and the stuff won't stop. There is never a moment of peace here. I don't know how long this waking up has been, but I'm ready to rest again.

Endless Doctors and Technicians and Nurses and Specialists have been in my room since I woke up. There have been so many people in here constantly. There has been so much talking in here. There has been so much activity in here. There has been so much of *everything* in this little room.

Throughout all the noise, everyone has been asking the same questions, and everyone has been touching me. Everyone has been in my face and it's just too much for me.

I don't want to talk anymore, and I don't want to be touched anymore. I don't want my legs moved while I close my eyes, and I don't want my arms raised as I open my eyes. I don't want to be lifted, and shifted, and rolled, and changed anymore. I don't want to hear about my movements, and I don't want my memory tested again. I don't want to hear about myself anymore because I'm not that interesting. Plus, I'm really not listening anyway.

I'm humiliated and exhausted at once. But no one will actually tell me what happened, or what I did wrong to end up here. No one answers any of MY questions; they just expect answers to all theirs. And back and forth we go.

They ask me a question which I answer, and then I ask them a question which they do NOT answer. Well, I'm not talking anymore and they can't make me. I'm tired, and I want to be left alone.

Where's Marcus? Why hasn't he come for me? Where is my mother? Why hasn't she come to claim me? Why am I here? These are such simple questions really but no one will answer me.

*****

Waking, I know there's someone in here, again. I know I'm not alone and I totally don't want to do this anymore. Why can't I just be alone? I wish I could go back to my sleepless dreaming sleep again. At least there I was alone in my head. Well, except for all the talking and noise and stuff, I was alone.

Opening my eyes slowly, I prepare for the newest person to invade my space. Looking, I see the woman again with the atrocious Brooklyn accent. Sitting beside me in a chair, she looks so happy to see me awake. Ugh... here we go again.

"Good morning, Suzanne. How are you feeling?"
"I'm *fine*. Why?"
"I'm just checking. Why do you seem so agitated? What's wrong?"
"I'm not agitated. I just don't know you, and you keep talking to me like I DO know you, and I don't. That's all. Why are you here again?"
"I'm here because we're friends and I've missed you. And because I wanted to see you when you woke up. I wanted to try to talk to you before the others arrived." The others?
"Um, okay, I don't mean to be rude, but why do you keep saying that? I told you before that I don't know you. I told you that before, like yesterday, or last night I think, but you keep saying

that I do know you, but I'm not your friend. I don't even know you, I'm sorry."
 Wow, I really do feel frustrated and tired and kind of angry at her or something.
 "Please listen to me, Suzanne. I promise you DO know me. You just have to remember me. You know me very well and we're very close friends. You stayed in my apartment in Manhattan. We went shopping, and I even lent you my car, which I never lend to anyone. We *are* friends- very close friends actually, I promise. Just trust me, okay?"
 "I do apologize, but I *don't* remember you and I *don't* trust you. Again, I don't mean to be rude, but would you mind if I had a little privacy?"
 "Oh god... *Please* Suzanne. You sound like *her* again. You are all polite and reserved, and actually kind of annoying sounding." *Seriously?* "Can't you just tell me to leave you the fuck alone? Or tell me to get the fuck out. Or even tell me to fuck off! Just please, tell me something!" Wow. *What?*
 "I'm sorry, but I don't speak that way. And I don't want to be rude to you, but please give me a little privacy. Do you know where my husband is?"
 "Suzanne, you DO speak that way now if you want to. You say 'fuck' now if you want to, and you say 'shit' a lot. Actually, you mumble 'shit' all the time and it's very cute coming from you. You say bad words *out loud* now, Suzanne. You do, I promise. You aren't like your old self anymore, I swear. You are fun and silly and cute, and even a little sarcastic, thanks to me and Kayla. You are *fun* Suzanne, and I miss you. Do you remember any of this?"
 "I'm sorry-"
 "STOP SAYING *'I'M SORRY'!*" Flinch. "Sorry. I'm sorry, it's just you worked too hard to stop saying sorry to everyone all the time. You have changed, Suzanne. You're really different now. Do you remember? Do you remember changing? You aren't *her* anymore. You are Suzanne now." Wow, as if I don't know my own name.

Staring at me, this woman seems to be waiting for something. What does she want from me? Actually, she seems kind of crazy and confused. I think she must be crazy. She doesn't know me, and she doesn't know what I say or do. She must be delusional, I think. I wonder what I can do to get her out of my room.
  "Please, Suzanne... remember me. Just try to remember. I'm tied with the other Kayla as your second-place best friends. We're tied in second- me and Kayla. We're *your* two Kaylas. Please remember me if you can- just a little."

  When she bursts into tears, I think I feel bad for her. She looks so lovely, but kind of gross when she cries. I definitely feel bad for her because it's clear that she's TOTALLY insane. I'm pretty sure I don't feel scared of her though, just bad for her.
  I wish I could help her. She obviously needs help, but I'm not sure what to do for her. Where is a doctor? Maybe a doctor can get her out of my room. Maybe a doctor can help her. Maybe I should page a doctor to my room for her.
  "Um, excuse me, but do you have someone you can talk to? Do you have a doctor who can maybe help you a little? Maybe if you find your doctor he can help you find your friend," I whisper, so she won't get mad at me again.
  "A doctor? *You're* trying to get *me* a doctor? You have no idea how fucking funny that is under the circumstances, I realize. But it IS quite funny. I don't need a doctor Suzanne, but you obviously do. You don't know anything, do you?"
  "I'm sorry, but I have no idea what's wrong with you, or what I've done to upset you. I'm really trying to be nice here but you seem so sad and confused. I just thought you could use a friend, or maybe a doctor to talk to so that maybe you won't look this sad anymore."
  "I'm not sad, Suzanne. Well *actually*, I'm devastated, but you don't know why, do you? So really, my devastation is kind of a moot point. I don't need a doctor, but I do have one should the need arise. I do however need my friend back. I need you, but

you're not here with me are you?" Holy shit! This woman is nuts.
"Okay miss, I'll get a doctor for myself, and maybe I can get a doctor for you too. Would you like that, um...?"
"I'm KAYLA! New. York. Fucking. KAYLA!! Fuck, Suzanne, THINK!! *REMEMBER* ME!!"

Shaking, I'm at a total loss. I don't know why this woman is here, and I don't know why she's so mad at me. I don't know what I did to upset her and I don't know why she's still here. What the hell do I do? Lie!
"Oh, I remember you now- of course. You're my friend from New York who I visited in Manhattan. I remember now. We had fun shopping and driving around. Thank you for coming to see me but would you mind if I had a little rest now? Would you mind if I was alone for a few minutes? I'd love for you to return another day, though. Thank you for your friendship, um..."
"*Kayla...*" she moans. "My name is Kayla, but you always called me New York Kayla, or 'this Kayla' when in New York or 'that Kayla' when in Chicago. I am your second best friend, tied with Chicago Kayla. I. Am. Kayla. I am *your* New. York. Kayla." Oh my god. *This* Kayla is certifiable.
"I know that, I really do. You're my New York Kayla. I remember now. Thanks for visiting me New York Kayla, but can I please be alone for a few minutes? Would you mind, um, New York Kayla just giving me a minute or two alone?" There, I think that was convincing. Jesus, my heart is pounding again.
"Sure, Suzanne, I'll leave you alone. Have a little rest, and maybe when you wake up again you'll remember me. Maybe after another rest, you'll remember us. Go ahead and have a rest."
"Thank you New York Kayla and I do apologize for upsetting you, but that was never my intention."
"I know it wasn't your intention, Suzanne. It's never your intention to upset anyone, but you always do anyway." *What?*
"It seems like every single minute with you is upsetting to those of us who love you, for those of us who care about you. All you do, though NOT your intention, is upset us. But please, don't

apologize- *please* don't say 'you're sorry'. I hate it, and so does everyone else who loves you. All of us who you can't remember hate it when you say you're sorry to us."

"Um, okay, I won't apologize anymore. Thank you New York Kayla. I'll try to be better next time we see each other so I won't upset you anymore. Thank you, and I promise I remember you now."

"Sure you do."

"I do, New York Kayla. I promise."

"Well, Suzanne..." she practically snarls at me. "If you honestly remembered me you wouldn't call me 'New York' Kayla to my face." What?! I swear to god, I don't get this woman. At all. "If you *really* remembered, you would know I am *just* Kayla when we're talking, unless I'm with the other Kayla, or when you're talking about us to someone else. When talking to me I'm just Kayla- your *friend* Kayla. To my face you just call me Kayla because it doesn't make sense to call me *New York* Kayla to my face."

Shaking her head, and wiping her eyes JUST Kayla rises from the chair without looking at me. Turning from me completely, she seems awful walking toward the door. God, this woman is just so sad suddenly. It's almost heartbreaking. I really hope she gets the help she needs and I really hope she finds her real friend soon. I hate seeing her leave looking so broken.

"Bye, Suzanne. I'll see you later. Um, I still love you..." she whispers from the doorway.

Wow, what a sad thing to hear. I don't know who she loves, but I hope she finds them soon. I hope her real friend can be found.

Maybe when a doctor comes in, I'll tell them about her so they can help her. Maybe she's just lost or can't find her room. Oh! Maybe her friend died and I look like her or something so she's crazy with grief. Maybe she's just lonely and needs a friend. God, I hope she finds a real friend soon so she's not so lonely anymore.

Ugh, I don't want to think about her sadness anymore because now I'm kind of sad myself. I feel lonely and just *weird*. I hate all this quiet, but I hate all the noise too.

I wish Marcus would come to take me home. I want my own house, with my own sunroom. I want to go home and be safe and NOT sad in my own home. I just want to go home so I'm not sad anymore.

Closing my eyes, I try to exhale all that Kayla stuff. I feel terrible for her, but she makes *me* feel terrible, which really isn't fair. I'm stuck in this hospital bed with tubes and IV's and stuff all over me so I can't move or get away. I'm trapped here, but I'm trapped awake this time.

Maybe if I fall asleep, I'll fall back into that long dream I had. Maybe I'll float away and dream about Marcus and my parents again. Maybe I'll float away and dream about things I actually understand.

Maybe I'll just float away, completely.

CHAPTER 11

MAY 13

Waking, I feel like I'm not alone. I'm never alone, but *feeling* not alone is way creepier than *knowing* you're not alone.
Shifting slightly on my bed, I can't believe how stiff my body feels. It's like every muscle I have is all tight and like scrunched up, or something. Ugh.

"Here, let me help you sit up a little."
Opening my eyes, I see Dr. MacDonald again. Huh. I wonder if this guy sleeps.
"How are you feeling, Suzanne?"
"Fine. Stiff, actually. My whole body is tight and kind of warm."
"Well, you've been asleep for a while, so your body needs to adjust to movement again, but it'll come. You have to start Physio-Therapy as soon as you can to stop any further muscle atrophy, but otherwise, it'll just take a little time and all the muscle tightness should start to fade. Generally speaking, muscle atrophy begins within weeks of immobility, but you shouldn't have any long-term issues with muscle degeneration or muscle weakness."
"Oh, good. Um, how long was I asleep? No one has actually told me what happened to me."
"A little over 12 weeks."
"Oh. Wow, that's so long. Am I okay? I mean, *am* I okay?" Duh. I sound so stupid.
"Yes, you're okay, and you're going to be better now. You were in another coma for these last 12 weeks but you seem to be relatively well now." A coma? *Another* coma? What the hell

does *that* mean?

"I don't remember another coma Dr. MacDonald. Was I little or something before?"

"No. You were in a medically-induced coma last year for a few weeks after you had a brain aneurism rupture. Do you remember anything about that time?"

"No, I'm sorry." Holy shit! 2 comas? What the hell is wrong with me?

"It's alright. No need to be sorry. You were quite sick last year, but you made a remarkable recovery. Do you remember anything about being sick last year?"

"No. I'm... I don't remember being sick at all. Where's Marcus?"

I'm starting to feel a little uncomfortable with this doctor. He keeps looking at me so intensely, but he's also so calm and relaxed that I'm feeling like I'm doing something wrong but he doesn't want to tell me what it is. Why doesn't he just tell me what he wants?

"Marcus had to go away for a few days. He's very sorry to not be here with you, but he couldn't put off the trip, so he sends his regards. I'm sure he'll be here as soon as he can though."

Why doesn't that surprise me? I can't help but giggle a little. I mean, come on! Your wife wakes up after 12 weeks in a friggin' coma and you can't get out of a business trip? Who does that? Speaking of colossal disappointments, where the hell are my parents anyway?

"Are you okay, Suzanne? You seem a little nervous or something. Marcus really does wish he could be here, but he had to straighten a few things out first."

"I'm sure he did. Where are my parents? Have they been here?"

"Do you want them here?" What? What a strange question. Of course I ... DON'T! Ha! Oops. Giggle.

"Suzanne, would you like your parents here? It's okay to answer truthfully. You can be honest with me. I promise you can confide in me and I won't tell anyone anything you tell me."

"Of course I do. They're my *parents,* Dr. MacDonald."

"Suzanne, do you really want your parents here?"

"Yes. I miss my mother." Giggle again. Shit. As if I miss her. "I'm sorry. I'm not sure why I'm laughing."

"Suzanne, do you really want your mother here?" He asks again very seriously.

"Um, no. Not really," I whisper. Shit.

"It's okay; I promise you I won't repeat anything you say to me. Do you know why you don't want your mother here?"

"No, not really. My mother is very intense and uptight sometimes, and I think she'll be mad at me for being in a coma, which sounds weird I know, but she's like that. I think she'll be disappointed in me for being in the hospital because I was in a coma, so she won't be very nice to me." Exhale.

"I understand, *though* being in a coma is a fairly good reason for being in the hospital, wouldn't you agree?" He asks while smirking at me. This guy is kind of funny.

"Yes, a coma sounds like a perfectly reasonable reason for being in the hospital but my mother isn't always so perfectly reasonable. So I try to never do anything wrong. And I think being in the hospital is wrong somehow, or at least *she'll* think it is. So I'm a little nervous about seeing her. Do you know when she should arrive?"

God, I'm going to have to prepare myself for her arrival so I'm not so scared when she gets here.

"Suzanne, your parents won't be visiting you anytime soon. They're unavailable at the moment so they can't be here with you. That may be disappointing, but-"

"Oh, it's not! That's awesome. I really don't want to see her, so this worked out perfectly."

Yes! My mother won't be here, so I'm okay for now. I wonder what they're doing, but then again, maybe if I know what they're doing the doctor will find them and tell them I'm awake and then she'll come here. It's probably best to not ask.

"Would you tell me when she's coming for me though? Would you please give me some notice so I can prepare myself for her? Is that okay, Dr. MacDonald?"

"Absolutely. I promise to let you know."
Staring at the doctor he smiles at me and I feel like maybe I can trust him. He seems like he'll tell me when she's coming for me, so until then I'll try to relax a little.

"What are you thinking about, Suzanne?"
"Nothing. I'm... nothing. I'm good. How did I get here? What happened?"
"You had a car accident. Do you remember that?"
"No... I don't think so."
An accident? Shit, I hope I was driving my car and not Marcus'. He'll kill me if I damaged his car.
"Was I driving Marcus car in the accident?"
"No, why?"
"I was just wondering."
"Why were you wondering?"
"It's nothing. I was just curious."
"Why were you curious?" God, this guy is so pushy, but he does it all calm-like, so it's kind of hard to ignore his questions when he sits so calmly waiting for my response.
"Marcus loves his car. I just wanted to make sure I didn't damage it so he wouldn't be mad at me. That's all."
"I wonder if he would still be angry at you if you did crash his car, even though you were seriously injured, AND you've just woken from a coma. Don't you think he would care more about your safety and health than for his car?"
"No, not really." Ooops. "Oh, of course he would, but he would still be disappointed if I crashed his car." Ugh. This still sounds bad. "No, I'm sure he wouldn't be disappointed. Marcus will be thrilled that I'm better now, I know he will be."
"Are you sure?"
"Of course. Marcus loves me, and he would choose me over his car. I'm sure of it." Am I?
"Well, that's good. And you can relax because you didn't crash his car, though even if you had you're certainly worth much more than a car."

Looking at the doctor, I'm suddenly overcome with emotion. Why the hell am I crying? He was just being nice, and I'm crying over his niceness? I'm *crying*?

"Are you okay? Why are you so sad suddenly?"

"I'm not sure. You just said something nice and it made me cry, I think. It's pathetic really, but hearing Marcus would pick me over his car feels good. I know it's probably stupid to you but it means something to me, I think."

"That's not stupid. Everyone wants to know that they're valuable to someone else. Everyone wants to feel important to someone else. And everyone, myself included, wants to know they're more important than, say, *a car*." Smirk again.

Giggling, I whisper a 'thanks' to him for being nice to me, and just stay quiet for a minute. It's like I'm basking in his simple little nicety. Why does his nice seem so important to me?

"Why are you still here?"

"I'm your doctor, Suzanne. Your private physician, actually. It's my job to be here with you, but even if it wasn't my job I would be here regardless. Do you remember anything about me, Suzanne? Do you remember that I'm your doctor?"

"Yes, you told me that. But I don't understand why I have a personal physician." Who does that?

"Last year when you were very sick I became your doctor, and I'm still on retainer as such." Wow, really? "You needed me then, so I've been your doctor and your very close friend ever since. I've been waiting for you to wake up so I could help you get better again. And I'm thrilled that you're finally recovering. Is there anything else you want to know? Is there anything else you want to ask me?" Huh. Only like a *million* questions.

"Why don't I remember you from before?" I whisper.

"Suzanne, you are suffering from a form of presumably temporary memory-loss. Many, if not most patients who find themselves awake after a coma have a mild to moderate form of amnesia, and it's quite normal. In theory, comas lasting even weeks can result in post-traumatic amnesia, or PTA, that lasts months; with a recovery rate occurring over weeks and months, or more severely over the course of years. It's almost as if, for every week in a coma, patients need approximately that many months to retain all their previous memories...

"But it's very rare for patients to have long term memory loss, especially after such a short time span as you were in the coma. Again, PTA is very standard and your memory loss is almost certainly short term. Some patients literally wake up a few days later with all their memories, or again, some need a little more time for the memories to eventually return."

"Okay... So maybe soon I'll remember you?"

"I trust that you will. We were very, very close, therefore I'm confident you'll remember me sooner rather than later. And I promise, once you remember your past you'll see that I can be trusted, and you'll probably relax a little while you recover fully. Do you have any more questions for me? Feel free to ask me anything, as I said earlier."

"No, I'm good, but I'm kind of tired now. Do you mind if I sleep for a little bit?"

"Not at all. Suzanne, you're going to sleep frequently in the next few weeks, which is also standard for post-coma patients as well. You may also feel confused or depressed from time to time, which is also quite typical, and something we'll monitor closely in the coming weeks. But if you should feel overwhelmed or depressed, please let me know immediately so I can help you at the onset."

"Okay. Thanks for telling me. I didn't want to seem all dramatic for feeling kind of tired and sad."

"You're not dramatic. You're just dealing with a new challenge, and you'll need my help along the way, which I'm here for."

"Thank you Dr. MacDonald. You're very nice to talk to."

Smiling, he says, "You used to always tell me that, you know? Actually, you told me frequently how much you loved me and our friendship, and I find I miss you terribly."

Looking at Dr. MacDonald, he seems so sad that I again feel overwhelmed with sadness. I feel bad that I don't remember him, but I DON'T remember him. God, I feel terrible for making him look like that.

Whispering, "I'm so sorry I don't remember you..."

"Suzanne, *I'm* sorry. I didn't mean to upset you, or to put any undue stress upon you. I just miss you, but I'll refrain from sharing like that again. We always spoke so freely with each other that it's hard for me to hold back now. That was a mistake on my part, or as you used to say a 'Doctorly mistake', and I won't make it again."

"It's okay. I just hate seeing people look sad; it kind of bothers me and makes me sad too. I'm sure I'll remember you though, I promise."

"I'm going to leave you to rest for a while, but I'll come back soon to talk with you."

When I nod, he rises from his chair, and gently touches my leg as his goodbye. Smiling, he leaves me alone.

Wow. That was intense. But I get it. I know him; I just don't *know* know him. That would be upsetting to anyone- to know that you're known but to be unknown. Anyone would feel sad by that. I know I would.

When I wake up again, I'm going to try really, *really* hard to remember him. Dr. MacDonald seems like someone I should remember, so I'm going to try hard, so he doesn't look like that ever again. Maybe when I remember him, everything else will make more sense to me.

CHAPTER 12

MAY 16

I don't even know how many days I've been 'awake', but I keep feeling this weird sense of déjà vu mixed with a total confusion about who I am and what I'm supposed to be. From what I'm told this is a very normal confusion, but it's still so mentally exhausting for me.
I wish I knew the reality everyone keeps telling me about. I wish I understood what everyone is telling me about myself, but I don't. Usually, I'm just constantly confused and totally overwhelmed. I really wish I understood my life as it has been repeatedly explained to me.
It doesn't help that the people I actually DO remember, Marcus and my parents are nowhere to be found. I mean honestly, your wife and daughter wakes from a coma and you don't even visit her. Why wouldn't they visit? If ever I had questioned my importance to them before, I'm fairly sure I have my answer now.

*****

Trying to turn my heavy body which still doesn't obey me very well, I see a man beside me. Staring at his smiling face, I'm shocked. *Well, hello there handsome...* Ha! What the *hell?*
This guy is so attractive; actually he's kind of beautiful for a man. Oh god, I feel like I'm going to start laughing. Shit. No. No.

No. *Argh...* This giggle is gonna burst out any second now... Shit. I can't help but just silently stare at him while fighting this strange fit of laughter inside me.

Still smiling at me he whispers, "Hi, Suzanne. Remember me?" Ugh... Here we go again. Again.

"No, I'm sorry." And there's the look.

"It's okay. Just think hard, and I'm sure you'll remember me." Yeah, I'd like to stare at this guy *all* friggin' day. Holy Hot Pants, Batman! Giggle.

"I'm sorry, I don't remember you. Are we friends?"

Grinning, he winks at me. "Yes, we're friends, and lovers, and actually kind of engaged, unless you've change your mind, of course. I'm Z, and you are my Suzanne."

Stunned, I have no words. Looking at this man, I'm sure he's teasing me. He must be a doctor or a Shrink. He has to be. Actually, he looks like that tall, smooth, deep-voiced doctor type from all soap operas. There is NO WAY I know this guy... Marcus wouldn't allow me.

"My fiancé, huh? I'm sure. When is the wedding? Oh, and is Marcus- *my husband-* invited?" Giggle.

"Look hard, Suzanne. Please, just try to think back. I know you'll remember me. I am very much in love with you, and you with me. We were together in New York before your accident. You were with *me* in New York, not Marcus. You aren't with Marcus anymore." *What?!* "You left Marcus and you came to me in New York. You are mine now."

"Z..."

Looking, I'm startled to see Dr. MacDonald in the corner. I didn't even realize he was here, too. What the hell is going on?

"Suzanne, can you try hard to remember me. Just stare at me, love. Maybe if you just stare at me, all your memories will come back to you. You love me very much, I promise."

"Really? Well, I find that hard to believe seeing as I'm married. And I'm not the cheating type. And I'm not someone who loves other men. I love my husband."

"Actually, you don't love him- not like that anymore."

"Suzanne, Z is telling you the truth. You had left Marcus before your accident, and you came to New York to stay with your friend Kayla, and then you went to be with Z."

Something about this whole thing seems so wrong. I can't explain it, but I'm getting kind of angry now. It's like I'm covered in their lies and I'm not sure why they want to do this to me. I'm not sure why they want me to believe these lies.

"This isn't fair," I whisper. "I don't remember anything, but you're both trying to tell me lies, and you're trying to make me believe in lies. Why are you doing this? And no offense Z, but you are *way* out of my league and not someone I would ever know, never mind someone I would love. So could you please just leave me alone now?"

"Suzanne, trust me. I'm not lying to you, and neither is Z."

"Okay, I'm really tired now, so would you mind leaving me alone?"

"Suzanne, *please...*"

Taking my hand suddenly, Z bends his head against me and kisses my hand while keeping his face hidden against my bed. What the hell? And what the hell kind of name is Z, anyway?

Oh my god, this is so weird. I'm mean, come *on!* As if I would be with this guy. As if I would leave Marcus- I'm not allowed. My parents would have been pissed at me and Marcus would have found me and taken me back anyway, so what would be the point?

None of this makes sense, and yet I had believed Dr. MacDonald about everything else before. I had believed him, and now I don't feel like I can trust him at all.

Pulling my hand away, Z lifts his head. Oh my god... His eyes are swimming with tears.

"Suzanne, we had only one night since you were sick- one fucking night," he croaks. "I have known you almost exactly a year and I've waited for you for that entire year to come to me, and then you did come to me, and then you were lost again. Please, love. Just try to remember me. We only had one night."

Giggling, which I can't seem to stop, I ask, "One night together, huh? And already we're engaged? That seems a little sudden, no? I mean really, not only do I leave my husband, which I don't believe for a second, but I have a one night stand with you and we're engaged? Do you even realize how absurd your lies actually sound? I mean, come ON! At least make your lies believable!" What an idiot, I swear.

"We had one night together, but we were together *emotionally* for months and months."

"*Emotionally?*" I scoff.

"I helped you when you were sick, and you became better, and we were finally together. And by the time you came back to me, you were ready to start your life with me."

"Really? Okay. Well Z, I think you're full of shit, and I'm not sure why you're doing this, but-"

"I'm not full of shit! Ask anyone! Ask the other doctors. Ask Mack. Ask the Kaylas. Fuck! Ask your grandfather- he'll tell you. It was your grandfather and I who stopped Marcus from hurting you! It was us who saved you!"

"Z, please calm down. I think you may be scaring Suzanne."

"Yeah, *Z!*" I yell.

"Good! I'm sorry Suzanne, but you need to wake up and remember me and our life and YOUR life. You need to wake up and remember. We have some big changes ahead of us. We have many plans to make."

"Really? And what are those plans, exactly? Are they wedding plans? Or maybe they're plans which will conveniently convince me of your lies?"

"No."

"Because right now everything you say is a lie. I know it. First of all, I would never leave Marcus-"

"You did."

"Uh huh. Whatever. I would NEVER leave Marcus, and I would NEVER be with another man."
"You were. You were with me, you just don't-"
"Yeah, I don't *remember*. Convenient. And my grandfather? I haven't seen or spoken to my grandfather in forever, like 16 years or something. He wasn't even at my wedding to MARCUS- my *husband*. So again, no offense, but you are Full Of Shit, Z." Ha!
"Suzanne, please-"
"Nope. Get out! Get the hell out of my room. I never want to see you again. I have no idea what you and Dr. MacDonald are doing, but-"
"Mack. What Mack and I are doing."
"Fine. MACK! Whatever you think you're doing is pointless. I know who I am. I know I'm Suzanne Anderson, and I know Marcus is my husband, and I know I don't have anything to do with my grandfather or any other man, or anything else you're trying to tell me. So please, get out of my room."
"Suzanne, please listen to me. I-"
"Not a chance. Seriously, get out of my room. Now! And take Dr. Liar MacDonald with you as well."
"Suzanne-"
"Oh, Fuck *Off* and take this asshole with you and get out of here. I don't know why you're doing this, but I need you to stop!" Ugh...
"Suzanne, take a deep breath. You're starting to panic a little, and I need you to breathe in and out slowly for me."
"Panic? *Really?* Well, that's YOUR f-fault!" Shit.
"Suzanne-"
"No!" Gasp. "Stop talking! Just don't t-talk-"
"Listen to me. I love you desperately-"
"NO!" Screaming, I finally move a little from my helpless position and grab my face in my hands. If they can't see me, I can't see them!! I've had enough. Holding tightly, I suddenly feel my face.
Oh my god, what the fuck is this? What. The. FUCK. Is. *THIS?!*

Screaming, I start thrashing as best I can. Holding onto my face, I can't believe what I feel. What is this? What have they done to me? Hysterically, the panic threatens to overwhelm me! What have they done to me?

Screaming, "What did you do? What's w-wrong with me?! What *IS* this?!"

Oh god, I can barely breathe from the fear. What did they do?

Feeling arms holding me down, I can't look. What is this? Touching, I'm shocked and stunned and horrified at once. What is this? My face is all bumpy, and weird, and hot, and, and *WEIRD!* What the hell *IS* this?!

Screaming, I feel the arms tighten around me. I think someone is on the bed. I think I hear talking but I can't stop screaming. I hear the raised voices and I feel a weight on me. But I can't hear their words.

Gasping for breath in between screams, I'm numb. There has never been a moment like this in my life. I now know true horror.

Gasping, I beg, "What- did you- do- to me?"

When there is only silence, my screams begin again. Moving my legs, I fight the arms binding me to the bed. Screaming, I try to fight them. Screaming, I try to erase this.

Knowing I have only seconds before they put me away, I gather my strength for one last rush of panic and then I'm free. Looking with terrified eyes, I see their horror staring back at me.

Dr. MacDonald, and Z, and a nurse have me surrounded. They're staring at me. They're doing stuff to my body, and to the tubes and to the wires. They're staring at me with horror.

I see them shaking and they look horrified, so I think they must be horrified because of me. But there is only silence in my room as I try to breathe throughout the screams inside my head.

Whispering, I beg again, "What- did you do- to my face...?" As I feel the blackness consume me.

CHAPTER 13

MAY 19

Holding my face, I slowly wake up again. I don't know how long I've been asleep this time, and my memories of falling asleep are fuzzy at best. But I know what I'm doing in this moment- I'm struggling.
Right now touching my face, I can barely breathe. With my eyes closed tightly, I'm slowly feeling the skin on my face. I'm stunned but desperately trying to breathe through this. I know what I feel but I can't *believe* what I'm feeling. This is just so wrong. This is so horrible.

"Suzanne... it's me. Chicago Kayla. Can you talk to me?"
The infamous Chicago Kayla all the others talk about? Well, this should be interesting.
Opening my eyes, I'm stunned. Holy *shit!* I know her. Finally! Someone I know. Kayla Lefferts.
"Hello, Kayla. I remember you from work. Ah, how are you?" Why is *she* here? I swear to god, my days just get weirder and weirder.
"Suzanne, I'm here because we're best friends- well, I'm one of your 3 best friends," she grins. Three, huh? *Whatever.*
"Okay. Well, thank you for visiting, but have you seen my husband Marcus? I've been waiting for him to visit me since I woke up."
"Marcus isn't here right now, but I'm sure he'll be here as soon as he can. Do you remember me, Suzanne?"
"Of course. I just told you I know you from work." Duh. Thank god she's hot 'cause she's not too bright- I feel better now.

Ooops. Catty. Giggle. Ooops again. Shit.
"Why are you giggling?" She asks with a smile.
"Oh, no reason."
"You can tell me, I'm cool. *We're* cool, Suzanne. And I wasn't joking about being one of your three best friends. Unlike the other Kayla, I'm not intimidated by being tied with her as your second-place best friend, behind Mack of course. Honestly, you can tell me or ask me anything."
Okay, she seems like I remember, but she and I weren't very close. I mean, I always spoke to her at work, but I would NEVER confide in her. She and I weren't like that. I'm not like that with anyone.
"Do you remember me from before the accident? Or just from *before*-before, like when we worked together?"
"I remember working with you, certainly. But I'm not sure about the 'tied as best friends' thing. I know that other Kayla and Dr. MacDonald keep telling me things, but I don't remember them at all. Um, when did we become best friends?" Again... weird.

I find this whole thing very hard to believe. It's so strange that I would be friends with Kayla Lefferts, never-mind *best* friends. She is totally not my type of friend. Not that I *have* a type of friend or even, you know, *a* friend really... Giggle. Shit.
"You're giggling again, which for you is actually a very bad thing. You only giggle when you're stressed or wiggy, or like losing your shit, or something. You never giggle when you're okay. Are you okay, Suzanne?"
"Ah, not really. I keep learning things that are too much and too hard to believe, and quite frankly, rather insane to me. But the things I expect are not happening either. I have no memory of all you 'friends' of mine, and yet my parents, and Marcus aren't here either. So it's very strange that they aren't here, and it makes the other stuff you people keep telling me more believable, but at the same time it's all so *un*believable that I'm having a hard time understanding anything. Why is my giggling bad?" Giggle. And

THIS is me...

there it is again.
"As I said, you only giggle when you're crazy, which I'm hoping you're not. I don't want you to go there again." *Again?*
"What does THAT mean?"
"You were out of it last year, but you recovered! You did, I promise. It's just you giggled a lot back then and it was so unlike you that we knew something was wrong. Well, *I* knew, and I guess Marcus and your parents knew, but then you got sick, and then you got better. Don't get me wrong, you totally laugh when things are funny, and when Kayla and I tease you, you giggle as well- I'm talking about this random, spontaneous giggling, which you seem to be fighting even right now."
And I really am. Right now. I feel all this pressure to just burst out laughing at everything she's saying, but I think she wants me to clamp down on the hysterical laughter that wants to swallow up the room. I want to just laugh at all this confusion. Okay. Change of subject desperately needed.
"Ah, that man, Z...? Um..." Blush.
"Z. Mr. Z Zinfandel. Totally yes," she smiles. Gulp. *Really?*
"Yes, what?"
"You and Z are very much together. You and Z are a couple, or were a couple- are *trying* to be a couple. He loves you very much and he's been by your side this whole time. And you love him very much. Christ! I'm half in love with him myself. I swear he is the sexiest, funniest, yet most intense man I've ever met in my life. I just adore him, especially for you. He is amazing, Suzanne. And I'm not kidding- if you and he don't work out I'm throwing myself at him," she smiles at me again. Wow. How weird. How do I even respond to that?
Whispering, "But I'm married to Marcus. I don't understand."
"I know you don't remember this, but you left Marcus. You really did leave Marcus in February. You and Marcus are over, or were over. I hope ARE over. You tried to make it work though, Suzanne. You tried very hard, but you finally left Marcus in February and he is well aware of this, regardless of what he tells you now."

But I don't believe her. I really don't. I mean, that guy was super-hot, so how would I even meet someone like that? This whole thing reads like fiction. I wish to god Marcus would get here so he could tell me what's actually going on. I know people don't generally band together to mess with a total stranger's head but other than that theory, I've got nothing.

I don't know these people, and I don't believe I would ever leave Marcus. Marcus loves me, I know he does.

"Marcus loves me, Kayla. I know you didn't really know him, but he does. Mr. Shields knows him and he'll tell you. Marcus and I have been together for a long time now. And he loves me very much," I tell her desperately.

Staring hard at me, Kayla looks like she wants to say something. Actually, I can tell she really wants to say something but won't or can't. Or maybe she shouldn't. Or maybe she doesn't know how. I'm not sure, but her sudden silence is unnerving.

Suddenly desperate, I beg, "What is it?"

"It's not my place to tell you this, though I want to very much. You have so much to talk to Mack about. Actually, you, Mack, Z, and even Marcus have a lot to discuss, and though it's killing me not to tell you, I can't. Trust me, you're gonna need Mack badly. I just hope you remember Mack soon so you remember your love for him, so you can be 'Mack and Suzanne' again because you're really awesome together, and Mack totally gets you."

"But you said I was in love with Z."

"You are. You and Mack are inseparable *friends*. You both love each other very much but as dear friends. Mack is with the other Kayla, though I'm trying to get him for myself as well." Again with the smirk. What is *with* her?

"I'm joking, Suzanne. Z is yours and Mack is Kayla's, and I'm just joking. I always threaten those 2 men with dating them but I'm totally kidding. Please don't look at me like that. You have this look of disgust on your face, and you never do that. You don't judge me like every other woman does, and you *know* I'm kidding and not half as bad as my reputation is."

"Actually, I *don't* know that because I don't remember that. But truthfully, it's hard to believe anything you say because I only remember you from work. And at work you were always so explicit and promiscuous and very, very verbal about it."

"Suzanne, please. I'm NOT like that, and we're very good friends now, I promise. You don't even work at Petri-Dunn anymore-"

"What?! *Why*?!"

"Oh fuck, I'm sorry. I'm not supposed to tell you things you don't remember yet. Shit. Okay... Ah, you quit your job but you're okay! You *wanted* to quit."

Okay, breathe. What the hell is going on? I must have mental overload, I think. I can't possibly process anything else right now. I'm unemployed. I'm estranged from my husband. I'm *in love* with another man. I have all these 'friends' and my husband and parents haven't even been here to visit me yet. What the hell is going on in my life??

"What's wrong with my face?" Wow. Where did THAT come from?

"You were in a car accident and you sustained some damage."

"Is that why I'm in here?"

"Yes and no. You were in a coma because of brain trauma as you know, and while in here you've also been treated for the damage to your body caused from the accident."

"Is it really bad?" I whisper.

Shaking her head she says, "It's not great, but it's not as bad as it probably feels to you. Would you like to see it?"

"NO! God, no."

"Okay. Whenever you're ready though, let me know and I'll get you a mirror."

"Is that why my arm and leg have those tight bandages on them?"

"Yes. You were hurt on one side of your body, your left side, so you've been recovering from the trauma to your body while in the coma. I know it doesn't seem like it, but it's really not as bad as you're probably thinking." I'm sure it IS as bad as I'm thinking.

"I don't want to see it. And I really wish you weren't looking at me so much. If I had known I was messed up I wouldn't have talked with all those other people. I don't really want anyone to see me. Would you mind leaving now? I'd like to be alone for a while."

But as I try turning away from her she suddenly yells, "Well, that's tough shit! If by 'the others' you mean Mack, Kayla, and Z, then you're going to be very disappointed. We've been here constantly since your accident. We have talked with you, and held you, and hugged you and begged you. We have been the constant for you since this all began- actually even before the accident we were with you whether you remember us or not.

"... So please don't give me the 'I am an island- I just want to be alone' bullshit, okay? Just spare me 'cause I'm way too fucking tired of all the Suzanne *drama* to have any patience left. At this point you're lucky I'm even remotely civil with you."

Oh my god... I'm stunned. What the hell is she talking about? And how cruel can one person be? I'm not trying to be anything. I'm just confused, and lonely, and I don't know these people like this so I don't want them here. *And* I'm ugly now. So naturally, I don't want them to have to look at my ugliness.

Bursting into tears, I suddenly close in on myself. I don't want to keep doing this. If by 'Suzanne-drama' she means being in a car accident, then how mean! Honestly, it's not like I asked for this. It's not like I want any of this. I don't even know what I look like, but I know I don't want it. Why is she so mean to me?

"Oh, shit! I'm so sorry Suzanne. I know I'm a total bitch but I swear I'm not usually with you. Just with everyone else. Ask Mack and Kayla- they'll tell you," she exhales. "I'm just so tired and scared all the time with you because there's never any peace around you. And I'm never sure how to handle it all so I act like a bitch usually. Look, I don't really do *warm and fuzzy* so I'm mostly hard and bitchy, but that's my shit NOT yours. Please don't cry

Suzanne. Please. Plus, Mack and Kayla will be pissed at me for fucking you up, and Z will absolutely kill me."
Looking at her, I just can't understand this Kayla as the Kayla I remember. She was always so strong and tough and awesome at work. She was never sorry, or tired, or scared. She was just the funny, kind of slutty Kayla from work, who I always talked to because no one else really did. Except for the men, of course.

"Look Kayla, I'm okay. But I'm really tired now, so I *really* need you to leave. I'm not trying to be all *dramatic-*"
"I'm sorry, I didn't mean that."
"It's fine. Forget it. I'm just exhausted, so please leave me alone. I need to sleep badly. Okay? But thank you for visiting, I really appreciate it."
"Okay Suzanne... But I'm really sorry I upset you. If it makes you feel any better I'm going to tell on myself to Mack and Kayla, AND I'm going to kick my own ass afterward."
Okay, I don't even know what that means, but it's kind of funny.
"Okay. You do that, and I'll see you some other time. Thanks for stopping by."
"I'm coming back tomorrow, I promise."
"Okay, thank you. Good night."
Leaning in, Kayla suddenly hugs me, which actually makes me tense right up and even flinch a little. I suddenly feel so trapped and uncomfortable; I can't wait for her to leave. This feels so gross to me.
"Goodbye Suzanne. I miss you."

Leaving my room, I see her tears and again I know I'm supposed to feel something for her sadness, but I really don't. It's like I'm heartless or numb to her upset, which I think is good. If I felt like shit on top of the mental aerobics I'm suffering I think I may just lose my mind. There is only so much I can take.
Exhaling a big breath, I once again find my hand resting between my cheek and the pillow. Touching my face, I feel the bumps and weird skin. I swear it feels hot on my fingertips. Strangely, the

pattern feels almost interesting as I touch it with my fingers, though clearly not interesting enough that I want to actually look at it.

I wonder what I look like now. I wonder how many layers of gross I've added to myself. I wonder if I'll be known now as 'The short, big-assed, wide-hipped, ugly-faced Woman'. Giggle. Shit, I really am mental sometimes.

Closing my eyes, it's time for me. This reality sucks, so maybe my dream reality will be easier to handle. I mean really... How much worse can it get?

Ooops, probably just jinxed myself. Ha! Dammit.

CHAPTER 14

MAY 23

Thinking again about that man Z, I'm almost excited. It's so weird to try to understand and remember a relationship I don't know at all. It's even harder trying to forget the relationship I DO know with Marcus simply because strangers tell me it's over.
　Moving slowly, I turn to my left side and there he is. Wow! I just think about him and he's here? I wonder if my power reaches beyond just him. That would be an amazingly useful power to have. Think and you shall receive. Giggle.

　"Suzanne... How are you, love?"
　"Ah, good. I'm sore and a little uncomfortable, but okay. Why are you here?"
　"I'm always here. I've been here since your accident. I followed you from New York, and settled into Chicago while I waited for you to wake up." Oh.
　"Thank you...?"
　"Suzanne, you don't need to be polite, and you don't need to be kind. Just be yourself. Talk to me however you like. However you need. I know you're struggling with all this information and confusion. Would you like me to get the nurse for more pain meds?"
　"I'm so sorry... but I really am confused. This is all too much for me, and no I don't want more medication. I think it confuses me more."
　Smiling, he says, "We can take it slow if you want. We can just talk, and maybe we'll trigger a memory, or maybe you will slowly begin to remember on your own. As I understand it, Mack says you could just wake up with your memory, or you may slowly

remember little details over time."

"He told me that, too. Um, why are you here though? This must be so boring for you."

As I speak, I find myself reaching for my own face. I find an intense insecurity forcing me to cover my face from him. He is so good looking- SO good looking and I don't want him to see me ugly like this.

When he leans forward to take my hand, I flinch and move deeper into the pillows. I don't want him to uncover me, and I DON'T want him to touch me.

When he slowly moves back into his chair, I relax. He smells delicious, but way too close to me. He's invading my personal space and he's keeping me from exhaling, I think.

"Suzanne. You never have to hide from me. Ever. Though you don't remember me yet, I love you very, very much. I love all of you, every piece of you. You and I have been to hell and back, to *temporarily* into hell again. But I'm not leaving you, so please try to trust in my words even if you can't remember me yet."

Silently, I nod and just take him in. I think he's pretty tall, and he's got a great body, and he dresses fantastic, and he's just so awesome to look at. His eyes are the loveliest dark brown I've ever seen, and his lips are those awesome full guy lips that every woman wants to kiss, and his skin looks warm, and naturally darker, I think. He seems Italian or Greek or something with that coloring.

"Are you Italian, or Greek?" What a stupid question, but honestly, it's all I've got right now.

"I'm half Italian and half American. My Italian side is deeply Italian, but my American side is the classic British 'once upon a time' mix." Smirking, he questions, "Why do you ask?"

"Um, you have lovely tanned skin, and your eyes are beautiful." Holy shit! Did I just say that?

"Why, thank you," he grins.

Grinning and mumbling a 'you're welcome' I pause.

When silence descends on us, I feel lost again. I want to know so much but I don't know what to ask him?

"Would you like me to tell you a little about us, Suzanne? Would you like me to explain you and me?"

Exhaling, I nod, "Yes, please."

Smiling at me once again, he says, "Well get comfy, love, because you and I are a beautiful story." Oh!

Turning a little more to my left, I settle my face deeply into my pillow. Clasping my hands under my cheek, I'm almost excited to hear Z speak. His voice is deep and dark and his eyes totally mesmerize me.

"Almost exactly a year ago, you and I began a kind of pseudo-relationship via email when you were having problems at work and problems with your husband, and I quickly found myself intrigued by you. You are, or *were* very proper and reserved and you were wrapped so tightly, I found myself curious about *unwrapping* you," he winks. Oh *shit*. I think I just blushed.

"Anyway, we spoke on the phone frequently, and eventually we met up once you left your husband. And when we met, I was drawn to you the very moment I kissed you. Actually, the very moment I saw your photo I was intrigued by you. But the moment I met you in person, I was done. There was something about you I couldn't understand or deny. I was so attracted to you that I was rather shocked by the intensity of my initial attraction. And once you left your husband, I knew I had my opening with you."

I don't even know what to say to this. There are no words. It's impossible for someone like him to feel like that for someone like me. It doesn't make sense. I'm just me, and he is SO him.

"I really left Marcus?" I beg, instead of stating the obvious.

"You really did, Suzanne."

God, he says that with such conviction, I believe him totally, but it's just so unbelievable that I would do such a thing. What could've happened?

"Do you know why I left him?" I beg.

"I do, but I'd rather you talk to Marcus about that. If you need

me to tell you I will, but I feel like that's Marcus' story to tell you."
"Okay, I'll ask him. Thank you."
Nodding, he continues...
"Suzanne, you were very intense and overwhelmed, and so scared by the events in your life that I instantly wanted to help you. God, I just looked at you and I wanted to ease all your upset. I wanted to be the man who eased you from your loneliness and from all your pain. And I *was* that man for a very short period of time for you.

"...There was such a sadness in you, and I needed to be the man who gave you some peace. Not that the feelings were one-sided, because this time was exceptionally intense for me as well. I was stunned by the depth of my feelings for you. I was simply overcome with the need to protect you, and to just *love* you. For me it was so fast. It was way too fast and intense, and though I never fought my attraction to you, honestly, I *was* shocked by it."

As his words set in, I feel something stir inside me. I'm not sure what it is, but I kind of hope it's the return of my memories.

"... You were just this little lost woman who I met, and within seconds I wanted to be everything to you. I wanted to be your lover, *of course*, but I wanted more. I wanted to be the man who helped you, and pleased you, and healed you. I wanted to be the greatest love of your life." Oh My *God!*

When there is only silence, I realize Z seems to be collecting himself. He's shaking slightly, and he's breathing heavier, and he also seems to be struggling with all this information, just like I am in this amazing moment.

It's like he's trying to hold back a little. I wish I could help him, but I'm afraid if I speak he'll stop talking, and I really, *really* don't want him to stop speaking. This is an amazing story to hear.

"You became sick shortly after our first meeting, but not before I had fallen in love with you. You became sick, and I became desperate to help you. I *needed* to make you better. I found I couldn't even function myself with you so rapidly declining."

"What was wrong with me?" I whisper.

"Well, you were having a nervous breakdown caused in part from a bleeding aneurism in your brain, which eventually ruptured." Really? Wow.

"It was during this illness that you remembered things you had repressed and you became more sick. It was also during this time of sickness that you met Mack, and shortly thereafter Kayla Rinaldi, the nurse from New York." So that's how I met her.

"Suzanne, you were just so sick, and I couldn't help you, and you wouldn't let me help you. And there was nothing I could do or say to make you let me help you. You wouldn't see me because you needed distance between us while you recovered, so I stayed away. Eventually, you were saved in the hospital, and you began to make your recovery.

"... But during this time, I was out of my mind with grief. Um, in your attempt to get well, you chose to push me away completely. I know you didn't do it to hurt me, and I understood your need at the time, but emotionally, I was just wrecked. By pushing me away, you almost destroyed me," he moans.

"I'm sorry-"

"Suzanne, you don't need to be sorry. You did what you had to, and I knew that at the time. I knew in my mind you were trying to get well. It was just my heart that was broken, and there was nothing I could do but wait for you to get well. And so I waited.

"... Months passed, and you slowly found yourself again, and then you found me again. Well actually, I chased you down but thankfully you chose to be caught," he grins.

"Then what happened?" Oh my god! This is the best story I've ever heard in my life!

Smiling, he wiggles his eyebrows at me. Wow. That was so cute. Blush.

Sitting closer to me, he continues.

"The night you came to me in my apartment in New York was without a doubt the best night of my life. You came to me well and sure of yourself. You came to me with strength and dignity, and with promise. I saw hope and need in your eyes. I saw you were finally ready for me."

Smiling again and shaking his head, he continues. "God, it was so overwhelming for me to be with you after waiting for so long. Actually, I was horribly pathetic that night, crying, and begging, while so desperate for you to love me again. I looked like a complete ass, but I didn't care. You were with me, and I was so desperate to make you understand my feelings for you that I didn't care what I said or did.

"...Thankfully, you weren't disgusted by my wretched display of emotion, and you chose to be with me anyway. You wanted to be with me, finally. We made love..." Holy SHIT! "... and you were with me completely. You were finally *with* me, and I was just stunned by the fact that I had you, and that you finally wanted me again as much as I had wanted you.

"... Um, I proposed during the throws of passion," he says laughing. "And though you agreed to marry me, afterward you did request a more suitable proposal, one preferably with some clothing," he laughs again as I smile.

"And we laughed and cried, and held each other, and just loved one another completely, without reservation or sadness.

"... Suzanne, you are the great love of my life. I know you don't know or understand this, and you probably have a hard time believing this but it is the absolute truth. I would give my life to save you. I would give anything and everything to have you back with me. You are absolutely IT for me."

"So what happened...?" I know this love story has to end- they always do.

"The following morning we were still together. You were mine and I was yours. We made a promise to each other; we both wanted this new start to our lives *together*. You wanted to be with me, as much as I wanted to be with you. We talked to each other and we loved each other physically and emotionally. We were together, and I was just so happy."

"But what happened...?" I beg desperately.

"Nothing happened and *everything* happened. After you promised to never push me away again, you left to meet Kayla for lunch, and that's the end. You were in the car accident, and you've been asleep ever since. I died the moment I got the call, and I've been dying ever since," he states so calmly while looking at me so intensely.

"I love you Suzanne so completely that I've become half insane waiting for you to come back to me. And though it's not your fault *obviously,* I'm just so lost without you. I'm devastated that you don't remember us yet."

"I'm so sorry."

"Please don't be. You have nothing of be sorry for, and I'm still here, and I'll wait for you. One day you'll have the memories back and you'll know this truth as I've told it. Until then, I'll be here waiting and hoping and reminding you at every turn that I love you, and that I'll always love you. And if we have to start over again, we will. I'll show you my love until you fall in love with me again."

"But, what if-"

"... You are IT for me, Suzanne. As cheesy as this sounds, you're the one for me. I love you, and I will never love another. So keep getting better, and one day you'll remember me, and you'll know I'm telling you the truth. You are the absolute love of my life. You are everything to me," he exhales.

Nodding, there is nothing else I can do. I have no words to give him, and really, what could I say? He is so sure and so certain of his love, and I know no different. What could I possibly say to this beautiful man who says he loves me?

"I hope I remember you soon, because that IS a beautiful story."

"I know you will, and so I'll continue waiting. Suzanne, there is nothing between us I won't wait for. There is no struggle I can't endure for you. I love too much."

"Thank you," I breathe on an exhale.

What do I do now? What should he do now? What the hell will happen now?

Well, for starters, I'd really like my memories back because if even half of what he just said is true, I WANT to remember him. God, I *need* to remember him.

No one has ever loved me like that, and no one has ever waited for me. I am just me, but Z makes me sound like I'm more than that. Z acts like I'm more than just me for him.

"Thank you," I whisper again through my tears.

"Suzanne, just come back to me and you'll see. I'm going to love you so beautifully; you will never feel confused or lonely again. You will know beyond any doubt that you have me to love you, forever."

"Okay, I'll try."

After a few minutes of silence, Z asks if I would like some time alone, which is EXACTLY what I want. I need to digest all this awesome. I need to start believing all this awesome. This is just too much to believe at once.

Bending to me, Z suddenly kisses my chest, but not in a pervy way. At first I didn't understand what he was doing so I flinched, but then I understood. He kissed my heart. Wow.

"I'll be back soon, love."

"Okay. Thank you again Z. That *was* a beautiful story."

"I'll see you soon," he says with a stunning smile as he briefly touches my hand goodbye.

Watching him walk away, I want to believe him so badly, it's nearly overwhelming. I *want* to be loved by him. Z just seems so intense, and sexy, and stunning, really. He's like a dream for me, a dream of such intensity, I don't even know if I *could* handle a man, or a love like that. But god, I want to try.

Closing my eyes, I try to picture making love with Z. I'm sure it wasn't very good for him, but I imagine HE was spectacular. He has that 'look at me! I'm an intense passionate Italian super sexy lover' thing going for him. He's like the hero from a novel who loves the woman until she can't breathe without him. He looks like he would be a novel lover, for sure.

  Closing my eyes with a little smile on my lips, I imagine us as lovers. I imagine us as a couple. How amazing would that be? It's almost too amazing to believe. Actually, it IS too amazing to believe, but I'm going to try anyway. How could I not?

CHAPTER 15

MAY 28

Okay, so I'm awake AND tired again. I know it's only been a few weeks and every single Doctor I meet explains recovery, and the slow progression back to being myself, but I'm so tired of all this work.
After another trip to another room- the Physiotherapy room, which incidentally is filled with mirrors WHICH I AVOIDED, I'm finally wheeled back to my room again.
Dr. Mirabelli, the Doctor of Physiotherapy, or the DPT Specialist, has promised that if I work really hard at the physiotherapy I may have perfect use of my left leg again. I'm not too sure about all the damage because I just can't seem to face looking at it yet. And even though my leg is bandaged with those tight meshy white bandages a few times every day I still haven't been able to look at it.
Apparently, the Physio is supposed to strengthen my legs, and then I'll be out of the hideous wheelchair they've been using to get me around. I hate the wheelchair, but I can't even really feel my left leg very well, except for this constant pain that just simmers on the surface, so I need it still, because right now the pain is *almost* more annoying than it is painful.
Resting on my bed, Dr. Mirabelli has finally left me alone. She is very kind, but very intense sometimes. She reminds me of the other nurse Kayla and Kayla from work with all her demands and her 'take no prisoners' attitude, but she's still really professional and nice to me.
Maybe she's another Kayla? Huh. Wouldn't that be insane! Kayla Lefferts, Kayla Rinaldi, and Dr. Freakin' Kayla Mirabelli. I swear to god, I'd start laughing. I should ask her first name. Then

again, if she actually IS another Kayla, I think I'd lose my mind... totally and completely. What is *with* that name, anyway?!

*****

Getting comfy, I relax into another semi-rest. Christ, I need it. All these physical exertions and tests, and mental tests, and emotional exertions have worn me out. Closing my eyes, I'm ready to sleep until I hear the door open again. Argh...
Turning my head- MARCUS!
"Marcus! Where have you been?" Oh my god! He's finally here! The relief I feel is overwhelming. Bursting into tears, I reach out for him as he races to my side.
"Suzanne, I'm here. I'm so sorry, honey. I'm so sorry I wasn't here when you woke up. There was a situation I was in the middle of but I tried to get away. I swear I tried! I just couldn't get away until now. They wouldn't let me until now!"
Grasping his arms as tight as I can (which really isn't very tight) I weep on his shoulder while releasing all the tension and confusion I've endured since my awake.
"I'm so glad you're finally here. What the hell is happening? All these strange people are visiting, and Kayla Lefferts from work is saying all this strange stuff, and there's a really nice doctor, and this other guy..." Ooops. Don't go there! "Anyway, I'm so confused all the time."
"I know, honey. I know. I'm so sorry and I really did try. But I'm here now. Oh god, I'm so glad to see you awake. I've missed you so much. You are everything to me, Suzanne. *Everything!*"
Marcus is suddenly just sobbing all over me. His breath is hitched, and his sobs are mixed with groans of agony. He sounds terrible. THIS is terrible.

"It'll be okay, Marcus. I'm awake now," I say while patting his back.

"I can't believe you're awake. They t-told me. They said you were, but I just couldn't believe them. I thought you were gone for sure. I was ready for it. I knew you were gone. I knew you had died already so I said all my goodbyes." He did? Um... not too sure how I feel about that.

"You did?" I question.

"Yes, but its good now. You're here. You're alive and awake. So I didn't make a mistake."

What mistake? Holy shit, I suddenly feel more confused than I did before.

"What mistake? What did you think before?"

"It doesn't matter anymore. You're awake and I'm so happy to have you back. You ARE back with me, right Suzanne?"

Looking at his face, he seems kind of weird to me- all manic and desperate, or something. He's even holding my arms really tightly. Actually, he's kind of hurting me now. Um...

"Marcus, what's wrong? Why are you acting so weird with me? Of course I'm back. I mean, I'm out of the coma so I'm going to be alright now, right? I mean, I know my legs are weak and my arm is hurt, but Dr. Mirabelli says I can get my body working again with lots of Physio. So it'll be fine. I'll be fine, right Marcus?"

"Yes, everything is fine now. You remember ME, so everything else is going to be fine. I knew you'd remember me. I told them. I told them all you would remember me but they didn't believe me! They didn't!"

"Who did you tell? My parents? Where are they anyway?"

"Your parents are on a cruise," he replies quickly.

"A cruise?! Oh... do they know I'm awake?"

"No, not yet. Your parents can't get off the ship right now, so there's no sense telling them because they can't get to you anyway. But I'll tell them soon. Don't worry." A cruise? *Really?* Ah, my mother can't get off a cruise? As *if.*

"Marcus, that doesn't make sense. My mother is, well, my *mother*. As if she couldn't get off a cruise if she wanted to. Why are they on a cruise anyway? I mean, I was in a coma. Why wouldn't they postpone it?" *Seriously?*

"Non-refundable tickets," he replies quickly.

Marcus is suddenly all tense while just kind of staring at me. Non-refundable tickets? What the hell? *Non-refundable tickets?*

Bursting out laughing, I'm totally shocked. My mother is rich! My parents are rich! My parents are **THE** Beaumonts for Christ's sake! What the hell kind of cruise is it anyway?

When Marcus starts shaking me, I silence. Why the hell is he shaking me? I'm just laughing. I mean, who wouldn't? My parents would rather be on a cruise then wait around for, oh, I don't know... their daughter to wake up from a coma? Who *does* that?

"Stop laughing Suzanne. It's very odd, and there's no reason to be laughing." Oh! Instant silence.

"Sorry, Marcus. I'm sorry I'm laughing, but I find it strange that my parents left on a cruise when I was in the hospital. And non-refundable tickets? My mother wouldn't care about that. I'm sure she could have a helicopter fly out to the main deck to pick her up if she wanted. Don't you find that strange?" Giggle.

"Well, as I said, they don't even know you've woken yet, so it's not all that strange. And they booked the cruise months in advance, and your chances of waking were slim to none, so I'm sure they just needed a get-away."

A 'get-away'? From a comatose daughter? Yes, how very taxing for them to have to stare at me while I SLEPT. Jesus *Christ!* They are so messed up.

"Anyway, I'm thrilled you're here, and I can't wait to get you home. Did the Doctors say how long you'll be here? Did they say when you could leave with me? I've missed you terribly."

Thank god somebody cares, even if it's Marcus. Wow. Ooops. That was very ungrateful, I think.

"No, I don't know when I can leave. I'm not even sure of all the details yet. I know my leg and arm were hurt in the car accident, and I know I need physiotherapy because I'm not very strong yet, but other than that they haven't told me much. But I'd like to go home soon, if that's okay?"

Crying again, Marcus nods yes. Taking my right hand again, he begins kissing my fingers and rests his head on my hand on my stomach.

Kissing my stomach, Marcus seems to exhale all his tension. He seems so relieved that I'm awake, and so genuinely happy that I've suddenly never been more grateful for Marcus in all the years we've been together. Thank god I have him in my life.

"What's wrong Marcus? You seem so upset. And you're not usually this emotional," I question.

"I'm just very pleased you're awake and you remember me, and you want to come home with me. That's all." Huh?

"Where else would I go? Where else *can* I go?" What a strange thing to say.

"Nowhere. Of course you want to come home with me, Suzanne. Just make sure you tell all the doctors and anyone else who stops by that you want to be with me, okay? Make sure everyone knows that you want to be with me, your husband."

"I will. But what's wrong? You're telling me things that are so common sense that I feel like they don't make sense. Shit. Does that make sense? Oh! Sorry for swearing." Shit! Ugh...

"It's okay, Suzanne. But please watch your mouth in front of others. I wouldn't want you to get a bad reputation." *Seriously?*

Well, there's my Marcus. At least Marcus is still Marcus, even if every one of those *other* people keep trying to tell me otherwise.

"Marcus? Who are all those people? Dr. MacDonald told me he's my personal physician, and the nurse Kayla said she's my good friend from New York. And Kayla from work says she and I are best friends, which seems really weird. And there's this other man who has visited me. Why are they coming here? Do you know why?" Please know. I have got to make sense of all this confusion.

"I'm sure the man you're talking about is Mr. Zinfandel. He's close personal friends with Dr. MacDonald, your old co-worker Kayla, and also with the nurse Kayla. They're a *charming* little 'foursome' who have been trying to keep you from me," he sneers.
"Why? Why would they keep you from me?"
"Well, Mr. Zinfandel has become a little obsessed with you..."
"Why? When? I don't remember him."
"I know you don't. But he knows you and your family and he's been working with your grandfather to keep you from me."
"Marcus, that doesn't make any sense. I'm no one. I'm just... no one."

Staring at Marcus, I'm desperate to understand *something* around me. Nothing makes sense to me. Nothing! I mean I get I was in a coma, but something should make sense, shouldn't it?
The last I remember I was working at Petri-Dunn, and spending my evenings with Marcus. There was no time for anything else. I wasn't allowed to do anything else. When did all this happen?
Marcus looks as perplexed as I feel. His eyes are darting around the room, and he won't make eye contact with me, not that I actually mind, but still. What's going on?

"Marcus, tell me what's going on, please..."
Inhaling deeply, Marcus finally turns back to me. Looking straight into my eyes (which I hate) he exhales on a rush, "Um, I don't know how to say this to you, but you were attacked by Mr. Zinfandel and Dr. MacDonald and those two Kaylas are his friends, and they're trying to cover it up, and they're trying to confuse you so you don't remember the truth." *WHAT?!*
"But they said I left you. They said you-"
"Do I seem like a man whose wife left him? Remember Suzanne, you're confused right now and they're lying to you to protect their friend."
I suddenly feel so scared of everything my stomach is in knots. Everything is just so confusing and painful inside me.

Why would they do that to me? Why would that man attack me? He said he was in love with me and that he would wait forever for me to remember his love. He said we were in love. He said we were a beautiful love story.

Looking at Marcus, I'm struggling. What happened? What does that mean- he *attacked* me?

"He attacked me?" When Marcus nods, I'm shocked. When? How? Oh, god... How bad was it?

"Did he r-rape me?" I whisper

"Yes, he did. You're married to me, but he forced himself on you. He raped you and-" **WHAT?!**

On a gasp, everything starts spinning. Everything is moving all at once. It feels like an earthquake all around me. I reach for the guardrails and try to hold on. What the hell is happening to me?

Looking at Marcus, he's reaching for me and speaking, but I can't hear him. All the noise is so loud in my head. There's so much noise that I can't hear Marcus anymore. Grabbing for me, I turn my head and see the bad man standing in the doorway with Dr. MacDonald. Oh *GOD!*

My mouth opens on a silent scream. Wider and wider, my mouth screams. But there is no sound. There is only this chaos of noise in my head. Screaming silently, I shake my head at the man.

There is no help for me. There is no one here with me. I am alone in my head, and It's. Just. So. Loud. I need help!

Looking fast, I see the bad man hit Marcus, and I see the Doctor push the bad man away. I see them stop and look at me. I see them watch me, but all I hear is sound.

Staring at the bad man I remember the pain. I remember all the ripping and the tearing and the screams and all the RED! There's red everywhere! I'm covered in it!

The noise is overwhelming, and the red is blurring my vision. I am so lost but there is nothing in me but sound. I can't feel anything. I can't feel at all.

As the bad man reaches for me, Marcus stands deathly still with his hands over his ears. He's not helping me!
The Doctor is beside me, doing stuff to my body and tubes and buttons. He's touching me all over while his lips move like he's talking to me. Shaking my head no, I can't hear him.
The bad man is beside me and I think he's yelling at me. He is shaking me, but I can't feel him. I will never feel him again. I will never *feel* again.

Closing my mouth and staring at his dark eyes my sudden silence seems to silence the entire room.
"Please, d-don't rape me again..." I beg on a gasp.
Letting me go abruptly, the bad man steps back with his hands raised in surrender. Suddenly bending at the waist, he seems to scream in agony.
I think I hear him scream but watching him with wide eyes, I'm appalled by his performance.
Turning toward Marcus, I'm appalled by his silence.
Reaching out to Dr. MacDonald, I beg, "Please help me..."
Suddenly screaming in the agony of confusion and fear again, I shake as the doctor reaches for me.

Gasping a final breath as he grabs me, I close my eyes and disappear into the darkness.

*****

When I wake up everything hurts. From my head to my toes I think I'm in pain. What the hell happened...? Oh! Jumping, I turn as quickly as my sore neck will allow finding him waiting for me, but-

"No one else is here with you." Exhale...
"Hi, Dr. Robinson," I groan.
"Hi, Suzanne. Are you in pain?"
"Yes. Everywhere," I admit on a gasp.
Smiling a Doctor-smile, she walks closer to me with my chart.
"How are you feeling, besides the pain?"
"Okay, I guess... What happened to me? I'm confused about everything again, I think."
"Suzanne, I'm unsure of what was said to you, specifically when your husband visited, but he has indicated that he may have frightened you, which was actually quite obvious to everyone who saw you a few hours ago based on your panic-attack and the near psychotic-break you suffered."
"He told me that man Z hurt me and that he attacked me."
"Do you remember being attacked or hurt by Mr. Zinfandel?"
"Not really, but I think I do remember being attacked, I think. There was this feeling all over me that felt really painful and awful, and... Do *you* know if he did hurt me?" I ask quietly.
"No, I don't think what Marcus told you is true. From what I understand and from what I believe to be true, Mr. Zinfandel has never hurt you."
"Oh." Okay. This is good.
"Suzanne, I have been involved with your case since you were transferred to this hospital, and I have worked closely with Dr. MacDonald throughout your stay. The details and events Marcus told you may not be as he said, and I think you need to discuss them with Dr. MacDonald. I believe you'll be surprised by your reality, versus the reality your husband may have painted for you."
"Why would he tell me lies...?" I beg.
"I don't know for sure, but I suspect Marcus may be having his own rather difficult *issues* at the moment."
"Oh."
"Would you like to speak with me and Dr. MacDonald together?

You may feel more comfortable with me in the room because I have no past with you to cloud any perspective." Yes? No?

"Um, okay..."

"Good. I'll speak with Dr. MacDonald first, and join him in your room in a few minutes."

After exhaling, I try to strengthen myself as she nods and leaves my room.

Oh god... I hope this goes well, because I think I'm about to lose my mind.

CHAPTER 16

Waking up alone again, I'm still unbelievably relieved by my newest reality. My biggest reality shift being that seeing Marcus was a huge mistake.

I've learned from Dr. Robinson that Marcus is having his own issues with this situation and that the things he told me were not true at all. After speaking with her, I did invite Dr. MacDonald back into my room so the three of us could speak together.

After a few tense moments after he entered my room, I struggled with believing *anything* Dr. MacDonald said. But with Dr. Robinson's help I eventually relaxed a little and slowly starting listening to him instead of fearing and disbelieving him.

Learning Z didn't hurt me, or rather, *believing* Z didn't hurt me was a huge relief. I didn't want to believe that of Z. He had always seemed so honest about our 'relationship', and so loving toward me each time we had spoken in the last few weeks, I really didn't want to believe he was the monster Marcus told me he was.

After we discussed Z, I was grateful to both my Doctors for helping me understand a little more of the struggle Marcus was having with the fact that I apparently left him.

I still don't remember any of the actual details of leaving Marcus, but I believe Dr. MacDonald and Dr. Robinson were telling me the truth, especially since both said there is a letter as proof, *and* that I could ask my grandfather, should I desire to- which I don't. So learning Marcus was struggling made the things he told me more believable as lies, for which again, I was very grateful.

Dr. Robinson is a good Doctor who I really like. She told me she has been working with Mack since I was transferred to Chicago, and she seems to think Mack is a wonderful doctor as well.

I like her and knowing she wasn't friends with that group before I was transferred here helped me believe her claims against Marcus and the explanations she offered me for his behavior.

And so I've calmed down and tried really hard to remember the four people who claim to be my 'real' friends. The four people Marcus said weren't my friends but who were actually here to hurt me.

And now that I have seen them all individually since that day last week, and they have each told me the same stories of how we met and of how close we are as friends, I'm trying very hard to relax with them through all the endless confusion.

It was hard when I saw Z again even WITH Dr. Robinson and Dr. MacDonald in the room, but I felt safe enough to listen to Z explain our relationship again.

I felt instantly relieved to hear his story hadn't changed at all since he first told me about 'us'. I was relieved that he didn't seem angry with me or angry with Marcus even. Z just sat beside me, without touching me, as he told me of our beautiful story once again. And I did believe him, eventually.

And so I'm back to visits from Dr. MacDonald- *Mack*, the Kaylas and even Z, often. I'm trying to remember them and they seem to be very patient with me and my questions and with my lack of memories or acknowledgement of all the things they tell me are true.

They seem like really nice people, who I actually *want* to know.

CHAPTER 17

JUNE 4

Time is so hard for me now. When I'm alone the days and nights drag on and on, but when I have all the visitors and the doctors, all I want is my solitude.
Not that I haven't enjoyed *re*-meeting these people, but I'm just not used to them like I guess I should be. Sometimes they act like I remember them, and tell me stories about something I said or did but I don't remember the story so it's a little awkward for me at times.
Sometimes they talk to me in a way that's totally personal and inappropriate like I'm okay with it, but I'm not. I don't remember them at all but they behave as I should. Then again, maybe they're acting normal to me to help trigger my memories. Actually, that's probably exactly what they're doing. That makes way more sense than thinking they're just insensitive people who like to confuse me and make me blush.
God, I wished I remembered them so I could find some comfort in their constant visits. But as it is I usually feel confused and then kind of depressed again once they leave because they're all such great people and they seem to have a real bond between them.
When I asked about their friendship Mack once told me they are *my* foursome and once I'm better and remember them all, our group will be a close 'Fiver' as he called it. In theory I'd like to be a part of a 'Fiver'. I'd like to have people I was close to, but in reality I'm nervous I won't fit in. I'm scared I'll be the *very* odd man out in their awesome group of five.

THIS is me...

So when Mack asked me yesterday if we could all have breakfast together before New York Kayla flies back home later, I was taken by surprise and agreed, but I've dreaded it ever since. I'm not too sure how I feel about them all here at once. And I'm not too sure how I feel about eating with them all around me, which I know is weird. But I can't help it. Eating with people bothers me, though I don't know why.

But I said yes, so I have to suck it up. God, I've spend most of my life sucking it up for my parents and Marcus- you'd think I'd be used to it by now.

*****

Waiting, it's almost 9:00 and Mack said they would all be here by then. So naturally, I find I'm totally anxious, though again, I'm not sure why.

So far, everyone has been very nice to me. There has never been a moment of mean, except for that confusing time with Mack and Z and that one time Kayla yelled at me. Other than those few little incidents they've all been nice to me throughout these past few weeks, especially while I struggle to adjust to my new body, and try desperately to gain my memories back.

While waiting, I asked the nurse earlier as she helped me bathe and change if I could wear other clothes, but she said I didn't have any here of my own. As consolation, she did bring me a beautiful robe to wear over my hospital gown, which does make me feel a little better.

I really hate lying in this bed all the time, and I *really* hate lying around all day in this hideous hospital garb.

I still haven't seen my face or body yet, but I tried to fix my hair so I look somewhat nice for the friends when they arrive. The nurse last night even brought me brand new mascara which I maybe shouldn't have, but she brought it to me anyway.

God, I was so grateful I almost cried. But when she asked if I needed help applying it, I quickly declined her offer. I'm not sure what I look like, but I certainly didn't want her to have to be so close to my face while applying mascara.

Anyway, I have on the beautiful robe, and I managed to put on mascara without a mirror, and my hair is all brushed and down, and now I just have to wait for the friends.

Looking at the magazine beside me to kill time, I'm struck by the gorgeous actor on the cover and I think of Z immediately.

Actually, I think of them all because each of those four friends are very attractive people, but in totally different ways. If I could remember, I'd think I was probably really insecure around them. They are just *way* better looking than I am- or *was*.

God, it must have sucked for me standing with Mack and especially with Z when both men are super attractive, making me so plain beside them.

And I can just imagine how I felt if I was ever out with both Kaylas. We were probably described as 'The Two Tall Hot Chicks... and their friend'. Giggle. *Seriously?*

When I hear the knock, Kayla is already poking her head in.
"Hi Suzanne. Are you ready for us?" Nope, not now... HOTTIE!
"Um, sure. Good morning," I say shaking.

When both Kaylas pause and just stare at me, I'm more than a little uncomfortable. What's wrong? Ugh. I hate this feeling of insecurity when it grips me tight.

Looking at Kayla, I'm still amazed that we're friends outside of work. She is just so awesome. And honestly, I can't imagine what the hell she sees in me.

The other Kayla is pretty awesome too. When she laughs she can melt me with her smile. It's like her smile gets into my skin, and then she says something totally ridiculous, or very sarcastic and inappropriate and I don't know what to do with myself. I must seem so freakin' boring to them both.

"Z and Mack should be here any minute. How are you feeling? Are you okay?"
"Yes, I'm good. Thank you."
"Are you *sure,* Suzanne? You seem a little off this morning."
Off? *How?* I've barely spoken. What the hell is New York Kayla talking about?
"Why did you ask me that? How do I seem off? I've barely spoken," I laugh nervously.
"Nothing. Everything is good. You're fine, Suzanne." What?!
"I know I'm fine- but *you're* freaking me out a little. What's wrong?"
Waiting, work Kayla charges past the other Kayla with a smile. "Nothing's wrong- you're good. And you look very pretty this morning. Did you dress yourself?"
"Yes. Why?" What the HELL is going on?
When I see the other Kayla smile at me while taking her cell out of her purse, I'm worried. Kayla's smile isn't the good one- the melt me and make *me* smile-smile. Winking at me as she turns back toward the door with a 'one minute, please' finger in the air doesn't help me either. Something is definitely wrong.
"Suzanne! I asked how you slept last night."
"Oh. Good. Why?" Ugh, I can *feel* something is wrong.
"Just wondering. I hope you're hungry. Mack and Z managed to get absolutely *everything* for breakfast. When I heard the list I laughed but my thighs screamed. I think I'm gonna gain 15 pounds this morning but it'll be totally worth it I'm sure."
"Really? Why?"
"'Cause it'll be so delicious." Oh duh. Why the hell are we talking about food anyway?

As Kayla begins moving around my room, clearing the bedside table and the hospital table, she keeps smiling at me- like *constantly* smiling, which of course freaks me right out. I'm not sure what's going on, but work Kayla isn't relaxed like she usually is, and she's working way too hard trying to *look* relaxed while still being really busy around my room. I wonder when the other Kayla will be back.

"Suzanne, you're going to be okay, you know."

"I think so too. Why are you acting so weird this morning? Did I do something wrong?"

"I'm sorry if it seems that way. I'm not trying to act weird, and I'm sorry if you feel that way. And no, you've done nothing wrong at all."

"You ARE being weird and it's making me feel insecure and kind of nervous."

"Shit. Sorry. I'm good, I promise. I'm just going to clear everything away for the food, okay?"

"Sure..."

When my door opens seconds later, Mack and Z are standing together in the doorway.

Jesus! This is like every woman's fantasy or something. Giggle. Two super-hot men standing in your doorway, both looking at you so expectantly. Both looking totally edible. Huh. I wonder if *they're* my breakfast. Oh shit! Giggle.

"Hi Suzanne. How are you this morning?" Mack asks rather seriously.

Smiling, and still giggling a little, "I'm good. And you?"

"Excellent. I hope you're hungry?"

"I am. Are you and Z my meal?" *WHAT?!*

"Um, no." Silence. Dammit. No one is moving. Shit.

"*I* can be your breakfast if you'd like," Z replies with a wink. Whew... that could've been totally awkward for a minute there.

Bursting out laughing, I'm grateful he's so playful with me. "Well, come on up here then and let me taste you!"

"Alright... take off that robe and let's get to it," he laughs.

Still laughing I hunch over my bed and suddenly touch my

face. Oh GOD! I forgot. Jolting, my laughter silences immediately.
I forgot I'm gross! Shit, why would I forget that? *HOW* could I forget that? Here I am talking, and kind of flirting with these two gorgeous men and I forgot I'm all disgusting. I'm so pathetic and I'm so ugly. And I forgot.
In the silence that follows, I hear Mack speaking quietly to the friends in my room.
Turning to me he says, "Suzanne, Z and the ladies are going to leave for a few minutes, okay?"
"Why? What's wrong?" Covering my face with my head down, I stare into my lap.
"Nothing at all. I just want to talk to you for a few minutes."
"Why? What's wrong?" Gasping, my breath is getting all weird in my chest.
"Suzanne, I want to spend a little time talking with you, that's all. And there is absolutely nothing wrong."
"Why are we going to be alone? What did I do wrong?!" I sound a little loud now.
"Suzanne... I need you to breathe slowly for me, and just relax, okay?"
"What's wrong?! Just tell me!"
Looking, I see Kayla touching Z's arm as they turn their backs to me. What the *hell*? In front of me? *Seriously?* So not gonna happen!
"Hey **SLUT!** Are you gonna fuck *him* too?!" Ha! She jumped. The Whore!
"Suzanne... I need you to look at me for a minute. Just look at *me*, Suzanne. Now." Ignoring Mack, I seem to panic again.
"**Z!** Z, please don't go with her. I dressed up for you. I did my make-up and dressed up for you. Look! I'm dressed up! Please look at me! I'm pretty. Oh! *Well,* I'm not *actually* pretty anymore, but I tried. Doesn't that mean *anything* to you? I tried to be pretty. I tried for you!"
"Suzanne, stop! I want you to look at me- not at Kayla and Z. Just look at *me*, Suzanne!"

"She doesn't love you Z," I moan. "She just wants to fuck you. She just wants you to be her 'hot new screw', you know? That's all you'll be. Ha! I remember you now, Kayla. You're Kayla the whore. Kayla the man-eater."

Singing, *"Kayla on her knees... Kayla in the bathroom stall... Kayla, Kayla, Kayla... Kayla is a whore."*

Smiling and rocking, this is the most fun I've had in ages.

"What's wrong, Kayla? You don't like it? I always sing it for you. *'Leaving out the door... Kayla is a whore...'"*

When she turns to me she's actually crying. *Whatever*. She takes and takes and everyone lets her. She fucks everyone! She's a slutty whore-bag who no one trusts or likes, and *she's* crying to me?

"Suzanne... Please–"

"Please, WHAT?! Watch you fuck another man who loves me? No thanks. You've already fucked my husband, why not my no memory of him-sexy as hell- *fiancé*? You know what, Z? Go for it. I'm sure she's much better at fucking than I am anyway. She HAS had extensive practice, right Kayla?"

"Suzanne! Enough! Do you remember Kayla sleeping with Marcus? Do. You. Remember?"

Staring at the dirty whore, I scream, "Yeah! How could I forget?! What the fuck are you doing here anyway?! Fuck off, WHORE!"

Closing my eyes from the room, I still sway and sing my awesome song while the rage builds inside me.

"Kayla is a whore... Fucks on the floor... Always begs for more... suzanne the little whore... lying on the floor... begging no more... they fuck her till she's tore... suzannes a little whore."

I know someone has me in their hands, I know I'm being held and squeezed, and I hear all the sound in my room.

There's yelling, and crying, and talking, and begging, but I don't care. They can't make me hear this. They can't make me feel this.

"I'm a little whore... lying on the floor... ripping, burning sore... always hurting more... fucked and fucked some more... suzanne the little whore..." **OH!**

Opening my eyes, Mack is talking to me, and Z is holding me, and Kayla is hugging other Kayla, and 2 different doctors are moving around the room looking at me. But the silence in the room is so loud in my head; I don't know how to silence the noise.

There is so much sound, but I understand nothing. I have only my song in my head.

I hear my little girl voice again on the billiards-room floor. My vision is blurry and my body is bloody and sore. And I don't know how to stop this anymore.

So opening my mouth, I scream as loud as I can until finally the painless darkness engulfs me.

CHAPTER 18

JUNE 5

I remember from before the beautiful song "I'm in here" by Sia. I remember every word I heard but I didn't know then I would feel the song as I feel it now. That song is my song in this moment. If I could thank Sia for her words, I would. I would tell her she sang my exact thoughts. *Her* words, to *her* beautiful song are my exact words in this moment.
 Oh, god... I'm just so *sad*. There is too much to think and feel and remember this time. There is just too much this time.
 I want to beg everyone to STOP. I want everyone to stop what they're doing and listen to "I'm in here" by Sia because that is all I am in this moment. Those are the only words I have in this moment to explain the oppressive depth of my despair.
 I'm drowning in my memories. I'm dying from my memories. My memories are suffocating me so slowly; I can actually feel the life draining from my body this time.
 Sia sang it before I understood it. Her song is my pain in this moment. I wish I could play her beautiful song to everyone I have ever known so they can understand exactly what I feel in this final moment. I want everyone to listen to her beautiful words so they know what I feel in this moment. Her exact words have become my life and death in this moment.
 No one has ever known me, and no one has ever understood me. No one has ever known why I'm like this because no one has ever truly known what my life was really like.

THIS is me...

*****

I know I'm sleeping and dreaming, but I can't seem to wake this time. This time I'm fully trapped in this movie-like fast forward showcase of my life. This time I see it all... and it's truly horrific.
Starting from childhood, I remember my mother. I see her hatred for me. I *feel* her hatred for me. But there was nothing I could do then, I see that now too. There was no pleasure to be had from me for her. She always hated me. It's so clear to me now.
My father also plays out in these memories- so cold and quiet. With not a word spoken to me, my father stands in front of me. I am always the little creature in the room my parents wanted to poison. The silent life I led in their home is whipping by my memory vault. I am silence and sadness.
Watching, I see me so young and quiet suffocating in the loneliness. I wanted to be spoken to so badly. I wanted them to see me without hate and indifference. I wanted to be known and acknowledged and seen in their lives, but they never did know me, or acknowledge me, or see me. I wanted to be loved. I wanted to be held just once so badly I cried throughout my nights and silently hid my pain throughout my days.
Awake, they never knew how much pain I felt. But asleep I couldn't stop the pain from soaking my pillows. I was just so lonely, even with my parents right there in the room in front of me. I was the Creature.

Dammit, even my school reality plays out now. I'm alone. I sit alone. I eat my pitiful little lunch alone. I am *always* alone. It's a wonder I even know how to speak. It's more amazing still that I know how to socialize perfectly. God, I was just so lonely. All the time.
I remember a grade school teacher making us watch the movie "Cipher in the Snow". I remember leaving the darkened quiet

classroom afterward to sit in a bathroom stall while I cried my eyes out.

I was so sad for the little boy, Cliff. I was so sad after he collapsed and died. I remember how sad I felt, never knowing what became of all the people who ignored him. I remember crying alone in the bathroom for at least an hour before a teacher found me and made me return to my classroom. I was so sad, but I was scared too.

I kept wondering if I was just going to die one day from the loneliness. I remember wondering if my parents would find me dead in my bed one morning. I remember kind of wishing they would find me dead so that I didn't have to be this sad and lonely anymore.

I had no friends and no one spoke to me because I was The 'Snobby' Suzanne Beaumont. But I was never a snob, I was just lonely. I was awkward and sad and I didn't know how to have a friend, so I never had one.

And now I see the abuse. God, the first time was so awful and frightening. My mother dressed me and left me in the room alone. I remember crying and I remember begging to get out... And then I remember *him*.

The first time for me was forced oral sex. Choking and gagging and screaming around it, until he slapped my face hard, forcing my jaw open with his fingers digging brutally into my cheeks.

And then I stopped fighting. I didn't move. I closed my eyes as he continued gagging and choking me throughout my silence.

Oh god, the horror and the shame, and the absolute truth of my mother- SHE did this to me. She set it up. She watched me and she encouraged this for some awful reason in her twisted mind. This was *all* her.

Sadly, I remember the first anal abuse. I remember the screaming agony, until there was only black darkness. Thank god for the darkness. There was no known pain then, and afterward my memory was inconsistent, at best.

I loved blacking-out because I never knew what they actually did to me; therefore I wasn't sure of what *exactly* I should be ashamed of. I loved the darkness because it was my only ally on these brutally long, excruciating nights.

Ah, yes... now my movie fast-forwards to Dr. Simmons, the truly *amazing* Psychiatrist that he was.

Jesus... being forced into his hospital was the turning point for me I think. I'm almost sure the memories went away after visiting his hospital. I wonder what he did to me. I wonder what was done to me to make me forget.

Strangely, he never penetrated me though-not even once. He did however, force me to endure his desires. He kissed and fondled, and would perform sexual acts *to* me like he was hoping for a response from me.

God, it was so gross and I could do nothing to stop it. Between his strength and the straps around my wrists and ankles and the medications in me, he could do to me as he liked. And sadly he did.

When it was happening I would just turn my head to the side, stare at the bathroom doorway looking at the red, and sadly, wait for him to finish. My body was lifeless. I was nothing living, but the chaos in my mind never ended. I was a broken deadened body that could not move, and did not feel.

And again, my memories seem to jump forward to Marcus. Marcus was the most wonderful thing that had ever happened to me. He was so kind and calm and gentle to me. He held doors open and cared enough to order my food. And he would smile at me often.

Marcus would simply smile and I felt such a strange contentment with him. Marcus rarely yelled at me, and he never acted as though I was someone born for his hatred. He took me as his wife and seemed to enjoy me in his life. Marcus was a blessing from the nightmare of my parents. He was a lovely kindness in all my darkness. God, I miss him in my life.

I wish I could stop this reel. I wish to stop this show with Marcus. I want this movie to end with my memories of a decent man who loves me. But I never get what I want, certainly not in this life.

Why was this my life? I wish I could ask someone. I wish there was someone *to* ask. It's strange remembering everything I think my brain must desperately want me to forget.

How do victims do this? It's such a sad question to ask but I don't know the answer. How do other victims of sexual abuse learn to move past it? What IS moving past it?

I know I'm not alone; I *know* that, but I just *feel* so alone. I don't know how to forget the feelings and the pain and all the darkness that surrounds my life. I don't know how to do it, and I'm scared to become a person obsessed with the darkness.

I don't want to be a woman who constantly thinks of the bad. I don't want to be a woman *consumed* with all the bad. I don't want to be a woman who cries and screams and prays for darkness all the time, just to ease the pain of her memories.

But how do I forget? What will make my horrible memories go away?

I wish I could ask Mack. Oh! My Mack. God, I remember him now. He's Mack, not Dr. MacDonald, and he wasn't lying. He IS mine. Holy shit! How could I have forgotten my Mack?

Now *this* I regret. I wish I had remembered him immediately. I wish I had awoken to the memory of his love and strength. I probably wouldn't feel so lost if I'd just known who to love and who to take my comfort from.

Mack is here, and I can start again, *again.*

Now I see them. My crazy sarcastic sexy as hell Kayla from New York, and my crazy sarcastic man-hungry Kayla from Chicago... and Z.

Oh, Z. Now I remember him. Z's my lover. Oh god... I remember him now. He IS my lover and he loves me. He actually wants me. He even wants to marry me. Wow! How could I forget that? I mean, I know I was in a coma, but still... who could forget such an

THIS is me...

awesome, sexy, beautiful man loving them? I swear I'm a moron sometimes. He loves me and I want to love him back. I think I even remember loving him back.

Oh! I remember loving him back in New York. He was sexy and kind, and really, *really* awesome at all the sex stuff.

Christ! He knew exactly how to touch me, and what to say, and what to do. I remember sex with Z was loving, and amazing, and unforgettable. Huh. Maybe Mack should've started with the Z sex-stuff. I probably would have remembered my life sooner.

Remembering Z, I'm overcome with my newest reality. I have to change again. I have to get better again. I have to start feeling all this life again. God, I have to wake up. Again.

This movie has been long and exhausting, but I think it's my time now. I think maybe I should write the script of my life from now on. Finally, I should try to be my own Director.

I want to be the person who yells 'action' during the good times, and 'cut' during the bad times. I want this movie of my life to have a Hollywood ending. I *want* the happily ever after. God, I have to wake up now and take control of my movie. I know that now.

Of course, I don't have a freakin' clue how to start. And I don't know how to make this horrible movie into a love story, but I want to try. I really, *really* want to try this time.

I want a happily ever after. Everyone wants a happily ever after. Even the people who hate them; those who scoff at the perfectly cheesy endings, those who make fun of happily ever after's, deep down kinda want them I think, because nobody wants the ending to be more depressing than the story was. No one wants the ending to feel worse than the horrific journey to get there.

So that's what I'm going to do. This is it. When I wake up again from this nightmare, I'm going to try to live this life well, with the people who love me. I'm going to forget the monsters, and I'm going to love the angels instead.

I'm going to write this script by my own hand, with the words I've always wanted to say, and with the love I've always wanted to feel. I'm going to close the book of my past, and I'm going to write a new book filled with my new future.

I'm going to wake up now.

THIS is me...

THIS is me...

NIGHTMARES

CHAPTER 19

JUNE 6

Opening my eyes, I'm relieved to still remember. My dream is fuzzy, but my memories are clear. I remember all the bad, and I remember the little bit of good I've had. I think I remember it all now.

"Suzanne... Welcome back. How are you feeling?" *Should I? Shouldn't I?* No, dammit. I'm not gonna mess with him.

"Hi, Mack. Um, I remember," I confess.

Staring at me for seconds, Mack seems to collect his thoughts. "What do you remember, Suzanne?" Oh, he looks so hopeful, though I can tell he's fighting the urge to hope.

Taking his hand in mine, I squeeze as tight as I can. "I remember you Mack. I remember everything. I must have been asleep for a long time, because my dream was really long, but I remember everything now. I remember all of it."

Guarded still, he asks, "What exactly do you remember, Suzanne?"

"Oh, Mack, I remember how I felt about you. I remember you're *my* Mack. You're my person. You're my Mack, and I remember loving you very much."

"What else do you remember?" He asks way too calmly.

"Everything. All of it. I remember my Kaylas, and I remember Z. It all came back to me Mack. I remember leaving Marcus, and I remember how my parents treated me. I remember all the bad stuff and I remember what was done to me when I was young by my parents and the men. I remember it all. I remember *you* all."

Exhaling a long breath, Mack is silent. Still staring at me, he doesn't seem entirely convinced, but he *does* seem hopeful now.

"When did the memories return?"

"I don't know. Just now I guess. I was dreaming and then I was remembering. It was like a movie that played out. My horrible autobiography. My life in sections, and chunks. Mostly bad stuff, and awful loneliness, but then I remembered you, and the Kaylas, and Z, and even the good Marcus. I think I remember everything now."

"Do you remember what upset you recently?"

"No. I was just sleeping for a long time with all my memories playing out. Why? What happened?"

"Do you remember the last three weeks? Do you remember waking from the coma?"

"Yes. It's all weird though and kind of fuzzy because I was so confused but I don't know why I was confused because I remember everything now, but I guess I didn't really remember then. I don't know. Everything is all weird. I remember hearing I was in a car accident, and that I was in another coma, which is so messed up. Another coma? How very *dramatic* of me," I giggle.

"Yes, highly dramatic Suzanne. Though the first was medically-induced, this second was from a brain trauma. But still- two comas in a year? That's a bit much wouldn't you agree?"

"Yes, Mack. Yes, I would. Have I barfed at all?" I grin.

"Once or twice, but you're handling all this very well considering. I would request that you stop with all the psychotic freak-outs and drama however, because the Kaylas are getting a little pissed." Smirk.

Ha! There's my Mack. Doctorly and dorky all at once. Actually, he seems a little sarcastic too. I wonder if he realizes the tragic influence Kayla has had on him.

"How's Kayla?"

"She's good, Suzanne. Actually, she's thrilled you're awake, but she'll be ecstatic that you finally remember her. The other Kayla is just as funny and hard and Kayla-like as ever. Well, except with you of course. With you she's kind of a pushover, though she'd hit me for saying that."

Smiling at Mack, I think I'm happy to hear that the Kaylas are okay. I think I'm relieved that they still care about me.

"How are *you*, Mack?"

"I'm really good. And I'm so happy you're back with us. We've been very worried, and this stretch with you has seemed endless. But otherwise, I'm very well."

"Was it really bad?"

"It was sometimes, yes. I think because you were so confused and felt such a lack of control you panicked often. You were very easily agitated and you tended to lash out frequently."

"I'm sorry..."

When Mack takes my hand, I can help but ask. I just need a little comfort. I need some Mack-like comfort.

"Would you please hug me, Mack," I beg on a whisper.

"God, yes..."

And when he takes me in his arms, I feel how gentle he is. I know he's holding me gently, but I don't want that. I think I need a hard, 'I'm awake now' hug. I need Mack to strengthen me.

So pulling tighter, I squeeze Mack with all I can. Holding on tightly, I'm waiting for the comfort to envelop me. I'm waiting, but I feel nothing but the physical hug.

"Um, I can't really feel you, *emotionally.* Does that make sense? I know you're hugging me and I know I want it- I know I *need* it actually, but you feel like a stranger or something. Is that normal?"

"Suzanne, your emotions are going to run the gauntlet for the next while. You're going to be depressed, and scared, and overwhelmed, and an endless combination of a multitude of emotions. You may even experience a sudden sense of euphoria, which is also common.

"...You have been trapped unaware, and then you were awake with no cognizant memory of your life, and now you're awake *with* memory. You may feel happy or sad, or nothing at all until this all settles. There is no right or wrong way to feel right now.

Honestly, it's pretty remarkable that you have your memory at all, at least this early after waking. Generally speaking, PTA patients- post-traumatic amnesia patients- can take months to feel and to remember their previous lives, or they may never regain all their memories, nor can they heal entirely. The short timeframe for which you experienced your memory loss is amazing. So please don't worry. You're doing very well."
"Okay." Silence.

Staring at Mack again, I feel like a bit of a fool asking this, but...
"How's Z?"
"He's good Suzanne. Well, that's not entirely true. Right now I can almost feel him climbing the walls outside. He's just itching to get to you, but otherwise he's good." Oh!
"So he's still interested in me? Um, even though I'm highly dramatic?"
"Most definitely. Probably *because* you're highly dramatic and keep him on his toes, Suzanne," he winks.
"That's probably a very bad joke, Mack."
"I'm sure it is, but that's me. And Z will just have to deal with it. Would you like to see him?"
Gulp. I do want to see him. I know I do, but I feel scared, or intimidated, or nervous, or something. Seeing Z makes everything back to normal, but I don't really *feel* back to normal just yet. Z will want me to be normal, and I'm not sure I am yet. Shit.
"I do, but can I just have a minute. There's still so much to understand. Is that bad?"
"Not at all. I'm sure you're very confused and exhausted, and it's perfectly reasonable to have reservations about certain things. Do you want to see the Kaylas?"
"Not yet. I'm not sure why, but I feel like I'll let them all down if I'm not perfectly normal yet."
"You wouldn't let anyone down, but I understand your fear and hesitation. Please, don't worry Suzanne. You get to do this at your own pace. No one expects miracles from you, and no one is

expecting you to just jump right back into your old life. You've got however long you need."

"Thanks, Mack. I remember you always say the right thing. Can you just stay with me for a few minutes? I don't think I want to be alone yet."

"I'm *always* here Suzanne. I'll stay as long as you want. Do you want to talk? Do you have any questions for me?"

"A million, I think. Um, what happened, exactly? I know there was a car accident but that's it, I think."

"You were at Z's apartment. Do you remember that?"

"Yes. I remember I spent the night with him and it was amazing."

"That's what Z says as well," he grins. "Anyway, you left Z's to meet my Kayla for lunch and you were involved in the car accident. Do you remember the accident?"

"No. Was it bad? It's okay, you can tell me."

When Mack pauses for a minute and looks down at his hands, I suddenly think this'll be bad to hear.

"Yes, it was very bad," he says on an exhale. "You were pronounced at the scene, and then pronounced with minimal brain function on the operating table. But true to form, you pulled through again."

"Pronounced? Like *dead?*" Gulp.

"Yes, like dead."

"Wow. That's messed up, huh?" Giggle. "Sorry. I'm not sure what to say. It's so weird to hear that kind of stuff. I mean, *really* weird."

"I'm sure it is but you're handling it very well."

"Thanks. And then I was in another coma? Do I have any brain damage?" Giggle again. Shit. "I'm sorry. This is just so strange. I mean who asks these questions? It seems like I'm the only freak in the world who all this shit happens to. And I think I'm one of those people who probably laughs when stressed, like at a funeral, or something."

"You are totally that person. I could see you bursting out laughing at a funeral due to the stress, for sure. You are very

strange Suzanne, but in a very endearing way," he grins again.
Smiling back at him, "Thanks, Mack. That's probably a horrible thing to say, but I love it. Probably another weird Suzanne-ism, I'm sure."
"Yup. You're filled with them. How are you feeling?"
"Better, but not great. It's like I'm seeing and remembering everything in a haze. I *know* everything now, but I don't really feel it. It's like I'm looking at myself, but not really seeing myself."
"That's normal. You've been under much stress Suzanne, combined with confusion and a lack of memory. It's very normal to feel a little unlike yourself at this point."
"How long have I been awake from the coma?"
"Um, around 3 weeks."
"Really? Wow. What was I like? I only remember last night, or my dream, or whatever that was. Was I normal that whole time?"
"You were awake, but you had no memory of your most recent past, approximately the last 2 years or so from what I could ascertain. It was hard to gauge, so things were quite difficult for you, and for us. But Z and the Kaylas and I never left your side, though it was very hard at times."
"I'm so sorry."
"Don't be. Ever. Nothing you did or said is to be apologized for. You were struggling and we knew that. Anything you said was to be expected from someone struggling as you were. I'm just thrilled you seem so well right now. I'm thrilled you seem to be returning as Suzanne."
"I think I'm back. Was I really bad?"
"Sometimes, yes. You had a few episodes which were very painful for us, and you lashed out at Z and especially at Chicago Kayla once. But we knew these episodes weren't your fault, and Kayla and Z don't blame you for them. Again, they're going to be just so thrilled your memory has returned. Z is going to be beside himself with happiness. He has been so amazing, and patient, and loving to you during this time. He has been amazing to all of us, *for* you." Oh.

THIS is me...

"Should I see him now?"
"Are you ready to? Would you like me to stay? I could give you privacy, or I could stay in case you both become overwhelmed. The choice is yours Suzanne." God, Mack is so awesome.
"Is it really bad of me to wait just a little longer before I see him- NOT because I don't want to, but I just want to make sure I'm feeling better for him, or like, feeling *something* before I see him. Is that okay?"
"Absolutely. But I'm going to go talk to him for a few minutes. I want to put his mind at ease, then I'll return and stay awhile with you if you'd like."
Nodding, I exhale again.
"May I have another hug, Mack?"
"Absolutely," he says taking me into his arms.

This awake has been much calmer than I anticipated. This one hasn't been all confusing and manic. This awake has been as I hoped- calm and steady with my Mack while I wake up to my life.
Letting me go, Mack stays close to me watching my face as all the information sets in. I'm okay. I *am* overwhelmed, but I'm okay. So smiling with a nod, I let him leave me alone.

*****

When Mack returns I feel the need to confess.
"Um, I think I remember Marcus said some things about Z, but I confused it with the other stuff that happened to me. I remember now Z didn't hurt me."
"What exactly did Marcus say to you? He won't tell me specifics, and I still need specifics in order to help you."

"It really doesn't matter. I remember being with Z- by choice. I remember him now. Is he okay?"

"Yes, he's fine. He's still waiting outside if you'd like to speak with him. Are you ready to speak with Z now? Or would you like a little more time?"

"I'm sorry... but I can't yet. I think I remember something important Marcus said to me and I can't talk about it yet. I can't Mack. And I'm afraid it's true, and I'm afraid talking about it will make it true, and I don't want it to be true."

"What Suzanne? What don't you want to be true? What did Marcus tell you?"

"I can't tell you because it shouldn't be true. Actually Mack, do you mind leaving now? You're still awesome, I swear... but I just need to think about things a little by myself. Is that okay?"

"Its okay, Suzanne. I only ask that you talk to me as much as you can, so I can help you. If you start closing down and internalizing all this information and your new reality, I'm nervous you may become caught up in it all again, instead of slowly moving past it. Does that make sense? I just want you to be emotionally well, Suzanne. That's all I want for you."

"I'm good. I'm just tired. Can I talk to you later?"

Rising from his chair, Mack smiles his lovely smile at me. "Of course you can speak to me later. I'll see to Z, and I'll come back in a few hours. Rest well, Suzanne. You really are doing amazingly well considering all you've been through."

"Thanks, Mack."

Leaning into me, Mack gives another Mack hug, as only he can. Holding him as tightly as I can, I try to take his awesome into my body. I would love to be as calm and supportive, and smart and wonderful as Mack is. I would love to be a Mack to someone else. I would love to be needed by someone else, as I need him.

Releasing me, Mack kisses my forehead gently, squeezes my hand on the bed and walks out of my room.

And without knowing why, I'm totally overcome with sadness again the moment he leaves me. I can't stop the tears, and I can't stop the sad from overwhelming me. I don't even know *why* I'm sad. I just am.

But sadness is something I'm totally familiar with, so I embrace it. There's no sense fighting something I've always had, and so I give into the tears and sadness.
Eventually, I feel myself falling asleep again to the comfort of my tears.

CHAPTER 20

JUNE 9

Reading a lame celebrity mag, I'm surprised by how unattractive some actresses are without all their make-up and airbrushing. Seeing their before and afters gives me a little hope. Maybe with tons of make-up and endless airbrushing I could look attractive again. I doubt it though. I doubt I'm that talented with an airbrush.

I haven't actually seen my ugliness yet but I feel it constantly, *obsessively* with my fingertips, and I doubt make-up can cover up an ugly texture. Plus, it's not like I can walk around with my own personal Air-Brusher. Can I?

When I hear a knock on my door I inhale a big breath. Please be Mack. *Please.* Mack seems to be the only one I can see without panicking even a little so far. Even the doctors I've seen over and over again still freak me out a little.

Turning, I watch Z enter my room. Whooooosh. Christ!

"Hi Suzanne. I hope you don't mind me visiting?"

"Um, no. I guess not. No. I mean, its fine to visit. It's fine." Babble. Babble. What a loser *still*. Giggle.

"What's so funny?" He asks with a grin.

"Oh, not much. I'm still a loser, that's all. I find it funny how I can go through all these things, one after another, and yet I'm still the same loser I always was." Giggle.

"I don't think you're a loser."

"Well then, you must be a loser too." Giggle. *Seriously?!* THIS is my big loving reunion? Total LOSER!!

"I'm not sure, but I doubt either of us are losers," he smiles.

"How are you today?"
"Good. You?
"I'm very well. Actually, I'm thrilled you're awake and lucid and that you remember me. I've been waiting a long time for you to remember me."
"I know. I'm sorry-"
"Suzanne, please. I can't even begin to explain how happy I am that you're back. Don't be sorry, love. Just tell me you're back. That's all I want from you. That's all I *need* from you."
Looking at him, I'm totally overwhelmed by him. He's just so much. He seems to even take the air from the room. He looks so handsome, and together, and normal, and just so like the Z I remember.
When I begin gently crying, he takes my hand but doesn't speak. I wish I could explain this to him. I wish I had the words. He's the same. But I know I'm not.
Whispering to me, "What is it, love?"
"Um, I remember you, Z. I remember all our time together, and I remember the way you were with me, but I can't really *feel* the way I felt for you back then. Not yet anyway. Does that make sense?"
"Yes..."
"I remember you though! You're so amazing Z. But you're too much for me, I think."
"No, I'm not. I'm just right for you Suzanne- I am. Don't do this, please. I just want to sit beside you, and you don't have to do or say anything. I just want to be near you for a while. I'm not too much. I'm really not," he pleads.
"Okay. You're not too much. Maybe it's just all *this* feels like too much or something. Please, don't be upset, Z."
"I'm not upset. I'm emotional, and thrilled to see you, but I'm not upset."
"Okay..."

Still holding my hand, Z leans forward a little and stares deeply into my eyes, which of course makes me turn away. I hate that.

Even with Z. Eye contact is just too personal.
"Don't Z... I'm ugly now," I suddenly shake and sob.

Shit! Z jumps on my bed so quickly I don't even have time to react or flinch before he's holding me tightly, while lying against my side in the bed. Fighting his arms for a second, he completely overtakes me. Holding me tightly, he begins shaking too.
What a mess this is. I don't know what to say to comfort him. I still have no words for him. Why can't this be easy? Why does everything have to be so intense and dramatic? Why can't I just have normal emotions with normal people under normal circumstances?
"Z..."
Moaning, "I'm sorry, Suzanne. I have felt every emotion there is for you during the last 3 months. I have been so low I thought I would die in my sleep beside you. And then I've been so hopeful I found the reason to come back and sit here watching you struggle to come back to me. I watched and waited as you struggled to live again. But I just need a minute. I just have to hold you for a minute so I know you're back. Please?"
"Alright..."

After forever, I feel Z wiping his face against my pillow. And when his breathing returns to normal, I know this upset is almost over. I just wish I had the best words possible to give to him, but as usual I don't. I have only my silence to offer him.
"I'm sorry for that, Suzanne."
"I don't mind."
"No, I'm very sorry. I think I've got all the emotion out of my system now. I'm ready for anything you want or need." Huh. As soon as he says 'need' I suddenly go to a dirty place.
"Would you give me a kiss, Z?" I say so quietly I'm sure he couldn't possibly hear me, but then he moves me slowly until I'm flat on my back again while he leans over my body.

Looking down at me, his eyes are so shiny and beautiful, just like the pretty marbles I remember from *before*- before.

Taking my face in his hands, I flinch for a second until he stops moving. Slowly, he begins moving closer and closer until his lips touch mine.

Oh! I forgot. Dammit! How could I forget this? Z's lips are amazing against mine. They're so soft and full, and opening my mouth, he slips his tongue inside, a slow and sexy slide of his tongue until I hear myself moan.

Kissing him deeply in return, I'm instantly back with him in his apartment. I remember the love and the passion between us then. I remember the feeling. I remember it all.

Suddenly, I have never wanted anything so badly in my life. If I could kiss Z forever I would. I would erase my life, and forget the tragedies, through his kiss. I would close the door on my horrific past. And I would spend every moment like this, kissing this most amazing man, *forever.*

Moving my body closer to him, I find myself moving against him in a rhythm of sex. I want to be touched and I want to be loved. I want to be reminded of what we had. I want to feel the passion we once shared.

Lifting my arms to his back, I slip my hands under his shirt and pull him even closer still, until he leans over me with a leg resting between my thighs. Rubbing myself against his leg, I want to *feel* this. I want to have a new memory between us. I *need* a new memory between is.

"Z... please touch me," I beg.

Pulling away from my lips, he asks, "Um, here? Suzanne we could be caught at any moment, and I'm not sure you're ready, and I'm not sure I'm ready and... *Really?*" He looks stunned.

"Please touch me. I don't care if we're caught, and I'm totally ready."

"Ah... This seems really inappropriate, like I'm taking advantage of you. It feels kind of wrong, Suzanne. I don't want to hurt or scare you by touching you before you're ready."

"I'm not scared, and I want you very badly. I want this. You aren't taking advantage of anything. You're with me and you love me."

Looking at me again, Z seems to be struggling with my request. I mean, I get it. It IS a little odd for me to be so aggressive, but I want this. I want Z to touch me. I want that feeling he gives me again.

Nodding and staring at me for seconds, Z seems to make up his mind. Yet when he kisses me again, and his right hand touches my breast, I jump underneath him.

Not wanting him to stop, I begin pushing myself against his thigh harder, and I can't believe how aroused I suddenly feel. I want him inside me again. I want his fingers and his tongue. I want him to enter me. I want him to make me feel all his love for me.

Moaning, I feel his hand move under the covers to me. Touching me lightly under the hospital gown, I try to push against his hand. Rubbing myself against his hand harder, I'm just desperate for him to enter me.

"Please..." I moan.

When I feel his finger slip inside me, I'm done. Gasping and rocking against him, I want this so badly, I don't even care how trampy I look. I don't care if this is bad timing. I don't care if I'm too aggressive. I want this with Z. I want this memory with Z. I want this *release* of all my sadness and confusion with Z.

Moaning and writhing against his hand forever while we continue kissing, I feel the pressure gradually building. I know this tightness and I know this intensity. Kissing him deeper, my hands pull him onto my whole body as I writhe against him.

He is so good to me. His hands and fingers are so amazing. He knows what to do, and he knows what I need. *This* is what I need.

Oh god... It's coming. I'm almost there.

When Z slowly pulls away from my lips and kisses my eyelid and then slowly my scarred cheek, it's all over. The spell has been broken.

Gasping, my hands fly to my face trying to cover it up. Oh, GOD! Not my face. He made me forget about my face.

Bursting into tears, I push his hand away from my body and quickly flip to my side away from him as he stays still and quiet above me. Fuck! *Why?!*

"Suzanne... *please.*"

"I'm okay. Its okay, Z. I wish you hadn't done that though. I wish you had ignored my face. Why did you do that?! Why my face?!" I moan.

"I was showing you how much I love you. How I don't care about anything but you. There is nothing between us-" he tries to soothe.

"Actually, there is *everything* between us. Just forget it. I'm sorry. You didn't do anything wrong, but I need a minute, okay?"

"Please, Suzanne, just talk-"

"No. Its fine, Z. But please give me a little time. I just want to be alone for a minute."

"I understand, but I need you to hear me first. Please listen to me Suzanne."

"Yup. Go ahead." Shit. I sound all bitchy, but I'm just freaked and grossed out.

"I still see only you."

"Okay. Thanks."

"Suzanne-"

"I *said* thanks. *Okay*? Please Z, just give me a moment."

When I feel him climbing off the bed, I realize just how tense I really am. I didn't realize everything was so tight. I didn't realize I was barely breathing. I didn't realize I was so destroyed over this.

Watching him walk to the door, I'm scared I can't come back from this, but I'm not going to push him away this time. I'm not! I still want him, and I still want his love. I just need a moment. *That's all this is.*

Calling out to his back, "This isn't our end, Z. I just need a minute. That's all this is, I promise. I want you, I really do. I just need a moment to deal with all this ugliness."

"This *isn't* our end, Suzanne. I love you too much to let your panic end us. And I know you need a moment, I've *always* known when you need a moment, and that's the only reason I'm leaving right now- for THIS moment. I'm giving it to you until you're ready for me. But I'll be back after you take your moment. I'll be back to love you again."

"Thank you," I whisper. God, he's amazing.

"Suzanne, I'm the strength right now when you're not able to be, but we'll balance this out. I need you to listen to me closely though, Suzanne. Are you listening?" I nod. And I am listening. His rich deep voice will make me *always* listen to him.

"I see NO ugliness in you and I never will. You're my Suzanne, only." Oh! "So take your 'moment' and know I'll be back soon. I love you, Suzanne. I love you too much to let you end us over a moment of panic."

Crying again, I can only nod. Who talks like this? What man openly cries for the woman he loves without looking weak or unattractive? What man says the novel lover words without looking pathetic? No one! Only Z could break into me with words like those, so beautiful and sincere; words that I actually *feel*.

Wiping my tears as the door closes; I feel my gross face again but suddenly I don't care. In this moment, I almost believe I *am* Z's beautiful Suzanne. I almost trust in nothing more than his words. I almost forget for a minute how very hard this life of mine really is.

CHAPTER 21

JUNE 9

Turning my head when I wake up, I look directly at Z and Mack sitting side by side in chairs waiting for me.

When Z smiles, I remember everything from last night. Wow. That was so intense and so very unlike me. Suddenly, I'm horribly embarrassed by my sexual need and aggression.

"Hi," I croak in my even raspier morning voice.

"Hi, Suzanne. I hope you don't mind that I'm here. If you need me to leave I will. If you need another minute I'll leave. I know you're trying to process everything, and that I may be too much for you just yet, especially after what happened last night. So the choice is absolutely yours."

Mack suddenly turns his head toward Z with the question 'what happened last night?' written all over his face. Blush.

"No. It's okay. I thought about you all night, Z. And I'm going to try to take my moments as *infrequently* as possible. I really do want you in my life." There. I said it. Thank god, he seems happy with my words going by his smile. "It's really good to see you again," I grin.

"It's really good to be seen," he smirks.

Reaching out for his hand, Z gladly gives it. Holding it tightly while just taking him in, I think I feel happiness in this moment.

I'm so glad he doesn't cave under all my shit. I'm so glad that when I need a minute he comes back to me. I am so unbelievably lucky to have him in my life, I know now. Not that I didn't think I knew it before, but now I *really* know it.

"Suzanne, I have to talk to you about something very important. I wish I could give you more time, but I really can't. It involves Z, but if you'd like privacy with me he has agreed to leave us."
Mack looks so serious, I'm just dreading this conversation, and I'm pretty sure I know what it is- the damage from the accident.
"Go ahead, Mack. Just say it." Shit. I'm so scared.
But it's Z who speaks. "Suzanne, I need you to try to stay calm for a minute, okay?" Ugh. This can't be good, but I nod anyway.
After a huge inhale, Z squeezes my hand tighter and says, "You and I are going to have a child." Silence. "You're pregnant with our baby." Nothing. "Um, we're going to be parents." And *stillllll* nothing.
Is this shock? Is this what being stunned feels like? Huh. I feel nothing. Actually I *feel* nothing. Is nothing a feeling? I should ask Mack some time.
Mack slowly moves closer to me, almost like he's afraid of my reaction to movement or something.
"Suzanne? Did you hear Z?"
"Talk to me, love. Did you hear me?" Yup. I heard.
Silence. Well this sure as fuck is NOT what I thought. Jesus CHRIST! Looking between Mack and Z they seem to be waiting for me speak. Why the hell is it always me who has to react, or speak, or like, *function?* What the fuck? This is totally unfair.
"Suzanne, you and I made a child, and though you've been through so much, the baby is doing well. They've been monitoring its development, and trying to regulate your medications according to your pregnancy. Um, that's why you physically have so much pain still. I'm sorry, but they couldn't give you the really good stuff with the baby inside you," he grins.
Is he making a joke? Is this funny? I don't know. I still feel NOTHING! Blink.
"Suzanne this is a shock, certainly for you right now. It was a shock to Z as well. You don't have to say anything if you're not ready. There are no expectations here, right Z?"
Looking, Z nods with a smile. No expectations, huh? He looks

pretty expectant, and I'm EXPECTING! Ha! What. The. *FUCK?!* Giggle.

"Well, *shiiiit...* This is a surprise." And that's it. That's all I've got for words.

"Suzanne, I know you're probably a little freaked out."

"Ya think?!" I giggle.

"Please, love. This is a good thing. This really is amazing and wonderful, and just *amazing...*"

"For you."

"For us."

"Yeah, right. How the hell is this amazing for us? What the hell am *I* going to do?"

Sitting closer to me Mack asks, "What do you mean? What can't you do?"

"Well, I can't have a baby, that's for sure!" Holy SHIT! As *if.*

"Why can't you? Why can't we? I'm here, Suzanne. I'm not going anywhere I promise, and I'll take care of you and the baby, I promise. We're going to be okay. I know we will."

"Uh huh."

"Suzanne, please don't do this. I know you're freaked out-"

"You know nothing, Z. You don't have a clue how I feel. *You might think this is awesome, but I sure as hell don't.*"

"Suzanne... please."

"Please, what? What can I possibly say right now? What do you want to hear Z? You want me to say I'm happy? You want me to BE happy? Well, I can't and I'm not. I *can* lie though, if you want."

Turning away from them, I just need a minute to myself. I need to feel this. I need to feel something, but there's nothing good right now. There is panic, and shock, and even sadness, I think. But I don't feel anything good about this.

"Suzanne... just take a little time to get used to this. I promise you'll be happy. I promise we'll be good."

"Don't make that promise Z. Don't do it, because we're not going to be okay *I* promise. How can you be so fucking stupid? *Seriously?* I'm mental half the time or in a coma the other half.

What makes you think I would possibly want this, or that I could possibly *do* this? I'm fucked UP!"

"You're not fucked up. You're just in shock, but that'll pass, I promise."

"Okay, sure."

"Suzanne, look at me. Would you like Z to leave us for a few minutes? Would you like to talk to me alone? It's okay. You can talk with me about this without Z if you need."

Looking over, Z looks so hurt right now and I wish I cared, but I honestly don't. Right now I feel nothing but disgust. I think I actually hate him for this.

Yelling loudly, I can't control myself. "Why did you DO THIS TO ME!?"

Flinching, Z seems to stumble over his words. But finally, he speaks. "I didn't do this TO you. We did it together. Call it an accident, call it a mistake, or call it a miracle. We love each other and somehow made a life together. Do you remember our night together? Do you remember how amazing it was? Well, *that's* how this happened.

"... Suzanne, I love you, and I'm going to love you forever, and I'm going to love this child forever. Yes, it's a shock- I was shocked too, but after a minute of shock I realized I wanted this. I want you, and I want this baby, and we're going to be okay."

"No, we aren't."

"We are. There's nothing I can't handle with you. There's nothing we can't handle together. And there's nothing I won't do for you, because you're everything to me, Suzanne."

Crying finally, I beg in a whisper, "Then please make this go away..."

Flinching again, Z looks like I hit him. I swear to god, he exhaled a huge breath and sat back in his chair. Looking at me stunned, he seems wordless but I have to finish this.

"Z..." Mack tries.

"No, Mack. This is between Suzanne and me. Right, Suzanne? This is *our* decision because it's *our* child we're talking about."

"Z, please? Please don't do this to me. I really don't want your baby. I don't want *a* baby. Please Z, I'm begging you. If you love me like you say you do, please make this go away. If you love me at all, even a tenth of what you keep telling me, then do this for me. Please make this go away... if you really love me," I whisper.

After a moment of silence, Z seems to groan, "Wow. You would use my love for you against me like THAT? That's pretty nasty, Suzanne. I'm going to go with the assumption that you've just been thrown for a loop here, and that you're not seriously throwing my fucking love for you in my face. I'm going to assume you couldn't possibly be serious-"

"I am, Z. I'm dead fucking serious. Get this thing out of me!"

When Z suddenly jumps up from the chair it tips over behind him, and I flinch. Suddenly, I'm scared to death he's going to hurt me. Shit! Covering my head with my hands I wait for the blows. Waiting, I can't even breathe from the fear.

"Suzanne. Stop! Z would never hit you, and I'm not sure why you're behaving as he would. Are you confused right now? You seem to be struggling with your past and with your reality right here and now. Suzanne, please talk to me."

Opening my eyes, I see Z standing beside me, *not* looking like he's going to hurt me.

Exhaling, I breathe, "There's nothing more to say Mack. And I'm not confused- I'm desperate. I don't want this and I want it out of me."

"NO!" Z roars in the quiet room.

"Whatever, Z. This is MY body and I want it out," I say glaring at him.

"Not gonna happen, Suzanne. You're just freaked out, and you'll feel better later after you think about this. After you take another moment."

"No I won't, Z! This is way more than 'taking a moment'. This is horrible! Mack I need him out of my room now. Get him out, Mack. NOW!"

"Suzanne-"

"Mack, get him out of here. I don't want to look at him

anymore."

"Suzanne stop talking about me like that. I'm not a fucking monster! I'm Z! Look at me, love. LOOK! I love you and I'm here for you. I'm *always* here. I've always been here no matter what happens and no matter what I go through with you, I'm always here."

"BUT I DON'T WANT YOU HERE!! Christ..." Catching my breath, I beg, "You're just not listening to me. Please! Listen. To. Me."

Desperately, Z moves to me trying to take my hand, but I pull away from him. I feel nothing for this man. I don't find him kind or attractive or loving. I feel nothing but disgust. And if he touches me again, I may lose my friggin mind!

"Suzanne, I love you!" He yells, sounding all manic himself.

"I'm sorry for that."

"Listen to me, please. We can have a wonderful life together. We *will* have a wonderful life, I'm sure of it."

"Please stop, Z-"

"Suzanne, if you do this you'll kill us. You will kill our child and kill us. I can't live with you doing this. I *won't* let you do this. So be sure. I'm not above forcing the issue if I have to. But I really want you to understand something- I will absolutely NEVER forgive you for this. I won't. And saying that breaks my heart after all you've been through, but I will NEVER forgive you, and I will NEVER be able to love you again after this."

"Z, Suzanne just needs some time-"

"No she doesn't!" I scream. "Suzanne doesn't need any more time with this. Suzanne has made her decision. *Suzanne* is sorry to hurt him, but she's making her own decision about her own body this time. No one else gets to do things to my body that I don't want to happen! YOU SAID SO!"

Staring right into Z's eyes, I come clean. "I don't think I love you anymore. I'm sorry that you've wasted so much time with me, I'm truly sorry for that. I wish I could give you that time back, but-"

"Suzanne. Be sure you're thinking clearly right now because some things can't be unsaid. And some things CAN'T be undone,"

Z moans.

"Yeah? Well this can. I'm sorry Z, but I'd like you to leave now. You don't understand, and clearly you'll never understand. So I really don't think there's any more to say between us. I do thank you for all the time you put into me though."

"*Time I put into you?* Jesus fucking *Christ!* It wasn't 'time'! It was LOVE, Suzanne. I loved you! That's what I did, and now you're breaking my heart and destroying our lives. Give me the baby then. Give me my child if you don't want it, or me. I'll love it. I'll care for the baby. I want this so much," he practically begs me.

"No."

"Be sure, Suzanne. Be absolutely fucking sure about this, because I can't come back from this. I WON'T come back. Not this time. I will walk away forever this time."

Looking at him, I say the words he has to hear.

"Z, you are amazing and I will always love your memory but I really need you to leave me now. You have helped me so much but I just can't give this back to you. You keep saying be sure, and I am. I don't want a child, and I don't want to be with you when you'll never forgive me for this. I don't feel *anything* right now, least of all for this thing inside me-"

"It'll come, Suzanne," he pleads desperately.

"No it won't. And of that I'm absolutely sure. You should leave now. And I'm really, truly sorry for all this. I'm so sorry you ever met me and ever loved me. Thank you though. I remember how much you meant to me, even if I don't feel it anymore."

"Fuck you, Suzanne! *I'm* fucking sorry I ever met and loved you. Marcus was right! Loving you has been the hardest thing I've ever done." Ouch. Low-blow, but considering the topic I'll just have to take it.

"Sorry-"

"Suzanne, think about what you're saying," Mack finally jumps in.

"Forget it, Mack. Don't try to change her mind. Don't try to be the hero for her again. Suzanne has made up her mind, haven't

you, love?" Nodding, I have no other words for him.
"Okay then. Good bye, Suzanne. I truly wish you well in life, but I'm through looking like an ass for a woman who doesn't want the love I can give her. Be well," he breathes while touching my hand briefly before he walks out the door.
There was no dramatic backwards glance. No last attempt. There were no final words or confessions of love. He just left, completely finished with me, silently closing the door behind him.

Exhaling... I'm done. The sadness is overwhelming but it doesn't change the fact that I made the right decision. There is NO other decision *to* make. There is just nothing.
Crying, Mack tries to take my hand but I pull away from him as well. I want no comfort. I want nothing to soothe me. I want to embrace this pain for eternity.
Z is gone. Finally. Z left, as I always knew he would. I may have provoked it, but I was always going to anyway. This just saved him from putting in any more time and effort before he left me eventually. People like him shouldn't love people like me anyway.
Crying, my whole world seems to shift. I have a plan and I have to move forward. I want no one else to have a say, and I want no one else to help me. This is it for me. This is *my* life to live as I choose. I have to write this script with my own hand now.
"Mack?"
"Yes?"
Looking up at him hovering over me, I say as clearly as possible, "I am dead fucking serious. I want this out of me. Now."
"Um... It's too late, Suzanne." Oh! Gasp.
"Then I want you to leave me with this nightmare. Get out Mack and leave me with this. I want to be alone for a while so I can swallow another nightmare someone else has caused me and my body... again."
Exhaling, I see the tears in his eyes, but as Mack nods his head and walks from my room I. Just. Don't. Care.

Desperately, my mind spins. There are all these terrible thoughts in my head. There are all these terrible self-mutilations playing out in my mind. There has to be someone who can help me.
There has to be something I can take or something I can do to myself. Something! Maybe herbal medicines, or coat hangers, or falling down stairs, or swallowing bleach. Something has to work! It can't be too late. It can't!
Shit! I'm. just. so. desperate. What the hell do I do now?
Bursting into tears, my mind won't stop spinning and panicking. And I'm just so completely alone with this nightmare.
Oh god, somebody help me. I CAN'T do this anymore!

CHAPTER 22

JUNE 10

Waking, I can't believe what I've been told because I'm still stunned. I'm awake and yet my world is so black with these thoughts and desperation. I hope to god I never live this nightmare. I CAN'T live this nightmare.
Turning my head, I see Mack waiting silently beside me in a chair. Oh god, I don't want to learn this truth. I don't want to know for sure. I hope they were lying. A lie right now would be the best news EVER.
Looking at Mack, well, actually kind of staring numbly at him, I just know it's the truth. Holy SHIT! How do I live with this? How do I tell him this? How do I make this go away?

"Suzanne, you're going to love this baby." And so it begins...
"How did this happen?" Oh, duh. Isn't that the stupid question all men ask with an unexpected pregnancy? Jesus! I'm still a moron.
Raising an eyebrow at me, I cut him off. "I know *how*, I just mean HOW? I was protected. It's never happened before. There's never been an accident before. It's never happened to me before. How did this happen?!" God, I sound all manic.
"Your meds failed? You forgot to take them? You were under stress? Who knows? There could be a multitude of factors, Suzanne." Shit! This is bad. "Suzanne, once the shock wears off I think you'll be very happy about this."
"Um, I really don't think so."
"You will, I promise. You're going to be so happy when he or she is born."
"No, I won't."

Leaning in closer to me, Mack takes my hand. "You will. I know it, Suzanne. When you see this baby, you're going to love it so much that this upset and shock will all be worth it, I promise."
"Mack, I really won't." Shit, he's not hearing me, at all.
"I really wish you would stop saying that. I know you and I know your capacity to love, and though you don't believe me right now, I promise you're going to love this little life which you and Z created together."
Oh, god. He doesn't know my capacity to love if he believes that even for a moment.
"Suzanne... I need you to listen to me for a minute. Please. I know you, and though this is another shock to you, this baby is going to be amazing for you, AND for Z. You will love this baby-"
Snap!
"NO, I WON'T! Don't you get it? I won't love it or like being its mother. I don't want to BE a mother. I don't want his baby. I don't want anyone's baby. I don't want a baby at all. I'll fuck it up, or hurt it, or torture it, or just, like, *hate* it. I know I will because that's all I know, so that's what I'll do, okay?!" Shit! Breathe.
"That isn't all you know. You know love and friendship. You know a better life than you had before."
"Yeah, I may *know* it, but I don't *feel* it, okay? I feel nothing. There is this awful thing in me that I feel nothing for and I know the feelings aren't going to come. I'm not going to feel it."
"You will, I promise." Oh god, he still can't hear me. What do I do?
Moaning my words, "You're wrong, Mack. I won't ever feel this."
"I honestly believe given time you will, Suzanne. By the time this baby gets here you'll be better, and maybe all your feelings will have returned. You'll know pleasure and happiness again, instead of just this sadness and depression. You will feel your baby and you'll love your baby." Ugh.
"Fuck! Would you just *listen* to me? I WON'T feel anything for this kid. NOTHING! I don't feel anything now, and I won't in the future. I want it out. I don't want this- I'm sorry. I'm probably a

horrible person, or a bitch, or even evil like my parents, but I WON'T feel anything, I promise. There is NO feeling in me. There is nothing.

"... Look, I know you don't understand. I know no one will understand. I don't think most women are even capable of understanding what I'm telling you, but I DON'T want this. I really, *really* don't. Having a baby was *never* something I wanted. *Ever*. I'm just not one of those women. And I know everyone will judge me and maybe even hate me, but I can't change that. Most women are thrilled when they find out they're pregnant, I know that. People think it's a blessing, and the most wonderful thing on the planet. But I don't! I never have! I'm sorry if that makes me bad, or evil, or selfish, and I know I'll be judged by everyone, but I don't want this. I really don't.

"... Mack, I know who I was trying to be, but I don't feel like her anymore. I just want to wake up for once and not feel like shit. I want to wake up and not BE shit for once. Having a baby is not going to change me, and it's not going to make me feel better, or feel love, or even feel Z anymore. I'm sorry, I know he loves me, and I remember that I love him, and though I *know* everything, I *feel* NOTHING!! There is nothing inside me anymore. And there is certainly nothing in me to give to a child."

"You love me. I know you feel that."

"Yes, I do. I feel you Mack, but not like I remember I did before. I know the way I used to feel about you. I remember the crazy desperation for your friendship and love. I remember holding onto you because you were the only good thing in my life at the time, but I don't feel that way anymore. I know what I felt, but I don't actually feel that anymore. I do love you, again I guess, but it's different. There is a comfort with you, but not a heavy desperate feeling for your love and friendship or an intensity of feeling for you like there was before."

"It'll come back Suzanne. It just takes time. Your memory return is new, you WILL feel-"

"No. I think you're wrong. I think I'm going to live like this, kind

THIS is me...

of suspended in a memory of hope in the past by all you people in a way that is awful and depressing, and filled with upset and longing because of me. I don't feel what I once felt. I don't feel anything. And having the Kaylas around, or you, or even Z isn't going to change that. I don't want to hurt anyone anymore but that's all I do, because I can't *feel* anything."

"Suzanne, it'll take time. Once you're used to the idea-"

"No."

"Suzanne, just listen to me-"

"No. No, Mack. Listen to *ME*. I don't want this baby and I want you to make it go away. I want you to do it as my doctor. I want you to make it stop. I want you to make the appointment, or tell me who I contact to make the appointment. I don't care but I want this done.

"... I'm not meant to be a mother. Christ! I'm barely meant to be a person. But I always knew that before. I ALWAYS knew I never wanted to be a mother, I just didn't know *why* at the time. But I was very clear about motherhood with Marcus. And though he tried for a few years to change my mind, he eventually gave in and agreed to no children between us. I didn't know why I didn't want any then, but I remember now what happened to me as a kid, and I know that's why I don't want a child now."

"But you don't have to feel like that. You could change that."

"But I won't."

"Suzanne, you don't have to be like your parents were."

Snorting, "That's all I know Mack."

"No, it isn't! You know me and the Kaylas, and especially Z. You know good people now. You now know what it's like to be loved and cared for. We'll help you. We'll help you learn how to be a good parent. You don't have to be like your parents were."

"No. You're not listening to me."

Abruptly standing, Mack seems so frustrated with me. "I AM listening, but I'm trying to get you to understand that you don't have to be like they were."

"But I will be-"

"NO YOU WON'T! You can choose to not be like them. You can

choose to be good, and you can learn how to love a baby, how to love all of us around you. You can choose-"
"But I won't. And I wish you would listen to me. I wish you would *hear* me. I won't feel anything, and I can't be what you hope I'll be."
"I don't want you to *be* anyone, Suzanne- Just yourself." Yeah, right.
In the silence between us, I'm just desperate for Mack to understand. I wish I had the right words for him. I wish I could get through to him so I had his support. I wish he would hear me and support me so I wasn't alone with this decision.
"Mack, I'm not HER anymore. I'm not the woman who woke up last year and remembered. I am NOT her. I'm better and I'm aware of everything I did and went through to be better, but I don't *feel* anything. I don't *feel* like her anymore. I am NOT her. This is me..."
"You'll feel again, I promise. There are some medications we haven't tried yet. There are some cognitive therapies available. There are still things we can do to help you assimilate to your new life. There are choices we can make to help you feel better."
"Mack, I'm not going to feel this even if I do start feeling again. I'm sure of it. I *know* it."
"And what if you do start to feel again? What if your feelings and your memories become clearer? What if you emotionally move past this? What if you make a mistake now, a mistake you can never take back? How will you live with the guilt of making a decision now when you aren't yourself fully yet? What if you do this, and you realize it was a mistake afterward? There is NO turning back from that."
"Mack... please listen to me. HEAR me. I know this is the truth- I KNOW it! I need you to listen to me. I'm going to say something and I want you to try to be objective. I want you to try to understand what I've said. I want you to stop being a friend and I want you to just be a doctor listening to his patient for a minute. Then I want you to leave my room so we can both think about

THIS is me...

what I've said. I want you to listen to me. Can you do that? Can you listen to me, and then leave for a little while so we can each absorb what I tell you? Can you, Mack?"

"Of course, Suzanne. I'll listen and give you some room to breathe," he says while sitting back down in the chair beside me.

Waiting for me to speak, he's so calm. He IS waiting and he WILL listen, but sadly I know he'll never understand. He will never agree with me.

Making eye contact, I speak to him as clearly as possible. "I do NOT want this baby. I CAN'T have this baby. I WON'T have this baby. I cannot be a mother to anything. There is not enough good in me to do this."

Exhaling, Mack nods his head. "Okay, Suzanne. I've heard you. And I'll leave to think about what you've said before I try to convince you otherwise. I hear you, but I think you're wrong."

Nodding again, Mack stands to leave my room and I feel nothing but relief.

Exhaling, I know I must seem a monster to Mack. I know the Kaylas will be disgusted. I know Z will be devastated and hate me forever, but there is just this- the knowledge of who I was trying to be, but no feeling for her anymore. This is who I am now. This is who I turned out to be.

"I cannot be a mother to anything. There is not enough good in me," I whisper to my empty room like a mantra.

CHAPTER 23

When Mack returns a few hours later, I know I'm done. There is a pity on his face which must be killing him. I know Mack. I *remember* Mack. Mack tries to always help me, but with this I don't think he can.

"Suzanne, you are too far along to end the pregnancy," he says abruptly. "There is nothing any doctor will medically do to help you terminate this pregnancy because the baby is healthy and well." God, Mack is all robotic as he speaks. I think he truly hates me this time.

"I have asked on your behalf within this hospital and I've called many Women's Clinics in the State. I know you don't want to hear this, and I won't tell you all the things I believe to be true of you. I'm sorry, but you ARE pregnant and you have to accept it. You are too far along for a termination, plus Z would fight this legally before anything could be done if you attempt to take this any further."

He looks so disgusted, or angry, or maybe hurt by me, I'm not sure. For once I can't tell by Mack's face what he's thinking of me and this scares me the most, I think.

"Okay," I finally give in. "Um, how far along am I?"

"You're in your second trimester. You are 19 weeks based on conception being the night before you're accident on February 15th. You're due date is November 7th, and your baby is strong. Through all the trauma and against all odds, your baby has not only survived, but flourished," he whispers.

"Why did you WAIT so long to tell me?!" I suddenly accuse.

Moving back a step, Mack looks like I hit him. Well, too bad. I feel like hitting him right now. I feel like hitting anyone right now, or maybe hitting something. I don't know, but I'm really friggin' annoyed right now.

"We were waiting for you to become emotionally more stable. It never occurred to me-"

"It never *occurred* to you to tell me sooner?! *Seriously?!*"

"NO! It never occurred to me or to Z that you would feel this way. We didn't know. *I* didn't know. What would you have done even if I told you last month? Really, what could you have done?"

"I would have got rid of it!"

"Really? When you knew nothing about yourself. You didn't know any of us. You didn't know where your husband was. You knew nothing! But you would have been rational enough to end a pregnancy?"

"Yes! I would-"

"Suzanne, you would have done nothing. I wouldn't have allowed it!" What?!

"You wouldn't have *allowed* it? Who the hell are you to make decisions about my body when-"

"I'M YOUR DOCTOR! That's who. And there is NO WAY I would have allowed a patient of mine, under any circumstance to make a decision like that under the circumstances you were in."

"Well, thank you. Thank you for making a decision that has screwed me for life!"

"Suzanne, please... Think about what you're saying. If you had aborted the child earlier without knowing who you were, and you woke up later and remembered your life and it was a mistake- THAT would have been for life. This decision has options the other did not. You have choices-"

"I have NO choice- you took that away from me when you didn't tell me when I woke up that I was pregnant."

"It wasn't like that."

"It was *exactly* like that."

"No, it wasn't. I-"

"I don't care what you say. I'm sure you and Z, and everybody else is thrilled that I'm stuck, but I'm not, and I never will be. So again, thank you for screwing up my already screwed up life."

"Would you just listen to me?"

"No. I'm done. Talk to the wall. Talk to Z. Talk to anyone but me. I'm not interested and I'm way too pissed to even look at you right now."

"Suzanne... I honestly didn't know you felt this way. I couldn't have known. You were in the coma for the first weeks of the pregnancy, so I didn't know-"

"You didn't know... Well, thanks. Now I'm stuck because it never *occurred* to you to tell me there was a child GROWING inside me! I'm trapped because it never occurred to you to tell me weeks ago? How could you both do this to me?! How could the PT doctors, and the Neuro-specialists, and the nurses, and every other fucking person I have spoken to in all the weeks since I've been awake NOT tell me? No one thought I should know?!"

"I'm sorry, but I spoke with all your Doctors, and with everyone involved with your treatment and being your Court Appointed Physician and your *friend*, I had all the say on what you were and were not told. And it just never occurred to me that this would be a problem for you. A shock definitely, but not a problem. Honestly Suzanne, I just wanted you stronger and emotionally stable before I told you about this. Plus, I thought you knew about the pregnancy but was blocking out the reality of it. I knew Marcus told you before you gained your memory back, and I know you've mentioned your weight gain from time to time with the nurses. I know you wondered about the ultrasound and *why* they were examining your stomach instead of your leg." What? Shit. Do I remember that? Um... Actually, that's seems familiar, I think.

"So I was waiting for you to become more emotionally stable so you could deal with the reality of the pregnancy rather than the unconscious denial of it. I promise you it was never to hurt you or to 'trap' you."

Watching him closely, Mack seems to become more and more sad as he confesses to me.

Whispering to my Mack, "I believe you weren't trying to hurt me but it doesn't change anything, does it? I'm still hurt and I'm still totally trapped."

THIS is me...

Closing my eyes, I try to breathe deeply. Being hysterical right now isn't going to help with my 'emotional stability' issues. Shit! Lashing out at Mack won't change this situation either, I know that. But I'm just so freaked out I can't help it. What the hell am I going to do?

Opening my eyes, I really see Mack. God, he looks bad. This isn't going well for either of us.

"You look awful, Mack."

"I'm sad, Suzanne." Ugh. Dammit.

Whispering, "I'm sorry Mack, I-"

"I'm not sad for me, Suzanne- I'm sad for you. I wish you felt what I feel, and I wish you believed what I believe. I know you. I really do know you. And I know you can do this, but I AM sorry I waited so long to tell you. I thought it was best at the time considering your emotional struggle and instability and with the PTA at the time. As I said, it was never my intention to trap you."

Looking at Mack I do believe him. He isn't a bad man and he's never hurt me before, and really, what difference could the last 4 weeks have made? Nothing really.

"Oh, god... I'm so scared," I finally cry.

"I know. But you have us in your life to help you. And we will."

"Z won't. He's gone."

"For now. He's just hurt by your words. But he loves you very much. And given time, I'm sure he'll come back if you want him back. Z was so shocked when we found out you were carrying. He was stunned and then minutes later he was ecstatic. You were so lost to us, but unbelievably, there was a child growing in you that was his. Z suddenly felt like there was something good in all the bad we were experiencing with you. He was so excited and happy again, after weeks of just sadness and horror. Z couldn't breathe when you were in the hospital, watching you so physically hurt and so mentally lost to us, but the baby gave him a reason to hold on tighter. He loves you Suzanne, but he's devastated by your reaction to the news. Trust me, once he calms down he'll come back to you."

"I don't want him to come back. I'm sorry, but I really don't. I think I hate him for this, and I think I'm going to resent him for this forever. Even though I know that's totally unfair, I can't help it. I don't want this Mack, and that's not going to change."
"It may-"
"It won't. I'm going to resent Z for doing this to me and he's going to resent me for not wanting this from him. There is just too much to overcome this time."
"There isn't too much, Suzanne. You and Z can talk and find a middle ground with each other. You can work this out."
"I don't think so. Honestly, Mack... I feel nothing for him but a horrible resentment. And I wish that wasn't true, but it is. I don't want to see him, and if this thing is born I'll give it to him and he can keep it if he wants. But I don't want it and I don't want to be with him with it. I want no part in this."
"Suzanne, you can't possibly know what you'll feel months from now. You can't understand how you may change. You're making decisions now without the ability to foresee your future. You're *barely* here emotionally, and your 'normal' personality is mediocre at best. You're still struggling with all these new developments and changes. Your emotions are all over the place, and you're still struggling from one moment to the next. I can see it."
"I know that, *believe* me. I KNOW I'm struggling but I'm not struggling over this. This is an absolute for me. Whether I was in the accident or not, I would still feel the same way. Mack, please hear me."
"I'm listening, but-"
"There is no but this time. This is it. Since I can't make this go away, I'll do what I have to, but I don't want to do it, and the whole time I'm going to resent it. But tell Z for me he can have it if he wants it."
"It's a baby, Suzanne."
"Fine. He can have the *baby* if he wants it. I don't care. And if that makes me horrible, so be it. I'm a horrible person he never

should've loved in the first place. And now he's aware of it, and you're aware of it. Everyone will know now what a horrible person I am, but I. Just. Don't. Care."

"You're not horrible. Many women feel this way about motherhood. I know that, Suzanne. Chicago Kayla herself isn't keen on the idea of ever being a mother, but she does believe you would make a great parent. It's sad for us who love you because we don't see you as you see yourself. We honestly believe you're making a mistake."

"Well, you can believe what you want. You can all think terrible things about me-"

"That isn't what I said."

"It doesn't matter to me. I see you all and I remember loving you all, but I feel nothing for you anymore. You are this awesome guy, I *know* that, but I don't *feel* like you're awesome right now. I know it but I don't feel it. So I don't care what you think of me over this."

"I don't think you're terrible. No one does. We just think you're shocked and making bad decisions."

"Really? Well, I'm sure Marcus will agree with my decision and *he'll* take me back." Wow. Where did THAT come from?

"Are you really going there, Suzanne? Honestly?"

"If I have to."

"Now THAT'S a horrible thing, Suzanne. That's a truly selfish, awful thing to do. Marcus is all twisted up over you. He's not even rational anymore where you're concerned."

"Good. Then we should be just fine together." Even I flinch as the sarcasm drips from my tongue.

"This is probably the only time I have EVER been disgusted with you, Suzanne. Please don't do this. Don't use Marcus to fight against Z. It's so wrong, and it lets me know just how unstable you really are. You shouldn't be making ANY decisions, if this is the kind of decision you're willing to make."

"Oh, fuck off Mack! Don't judge me! You don't know. You know nothing."

"What the hell don't I know Suzanne? Tell me!"

"Marcus was always good to me, and he'll support me, and I won't be lonely while I have to suffer this! That's what."
"Jesus! Grow UP, Suzanne! You're seriously pissing me off and making me furious with you. I realize this is very unprofessional of me, but fuck it! You're being a total asshole right now!" WHAT?! Giggle. "Go ahead and laugh. I don't give a shit. Suzanne, you're an adult. You're a grown woman faced with a problem, but instead of dealing with it you're just copping out. Grow up. It's time. Running back to Marcus isn't the answer."
"It is for me!"
"Bullshit! Running to Marcus isn't good for you OR for him. I'm not sure you know this, but Marcus is really fucked up right now, Suzanne- not that you give a shit. Frankly, I don't give a shit about him but it DOES affect you, so naturally I'm all involved again."
Man, he's pissed! If it wasn't so shocking I'd probably be scared to death right now.
"Again, I'm sure you care about no one but yourself here, but Marcus is a fucking mess. When he found out about your baby Suzanne, he lost it and was going to strangle you!" What?! "Yeah, that's right. Marcus began moaning and advancing like he would strangle you and MY Kayla had to fight him away from you before she could get him removed from your room. Marcus even back-handed Kayla in the process." WHAT?! He did?
"So, as you can imagine, I'm not a fan of his, though I do feel sorry for him. And Kayla is amazing, I swear to god! Kayla talked with Marcus afterward, and she saw in him a desperation and sadness so deep for you that she asked the police to drop the charges, calling the hit an 'accident' but not before we had a restraining order put into place for your protection. I wanted to go after him, and Z damn-near killed him, but Kayla stopped us. That's why he's only been to see you once. THAT'S why it's a bad idea to get back together with Marcus!" Holy shit! Marcus?! "So, you'll have to forgive me if I don't support your decision to take on Marcus right now, out of some misguided desperation. It's a bad fucking idea. It's pathetic, really." Shit!

"Um, I didn't know," I whisper.

"Of course you didn't! We, *as usual* try our best to protect you from all the things that'll push you over the edge, if you will. But I think we're going about your recovery wrong this time. ME being your constant support system last year when you became better falsely led me to believe that I had to proceed the same way with you this time as well. But now I'm sure I'm wrong. Kid gloves are not working with you anymore. You're using me to help you make bad decisions and you're even willing to use Marcus to make a bad decision against Z." This sounds kind of like a break-up to me.

"Mack-"

"Let me finish, please." Gulping, I nod to him. "Suzanne, I love you very much, but I think that's made me kind of soft with you, and I think it's becoming very detrimental to your emotional wellbeing. I think I need to stop trying to be your friend first and your doctor second. I should have been your Psychiatrist first and I've failed at that, I believe."

Crying out, "You haven't! I swear. You're a really good doctor for me."

"I don't think so any longer."

"Are you leaving me?" I beg. Oh god, *this* I feel. THIS hurts.

"No, I'm not leaving you but I am going to be different with you. I'm not going to simply nod and agree to all your crap anymore. You need guidance, and clearly a firm *objective* hand before you make more bad decisions. You may even fire me as your personal physician, but I think this is for the best."

"I won't fire you!" Oh GOD!

"It doesn't matter Suzanne if you do. I think we should really look into having another Psychiatrist assess you. I don't think I'm helping you anymore."

"You are! Oh, god... Please."

"Suzanne, I think maybe-"

"NO Mack, please! Please don't leave me!" Gasp. Shit. I can't breathe.

"Listen to me-"

"NO! Listen to ME!" Gasp. "I need you. Please don't leave m-me! Please. I'm sorry. I'll do- whatever- you want. I'll have this b-baby, I swear. I won't go- back to- Marcus! I'll do whatever- you want- me to do! Oh, god. PLEASE! Ssstay with- me..."

"Suzanne, look at me. I want you to take a deep breath. I want you to try to calm down."

"Mack, p-please don't leave- me. I'll die again. I swear! You're all I have left- in this world..." Gasp. Pause. Gasp.

Grabbing for me, Mack begins shushing me. Making little soothing noises as he rubs my back, he holds me tightly as I panic fully. My whole body is convulsing with the fear. I'm so scared I can't breathe. I am so unbelievably scared of being alone; of being without Mack I can't function.

"Please, don't leave me..." I beg.

Soothing me, "I'm not leaving you. I just don't want to be your doctor anymore. It's too hard for me now."

"I'm so- sorry-"

"Suzanne, I can't balance this anymore and it's not helping you. And I want to help you again, but I think I need to do that as your friend only. I'm sorry, but I can't be your doctor anymore." Oh god.

"What does that mean?" I whisper through my ragged breath.

"It means I'll introduce you to another Psychiatrist, maybe even my own," he laughs. "But I can't be objective or on the fence with you anymore. I'm angry all the time and I'm losing my once clear perspective. I'm fighting with Kayla, and I'm fighting with Z, and now I'm fighting with you. I'm screwing up, and I don't want that for either of us."

Pausing, I desperately try to get my breath back.

"I'm sorry I'm so hard for you, but I'll be better I promise."

"You *will* be better. But I don't want that for me. I want that for you. You have to start making decisions for you now. Not for me. You can't live only for me, Suzanne. And you can't threaten to kill yourself every time I say or do something you can't handle. It's wrong and it scares me. And it's very unhealthy, Suzanne."

"But I need you," I moan desperately.

"I'm not going anywhere. I'm still here for you as your *friend*. I'll still visit every day, and I'll still be your Mack. But that's it. So prepare yourself, Suzanne. The gloves are coming off. Any attempt at professionalism is out the window. I'm not going to hold back anymore. And I'm going to call you on your shit now, like a friend would and should."

Silently, I hold Mack tighter for a long time. I don't want to ever let him go. I CAN'T let him go. So if this is the new Mack- I'll take him.

"I'm really sorry I suck, Mack. I swear I don't mean to, but this is me I think. I think this is what my life has made me, but I'll try to be better. I promise. I don't want to lose you and if you want to be only my friend I'll take it. God, I know I love you so much, I just don't really feel if yet, but I know it's there."

"It better come back soon, Suzanne. Otherwise, as Kayla says, I'll totally lose my shit," he whispers in my ear. Grinning, I hold him even tighter than I thought possible.

This is going to be hard. I think Mack with the gloves off is going to be really scary for me sometimes, but as I said, I'll take it. I know at this point I'm not strong enough to face this life without him, so I'll take anything he's willing to give me, even if it sucks. Even if it's really scary sometimes with the gloves off, I'll take it.

CHAPTER 24

JUNE

Since I've been awake, I've made remarkable progress apparently. I'm still slow and my body is still sluggish, but my mind is pretty good now. I'm still having physiotherapy twice a day, and I am getting stronger in my arms but my legs are still really weak, especially my left leg.

It's great that I've made so much improvement. It's great that I have my memory back after waking so soon from a coma. And though I'm pleased to know what my reality is, I sometimes wish I could *feel* a little more of my reality. Well, except for the physical pain I still get on my left side, and the fear I feel knowing I haven't looked at my body yet- that I don't want to feel ever, obviously.

It's almost funny how I've trained my eyes to NEVER look at myself, even by accident. I haven't seen my body or my face since I woke up, and so far I'm okay with that. It's almost a talent really- being able to function with perfect eyesight, and yet never once catch a glimpse of your own arm or leg or face, each and every day. Funny though, this 'talent' often leaves me suddenly looking upward or sideways like a moron, which I'm sure is quite amusing to those around me. Oh well, what can I do?

One of the Kaylas and/or Mack have visited me every day, and though sometimes I'm lonely, I'm never really alone, at least not physically. I just feel alone sometimes, even when they're right beside me.

It's strange, but I DO feel all the negative feelings all the time. I feel loneliness, and sadness, and even a kind of desperation often, but I never feel any 'good' feelings. I know I loved Mack and the Kaylas before, but I don't actually feel it anymore. I even remember my time with Z- which was an amazing time. But again, I don't *feel* any of it.

It's like I'm watching a movie in my mind, seeing all the images of my life, remembering all the images but never really feeling a connection to them, which kind of sucks. It would be great to actually feel what I know my life is supposed to feel like.

Mack has explained all my absence of feeling. He has explained repeatedly that what I'm experiencing is typical- almost a delayed reaction to the memories which so quickly surfaced, but again, his words though understanding and thorough and medically significant don't actually make me feel any better. Mack even explained that some people have a complete or subtle personality change, which I may have had. The onset of PTA memories can cause a person to know everything but feel nothing, which of course I'm doing.

Why couldn't it be simple? Why couldn't I just wake up and feel everything I'm supposed to feel? Why? Because that wouldn't be the way of Suzanne. Once again, I've learned if there's a hard way or a dramatic way, or a depressing way to do something then I'm going to do it. Tada!

I think the only thing that has been beneficial with this delayed sense of feeling has been learning about the trials. It seems every day Mack or one of the Kaylas has some news to tell me. They are never actually graphic, but they let me know generally speaking what was said and what's happened to some of the people involved. During these conversations, I'm grateful that I feel nothing. I'm pleased to hear of the convictions without reliving or re*feeling* any of the pain I went through back then.

A few months ago Dr. Simmons, 'The Pig', as Kayla calls him, changed his plea to guilty for a lesser sentence with no chance for parole, especially when 4 of 11 known women, excluding me, were scheduled to testify against him. His lesser sentence is still long enough Kayla says to keep him in prison for the rest of his life, and I'm glad to hear that.

God, Chicago Kayla told me about that trial with so much excitement it was almost funny. I think I should have been insulted by her lack of sensitivity when describing the courtroom, the jurors, the defense team, and Dr. Simmons himself. But then I realized she was more excited for my sake than for her own entertainment, and her insensitivity became almost laughable. I realized she was excited *for* me that he was convicted and I was never going to be forced to take the stand against him.

Some of the other people involved have already been convicted and some of them are still finishing their trials. There were conflicts of interests everywhere and not one person was to be tried together so it's taken longer than expected. Plus a few of the men are testifying against other men so the whole thing is a clusterfuck as Kayla says, for sure.

Kayla told me gently that Mr. Sheehan killed himself before his trial when he was fired from his position as CEO of his own company, and after his wife of 23 years left him. Apparently he couldn't handle the pressure he was faced with before the trial began. Whatever. I shouldn't be happy about it and I'm not really, but I feel nothing for his death either. He was a monster to me when I was little, and sometimes I think his quick death was almost too easy.

And finally, my mother's trial has begun after many ridiculous continuations, one even being due to my coma which is kind of a slap in the face. I was told her defense team actually convinced a judge to postpone her trial *because* her daughter was in a coma- which is pretty shocking.

My mother made some plea which actually has her testifying against my father during his trial afterward. And my father has lawyered-up so successfully that he has been able to delay his trial until early November, which is kind of annoying.

I would love for my parents to finally be convicted and sentenced so I can release all the tension I hold for them still. But everyone says I have to be patient. Even the D.A., Mr. Rose, says the case is a slam dunk, no matter how long my parents delay the inevitable. This whole thing is truly exhausting, and seems never-ending for me and my sanity.

Once, when I asked Mack what the delay was about he finally told me my mother's defense. Apparently, she claims she never hurt me, other than assisting my father in hurting me because HE forced *her* to do it. But her take on the events are NOT true, and I'm having a hard time dealing with that fact.

Part of me wants to rush the courtroom and scream she's a liar, telling everyone what my mother was really like. I want everyone to know of the physical and emotional abuse I had to endure as a child, and then the sexual abuse I had to endure from HER when I was a young teen.

But then the wimpy part of me just wants to let her lie, because inevitably she's still going to be convicted anyway, even if it's for a lesser crime. And though I think Mack secretly wishes I would come forward with the real story so everyone knows the truth about my mother, he (as usual) supports my decision to stay the hell away, whether he wants to support me or not.

Without a doubt, of my two parents I hate my mother much, much more. My father NEVER touched me- not even once by his own doing. I'm sure of it. He never hit me when I was bad, and he never sexually abused me as a kid. The only thing he ever did was make sure I was available for the men, which obviously I know is bad enough. But he was just so different than my mother. He didn't seem to do any of the things because he actually *wanted* to.

My father was very quiet, and if I was to assume anything about a man who never spoke to me, I would say he was the abused spouse, or rather the frightened spouse. Somehow my 95 pound mother scared my father into hurting me, which is just so weird yet still the truth as I know it.

I can't even explain it, but my father seemed to always just go along with my mother. Even when he would strip me and put me in the outfits for the men, it was because my mother told him to. While my mother prepared the room, or adjusted the camera, or entertained the men, she forced my father 'prep' me.

Even when my father would hunt me down for my mother-

dragging me by my hair to her room, he didn't ever speak to me or seem like he enjoyed it. He would take me to her, and he always left immediately when he got me to her room for my punishments. He was the accomplice absolutely, but I KNOW he was never the mastermind. She was.

Talking with Mack, I've come to the horrible conclusion that my mother really was a creepy incestuous pedophile, or something like that. I remember the way she would prepare my body for the coming invasions with creams and lubricants. And I remember how after the events took place she would violate me again with her fingers to make sure I was still a virgin.
I remember the way she would have me taken to the downstairs washroom, draw me a bath whether I was barely conscious or not. I remember how I would always be laid on the cold floor in the billboards room to recover before I could make my way slowly, painfully, up to my own bedroom. And once I made it slowly to my bedroom there were gifts, and there was always a huge meal waiting for me.
There was food, I swear to god! After all the agony and degradation, and the pain and abuse, that was probably the part that messed with me the most. Fucking food.
As a kid, I was never allowed to eat on my own, or by choice, or because *I was HUNGRY*. My mother monitored each and every morsel that entered my mouth. She dictated to any employees in our house AND to my father that I was never, EVER to be given food that she was unaware of. She was fanatical about it, and yet, after each of my horrendous abuses, or rapes, as Mack would call them, my mother made sure I had a huge tray on my bed filled with amazing food, and a bedside table covered with every sweet and desert imaginable.
Obviously, I would have taken never eating again over the abuse I suffered. But honestly, as a kid there was such a comfort in eating like a pig, choosing anything I wanted from the huge tray, grabbing handfuls of cookies, and licorice, and chocolates, and the

ice-cream, and anything else I had ever wanted, in that moment.
 Sometimes, just for a second, I forgot how bad the abuse was. Sometimes I almost, a little bit, kind of, thought maybe it was worth all the abuse just to eat without getting into trouble or punished, or having to listen to the verbal abuse I was so used to when I ate.
 And I know that was totally messed up! I KNOW it was. However, sometimes I was so grateful for the food because it comforted me. And yet other times I was scared to death the food was a trick.
 I was scared the food was a test to see if I would eat it, and then I would fail and my mother would be mad and have another reason to punish me again. But I usually only cared for a minute or two, and then I dove in and ate until I could barely move.
 One hour after I was placed in my room with all the food, it was ALWAYS cleared away by my mother. One hour. That's all I had. And though that sounds like a long time it really wasn't. Usually, I would stuff my young face full immediately, then I would spend the next forty-five minutes or so staring at all the food I wished I still had room to eat while I fought the nausea of my pig-fest.
 One time, I grabbed and hid a few cookies under my pillow for later but then my mother came in, counted the cookies, looked at me and seemed to know *somehow* what I had done. Within seconds she had forced me from my bed, found and removed the cookies, slapped me across the face but said not one word to me. The end. I never tried to hide any food again.
 And the day following the abuses everything would go back to 'normal' as it were. My mother would monitor each and every piece of food that entered my mouth, tsking or shaking her head if I ate too fast, or chewed my food too loudly, or drank my water too slowly. If there was anything I did in any way she could disapprove of, she did. And it would all begin again for me.
 Naturally, the next day, or if I was lucky 2 days later, I would have to use the washroom. With dread I would put this off until I had absolutely NO choice, but inevitably I would have to expel the food I'd eaten.

As you can imagine, having a bowel movement after the form of sexual abuse I endured was excruciating. Often I bled again. Often the stinging pain was so bad, I would sit in the bathroom crying, and bathing, going to the washroom again, crying some more, and bathing again until I was finished. It was horrible. It was almost a secondary abuse I had to endure days later without any creams to aid me or medication to numb me.

I've often thought about the food and I wonder why she gave it to me. I wonder what the point was. I wonder if it was a test, still. I wonder if it was a reward. I wonder if it was another sick punishment, geared only to mess with my head. I wonder if there was some psychological significance for her to feeding me full then, and only then. I wonder if she was apologizing FOR the abuse... though I highly doubt it.
To this day, when I eat food I always have a quick memory of the huge spread left for me after the abuses and I wish I could ask her- what was the point? It's like a continuous puzzle I will NEVER solve.
Why did she hate my body, call me fat, and countless other names but then have me abused and fed like a glutton. Strangely, this is my number one question I'm desperate to ask her, even above 'Why did you do ANY of this to me?' Which seems a little absurd, I know.

It really is shocking to remember all the things my mother did to me. She was just so disgusting and twisted, and filled with such hate for me. And though I know logically I couldn't have possibly deserved what my mother put me through, as the daughter and the victim, I can't help but wonder often what she would have been like if I'd been different, or had looked different, or had acted differently.
There probably would have been no difference no matter what I was like, but I can't help but question myself. I can't help but wonder if even a little, I somehow DID deserve everything she did

to me. Usually though, after confessing to Mack he helps me see the true reality of the abuse I suffered. The reality being my mother is a twisted Psycho who hurt me because she wanted to, NOT because I did anything to deserve it.

   God, this whole thing still makes me sick just thinking about it, but as I said, I'm thrilled to have a lack of feeling right now, because though I know intellectually the atrocities that were done to me I can't actually *feel* them, which is a total blessing. I hate the memories enough without having to actually feel the memories as well. Thank you side effect of PTA!

   Anyway, Mack and I have discussed this all again, and I'm okay this time. Thanks to my lack of feeling, he and I can discuss the physical and emotional ramifications of the abuse I endured calmly. We can talk about it all because I can't feel any of it anymore. We can talk about it while I decide if I want to actually testify against my mother. I have a month to make up my mind, and I'm grateful for this time.

   I hate her, but truthfully I'm still afraid of her which I know is stupid, but I can't change that. A lifetime of fear doesn't just stop because the monster goes away. I think she will be a nightmare for me until death takes me... and maybe even after that as well.

CHAPTER 25

JUNE 22

So I've been in the hospital for way too long. I know it, so I'm sure everyone else must know it. I think a normal patient would have been released by now to mend at home. I'm sure a normal person who woke from a coma nearly 7 weeks ago, even with the burns and the Physio-therapy requirements would have been sent home already. I know it, but I'm sure Mack has done this on purpose somehow so that I was mentally safe in the environment I've been accustomed to, or something like that. I'm sure Mack set this up on purpose, but it's time now. It's time to leave the safety of this hospital for the real world again.
   I have one giant step to take before I can leave the hospital for good though; I have to look at myself. I'm dreading this, but until I do, Mack is afraid that I'm not emotionally stable enough to consider leaving the hospital. I get it, but I'm totally not ready for it.
   I'm sure it's going to be brutal. I'm sure I'm going to panic when I see what I look like. I'm sure I'm going to fail this test of my emotional endurance. But today is the day we set. Today is my deadline. Today I have to keep my eyes open and look.

   When Mack arrives he steps inside my door and just waits for me to speak, I think. Wow, I find I'm speechless. Huh. Who would've thought?
   "Hi, Suzanne. Would you like to talk awhile, or do you want to get this over with. Rip off the band-aids, if you will?" Ha! Bad joke, but nice attempt. I can't help but smirk at him.
   Turning from him, I let my legs dangle from my bed until I slowly

touch the ground. Still not looking, I pull off my light, baggy pajama bottoms which his Kayla gave me, and just brace myself without looking. My boy boxer shorts are big enough to give me total coverage of my privates, but they're short enough to see all my leg, finally.

Lifting my long pajama dress over my head, I'm almost hyperventilating with the fear. I know I'm actually being strong, and I know Mack is going to say something to the effect any second now. In reality; though I look like I'm preparing myself, I'm actually scared to death of what I'm going to see.

"You're doing very well Suzanne. Would you like any help?"

And there he is- My Mack. Hanging onto the bed for dear life with my head bent, I try to absorb Mack's kindness into my bones while I continue to struggle.

Exhaling a hard breathe, I finally turn to look at Mack. Wearing only a tank top and my boxer shorts, I'm almost ready. And thankfully Mack doesn't move toward me, nor does he push me to move any faster. Waiting, we each just stare at each other for a very long pause.

Eventually, Mack walks to my side and takes my right arm to assist me. Though I'm doing really well, my left leg is still too weak to hold me up for long, and my mind is too weak to hold me up, period.

Taking my hand in his with his arm wrapped around my back, Mack starts the slow journey past the wheelchair I once used, to walk me toward the bathroom. Holding me steady, Mack places me on the little bathroom chair and just waits. Keeping his hand on my shoulder, Mack seems content to just wait. It's like we have all day, and he wants me to know that I can take my time with this. God, he is just so unbelievably comforting.

Ugh, I'm ready to see this, I think.

"Um, would you help me to the mirror, Mack?"

"Absolutely."

Lifting from the chair, I begin walking with Mack's help the 2 or 3 steps to my reality. Holding my breath, I'm nervous and shaking,

and so scared of what I'm going to find, I can't even open my eyes yet.
"It's going to be alright Suzanne, I promise. Would you like a little hand mirror first?"
"No. No hand mirror. I want to see it all."
"Okay. Take your time," he reassures me.

Holding my breath, Mack squeezes my shoulder tightly until I exhale and open my eyes.
Pause. Blink. Inhale.
Look. Blink. Exhale.
More pause. Blink. Inhale.
Looking harder. Blink. Exhale.
Longer pause. Blink. Inhale.
What. The. **FUCK?!**
Exhaling a burst of laughter, I keel over bending at the waist. Holy SHIT! I'm laughing hysterically, but when Mack tries pulling at me I fight him with my weak strength. I'm still laughing and I can't look at myself again as my hysteria continues. Dammit, my breathing is becoming difficult again.
"Breathe slowly, Suzanne."
Landing on my ass suddenly, Mack immediately pushes my head between my knees. I'm still breathing, and I'm still struggling, and I'm still laughing, and still breathing, and still laughing, and struggling, and laughing, and breathing and struggling... more.
But eventually, my laughter turns to infrequent bouts of giggles and I start breathing relatively well again considering the fucked up situation I'm in. Ooops, giggle again.
Another long pause follows and I find I just CAN'T raise my head as the shaking continues.
"You don't have to do this now. You can wait if you'd like. We can go back to your room and regroup if you need. It's up to you, Suzanne. Today was just the first attempt, but we can always wait a little longer if you need. We can set another deadline. We can delay this if you need to."

Breathing and pausing and shaking, I'm trying to fight through the leftover giggles. I need to get through this near insanity.

"Um, I remember once comparing myself to a Tim Burton character. Wow, I was so wrong then. *Now* I'm a Tim Burton character for sure. Now, I'm a monster." Giggle.

Mack waits for more, but doesn't speak as he slides his legs around me so they're circling my body. Leaning into him, I'm engulfed in a huge hug. Burying my face into his chest, he smells so good and comforting. He smells like my Mack.

Inhaling him over and over while I fight a growing nausea, I just try to breathe. Throughout forever on the bathroom floor Mack doesn't move at all. He just waits for me to resurface. God, I love him and his strength.

"I love you, Mack."

"I love you too, Suzanne, and it's going to be okay. You're going to be okay, I promise."

Slowly my shocked eyes begin crying as tears drip down my cheeks onto his shirt. Christ! I'm so ugly now. Well, at least my left side is. Giggle. More tears. Shit.

During this little sanity break of mine Mack sits quietly holding me tightly. I'm crying endless tears, but I have no hysteria left. This is like a complete submission to this ugly that is me. It's all over.

"Who will love me now?" I whisper.

"All of us. Everyone who meets you. The Kaylas, Z, me, even Marcus. We all still love you."

Looking up at Mack, he is just so beautiful to me and he always has the right words, whether I believe them or not. I think I really truly love him.

"Do you honestly love me, Mack?"

"Of course, Suzanne."

Lifting my head, I suddenly place me lips on his, but there's no reaction. In desperation, I try kissing him harder. Opening my mouth, I try to engage a passionate kiss from him with my tongue but there's still nothing. Turning into him and pulling his shoulders toward me, I try so hard to make him kiss me back, but Mack stays deathly still against me. There is just nothing for me anymore. So turning away, I begin to cry harder.

"Suzanne, we don't love each other like that. We don't and you know it. You are someone else's, and I'm someone else's, but we're together as dear friends," he whispers.

Suddenly desperate, I try to pull away from him when everything is just too quiet and still between us. But he holds me tight with his legs wrapped around me still. God, I feel so alone. He's still with me I know, just not like that.

Gasping, reality finally resurfaces and I moan, "I'm sorry. I didn't mean to do that. I'm not making sense right now. I think I'm just really scared of not being loved or something. I'm just so lonely... And now I'm ugly, too," I sob.

Hugging me tighter, Mack begins rocking me in his arms and kisses the top of my head. He doesn't let go, and I CANT let go.

"I'm really sorry. Please don't tell Kayla 'cause she'll hate me. I didn't mean to kiss you like that. I'm just so scared, and freaked out, and lonely, and, and, *ugly*. I thought you would kiss me back and maybe I'd be better. I thought you could kiss it all better, or like, kiss me so I felt there was more to me or something. I just wanted you to make me not ugly and lonely anymore."

"You're not ugly. You're a beautiful, strong woman-"

"I know what you're going to say, and I get it. I'm beautiful *on the inside* and all that crap, but nobody cares about that. No one *sees* that. All anyone is going to see is this- my left side as an ugly gross mess. I can't even look at it. I can't even see myself, it's so gross. I don't want to ever look at myself again."

"Suzanne, this is just the surface."

"I know that. But it's ugly and now I'm damaged on the inside AND the outside."

"You're not damaged, you have scarring, but you're healing every day."

"No, I'm not. I'm not healing. I thought I was healing before, but I wasn't. I was just changing. All the ugly is still inside me, but now it's on my outside too."

"Changing IS healing, Suzanne."

"No, it's not the same thing. I don't want this baby, and I don't want this body, and I don't want these memories, and I don't want this reality. I don't want this life, not like this. There is still too much to live with and too much to live through. There's too much to recover from and I can't be all ugly too. It's too much."

"It's not too much. And you CAN do this. You WILL do this. For no one else, not even yourself if you don't want to, but you will do this for me. I'm still holding you to your promise- your lifelong contract, Suzanne. You owe me, and I'm collecting. Suzanne, you are going to learn to live with this, and you're going to learn to enjoy this life again."

"I don't think I can."

"You will. In a few days, you'll get over this shock and you'll stop feeling sorry for yourself, and you'll learn to appreciate what you do have- *Who* you have. You will deal with this, just like you've dealt with everything before it."

"I don't think I can," I moan.

"I KNOW you can. You'll get better again, just like you did before, and you'll learn how to live with this new challenge-"

"*Challenge?* Christ, Mack- I'm hideous! What the hell?! Are you blind or something? Maybe if I enter a room with my right side forward and leave as I entered, I'll learn to live with this, but otherwise, this is just another example of '*What the Fuck?!*' in my life. Who lives like this? Nobody! The Kaylas have never had anything bad. You've never had anything bad. Nobody has! But me? I get the fucking ShitStorm of life. One fucking thing after another. Nonstop! It's like I was Eva Braun in a past life or something- like totally evil, and so I must suffer the greatest of karmic retribution or something in THIS life! What the hell did I do to deserve all this?! Tell me! Please!" Sniffling and pausing, I turn to stare at his face as I beg, "Christ! Answer me. What did I do to deserve all *this*?!"

"I don't think you did anything wrong, Suzanne. You have just suffered a series of events beyond your control, for which you must struggle, and get past."

"Oh, *fuck me*-"
"Let me finish!"
"Fine, FINISH!"
"Suzanne, you have to stop all this upset, and desperation and self-pity."
"But I am upset, and desperate, and full of self-pity! Look. At. Me."
"I'm looking! I see you, but I don't think you can see yourself anymore. You are beyond the face, Suzanne. You always were. You were intelligent and strong, and yes weak, but then strong again. You were loving and sad and beautiful, and you made us all love you so much that we your people, your two Kaylas, your Mack, and especially *your* Z- you have made us all die and weep for you for months! Months Suzanne!"
"But-"
"I'm not blaming you for the accident or for the coma, I'm just trying to get you to understand that we four people, and even that prick Marcus have been dying for you, each and every fucking day since the accident. We've been dying for you since BEFORE the goddamn accident. We love you, and we will do anything for you; we will care for you however you need because we love you with or without your beautiful face. But that's it! That's the only thing missing here; your flawless face. The rest of you is in there. Trapped in shock and sadness right now, but it IS there. I see it in your eyes- god, your beautiful eyes which seem to glow even brighter now through the facial damage. It's *you* we love Suzanne, not your fucking skin!" Flinch! "So please wake up. We will help you, but you need to wake the hell up now. You need to accept our help or you may lose us forever. You may finally find yourself as alone as you believe yourself to be!"

Holy shit! I don't think Mack has ever swore at me before. He's just too kind, or caring, or nice, or just too *Mack* to ever swear at me. Shit.

"But, I don't know what to do," I whisper.

Turning my face in his hands, Mack leans in close, kisses my lips gently and whispers, "Just wake up, and we'll help you. This life of yours is too big for just you to handle right now, but you have us here to help you. We *want* to help you. We have all given up so much to help you. So let us."

"I'm sorry, but I don't know what you're saying. I mean, I know you're here at the hospital, but what have you given up for me? Well, other than your sanity, of course." I grin, but Mack doesn't smile back. He looks so angry at me suddenly, I'm scared.

"Kayla has totally screwed up her job in New York so she could be here as often as she is on week-ends. I moved to Chicago for Christsake to be with you once you were moved; just so I could be near you when you woke up. I gave up my position at the hospital, and I've lost all my tenure to be here for you. Kayla cut back her hours at Petri-Dunn so she had more time to sit here with you, and Z... God, Z put his apartment on the market the minute you were moved to Chicago. Z picked up the very *second* the court agreed to Marcus' demand for the move. Z is here in Chicago, completely alone and stuck, just waiting for you to wake up for him."

"I'm sorry, but I don't know what you mean. I'm awake. I'm here. What am I supposed to do?"

"You're not here. You may be awake, but your desperation is keeping you from us and us from you. You are NOT awake yet."

"I am, I just don't feel anything but ugly, and desperate and lonely, and so sad again all the time. I'm just so sad again, Mack."

"I know, Suzanne. I know you're sad, but it's not like before. Remember before? You were having a nervous breakdown. But you are NOT suffering from that this time. This isn't a nervous breakdown. This is a shock that must be dealt with, that's all. You don't feel anything yet because you're still freaked out. But if you try to live past the obvious physical trauma you will slowly begin to feel again, I promise."

"How? I'm sorry if this sounds shallow or stupid to you, but I'm just so gross. I'm a girl, and I'm supposed to be pretty, or good looking, or at the very least decently plain. I'm not supposed to be hideous," I cry.

"You're not hideous."
"Oh, come on, Mack! Be honest with me. I AM hideous. I'm a girl who wants to be pretty, but I'm not. I want to be beautiful like grandma Tommy and now I'll never be," I sob.
"Grandma Tommy, Suzanne?" he questions.
"My mother's mom- grandma Tommy. She was so beautiful, Mack. Everyone thought so. She was so beautiful and special, and I wanted to be just like her so bad. I wanted to BE her so badly. She was the most amazing woman I have ever known. The most *beautiful* woman I've ever known. Everyone thought so. I have her coloring, but I don't look like her. And now I never will," I cry silently.
"You may not look like her but you ARE beautiful Suzanne. You are a light that I love and that everyone loves. Think of how many people have fought for you. Think of how hard we have *all* fought for you. Christ! Even Marcus, who I can't stand, has fought so hard for you- it's almost commendable, except for the fact that I hate him," he laughs.
Giggling, I nod my agreement. Marcus is a whole crazy complex issue for me as well. I love him like a friend, but dislike him like an enemy. His potential scares me but the memory of his presence comforts me as well. Christ! The Suzanne/Marcus adventure is truly exhausting.
Whispering, Mack asks, "Do you want to look again, Suzanne? Or is that enough for now?" Catching my breath, I nod, and then realize he doesn't know what I'm agreeing to.
"Okay. I want to see me," I exhale.
Standing slowly with me, Mack's knee cracks and I grin. Raising me gently from the floor, my legs are so weak I have to hold onto Mack for dear life. Turning me, I hide my face in his chest for another moment to collect myself.
Breathing slowly, I wait until I feel steady. But Mack doesn't say a word; he just continues to hold me until I'm ready.
After forever, I finally turn my head to look in the large mirror over the sink. Jesus *Christ!* It's as bad as I remember. It's

shocking really. It's like half my body was dunked in acid, while the other half stayed out in the crisp clean air. And my left thigh is totally warped, like a huge piece of it is missing.

"Explain how this happened exactly. *All* of it," I question while staring at my half burned, scarred face.

"Um, from what I understand, the truck hit the driver side door, shattering the window and door up against you. You were essentially crushed against the door, with your leg pinned underneath the front of the truck. The grill, actually. So no one from the other side of the car could just pull you out." Well, that explains the missing hunk out of my thigh.

"It was quick though, relatively speaking. There were police who heard the accident, so they and an off duty paramedic responded quickly. The fire department was third on the scene, followed by the paramedics. Within minutes, a small engine fire eventually started in the truck. So you were trapped against the front of the truck, while it started heating up and eventually caught fire.

"...The paramedic on scene attempted to amputate your leg to remove you quickly but the fire department arrived in time to put out the small fire. And though you were quite burned on your side in the process, it wasn't from the actual flames, but rather from the heat of the engine fire. Once the fire was out, the Fire Rescue Squad was able to remove the truck grill, the door, and eventually you. Again, I'm told fairly quickly."

Nodding, I'm so calm right now it's kind of freaky. I thought I'd be all nuts, or crying or something. But Mack was so calm relaying the information, I find myself calmly absorbing all the information from him in turn.

"What about the other driver? Was he burned?"

"No. He wasn't hurt, and he managed to get out okay."

"Oh, good. Why was I in a coma again?"

"Presumably, from the impact of the collision against your head and side. You were pronounced dead at the scene, but shortly thereafter you were found to be alive with a faint heartbeat, so you were rushed to Manhattan Mercy. It was then that Marcus received his call, and he presumed you were in fact dead, or about to be. And so he called Kayla, mistakenly telling her you had died. From there she called me, and I immediately called Z."

Pausing, Mack seems to be living a nightmare of his own in this moment. His eyes are so dark suddenly, I can only stare at him through the mirror in silence.

In a whisper I finally ask, "Was it really bad, Mack? Like for you? It's okay. You can tell me if you want to. I'm okay right now."

Exhaling, Mack groans, "Yes, Suzanne. It was really bad."

"What was?" The accident? My face?

"God, everything... There was just so much confusion and panic. We thought you were dead, and then Kayla and I couldn't find which hospital your body had been taken to. Then Kayla called Chicago Kayla who was screaming in her office, running from work to get to us. When I called Marcus, he was so calm- almost vegetative in his replies to my questions. And then I found the hospital you were taken to and the ER nurse told me you were in fact alive, though barely and already in surgery, so I called Kayla back and she met me at the hospital and Z... We couldn't get in touch with Z again."

Mack suddenly just stops speaking. Looking at me, his eyes are filled with tears, and he looks so pale I want him to stop.

"Its okay, Mack. You don't need to tell me anymore."

"Actually, I think I should. You need to understand this. You need to get it, Suzanne."

"I do. I promise."

"Suzanne we were so scared. So absolutely devastated, Kayla and I just stood together in shock. I called Marty who rushed to the hospital as well, but no one could reach Z. He just wouldn't answer his bloody phone."

"Once we knew a little about your condition, and once we knew the surgery would take a few hours, I finally left Kayla with Marty. I remember running down the hallway. I remember bumping into a man and apologizing. I remember nothing about the cab ride, and I remember nothing about reaching Z's apartment *but* the fear I felt."

"Mack, please stop. I-"

"No. Listen to me. Let me finish this, okay?"

Nodding, I stare at his beautiful face in the mirror while holding on tightly. Rubbing his back with my hand I'm desperate to comfort him in this moment.

"When I threw open Z's door, I had a moment of true terror. In the silence of his apartment, I was sure I was burying if not one probably two friends that day. I didn't know what I would find, but I was sure he was gone. Pausing for a moment, I turned my head and there he was. Sitting in a chair, with a bottle of liquor between his legs, his head was hung with his shoulders collapsed around him."

Oh god... I know Z doesn't really drink. Just a glass of wine once in a while, but he never drinks often or too much. And he would never sit with a bottle in his lap unless...

"When Z turned his head to me, I couldn't believe the look on his face. Z was death in that moment. That's all there was. I remember thinking if Suzanne isn't already dead- Z is dead right now in front of me. So I yelled, 'She's still alive! Z! She is still alive. She's in surgery, but alive.' And that was all it took. Z jumped from the chair and ran for the door. Pushing me out of his way he ran, and all I remember was how loud the door sounded as I slammed it shut behind us.

"... And that was it. He yelled and cursed at the cab driver, but we made it to the hospital quickly. And Z ran. I remember thinking, Z is running for her. If he can get there in time, she'll live for him. I remember thinking; this is what she'll need. Not me or the Kaylas, but Z. I remember whispering to Kayla, 'She will live for him.' And you did."

Oh god... This hurts my heart.

"Before Marcus arrived and took over control as your 'next of kin' Z was allowed to see you in between surgeries. Z saw you and spoke to you, and begged you and loved you. Kayla shook and wept listening to him speak to you, and Marty held us all together until Chicago Kayla and Marcus arrived. But Z made you live. I'm sure of it."

Crying, Mack turns his lovely face to mine and I hug him even tighter. Whispering, 'I'm sorry', Mack's shushes me again, and buries his face in my hair.

This is unbelievable. This is a movie. This is a scene from the best novel I have ever read. This is so beautiful in its tragedy.

Waiting for his nightmare to pass, Mack slowly shakes his head and continues this tale.

"You had massive cranial bleeding and swelling, and because of the blood thinners you had been on since the rupture last year, the bleeding wouldn't stop. You were taken back into surgery quickly, where..." pause "you were pronounced with minimal to no brain function, until the surgical Neurologist found a slight reaction to stimuli. So you were operated on while the Ortho team repaired the crushed bones in your leg, and the Plastics team began your skin grafting and skin repair for the burns, which were only 3rd degree on just under 30% of your body- the rest of the burns being 2nd and 1st degree, and already mostly healed today."

"Oh. It seems like so much more than 30%."

"Well, because part of the burn is on your face, you're focusing on that part and that's why you feel like you're burned more than you actually are... Not to diminish what you're feeling. It's just if the burns were covered, you probably wouldn't find them as noticeable, and therefore, they wouldn't seem as great as they actually are."

"It's just so ugly, Mack..." I whisper on a slight exhale.

"It really isn't Suzanne, and you're scheduled for more cosmetic surgery and more laser surgery to your face and neck in 2 weeks. The last facial graft will help hide more of the burn, and it'll help cover some of the red and white burn of your cheek and neck."

Staring, I'm absolutely mesmerized by my blue eyes. Well, actually, just my left blue eye. Surrounded by the red of my face and all the white crisscross-type skin markings, the blue looks like it glows. It's kind of freaky the way my eye seems to glow out of my face. I wouldn't say it's attractive, but more shocking. I can't help but stare at my own eye, so others must find it extra weird or totally freaky too.

Strangely I'm reminded of those tooth whitening commercials were the before teeth- all nasty and yellow- are surrounded by pink or bronze lipstick. Then suddenly the after 'whitened' teeth are surrounded by luscious red lips. But everyone knows red lipstick makes our teeth look whiter, so they're not *actually* fooling us. Ha! I'm still a moron sometimes, honestly.

"What are you thinking about? You're very calm and quiet Suzanne, and it's freaking me out here," he says with a cheeky grin.

Smiling, I gaze at his face in the mirror. "My eye looks really bright and kind of see-through now that it's surrounded by all the red."

"Your eyes are beautiful Suzanne- they always have been."

Gulping, I'm ready to stop looking for now. I have a lifetime to get used to this new, gross Suzanne.

"You must be tired from holding me up all this time."

"I'm fine. We can stay here for longer if you want. Anything you need, Suzanne. Don't worry about me," he says softly.

"I'm ready Mack. Please help me back to my bed. I just need to rest for a while, okay?"

Nodding, Mack tightens his grip on my arms and helps me walk out of the bathroom. Passing the wheelchair he continues until he helps me gently rise onto my bed. Getting settled, we both move my bad leg closer to the middle, and Mack helps prop me up against my right side as I settle in. Pulling the blankets over my body and up to my shoulders, Mack leans against my back for a minute.

Nothing is said. Nothing *needs* to be said. I feel him against me, and I just soak up all the warmth and love he gives me.

"Its okay, Mack. You can leave. I'm trying to wake up now."

"Okay, Suzanne. You go to sleep while you try to wake up for me." Grinning at his stupidity of words I giggle slightly, while

Mack laughs and kisses the back of my head.
Leaving my side, he walks across the room, turns once and whispers, "I love you very much, Suzanne."
Nodding, "I know Mack and thank you. I promise I'll start trying."
And with a smile he turns from me, quietly opening and closing the door behind him.

Once the door closes, I release the breath I've been holding and begin crying.
I'm impressed with my tears. They're the silent continuous kind of tears that don't really make a sound. They don't choke or gag me. They don't make confessions, or promises that can't possibly be upheld. They don't scream and cry to the heavens for all that is wrong. They don't beg and plead for redemption from this life. These tears just fall continuously, endlessly, yet quietly from my eerily bright, glowy blue eyes.
These are the tears I've had before and remember well. These are the tears of desperation for another nightmare I have to face, and will sadly be *forced* to face whether I want to or not. These are simple, continuous, quiet tears of desperate resignation for this crazy, horrific little life of mine.

CHAPTER 26

JUNE 26

It's been over two weeks since I last saw Z. Two loooong weeks. And I miss him terribly, I know I do. I had such a short period of time with him, such a limited time to kiss him and to just look at him knowing he loved me. And it was so amazing, but so damn short.

Things with the baby haven't changed for me. I still don't want it, and I still won't keep it, but I've accepted the fact that I'm actually pregnant now. I've had to.

Against my will, I'm getting a bigger lower belly which is a constant torturous reminder that there's a baby in my body. Oh, and every single person who enters this room talks about it, asks about it, or stares at it, so it's kind of hard to forget I'm knocked up.

Thank god, Mack and his Kayla are still awesome to me, even if they think what and how I feel is wrong. They talk to me and answer all my questions. I see Mack everyday still, but I've only seen Kayla for two days, twice in the last two weeks, though she does phone me from New York every single day. Mack and Kayla are still a constant, and though this helps, I *know* I'm missing Z.

A few days ago, Mack explained to me his conversation with Z over the baby. Mack told me that Z was no longer angry with me but that he *was* hurt and resigned to the fact that I wanted no part in this. Z apparently asked Mack to take good care of me and his child, until he could have his baby to care for himself; a baby he apparently wants desperately.

Mack was devastated telling me about their conversation- I could see it. And though he tried so hard to stay calm and detached, he was clearly shaken. I can just imagine how hard that conversation was for Mack, never mind for Z. I know how hard it must have been; and I'm really, truly sorry for that, but I still haven't changed my mind over this baby issue.

Every day I hope Mack was right and I change and I suddenly feel something for this baby, but I don't. It's like this never ending bad dream for me. This baby is a constant reminder of the love I had with Z- The *night* I had with Z. A night I clearly remember now in amazingly *graphic* detail.

God, I wish the memory of that night was enough. I wish I could call Z and tell him I'm sorry. I wish I could tell him I want his baby. I wish I could tell him I want him back in my life, but I can't. I no longer hate or resent Z, but I still hate and resent this horrible situation I'm in.

I even contemplated faking a change in attitude toward his baby so he would come back to me. But I knew Z and Mack would be able to tell I was lying, which would get me nowhere with Z, other than more heartache when he left me inevitably. And so I've stayed quiet about my feelings for Z so we can all move on.

Z has to move on from me. I *know* that, but I still miss him.

Sadly, I miss Chicago Kayla too. She still calls me but she doesn't visit anymore, and she doesn't act the way she used to with me.

Confused by her sudden absence, I asked Mack if he knew why she was distant toward me since my memories returned. Desperately, I begged him to tell me why my awesome Chicago Kayla was no longer so awesome with me. And eventually he sat down and told me what happened between us.

Once the disgusting tale of 'Suzanne and The **Red** Robe' was told I learned all I did and said to her, and I was absolutely horrified. Afterward, I collected myself enough to call Kayla. When she answered, I apologized immediately which she kindly accepted, but then she admitted regardless of my apology, things for her were different now in the aftermath.

She said she believes that like a drunk, my madness allowed me to say the things I wouldn't have normally said. When I told her she was wrong, she still didn't believe me. She said she forgave me, and she too apologized for not being able to move past my outburst, but sadly she just couldn't.

Kayla choked up and told me she felt betrayed by me, though admittedly it wasn't *really* my fault. She said she can't stop feeling like I betrayed our friendship with my disgusting words and with my honest thoughts of her. And though I swore she was wrong- that those were NOT my honest feelings toward her, she again said she just couldn't believe me anymore.

Kayla told me I hurt her deeply, though she knows it was caused by a very bad moment. She knows I didn't know what I was saying or doing, especially considering my mind was all wrapped up in past and present memories at the time, but again she can't forget. She even acknowledged the red robe I've heard about, and told me she knew things were going to get bad quickly- She just didn't think they would get bad for her.

And so I'm at a loss. I've cried to Mack and Kayla about *other* Kayla, and they each told me it'll just take some time to mend our previous friendship. They reminded me that she still calls me and still cares enough to talk to me, no matter how indifferent she may seem, which I guess is something. But it still hurts.

Everything hurts.

I remember the potential of the 'fiver' but it's gone now. Z is gone, and Kayla is essentially gone. I have a friend I miss. I have a man I miss. I know the love I'll never experience again. And I have a child growing in my body that I don't want.

Last week, Marcus even snuck back into my room and we had a good, long talk. Marcus admitted to losing it about the baby, and he admitted to telling me lies about Z. He admitted to his part in my confusion and upset. And he admitted to wanting to physically hurt me in that moment, which was really hard to hear from him.

Afterward, Marcus was so sad I think I felt terrible for him. Actually, I'm sure I did, but I also felt true fear of him for the first time. And when I admitted as much, Marcus was so horrified that I feared him physically; he bowed his head and cried a little, then eventually told me it was time for him to go.

He told me he loved me forever and that he sincerely hoped I had a good life. He said he hoped my baby was well, but he admitted that he couldn't be a casual observer to my life anymore. He told me he wasn't going to contact me again, and he didn't want to see me ever again, because knowing me was just too hard for him now.

After a rather desperate silence following his words he stopped crying, kissed my cheek, and left my room for the very last time I believe.

And so here I am. Z is gone because of my choices and refusals. Kayla is gone because of my madness and betrayals. And Marcus is gone because I can't love him as he loves me. My life has become one gigantic, semi-lonely Clusterfuck, as Kayla used to say.

*****

Waiting for Mack I have a very important question to ask him- a favor really. But it's big and I'm scared to death he's going to say no, but I've pulled up my big girl (and growing by the minute) panties and I'm going to ask it anyway.

Waiting, I'm almost hyperventilating over my question. I have other options, but this is what I want badly. This is the choice I want to make, and I really hope Mack is on board with me.

When I hear the knock, I practically jump out of the bed. Okay. Breathe. Yelling for Mack to enter, he smiles at me as he opens up the door.

"Hi, Mack!" Ooops. A little loud. Calm down.

"Hi, Suzanne. How are you feeling?"

"Fat," I laugh.

"You don't look fat," he smirks.

"Fine. Chunky again."

"You were never 'chunky', and you certainly don't look it now. How was the exam?"

"Good. It's still in there and *clearly* growing," I mumble.

"The *baby* is still in there," he prompts.

"Fine. The *baby* is fine and I'm getting fat, though I really never feel like eating, which is kind of warped. I mean, for the first time in my life I'm supposed to eat and get fat, but I have no appetite at all, which seems totally unfair, don't you think?"

"Yes, it does. You *are* eating though, right?" He asks me sternly.

"Of course. I'm gagging down every gross thing they bring me."

"Good. Now what's so important that I had to be here by 7:00am, versus my usual 8:00?"

Um... Shit. This is hard. Crap. Okay. Spit it out. Mack is always awesome with my insanity. This will probably be no different.

"Suzanne?" He asks expectantly, while sitting in the chair beside me. Oh!

"I just remembered you told me you always sit down when talking to me so I'm not afraid of your height! Shit! I forgot that, but it's true, right? You told me that, didn't you?"

"Yes, I did tell you that. And yes, it's true. Tall men intimidate you, and being 6'2 is certainly taller than you. Therefore, I try to always be lower or at least level to you when we speak so you're not scared or intimidated by me."

"You're so amazing Mack. Is there anything you aren't amazing at?"

"No, not really," he says so seriously, I burst out laughing. Looking at him, I know I'm right. I know it.

"Can I move in with you?" There. Gulp. Shit. Silence. "The final skin graft was good, and I'm not scheduled for another laser surgery for 4 weeks, and I'm walking better, and I'm feeling better, and I'm barely crazy now, and, um, please? They said I can go home now. Dr. Mirabelli was here late last night talking to me about the Physio I *have to* do when I leave or she'll kick my ass. And Dr. Robinson agreed I can go home now. But I don't really have one, a home I mean, and you're my best friend, and we get along so well, and I'm scared to be alone like this," I say pointing to my stomach. "Um, please Mack? Please can I live with you?"

"Suzanne, I don't think-"

"WAIT! Just listen. I know you have a 2 bedroom apartment that you're renting here, Kayla told me once, and I have lots of money, so I can pay for half of it, or even all of it, or we can get another place, or move back to New York if you want since I'm out of the hospital and Kayla's back in New York and you love it there. New York is your home, and you've given up too much for me already. Whatever you want."

Cutting me off, "Suzanne, I don't think-"

"MACK! I promise I'll be good. I promise I will obey you and do everything right. Please, Mack? Please? I won't be bad. I'll be the best roommate EVER! Please keep me. Please?"

"Suzanne, stop. Listen to yourself. You're being all manic and desperate again. You're speaking and begging like the old Suzanne would've. Stop. You're regressing and I don't want that."

"I'm sorry, Mack. Tell me what you want and I'll do it. I'll stop regressing. I'm sorry."

"Why do you need this? I'm still here in Chicago, and I'll still be your best friend, and I'll still visit you in your new place, which incidentally you've already rented and furnished. So what's going on?"

"I'm just scared, Mack. And I don't want to do this alone without you."

"I'll be with you..."

"NO YOU WON'T! You'll be living somewhere else, and eventually you'll stop visiting me. And what if something happens to me? What if I have another accident? What if Z's child gets hurt? What if I get sick? Who will help me?"

"Suzanne. I'm sure you know this isn't a good idea."

"I DON'T know that. I think this is an *excellent* idea. Please, Mack? God, I'm begging you. Please?"

"Um, I need to discuss this with Kayla."

"No you don't! She'll be fine with it! She likes me, and she would want me safe!"

"I still need to discuss this with her and I need time to think about it myself. Suzanne, this is a big step, for not just you but for me as well."

"Please Mack. I'll be a great roommate. Oh god, I'm begging you. I've thought of nothing else all night. I promise this is a good thing for us. Well, mostly for me, but I'll be so good it'll be a good thing for you too. When Kayla is in New York, you'll have someone to talk to. You'll have a best friend to talk to. I won't bug you, I swear!"

"Suzanne, what are you so afraid of?" Mack asks with his 'talk to me' face. Shit.

"Nothing. Everything. I'm afraid something's going to happen to me again if I'm alone."

"Like what?"

"Who knows with me? Maybe I'll fall in the shower, or I'll have another burst aneurism, or I'll go all mental. Really Mack, the options are limitless. I just know I don't want to be alone, but not like that! Oh, if that's what you're thinking-"

"I'm not thinking that, Suzanne. I'm just trying to figure out why you're so desperate for this so suddenly when you and I already found and rented you an apartment. Why didn't you discuss this with me before?"

"I don't know why now. Dr. Mirabelli made leaving official last night and I suddenly became scared. And all I could think about was being alone, and not being with people around, and not being with you. I thought of you all night, but not like *that*. I just thought since I see you every day anyway, why not be roommates for a while? If you hate it I'll leave, I promise. But please Mack, please let me come home with you. I really need you, and I don't want to do this alone."

"What about Z? Have you given any thought to talking to him about your fears?"

"No. I miss him, but I don't think being afraid to be alone is a good enough reason to try to be with him again. It just seems wrong somehow."

"I see your point, but he should be told. I mean, you're carrying his child and this'll make things awkward between him and I-"

"No it won't! Think about it. If he and I can't be together, then at least *you're* watching out for me. He'll be relieved by that."

"Suzanne, that's a little naïve."

"No it isn't!" Suddenly crying, I'm just desperate for Mack to say yes. I *need* him to say yes. "Please Mack. Please let me live with you."

When Mack just stares at me, I'm nervous. He's thinking too much. I think he's being all doctorly, analyzing this situation too intensely. Please don't think! PLEASE!

"Okay, Suzanne. You can live with me *temporarily* but we're treading some fairly heavy boundaries here. If I was still your personal physician I would be in a great deal of trouble. As it is, I'm sure others will think this situation WAY beyond appropriate."

"I know, and I'm sorry. But it's innocent. It's just two friends being roommates. It's just two friends sharing space. That's all, I swear."

"Alright, Suzanne. But I need another day. Can you stay here one more day before being discharged? I need to make a few calls, and I need to move around a few things. You've kind of sprung this on me."

"I know. I'm very sorry." And I am sorry to put him on the spot, but I'm way happier he's agreed. "Mack, are we okay? Are you mad at me?"

"I'm not mad. But I do have some thinking to do. I'm going to go now but I'll be back tomorrow at 10:00 so we can get you out of here and settled into my place, *temporarily*. Once you feel a little more secure, we'll have to discuss other options. We'll revisit the living arrangement and decide what's best for you. This is temporary, Suzanne."

"Okay. That sounds good. I'll take it. And thank you so much, Mack. I'm sure this is hard for you, but I just couldn't stand the thought of being alone yet. I'm too scared all the time."

"Its okay, Suzanne. We'll figure this out. We'll figure out what's best in the long run."

When Mack stands to leave, I'm nervous he's mad at me. I don't want to screw up our friendship. I CAN'T ruin our friendship. I probably made a terrible mistake asking him for this, but I had no other option. I need Mack right now.
Leaning into me, Mack kisses my cheek and exhales into my hair. I think he's totally freaked but keeping it together for me. Shit. I never thought about how this would affect him. Christ, I'm so selfish sometimes.
"Mack, I'm sorry," I whisper.
Smiling, he takes my ugly face in his hands, looks in my eyes and says, "Suzanne, we're good and we'll figure this out. I already know how nuts you can be, so there shouldn't be any surprises there."
Laughing, I give him a hug and finally exhale.
"See you tomorrow, Roomie."
"Uh huh. I guess I better remember to put the seat back down like I do when Kayla visits."
"Yes, please," I grin.
"See you tomorrow, Suzanne."
"I can't wait, Mack!"
"Uh huh. We'll see..." he grins again.

When he turns from my bed, I'm a little worried he'll change his mind overnight, but I don't think he will. He's too good a guy for that. He wouldn't lead me on then change his mind, if for no other reason than he already agreed to it. Mack is too good a man to disappoint me like that.

Alone, I exhale completely. The tension I felt all night is quickly vanishing, being replaced with calm and hope. If I have to do this for Z, I'm happy I have Mack to help me. I need him.
And though I know my decisions are ridiculously selfish right

now, I can't see any other way. These selfish decisions are all I have while I get through this newest challenge.

  Mack is my best friend, and he'll help me and keep me safe as no one else has before. I know I'll be safe with Mack.

CHAPTER 27

JUNE 27

After moving all my clothes into Mack's apartment from my other apartment, days after Marcus moved them into *that* apartment, we both exhale. Flopping on the couch, Mack looks at me like I'm totally insane again. Laughing, I know exactly what he's going to say.

Raising my hand I cut him off. "Don't say it- I already know. I'm a Clothes Whore, as Kayla calls me. I'm a certifiably obsessive clothes purchaser with an infinity for black. I'm freaky and creepy and completely off my meds where shoes and clothes are concerned... Am I close?"

"Um... close. How or *when* did you find the time to purchase all those clothes? Is that like ten years' worth?"

"Nope. More like 4 months' worth. I don't know. When I moved back in with Marcus there was nothing to do but shop out of boredom. You should see my iPad and Kindle. I one-clicked my index finger raw."

"Okay, I don't have a clue what that means, Suzanne, but please explain. You are seriously twisted with the clothing, but I would venture a guess that shopping fills a need, or rather a *void* in your life-" Ugh...

"Okay Mack, since we're roommates AND you're no longer my official doctor, how about we make a rule. I think unless I'm blatantly going off the deep end, we make a rule that while I live here with you as *roommates* you're not allowed to 'shrink' me, at all, ever. Unless of course I've gone nuts. Then please feel free to shrink me. Is that a good rule?"

Looking at me, and probably pondering my rule, Mack nods finally.

"Okay, I'll try. No *shrinking* while roommates, unless of course you start going insane, then I definitely step in. It's going to be hard for me to stay undoctorly with you though, but I'll make a serious effort to try. Good?"
"Thank you. Okay, so all my clothes are in my new bedroom-"
"From floor to ceiling-"
"And I'm starving. Do you mind if I make us dinner? It's been forever since I cooked."
"Not at all. Make yourself at home, but please don't feel as though you need to cook for me. I'm actually quite a good cook. Marty taught me a few tricks and tips over the years."
"Good to know. I'm sure I'll remember how much I hate cooking five minutes after I start, but tonight I actually feel like cooking." Weird.

Walking to the kitchen, Mack watches me closely, *analyzing* me I'm sure. I know it's going to be next to impossible for him to not get into my head every chance he gets because, well, that's all he's done for over a year now. I know he'll try, but I'm sure he'll eventually give me the 'talk to me' face I've become more than accustomed to.

Looking back into the living room, I see he's left the couch. Maybe Mack needed a minute himself to settle into this new arrangement. I doubt he's having second thoughts or even regretting his decision, but I'm sure it's still going to be strange for him having someone here all the time. As it was, he only saw Kayla on weekends, usually every, or every second week-end for 2 days, so I'm sure there's some adjustments needed.

When the chicken breasts are in the oven, I make a delicious cauliflower/broccoli salad and mix it with a sweet poppy seed dressing- my favorite. I'm so glad we grabbed groceries after leaving the hospital. Mack insisted that his kitchen was so bare the grocery store was mandatory, but I think he was testing me to see how I handled my first public appearance out of the hospital as 'Suzanne the Scarred'.

In the store I tended to have my head lowered, but I did remarkably well I think for my first time. I didn't cry or freak out, and though I saw people stare at me a little, it really wasn't as bad as I thought it would be.

I could usually look away from eye contact before I saw their faces transform into questions, or repulsion, or sadness regarding my face and limp. Usually, I ignored them and pretended no one even looked my way, which is what I've always preferred anyway.

After reading on my kindle, the chicken is done, but Mack still hasn't come out of his room. Walking down the hall, I hear him mumbling in his bedroom. Should I? Shouldn't I? Shit. I know it's wrong and an invasion of privacy and just WRONG but I can't help it.

Inching up to his door, I lean against it and listen to his words.

"Stop it Kayla... Not true...never... Would you just stop yelling, and listen to me for a minute! No, I won't... Are you seriously asking me that?... Yes, one time. One. When she was desperate and freaked out. ONCE!... Stop... Would you listen to yourself... Yes I've heard you for the last half hour and I'm exhausted with this back and forth... Yes, I said exhausted... I CAN'T! Jesus Christ, she was desperate and scared, and so sad I couldn't say no... NO, I couldn't! ENOUGH! Yes, I'm deciding this is enough... Grow up, Kayla!... Clever... Goodbye Kayla." Slam.

Holy SHIT! They're fighting because of me. Dammit! Running for the kitchen, I call out Mack's name so he thinks I've been there all along. Grabbing for the pot holders, my hands are shaking, my breathing is fast, and my heart is pounding. Shit! He's gonna know something's up with me. He can always tell. God *Dammit*.

Walking into the kitchen, Mack has a beautiful- but totally fake- smile on his face.

"Smells good. Thank you, I'm starving," he says with way too much enthusiasm.

When the phone suddenly rings, I jump and dip the left half of the pan of chicken. Catching it tightly again, my arm feels so weak from the shaking, I barely notice I'm stuck in the middle of the floor as the phone rings again. I just can't seem to move.

When the phone continues, Mack smiles and ignores it as the machine picks up. Hearing Kayla's voice from the living room, I freeze.

"*Pick up the phone, Mack! Pick it UP! You don't decide when I'm done talking. I do! And I'm not done fucking talking to you. Pick. It. UP!*" She yells.

Stuck in place, Mack takes my arms and leads me to the table. Helping me place the hot dish on the extra placemat, he seems to be studiously ignoring me.

"Ignore the message, Suzanne. Kayla and I are having a little argument, that's all."

"Sorry..." is all I mumble.

Mack doesn't know that I'm sorry me being here has caused his 'little argument', and Mack doesn't know I'm sorry that I selfishly asked him for this. Mack doesn't know I'm sorry that anything to do with me causes him any distress or upset of any kind. And that's what I'm sorry for. I'm sorry for anything involving *me* causing him anything bad. Dammit.

Dinner continues as Mack and I make small talk. There's nothing we can really talk about that seems safe now. I feel the very dark cloud over my first meal here. I feel the upset in the air. I hate that Mack is unhappy, especially over something *Suzanne*.

"I'm moving out in the morning," I suddenly state.

"No, you're not," he replies without looking at me.

"Actually, I am. It's good though. I really should learn how to do all this on my own anyway. Its fine, Mack. And I'm serious."

"Suzanne, that's not necessary. Kayla and my argument has nothing to do with you," he says, lying right to my face.

"Regardless, I'm moving out in the morning. I'm just a little tired tonight so I hope you don't mind me crashing-"

"Suzanne, seriously, its fine."

"I know it is. But I actually want this. I decided when I was cooking that I want to live alone. It's good. Honestly. And I've already decided. I'm just going to go turn in and then I'm leaving in the morning. But thanks Mack for having me," I smile my best smile for him.

"You're not leaving in the morning. I want you to stay and I'm not going to let you leave."

Smirking, "Well, unless you plan to lock me in, I AM leaving. I'm fine Mack, I promise. I just really want to move out, no offense. It's not you, I swear. But I feel a desperate need to do this on my own now. Um, good night Mack, and thanks," I say while quickly rising from the table.

Practically running for my room, I hear him call out my name, but ignore him and close my door quickly.

Well, this just sucks. I'm not ready to be alone and I don't want to BE alone. But what choice do I have? I can't screw up Mack and Kayla. I WON'T screw up Mack and Kayla.

When he knocks on my door, I open it with my best smile again.

"Mack, I'm super tired and I really need to sleep now, okay? Nothing's wrong, I just don't want I live here, that's all. Please let me go to sleep. I've had a really long day."

Exhaling a hard breath, Mack tugs his hair, which totally reminds me of Z. Oh! Not now. Not Z, *please...*

"Okay. We'll talk in the morning. Good night, Suzanne. And you're not leaving."

"Good night, Mack. And thanks for everything, always," I whisper.

Pausing, Mack stares at me like he knows what I'm going to do, until I gently begin closing the door on him with a parting smile.

This is good. This will be fine. I'll be fine once I get out of here. And Mack and Kayla will be fine *when* I'm out of here. This is good. I can do this.

Its 8:30, so I figure in 2 and a half hours or so, he'll probably go to bed, and then I'll leave. I really don't want all the drama in the morning, so I'll leave while he sleeps. I'm tired of drama all the time, so I'm going to make this move in-move out within 9 hours as anti-climactic as possible. I'll even write a quick note for him.

Grabbing my tote and finding my little black notebook I rip out a page and say my goodbye.

Mack,

Thanks for letting me stay here. I really appreciate the kind gesture. I promise this has nothing to do with you. This is ALL me. I just want to live alone for the first time in my life. I think it's time now.

I'll talk to you soon.

I love you, forever.

Suzanne xo

Waiting... at midnight I finally hear nothing. Jesus, it took forever for nothing to arrive, but finally it's here and I can slip out.

Collecting my purse and the keys to the apartment I rented, I quietly make my way to the front door. Leaving the note on the coffee table, I walk out of Mack's apartment, happy.

I'm doing my first unselfish thing in forever, and it feels good. I'm not even scared of my new apartment. I'm just happy I finally did something right for Mack. It's about friggin' time I did something good for him. Especially since he has done so much for me time and time again. This is a good thing for Mack and his Kayla, and maybe even for me, eventually.

*****

THIS is me...

Waking to a chaos of sound, I know I've been found. Between Mack pounding on my front door, and my cell phone ringing nonstop, my new neighbors are going to absolutely hate me.

Throwing open the door, I yell, "I'm completely okay, Mack. So just stop."

Stunned, Mack doesn't even know what to say. Looking at me like he's lost his mind, I take his hand while leading him into my place, park his ass on the couch, and sit on the coffee table in front of him.

"Suzanne-"

"Nope. You're not my Shrink anymore and I'm absolutely fine. I wanted to leave not just for you and Kayla, if that's what you think, but once I thought about it, I realized I HAD to leave your apartment for me as well. I didn't want to make you my *platonic* substitute for Z, who I can't be with. And I think we both know, and I'm sure Kayla is well aware that that's exactly what I was doing. *Unintentionally,* of course. I thought I wanted to live with you as best friends and roommates, which I did. But I also wanted you to fill the loneliness up because Z can't...

"... So because you are so loving, and kind, and just the most amazing man EVER you gave into me. Again. And quite frankly, for someone who said they were going to start calling me on my shit, you've done a pretty lousy job of it. You CAN say no to me, Mack. You *should* say no to me sometimes. Otherwise, I might start using you unintentionally. I might use you or take advantage of your Mackness, and I NEVER want to do that to you. I love you way too much to be a user or a jerk to you, even if it is unintentional."

When he sits forward to speak, I raise my hand in the classic Mack/Suzanne 'zip it' way and he sits back without saying a word. Good.

"So here's where I'm at. I came back here around 1:00am, and though it was dark and I'm not used to this place at all, I handled it. I slept on the couch right here *for now* but I'm sure I'll make it to my room in a few days. I took my meds and I actually fell asleep right away. There were no tears and I didn't freak out over this living arrangement. I'm not actually happy of course, but I AM okay. Okay?"

Nodding, and sitting toward me again Mack pulls me toward the edge of the table, between his spread thighs and hugs me so tightly, I can barely breathe. Exhaling into my hair, I feel him relax fully.

This is good. This is another new start. I think Mack may even be proud of me for this huge step which I did all on my own.

Pulling away, I kiss him gently on the lips. Nothing dirty and nothing too dramatic, but just a nice little kiss between best friends.

"You are such a doll, Suzanne."

"I know. I try..." I giggle.

Smiling back he asks, "So what do you want to do now? What's the plan?"

"I'm going to go pee because I'm dying here, and then I'm going to call *your* Kayla back and explain my plans, which both do and DO NOT include you. And then I'd like to go for breakfast with you. After that, I was wondering if you could help me go grocery shopping again but for my place this time. And then we need to pack up and bring back all my clothes again," I smirk at his groan.

"Other than the clothing situation, that sounds like an excellent plan."

"Good."

Standing and walking toward my ugly new bedroom I hear him call my name. Looking back at him, he's still sitting forward with his hands on his knees looking like he's struggling to speak.

"I was scared to death this morning, Suzanne. I didn't know what I'd find here," he whispers.

"Don't be. 'Life-long contract', remember? Whether I like it or not, I can't break my promise to you, and I never will. Plus, I'm stronger than that now. I have to be."

And with a dramatic flip of my hair, I turn my back on Mack and his laughter as I shut my bedroom door behind me.

Exhaling and leaning against the door, I suddenly believe every single thing I just said to him. When I was speaking, I pulled that speech right out of my ass but now I know it's actually true.

I want Mack and Kayla to be good, and I have Z's baby to care for. And I need to get stronger *on my own* to be able to do that. This is the absolute best thing I can do for me and for them under the circumstances, and I'm going to do it.

When I call Kayla, she cuts me off immediately and begs me to hear her out. When I agree and remain silent, she begins...

"Picture this: you love a guy who has a best *female* friend who is beautiful, and sweet, and pregnant and heartbroken and lost, and so sad as she goes through a very tough time in her life she breaks the hearts of everyone she meets. The guy you love picks up and moves to be near her and takes care of her constantly. You, the girlfriend never see him but he *always* sees her. You are the outsider and she is his main focus day and night. Though you love each other and the best friends SWEAR it's platonic between them, you know the beautiful, sweet, sad woman who he adores tried to kiss him passionately once. And though he told you about it, and explained the rather tragic circumstances that prompted it- at the end of the day you are with the man you love *sometimes* but HE is with the girl he loves and adores each and every single day."

Oh shit.

"Now imagine that scenario with Z and some beautiful, sweet, *pregnant,* heart-broken, best friend who he loves and adores, admittedly. A woman he leaves you for to move away to be with her, *platonically* of course, and tell me you don't absolutely freak the fuck out and become this jealous, neurotic psycho where he and the woman are concerned?"

Yikes. Now I've got it and I totally get it. In the silence that follows Kayla's sad little confession I can think of nothing to say. Eventually, through the heavy silence I hear her exhale her upset.

"But it isn't like that. Ever," I plead. "I swear when I say I love Mack and when he says he loves me it IS a totally innocent relationship based on affection and mutual caring, but that's it."

"I know... But I still get jealous. I'm a woman, I can't help it."

"I would never do anything with Mack, and I would NEVER hurt you like that."

"I know, but-"

"The kiss was just a desperate, random, strange, spontaneous ooops on my part. It wasn't even about kissing Mack, Kayla. In my warped mind, I wanted to kiss Mack to make me not ugly anymore."

"Suzanne-"

"Listen to me, Kayla. It could've been anyone in that intense moment. I just needed to not be ugly, and I thought if someone kissed me back then I wasn't so ugly. And believe me there was NO kiss-back. None! Mack became so freakishly still that I kind of woke up to what I had done, and I apologized immediately. The end. I swear. I was just so stunned at my ugliness, I didn't know what to do, so I panicked," I cry softly.

"You are NOT ugly. And I get it now. I'm sorry for being such an insecure Psycho. And I'm not mad, and I'll forget about it starting now."

"Promise?"

"Yes. But if you ever kiss MY Mack again, I'll knock you on your ass, Suzanne. Pregnant or not."

"I wouldn't dare and I wouldn't ever, I swear. It was a strange little fluky moment of fear and desperation on my part."

"Okay, I understand totally. I've done desperate before with a guy."

"Really?"

"Of course. Um, do you still want to live with Mack? It's okay if you do, I'm fine with it now."

"No. I don't want to for me, but I don't want to for you and Mack either. I'll be okay. I just need you and I to be okay."

"We are. I promise."

"Thank you Kayla for understanding, and for always being there for me. I love you so much."
"I love you too. Now go *platonically* kiss my Mack for me, and tell him I'll call him later to apologize for *my* version of crazy," she says with her best smile-voice.
"Okay..." I grin as she hangs up.

Thirty-five minutes later, after that rather dramatic phone call with New York Kayla, I'm still stunned as I join Mack in the living room.
"We're okay now. And Kayla wants me to kiss you for her, and tell you she'll call you later."
"I'm very sorry you had to deal with-"
"I'm not. I'm glad she told me her feelings. Honestly, I would have freaked out if I was her too. I just didn't think about anyone else and I didn't realize how she would feel, but now I get it."
"What do you want to do now?" Mack still seems tense.
"Eat a huge breakfast. You in?" I smirk.
"Absolutely," he grins.

Thank god Kayla can be a loser, too. Her insecurity truly shocked me until she laid it out for me in terms of me and Z. I *really* understand now and I totally get it.
She's even more amazing than I ever believed possible, because if it was me in her shoes with Z and some other female 'best friend' laid out in front of me the way she just described the situation, I would've lost my mind... Again.

CHAPTER 28

JULY 22

After loading the washing machine of my apartment sized washer/dryer combo, I'm done. Sitting with my decaf, reading a magazine, there's nothing left to do.

When you live alone, your place stays the same unless you change it. There is nothing to tidy if you keep everything the same. And there is nothing to fix up when everything is in its place. Cleaning and laundry are all I have to do each and every day, and obviously I don't do laundry every day. Nope. Laundry for one woman who rarely leaves her apartment is one load max, once a week.

So I'm done for another week, and I'm bored to tears. Mack isn't coming over today, which is fine! I'm absolutely fine with that. Mack isn't here and I have TV and magazines to keep me company. Oh, and my kindle. Thank god.

Some days the loneliness I feel is beyond overwhelming. It's a loneliness that is nearly debilitating. It's a soulless walk through my apartment alone trying to function, trying to just breathe, when all I want to do is to give into the loneliness while letting it consume me whole.

This is an agony itself.

But I was always alone, I remember that. My childhood was spent alone with my parents, and my youth was spend alone with my peers. My teen years were spent alone with my horrible secrets, and my marriage was spent alone with Marcus right beside me. I was always alone in my little world of pain. Alone is really all I've ever known, except within this past year.

Meeting and loving these few people of mine has saved me from the abyss. They are my lifeline from the depths of depression that would have killed me by now. They are my tether to this world, keeping me here, keeping me trying to live through the loneliness.

And I love them. Mack and Kayla, *other* Kayla and Z. I love them with every breath I take. I think of these four people and I realize they are all I have in this world. With these four in my life, the monsters are no longer waiting to strike, and my previous abusive nightmares are trying to stay in the past.

My four people have kept me alive. They are there for me. They are there to love me.

Mack is my constant. Still. I don't think Mack is even capable of leaving me now, or of loving me less. Mack is my forever friend, and I trust that. I *believe* he is my forever friend.

His dedication alone shows me the depth of his love for me and the depth and intensity of our friendship. He will not leave me- I know that without a doubt. I know I have found the one real person in this world who was made to help me. He was made to love me regardless of me being who I turned out to be. Mack is the one person in this world whom I never, ever fear. He loves me as his best friend and he has proven his love time and time again, whether I deserve his love or not.

And then there's New York Kayla. My Kayla Rinaldi. She is my reason to get up every morning. Kayla can beat the hell out of me with just words when I need an ass-kicking. She can call me on my shit, and she can soothe me when I'm *losing* my shit. Kayla has managed to put herself firmly into my heart in a way I previously could have only dreamed of. She has been the greatest strength in all my struggle; strength I could have only prayed for. She knows when to shake me and she knows when to hold me. She is the greatest friend I could have ever begged and prayed for. Kayla makes up for every friend I didn't have throughout my thirty years before her.

Other Kayla is still here to love me, too. She's just not *as* here as she was before, and I'm going to be okay with that one day. I'm going to except the relationship we have as friends now. I'm going to remember fondly the relationship we had, and I'm going to embrace this new, less intense friendship we have now, because really, that's all I can do.

I know if I asked her for anything or if I asked her to help me, she would in a heartbeat. I know she's still a champion for me. I know she's here- she's just not quite the same as she was. But that's okay. I'm going to be grateful for the friendship she does give me. She will always be my Chicago Kayla Lefferts.

And finally... there's Z. God, I miss him so much my heart aches constantly.

Everything I do, every person I see, every single thing I feel is about Z. He is *always* with me. Everywhere I go and everything I do is shared with him in my heart. My thoughts remain constantly on and about him. Z makes me, and sadly he breaks me. I miss him so much, I find myself gasping for air just to make it through my lonely days without him in my life.

I wish so many things for us, but I can't have any of them. Z is not in my life directly but I still feel him all day, every day. I feel him in each and everything I do. He is everything to me and it breaks my heart that I can't be with him, but I'm okay with this absence of him. I have to be.

This life between us is just too much to live with. The decisions made and this life lived is too great to overcome. Z and I cannot live this life with each other because the obstacles are too great to climb together. There is too much darkness and lost promise between us to ever live a life together.

I finally realize that and I'm okay now. I think I'm truly okay with the darkness. I've accepted it. I've lived a life so dark before him, that I don't know how to live in light *with* him. And though I wish I could, I know I can't live without the darkness. The light and the love between Z and I would eventually blind me and make me weak, and weakness is not part of me loving Z.

So I'll take the darkness and the strength. I'm most comfortable here anyway. I may not be happy and I may be so sad that I ache with gasping breaths of loneliness, but I'll take the strength and comfort I have in my darkness over the potential pain and endless heartbreak of a love tried and failed. This loneliness may be suffocating but at least it's familiar. This suffocating loneliness is all I've ever known, and it's all I'll ever know.

   This is my fate, and I'm okay now. I've accepted it. The choices made have brought me to this darkness, and I'm going to love this life as best I can with my only strength being my love of these four people- people who have changed my life and brought me some closure to my past.

   I may have little more than an empty cold apartment with an endless stretch of loneliness ahead of me, but at least it's mine. This is the life I have created. This is my life now, and I'm going to live it as best as I can.

   Through the darkness, I'm going to give my four people the most love I have, be it from close or from far. My love is theirs for the taking, and I offer it back freely to the four people who have helped and loved me through the nightmare that was my life before them.

   I'm okay with the dark loneliness now, because I still have the love of my four people surrounding me in my darkness.

CHAPTER 29

AUGUST 3

So I've learned one very important, life-changing reality the last 2 months I've been awake- Pregnancy is hard. It's so weird when I see other women behaving like this is the best time of their lives. They're so happy, people say they 'glow'. Well, I'm not glowing and I'm definitely NOT happy. This sucks.
 I would love to be all beautiful and wonderful and loving this, but I'm not. I don't feel beautiful and this is NOT wonderful. I absolutely hate this, I truly do.
 Never-mind the obvious; I'm getting huge. But there's so much else going on. Things ache. Body parts I didn't know existed hurt. I'm hungry but I don't want to eat. I'm tired but I can't sleep. And *I'm* having a good pregnancy, I'm told. I honestly can't imagine what this would possibly be like if I was having a 'bad' pregnancy.
 I wonder sometimes if I would feel so crappy all the time if I actually wanted this pregnancy. Huh. Maybe if I was happy that I was pregnant I wouldn't notice all these crappy side effects. It's good that I don't ever discuss this pregnancy with anyone, otherwise I might come off sounding whiny or annoying. As it is, people know how heartless I am about this, but I can't help it. I don't want this. Still.
 Honestly, I still feel nothing, but I've tried. I've touched my stomach and I've spoken to it. I've felt it move and I saw a picture of it once for a split second accidentally, but I still feel nothing. And that lack of feeling probably scares me more than just the thought of this whole thing.

I mean really... how can I feel nothing about a child growing inside me? *Z's* child, no less. But there it is. My horrific reality. I'm bad, and this time it's undeniable. I really am a bad person because I don't feel anything for this child inside me.

God, I need a distraction. I need to do something to stop all this thinking. I don't want to call Mack or Kayla, because I'm sure they're quite busy with each other, and I really have no one else *to* call.

Chicago Kayla is okay, but we're just not the same, and usually after talking to her I feel worse anyway because I miss her so much.

And so I'm going shopping... *as a distraction.*

I have to go shopping today alone because Mack is in New York for the night, and I'm left here alone, which is fine. Really it is. He's totally allowed to have a life, and I want him to have a life. I just hate that Mack having a life means I have less of a life. Ugh. Selfish Suzanne I know, but I can't help it. Mack is my Mack, and when he's not around I miss him.

So, I'm going shopping for underwear of all friggin' things. I swear to god- *underwear.* I'd like to pretend that only my belly is growing but it's simply not true. My ass is definitely getting bigger, and I really can't deny it anymore. My boobs are getting huge too. Quite frankly, I kinda like bigger boobs, not that they weren't big enough before, almost distractingly so, but before I could wear a nice black blouse and they didn't seem so big.

Now, I have huge boobs which I'm allowed to have, though this is slightly marred by the fact that my ass is bigger which seems totally unfair. My ass was always biggish to begin with and now it's bigger. Ugh... Pregnancy sucks.

*****

After checking my make-up and the best air-brush job I can possibly do with my limited resources, I hop in a waiting cab for the mall.

Fairfield Mall has department stores for big-sized underwear woman and there are even a few lingerie shops if I feel like torturing myself today, which I really don't. But why not go in and look... and yearn. Ha! I'm going shopping again, but with total sanity. Finally.

So I'm here and people have already noticed me though they're not staring too obviously. A few people have looked at me already but I've turned my head and hair to hide my face and I'm walking quickly. No need to give them a show for long.

I know I look weird. I know my face is scarred and still a little pink under the make-up and I know my limp is very noticeable which is my fault completely, but I couldn't help it. I had to wear a pair of killer heels for emotional support. I HAD to.

The problem? Balance. It's weird how a growing belly really does throw off your balance in heels. Actually, now that I think about it I'm kind of over compensating my belly by walking strangely with my spine pushed backward so I don't lean too far forward on these super high heels; heels which now seem a little ridiculous in my present condition. Dammit.

Okay, so shoe shopping first before bigass underwear shopping. Yay! Shoes.

Limp-walking to the closest shoe store, I notice it's clearly for older women, or for women who like comfortable shoes, or maybe for women who are already tall and don't need to flaunt their height. Huh. I see nothing greater than a 1 inch 'what's the point?' heel, so I quickly move on.

Lingerie store. Nope. Not ready yet. I need 'Awesome won't kill me' heels first. Okay. Hobble. Hobble.

Wow. Funky all black, black light, sexy funky, kinda Goth store. I *really* love black but I wonder how weird a 30 year old scarred, pregnant woman would look entering... too bad. I'm doing it anyway.

Ahhhh... Black. I love black. Black is good. Black hides my previously hide-able bodily nooks and crannies that are now amazingly less a problem since my boobs are bigger and my ass is huge, my stomach is growing and my face and leg are warped. Giggle.

"Can I help you find anything?" Jump. Yup, I'm still a loser.

"Yes... Do you have any larger sizes?" I had total confidence with that question- I'm proud of myself.

"Yeah, sure," says the poster-child gothic princess. Holy shit! I would kill to look like her any day. Every day. Always. Okay, maybe not now 'cause I'm too old, but when I was young like her I would've. Like if I had been able to dress myself at her age; I would have loved to be like her at least for a day or two. She's beautiful.

Following her to the back of the store where the music seems way too loud, I'm mesmerized by everything about her. She is so perfectly skinny. Her waist is tiny, she has a skinny girl butt, but amazingly she has smallish perfectly proportioned breasts as well. She's perfect and it's really nauseating to stare at her actually.

I wish *my* belly was flat and I could wear a small top that raises with my arms to flash the flat perfection of my stomach and waist. What the hell? Oh. She probably works out. Huh. Maybe I should eventually give that a try.

"Here's our Plus-Size section, and it's pretty good. We have a larger selection than most stores because even heavy chicks like looking good. Sweet shoes by the way," she smiles.

Oh my god, she's just so lovely. Her eyes are green and though her hair is dyed pitch black she doesn't look weird; she looks perfectly pale with green eyes that reach out and smack you in the face.

"Thank you," I whisper embarrassed. And why am I suddenly embarrassed? I'm not sure. I mean I know I'm pregnant, but I feel too old or too uptight to be here. There's something off, but I

don't think it's my sanity. I think I'm still okay with that.
"Let me know if you need any help," she smiles again. God, she's just so pretty, I wish I looked like her. Singing, she walks away.
What the hell is this song? It's horrible and not because I'm old. It just really sucks actually. There's no consistent beat, and the voice is strangely whiny and the music seems to put me on edge or something. But I'm fine.
Looking through some shirts I see nothing I like. Not one single thing. I'm too old for this club-type wear; and really, I would look mental trying to pull off most of this shit. Ha! Mack would have to commit me again. Turning, I spot the dresses and again I'm at a loss. There is NOTHING for me in here, even though *everything* is my black. Ugh.
Shoes? Ah, boots... I see a pair. Black, knee-high, side zipper, rich dark leather, 4' wedge-awesomeness. They look a little biker boot with a girly edge. They even have a side buckle on the ankle. Yup. These I can totally do.
Motioning to the lovely girl, holding up the boot and flashing 9 fingers she nods and makes her way to the farthest back. I'm excited. I always get excited with shoes, but I'm super excited this time. I love these boots. These are 'Suzanne with a twist' boots for sure.
When she comes back smiling, she leads me to a little bench seat. Pulling my boots out of the box they smell like new leather. Deep breathe. Oh yeah, leather scent in my lungs. I love this.
"You are so very pretty," I whisper. What?!
"Thanks," she replies easily.
Huh. I get it, she's super busy. The store is loud and there are enough people to make her have to split her attention between us, but still... 'thanks'?
"I'm serious. You have this awesome body and a beautiful face. I'm not weird or anything, but you're very attractive and I thought you should know."
"Oh, I know. Everyone tells me I'm gorgeous." *gorgeous?* "So I'm

over it, ya know?" Huh. Not really. I feel like I'm over *her* right now though.

Pulling on the boots, they fit perfectly. Yes! Standing, I'm instantly comfortable. These boots feel like slippers compared to my killer heels.

"Um, I'll take them and wear them out if you don't mind."

"No problem," she says as she takes my killer heels and places them in the boot box for me.

Following her to the check out, I think I'm a little pissed at her. I know she's young, like maybe 19 or 20 so she probably doesn't know anything about life yet, but still to be so blasé about her looks seems tragic. Oh! Actually maybe I'm the problem here because I'm too hung up on looks now. Shit. I'm fine. I'm not freaking out and my sanity is intact, totally. But I do feel annoyed by this situation.

"I used to be pretty too."

"*Really?*" Wow. Why the hell is she so surprised?

"Yes, really. Before I was hurt and pregnant, I was thinner and pretty too."

"Okay. Well, it's $163.39 for the boots," she says ignoring me. Okay, I'm more than annoyed now.

Pulling out my Debit card, I find I'm growing angrier by the second. Ugh. Calm down. I know this is my problem, I know it. She's NOT the problem, I am. I know it!

She still hasn't spoke to me at all. My card has been swiped, the boot box is in a gigantic bag, the receipt is in the bag, and my card is back in my wallet. I'm breathing and she's just ignoring me.

"Look. I know you don't know me, and I *know* you don't care about what I'm saying, but it's important. You may not always been so attractive, and it kind of hurts when you're not anymore, so, um... enjoy being pretty while you can." There I said it. Big exhale. I feel totally better now.

Pausing for a moment she just looks at me like I'm cracked. And in all fairness I don't know her and I'm desperately trying to convince her of something she doesn't understand yet, so I probably do seem a little weird to her.

Fake smiling at me, she says, "Okay. I'll keep that in mind. Have a good day," as she turns her back to me and walks away.

See, I'm fine. No freak out just because I was totally dismissed. I'm good. I'm wearing my awesome new comfy black 'Suzanne with a twist' boots and I'm okay. There is no freak out in sight.

Entering the large department store I need, I walk directly to the lingerie section. Buying new underwear is awful, but I've been trying to fit my fat ass and growing stomach into my old size for weeks and the elastic just rubs me raw under the belly which is not comfortable in the least. And the wedgie I get? Forget it. It's like my ass is trying to eat my underwear! Giggle.

When I get to the maternity section, I'm stunned. Every single pair of underwear is white, creamy beige or pink. What the hell? Where is my black? What the hell do I do with pink? I can't even imagine wearing white or pink, or creamy beige. Why? Oh god, if anything's gonna set me off, it's this. White underwear? This is complete insanity. Giggle.

Moving back to the normal section, I pick up a 3XL pair of BLACK underwear and exhale. These should fit for a while, and they'll probably go over my belly for a while too. Good. Grabbing 12 pair, I even throw in a 4XL just in case.

Walking to the bras I'm faced with the same problem. The maternity section has cute matching bra and panty sets in lacy pinks, whites and beiges. I swear to god, I'm gonna lose it over here. I want ONE black bra. That's it. Just one!

Walking back to the large sized non-maternity section I grab a 36DDD black bra and relax. If my boobs actually get this big I'm going to fall over anyway so who cares what it looks like. There is only so much fight against gravity one person can wage. There is only so much my back can handle before I face-plant. If I did actually grow to a 36DDD I'd probably be on bed rest anyway, right? God, I hope so.

Walking to the counter I'm fine. Still. I'm not losing it, and I'm not going to freak over anything. There's nothing to freak out over. I could probably call Mack and even tell him I'm shopping and I'm completely fine, but I don't want to interrupt the sexfest happening in New York.

Ugh, the girl in front of me is tiny and perfect. Another one? Seriously? Okay, so I may have missed the 'working out makes you look hot like this' memo, or maybe I threw it out by mistake with my take-out menus. Whatever. She's hot. Oh, and look- a matching WHITE lacy bra and panty set of course. Yuck. I'm fine. And she's awesome.

When it's my turn, I place my huge new underwear on the counter and smile at the middle-aged woman while totally embarrassed by my purchases.

"We have a large maternity section over there," she points with a lovely smile.

"I know. I was there, but you don't have any black which I absolutely require, so I'm just going to get these. Is that okay?" Why am I asking permission? Dammit.

"Oh, we usually have a few undergarments in black, but not many. Most women prefer the softer colors while pregnant." God. Why?

"It's fine. I'll just take these," I sigh.

Smiling again, thankfully the kind looking middle-aged woman named Kora doesn't say anything else to me about my undies. I mean seriously? Doesn't she know I just want to buy these tent-size drawers as quickly as possible and get them into the bag even quicker? Why is every single pair on a friggin' hanger? What is *with* that? Jesus, it's taking her forever to unhook, fold and bag each pair of my humongous underwear. Argh...

After paying with my Debit again I almost laugh at the bill. I never realized how expensive huge underwear were. At 12.99 each, times 13 pair plus my massive bra I actually managed to spend over two hundred dollars on underwear! Christ, even my new 'Suzanne with a twist' boots weren't that much and I'll have these babies forever! Unlike this underwear, which I'm going to burn in a few months.

Practically running... okay, *limping quickly* from the store, I exhale. I think that's it for me today. I'm still okay, but I'm feeling anxiety definitely creeping up, so I think it's time to end my solo shopping excursion before I'm not okay. I'm handling the few stares and double takes I'm getting, and I'm still okay. But it is definitely Time. To. Go.

Walking back into the main mall I need to go home. I know I'm getting anxious and I know I need a pill, but I forgot them at home because I'm an idiot. So far so good though.
Passing another funky clothing store, I figure what the hell? Shopping online fills a void in me, as Mack would say, but shopping in person is both exhilarating and nauseating at once.
Looking around, I see a decent array of black shirts, blouses, skirts and even jeans, NOT that I can fit into any proper sizes at the moment... but maybe afterward?
Grabbing a large, swingy cotton peasant-type dress in black, I think I found something I can fit into and actually wear today. It lands just lower than my knee so it'll look pretty cool with my new boots.
Maybe this whole shopping experience is my unconsciousness telling me that though I must stick with my blacks, it's time to branch out from my typical conservative wardrobe. Maybe this whole situation is my mind's way of telling me it's time to be different than I was. Maybe this is my way of changing my outer self to match all the physical changes I've had to endure these last few months. Maybe this is me trying to change who I am now. Maybe? I don't know but I'm shaky now.
Abruptly leaving the store, I know I *need* to get home. I've had enough. I'm starting to think in circles, and I'm not as clear as I usually am. Well, this is a step. At least I recognize I'm less clear in the head. Before, I didn't know when I was strange. I just was.
Pushing past people I'm just desperate to get back to the front

doors to hail a cab. I need to get home before I have to call Mack for help. I need to get home to my anxiety medication. Ugh. Why does everyone walk so slow in a mall when they know people are right behind them trying to pass?

Suddenly, feeling my arm tugged, I panic! Spinning around and covering my head as best as I can, I collapse on the floor to evade the men. Waiting for the blows, I breathe in short bursts as my mind spins.
Why does this always happen to me?! I thought I would be safe in a public place. I thought for sure I was safe!
"Mam, are you alright?" What?
Looking up I see a Security Guard standing over me, not a man. Well, not a bad man. What the hell?
"Yes, I'm fine. Why?" Crap, my voice is all raspy and breathy.
"Can you stand?" He asks kindly.
"I think so," I pause trying to stand on my own, but when he reaches for my hand, I pull away again. "Why did you touch me?" I beg.
"I was trying to get your attention. Do you need any medical assistance?" Um...
"No. Why?" Shit.
Looking around, this is so embarrassing. There are so many people stopping to look at me. I'm suddenly surrounded by gawkers and nosy bitches loving the show. Oh my god. I hate when people see me.
"Can you make them stop seeing me?" I whisper.
When the Security Guard leans down to me, I don't flinch this time. He doesn't look mean or angry, just concerned. Thank god. I couldn't stand meanness right now. I just need to get home.
"Let me help you up," he smiles kindly.
"Thank you."
Putting his hand behind my back and taking my right hand in his own, he pulls me to a stand with him. Listing a little to the left, he tightens his grip on me.
"I'm sorry my face is ugly now. It wasn't before. It was just plain,

but now it's ugly. I'm sorry."

"What's your name?"

"Suzanne Anderson," and looking I see his is Kevin. Didn't I just meet a Kevin? No, Kora. Kevin and Kora, cute. She would have to be his cougar though, because he looks about 30ish to lovely Kora's 55 years. Cool.

"Why did you touch me Kevin?"

"I was trying to call you to a stop. I called you a few times, but I don't think you heard me."

"Oh. Did you know my name then?" Shit. Do I know him?

"No. Actually, I said 'excuse me' and 'hey you' a few times but you ignored me," he grins.

"Oh. Well, I only answer to Suzanne now. That's what my name is, well always was, but IS... especially now. I am Suzanne Anderson, and nothing else. Now, I'm just Suzanne."

Looking around I see people still stopped near us watching and listening. Jesus! Could this be any more embarrassing? Turning my back to the people, I'm flush with a dark glass window of a knick-knack store.

Oh FUCK! I've done it again. Okay, breathe. Shit. There I am. Mascara everywhere, looking like a freak again. Shit. Shit. SHIT! But I'm okay. I *know* I am. How did I do this? I know better than this. I'M better than this.

"Kevin, I'm sorry. I screwed up. I'm not supposed to get this upset, and I'm not supposed to cry in public. I made a mistake but I didn't realize it until now. I have to go. I have to go home now before Mack and Kayla find out. Shit. Please don't tell Z. I'm fine now, I swear. I'm not freaked out anymore, I promise."

Feeling my body shaking, I'm just sick over this mistake. God Dammit! Mack should be able to go away for 2 friggin' days without 'Suzanne the Psycho' coming out to play.

"Mrs. Anderson, I need to talk to you in private. Would you please follow me, and we'll get away from all these people," he says quietly to me.

"I swear I'm okay Kevin. I'm just going to go home now. I'll flag a cab and be out of here in a minute. I'm fine. I'm not a Psycho. Well, not like *that* anymore. This is not a nervous breakdown either because Mack said. So I'm fine. I just forgot my anxiety medicine, but I'm going home to get it. Please..."

When Kevin bends back down he picks up my bags and looks back at me with sadness, I think. Oh, no.

"I'm okay, I promise. Please don't look like that," I beg.

"Mrs. Anderson, you have to come with me. The manager at Felice saw you steal this dress from the store," he says calmly lifting the dress to me.

Oh. My. *GOD!*

"I didn't steal that, I swear! I don't know how I have that. I would never steal," I scream. "I would never take something. I didn't do it. I didn't mean to. I don't know how I did that!"

Fuck. I can't breathe.

No longer looking so nice, Kevin takes my burned arm in his hand and says, "I'm sure you didn't steal it Mrs. Anderson, but you still have to come with me."

Bursting into tears I am just shocked by this situation. This can't be happening. Who *does* this? Who would want to? Just the humiliation alone is SO not worth the risk of shoplifting. I would never do this! I *didn't* do this.

Trying to pull my arm away, Kevin holds tighter. Oh god. Not my skin. Not my burns. I don't want him to feel them through my blouse.

"Please Kevin, I promise I didn't do this. I didn't realize I was holding the dress when I left the store, I swear. I have more than enough money to pay for it. Look at my new 'Suzanne with a twist' boots! They were over a hundred and sixty dollars!"

Quickly opening up my other bag, I grab all my underwear and hold them up to his face. When the huge bra drops to the floor I scoop it up and slip it up my arms so it's against my boobs and yell, "See! This sucker doesn't even fit yet, but I bought it anyway in case, and it was forty-five dollars. Look, all this underwear cost over two hundred! Look at all my new underwear! Why the hell would I steal a twenty dollar dress? And look at all my new

UNDERWEAR!" Ha! There. See! That makes sense.
Turning for a second I see a man looking at me like I'm crazy. Actually, he has a look of utter disgust on his face. Why?
"Don't look at me like that!" I scream at the man. "What did I do to you to deserve *that* look?" Christ! I still can't breathe.
Staring at Kevin again, I take it all in as he stares back at me silently. Holy SHIT! Ex*hale*...
I'm crying and shaking and barely breathing and yelling and waving humongous underwear around in the middle of a fucking mall with a gigantic bra against my chest, cupping my boobs. Besides Kevin, I see other people looking embarrassed too. Embarrassed for me or because of me? Who can tell? Jesus *Christ*... I'm a freak!
Whoosh.
Oh. My. GOD. *Again?* Oh, come ON! Why shopping? *Why SHOPPING?!* Why not at the dentist, or on a tall ladder, or at the gynecologist, or, or boarding a plane like a normal person? Why the hell must I freak the fuck out while shopping?!
I can't do anything right, no matter how hard I try. Wiping away the mascara on my cheeks with my hands, I know I've smeared my caked on cover the scars make-up, but what else can I do?

Exhaling all the crazy out of me, I sigh my defeat.
"I'm so sorry, Kevin. Where should we go?"
Picking up the bag from the floor, I throw all my underwear and my bra back in. Holding my huge boot box with my killer heels, I give in. What's the point? I've screwed up again.
"Mrs. Anderson, I'm very sorry," he whispers. God, he looks honestly upset by this.
"It's okay. You're just doing your job, and I must look like a crazy shoplifter. I get it. Can we just go?"
Nodding, Kevin takes my arm again and though I flinch a little at his touch I don't fight his grip this time. This time I give in. This time, I'm ready.
God, I need my anti-anxiety meds. I didn't even realize before

that they helped because I always took them because Mack makes me take them, but now I see I actually do need them.

I've often wondered if I was a junkie or like totally dependent on my meds. Well, I guess I have my answer now. I am and I totally do. And I am so screwed this time.

Walking quietly through the mall beside Kevin my face is lowered and as covered as I can with my hair. Kevin even tries to talk to me kindly a few times, but I just can't. This feels like walking to my mother when she was mad at me. I knew I didn't do anything wrong then but I was going to be punished anyway. Now, I didn't do anything wrong *on purpose* but it was still bad and I'm still going to be punished.

I am absolutely humiliated and sad that I failed this adventure. I wish I had been able to do this on my own. God, I don't want Mack and Kayla to be disappointed in me, but they will be and I know I'll deserve their disappointment this time.

When we enter a large room, there are other security guards and cameras and stuff everywhere. I see the monitors and I just know they all saw me freak out and I'm horribly embarrassed to be here with them.

When another man walks up to us, Kevin tells him my name. Shit. Here we go. Suzanne Anderson. Hopefully they don't have a clue I'm THE Suzanne Anderson- 'Mental case, Nut bar, Sexual Abuse Victim Extraordinaire'. Hopefully, I'm just some generic crazy shoplifter to them. One could only dream.

"Mrs. Anderson, do you know why you were apprehended by Security?"

"Yes. It appears that I shoplifted a twenty dollar dress, which I promise was a mistake. I didn't realize I was still holding the dress when I left the store. I just wanted to get home quickly because I was suffering from anxiety and I forgot my medication at home," I confess.

"So leaving Felice with the dress was accidental?" He looks like I'm a complete asshole liar.

"Yes, sir. I'm sorry." Great! Now I'm a child again, apologizing always. The sound of the words 'I'm sorry' make me sick. I hate this feeling. "I can pay for the dress, I promise. I have the money and it was a complete accident leaving the store with it."

"Was it?" Okay, head Security Guard Stanley looks like I'm a total lying loser, and I'm sure to him I am. I'm sure he's heard all these excuses before. I'm sure he thinks I'm just like every other shoplifter in the mall.

Again, I sigh my defeat. "You can call my best friend, Dr. Michael MacDonald and ask him. I have lots of money but I got confused and stressed and freaked out in the store and I just wanted to get home, but I didn't know I was still holding the dress when I left. I just don't understand. I didn't touch anything red..."

"Red?"

"Yes, *red*. Forget it. It really doesn't matter anymore. Nothing does. What do we do now? Do we call the Police?" Maybe Mack and Kayla don't need to help me. Maybe they don't need to know.

"Wait! Detective Rogers and Detective Bennici- Oh! And D.A. Rose know me. And they can tell you I have money, and that I'm good, and that I wouldn't steal anything, and that I'm Suzanne Anderson, and that I'm not a bad person." Thank god I thought of them. Please. Please. *Please*, call them.

"D.A. Rose? As in the District Attorney of Chicago?" Okay, I see the bullshit-o-meter going off in his head, and I can almost feel him trying not to laugh at me.

"Yes, him. I have his card in my wallet. Can I get it?"

"Sure," he smiles.

Looking at Kevin, I'm so sad I think I'm going to cry again. Actually, I think I was crying this whole time but just didn't realize it until this moment. It's weird how that happens. Obviously, I feel myself when I'm sobbing, but sometimes when I'm silently crying I don't even realize it until I'm covered in tears. I wonder if that's because the nerves are shot in half my face. Giggle. I should ask Mack if that's possibly the reason. Shit. Focus!

Going through my wallet I pull out my cash which is over a

hundred in bills and whisper, "See. I could've paid if I'd known," while I look for the business card of Mr. Rose. Finding it and handing it over to Stanley, I just wait. Huh. He looks surprised that I had the card. I should really ask if I'm allowed to call Glenn myself.

"Would you like me to call him? He put his cell number on the card for me."

"Ah, sure. If you want." He looks even more surprised. Wow. I feel a little less pathetic and upset suddenly as I start dialing.

When Glenn answers his clipped 'Rose', I'm instantly relieved. He has such a nice strong voice that has always been very kind to me the dozen or so times we've spoken. He doesn't seem to take shit from anybody though, which I guess he wouldn't as the D.A. of friggin' Chicago.

"Mr. Rose, this is Suzanne Anderson. I'm in some trouble and-"

"Have you been threatened, Suzanne?" He demands.

"No! Not like that, I-"

"Speaker phone," Stanley states beside me.

Nodding to Stanley I ask, "Mr. Rose, may I put you on speaker phone? I'm in the Security office at Fairfield Mall."

"Go ahead," he says as I hear shuffling on his phone. Putting my iPhone on speaker I just wait for a second. Christ! This is embarrassing.

"Please identify yourself," Stanley demands.

"This is District Attorney Glenn Rose. And your name is?"

"Stanley Hamilton of Amble Security stationed at Fairfield Mall."

"All right Stanley, badge number?" Yikes. This feel very testosterony suddenly.

"4-6-4. D.A. Rose, I have Suzanne Anderson here with me and she's been apprehended for shoplifting-"

Glenn suddenly barks a laugh, which amazingly makes me smile and prompts me to confess.

"It was an accident Mr. Rose! I started getting anxiety at the mall, and I forgot my medication and I left a store quickly to go get a cab so I could go home, and Kevin, the other security guard here grabbed my arm-" Kevin flinches.

"Are you hurt, Suzanne?" Glenn asks seriously.

"No, I just freaked out and fell down when he touched me but he wasn't mean, I just, you know how I am with men and touch and, and the other stuff. Anyway, Kevin showed me the dress I was still holding but I didn't mean to take it, I swear. I already bought a bunch of things, and I have more money in my wallet than the dress even costs plus, well, you know I have more money than twenty dollars, but I really didn't mean to take it. I *wouldn't* take it. It was an accident. And now I look like a thief and a Psycho-"

"Suzanne-"

"Wait. Please. I can pay for the dress."

"I know you can. What was the cost?"

"Twenty dollars plus tax," I confess.

"Are you are willing to pay restitution, Suzanne?" What restitution?

"Um, yes. I'll pay anything. It was a complete accident."

"Security Agent Hamilton, I would like you to take thirty dollars of Suzanne's money to the store in which the incident occurred and I would like you to please handle this matter discretely. I do not want Ms. Anderson's name becoming public and I will be very angry should this situation become known beyond just us. My office will NOT be pressing any charges and the Police do NOT need to be called. There will be no record of this event with her name anywhere. Ms. Anderson is a very important State's Witness and I need her anonymity to stay that way. Am I clear, Hamilton?"

"Perfectly," Stanley says a little jazzed. I thought he would resent this, but he looks almost excited that he's involved in something legal sounding. This is getting too weird.

I feel like I can finally breathe a little. I feel like I'm not in trouble anymore. I feel like I'm not a little girl facing her mother for her punishments.

"Where's Mack, Suzanne?" Whooooosh.

"In New York," I whisper.

"Okay. Go straight home and take care of yourself. Would you

like me to contact Mack or your doctor for you?" God no!
"No! I mean, no thank you Mr. Rose. I'll see Mack tomorrow, and I'm fine. I'm just going to go home with my new underwear." Oh! "Um-"
"And your new dress," he says laughing at me.
"Thank you so much Mr. Rose. I didn't know what else to do."
"Suzanne, you know we have a 'call me anytime' policy, and I'm pleased you finally used it. I'm glad I could help you. Go home Suzanne. And Hamilton!" Glenn suddenly barks making Stanley, Kevin and I all jump. "Make sure Ms. Anderson is escorted directly to a waiting cab immediately. I'll be checking in later to make sure she made it home safely. Understood?"
"Yes, sir. I'll make sure she gets home safely. Thank you, District Attorney Rose," Stanley says all stern and officially. What a dork. Honestly.
When Glenn hangs up I feel remarkably better. I wasn't arrested and no one has to know about this. I probably don't even need to tell Mack. Thank god.
Walking out with Stanley I realize I did learn two very important lessons today. First; Shopping is out without Mack, and second; I NEED my meds.
After getting in the cab with Stanley's help, I'm desperate to get home. This day has been shit, and I feel gross and cried out, and shaky and just desperate for the closed door of the boring place I call home.
I need my yoga pants and I need to park my fat ass in front of some Grey's Anatomy to release this failed attempt at normalcy. I need to order a pizza and I need to release this stress with mindlessness and food.

When I enter my apartment, I quickly remove my new 'Suzanne with a Twist' boots and exhale. Half expecting a message from Mack I make my way to the answering machine nervously. I hope Glenn didn't call him. I hope he knew I was embarrassed and decided to keep this between us- well, between us, and Stanley and Kevin.

With no blinking light, I'm free! Holy shit! I did it. I fucked up totally but I wasn't caught by Mack, so I'm okay. After these last 5 hours of completely mental I can finally exhale... AND take my meds.

CHAPTER 30

AUGUST

I've been in my apartment for nearly 7 weeks now and living on my own is okay. I'm actually surprised by *how* okay I feel about it generally. I thought I'd be all scared or nervous but strangely I'm okay. Of course I have moments of loneliness, but when it's real bad for me I read a book, or call Kayla, or shop online. Usually, I can distract myself into being less lonely, at least for a while.

One thing I really hate though is my actual apartment. It's just so ugly and lifeless. The walls are all beige and the kitchen tiles are beige. The carpets in the 2 bedrooms are beige. Everything is just so bland and neutral, which does NOT help my mindset right now.

I need something, well, some*one* to help because this apartment where I spent 95% of my time just isn't doing it for me. So since I can't paint right now in my 'condition', I'm going shopping today with Kayla and Mack to spruce up the place.

Waiting, I haven't seen Kayla in 2 weeks, but she and I still talk every day, and I see Mack every day for breakfast and sometimes for dinner, as well.

I feel bad for Mack most days because he's completely suspended in Chicago because of me. And I feel really bad for Kayla who is left alone in New York because Mack feels like he needs to be here for me. But I tried. I honestly tried to convince him to go back, and I tried to convince her to make him return to her, but neither was on board.

Mack said he would move back when things had settled, meaning *I* was settled, probably after the birth. And Kayla said she enjoys not seeing Mack every day because it makes their long distance relationship sex OFF THE CHARTS, which was *way* too much information for me, but she just laughed at my blush.

And so Mack is suspended, Kayla is horny, and I want to not be secretly happy that Mack hasn't left me yet, but I am. I look forward to seeing Mack in the mornings after my long sad nights, and I look forward to his spontaneous Mack and Suzanne movie nights, or card nights, or the shopping excursions we have from time to time which torture him.

And yes, I told Mack and Kayla what happened during my solo shopping trip. And amazingly, both were supportive and very, very kind to me. Neither yelled at me nor seemed to think badly of me. They each told me separately that I've done so well, but things are bound to 'set me off' from time to time which is both expected and 'normal'.

Mack gently lectured me about the importance of taking my medication always, which I understood totally. And Kayla said she wished she could have seen me because just the visual of me waving around huge underwear and wearing my gigantic bra over my clothes in the middle of a mall would have been hilarious to watch. And after I burst out laughing, I cried a little because of their understanding and kindness. God, I love them.

When Kayla suddenly walks right into my apartment, I'm stunned but laugh. She's just such a beast, and she doesn't even realize or maybe care that most people would knock before entering. She is Kayla, and she probably would find it weird if I didn't walk right into her place when visiting. She's just like that. At this point I think 30 different people have a key to her apartment, 'just in case' as she says. Regardless, she's a wrecking ball, but so sweet and kind to me, I couldn't love her more if I tried.

Waiting for it...

"Jesus! You're getting big." And there it is.

"I know. I'm going to be huge, I think."

"Yup. But your boobs like great," she grins. Ugh! Instantly looking at Mack I blush as she bursts out laughing at me. She is such a shit.

"Thanks, Kayla," I groan.

"Anyway, I know what you mean. This place is just so friggin' boring. I've hated sitting in here with you when I visit, but didn't want to hurt your feelings. Why did you buy everything the same? Why is everything so pale?" She questions while looking around my ugly apartment.

"Um, I didn't know what colors were safe," I whisper. "I mean, I know red is out, but I didn't want to be too dramatic in case something bad happened," I confess pathetically.

"Oh, come here..." she says walking toward me.

When she wraps me up in a huge hug I feel better instantly. She just has that thing about her. She is tough and strong and very sarcastic and kick your ass awesome, but she's also the most gentle, sympathetic people I've ever known. She's the perfect best friend for someone like me.

Whispering in my ear, she says, "You're okay with color, Suzanne. It's just red that's a problem, and we can make this living room better without any red. Just breathe and relax, okay? You'll be fine, and I'll shop this place fabulous in minutes. Are you ready?"

Releasing my tension I nod, and grab my purse for another shopping marathon with Kayla.

"But no hideous orange couches or crazy purple chairs. Understood?" I say sternly.

"Why not? You love my purple chair." And I totally do.

"I know but that's at your place, and it's the 'Suzanne purple chair' at YOUR place, but I don't want that in my apartment... It's just too weird."

Grinning, Mack nods his agreement behind Kayla's back making me laugh, until she gives me her funny death glare. Ooops.

*****

Four and a half hours later we're done and back in my apartment, and we did well, too. A few things Kayla picked out were completely insane, but otherwise she picked furniture, and pictures, and vases, and knick-knacks that were colored but not over the top.

God, I had so much fun with them. Mack and I were strangely the reasonably sane to Kayla's crazy *what the fuck?* moments. She even accused me and Mack of ganging up on her and being too boring for our own good. She teased and taunted poor Mack the whole time, and I could see he absolutely adored it.

And during our shopping trip I realized I was never sad or jealous watching them together. Okay, I was *a little* sad and jealous, but overall I just enjoyed watching them together. There was so much humor and laughter, and little reassuring touches between them that I watched with a sense of awe.

Kayla is just so *Kayla* and Mack loves her for it- you can see it all over his face. And honestly, though I of course thought of all I don't have, I was happier watching what they do have. They are just lovely together.

Today was about my apartment, but it wasn't about me, per se. It was just three friends shopping, having fun, laughing and living easily. I never once freaked out or needed a moment, and I never once lost my breath. I didn't focus on the few stares I received. And I ignored one woman who blatantly stared at me- The hugely prego, limpy, scarred chick. I was good, and it was one of the best days of my life, which is actually kind of sad, but the truth nonetheless.

When we open my door, Mack dramatically stumbles to the dining room table and proceeds to dump all the bags he had to carry for me. Kayla follows his lead, and I bring up the rear with my 3 bags. Suddenly the table seems filled with bags, and I'm excited to rip them all open.

"I'm going to call in dinner for us. Chinese?" Mack asks.

"God, yes!" Kayla yells as I nod as well. "And get double for

Suzanne!" What?! Ha!
  And as soon as Mack leaves for the spare room, we start. Blasting music from my iPad stereo, Kayla looks like she's on a total mission. Pulling and unwrapping and opening bags while shaking her ass to the music, within minutes there's stuff everywhere and it's just so much fun.
  Kayla starts running around my apartment at once. I don't even know what she's placing where, but she just keeps coming back and forth to the table taking more and more stuff with her when she leaves. Actually, I can barely keep up with all the unwrapping.
  Exhaling when I've opened the last bag, I look around and already my place seems a million times better. Even without the new love seat and chair she made me buy, everything looks great. Knowing the furniture is to be dropped off sometime before 7:00 tonight I'm suddenly super excited to see them arrive.
  "I love it already Kayla. You are so good at this, even with the color block you had to gently navigate around," I smirk.
  "It really is weird how much stuff has red in it, isn't it? I never noticed that before, but we managed."
  "We did. Thank you for helping me," I say as Mack walks past us for the kitchen.
  "I'm a New Yawker. I'll use any excuse to shop, and spending a fortune with someone else's money is really fun, though I'll admit I feel a certain possessiveness now about your apartment. You'll have to give me a key so I feel like its mine too, okay?"
  "Sure!"
  And for some reason Kayla's demand for a key makes me even happier. Really, it does. I love that she wants to have a key because it means we're as close as I hope to be with her. Giving her a key to my first apartment is special to me.
  "No tears, Suzanne," she whispers.
  Shaking my head, I smile. "They're good ones. Thank you for wanting a key to my apartment."
  "No problem. I figure since we're sharing my boyfriend, why not your apartment too." *WHAT?!*

Bursting out laughing, I hug my beautiful, tall, super sexy best friend and just feel happy. Today has been a really good day. This has been the happiest day I've had since I woke up. This is such a simple day, but I know it's a day I'll remember forever.

When dinner is over and the kitchen is clean, I feel absolutely exhausted. The movers brought my new furniture when we were eating, and finally plopping my huge ass in my new chair feels great. It's such a cool, velvety eggplant color, I love it.
It's kind of black for me, and kind of purple for Kayla. And judging by the look she gave me when I got to the chair first, I think she and I are going to fight over this chair whenever she visits.
"Do you mind if I spend the night here? I'm too tired to go back to Mack's."
"No! I don't mind... That's great. Mack?"
"Nah, I'll leave you two alone. I have a feeling you or me or both of us will be blushing before long with her. So I'll leave her to you, Suzanne."
Walking to Kayla on the couch Mack leans down and places a soft kiss on her lips. Watching, I'm mesmerized by the sweetness between them.
After the kiss, Kayla grins and asks, "Please sir, may I have another?" Just like Oliver Twist did, though she absolutely *slaughtered* the English accent.
When Mack leans back down, I can't stop staring at them. When I see him smile at her so beautifully, I'm just stunned by them. They are so easy with each other. They're so good with each other, and again, though somewhat jealous, I'm not overcome with it- I'm amazed by it because their love is so beautiful to me.
Walking to me, Mack leans in and kisses my forehead like he always does. Looking back at Kayla, she fakes a snarl at me and I laugh again with a cheeky 'He kissed me! He kissed me!' smirk of my own when Mack turns his back.
"Good night ladies. I'll see you in the morning. And behave,"

Mack threatens us.

"As if..." is all Kayla says under her breath as Mack turns to leave.

Once he's left us, I realize how tired I really am. Being almost 7 months pregnant, power-shopping, and eating way too much Chinese food has worn me out.

"Suzanne, why don't you go to bed? It's already 10:00, and I'm just going to watch a little TV before crashing myself."

"But this isn't a very good sleepover. We haven't trashed anyone, got drunk, or even did our nails and make-up yet," I grin.

"In the morning we're doing all that. No worries. Go to sleep, Suzanne. You look like shit."

"Jesus! You're brutal you know that?"

"I know, but I'm kind of funny."

"Uh huh. Kind of... Good night, Kayla," I yawn before making my way to my room.

Getting into bed five minutes later, I'm still happy. I'm totally, completely happy, smiling alone in my room. There is no upset, and there are no memories surfacing to torture me. I just had a good day from start to finish with my friends, and I'm happy.

Closing my eyes, I think of my new Kayla/Suzanne eggplant chair and I grin. Kayla wouldn't dare push a pregnant woman from the chair, would she? Huh. She might.

*****

"Suzanne, wake up. Suzanne, it's Kayla," she says at my side.

"What's wrong?" I rasp in my half sleep.

"You're crying and moaning, and-" Really?

"Oh... sorry."

Feeling my face, I'm wet and snotty, and obviously crying my eyes out all over my pillow. Gross. Watching Kayla walk into my bathroom I know she's in full nurse mode, which I don't want.

"Kayla! I'm fine. I'll do it," but she's back with a washcloth before I even sit up.

Handing the cloth to me she asks, 'may I?' as she crawls into my bed. Lying down on the pillows beside me, she lies on her side and stares at me until I mirror her exact position.

"What was it about? Which bad part?" Um...

Looking at her, and breathing heavily through the leftover upset, and knowing I can trust her, knowing I can tell her anything, I just spill it.

"I miss him so much," I exhale on a rush.

"And...?"

"That's it. I just miss everything about him. I love him and I miss him."

"And...?" She grins at my annoyed face.

"Okay, fine. Z and I have had one week of hell until I went away. One day of hell that made me send him away, and one night that was the most amazing night of my life until I went away again. That's it. One bad week, one horrible day, and one amazing night. But I love him and I miss him so much I can't stand this pain all the time. And I think I'm stupid for having feelings like this for a man that I've only really, if you take out the bad stuff, um... I've really only had one good night with him when I got better, but I'm in love with him, and I miss him so much I cry in my sleep because I hold it in all day."

After I confess, I just stop and wait, but *she's* waiting too. Dammit.

"Do you think it's weird, or unrealistic for me to think I'm in love with a man I've had one amazing night with after I got better 7 months ago? Be honest."

"When am I not?" She asks seriously. True. She's brutal sometimes. "Honesty, right?"

Oh god, I don't think this'll go well for me, but I nod 'yes' anyway.

"I knew with Mack. The millisecond I saw him at the hospital, I knew. He wasn't flashy, or smarmy or like an obnoxious, *I'M the Doctor*-Doctor. And when I heard him speak to a patient so kindly, I knew I was going to love him. I knew it, but I did nothing about it because I was actually afraid to."
"Really?" Wow.
"Yes, Suzanne. I was afraid to approach him, and Mack was too professional to approach me. So I just waited and watched and liked him from afar, until you pushed me down his throat and worked your magic on us. But I always knew I was going to love him one day. I think that's probably why I'm so amazing to you..." Smirk "... And why I put up with so much shit from you, and why I love you so much in spite of what an insecure, neurotic, crazy, pain in the ass you can be." What?! But then she smiles, and I know she's teasing me.
"Anyway, I knew with Mack the moment I met him, so why can't you love Z even though you've really had no time together? Z is smart, and kind, and selfless, and gorgeous, and *totally* not a typical rich New York kind of guy. And despite everything you've both been through, he loves you. I can see it. *Everyone* sees it. And he has made no secret of his feelings for you. Apparently, he and Marty even had a slightly heated argument over you once." Flinching, Kayla takes my hand.
"It's fine. *They're* fine. Marty just didn't get it, and he hated seeing Z in Chicago waiting on this girl in a coma, then waiting for the girl to know him, then waiting while the girl broke his heart over the baby..." Flinch again. Shit. I hate honesty.
"Anyway, Z apparently told Marty how he felt about you. He told Marty *everything* he felt for you. And finally Marty listened and understood and they're fine now, I swear. Marty is 37 and single, and actually perfect for Kayla, but that's another story..." Really? I never thought of that, but maybe?
"So you love a man who has shown you absolute devotion no matter what happens, and no matter what you put him through. So what's not to love? Why wouldn't you miss him? Z is tied with Mack in the unbelievably amazing male department as far as I'm

concerned. I love him dearly, and I wish for some peace for him, just like I wish for some happiness and peace for you."

Looking at her eyes, Kayla seems so devastated by this situation, which makes me feel more guilty and awful and just so sad for Z.

"I wish I could change, I really do. But I can't. And I don't want to fake it, and there's nothing I can do to change the way I feel about this pregnancy, and... Yes, I love him and I miss him but I can't be and do want he wants and needs. So I can't be with him like that."

"I agree. And that's why I haven't ever given you shit for all this pain you're causing Z and yourself. For once, though it kills me to see you both hurt this badly, I absolutely agree with you. I don't think you should be together based on faking feelings or because you pretend to be happy in a situation you're truly not happy with."

"Really?" I ask stunned.

"Yes. Mack wants you to be with Z. And obviously Z wants you to want him and this baby. But you don't want that, so I support you doing this the best way you can. Look, I don't know why you feel so negatively about this baby and I have no idea why you think you can't be a mother, but I also haven't suffered like you have so I'll probably never understand the psychological reasons behind you feeling the way you do."

"I can't explain it or... I'm not sure what to say anymore."

"I don't know if you're aware of this but your eyes are just devastating to look at, Suzanne, and they always tell us so much. Seriously, I can't even explain it to you. Yes, they're very beautiful and so blue they're gorgeous, but there's something else. There is something so sad in your eyes... No, not sad. It's more like painful or something. It's like we can see all the pain and the nightmares in your eyes. And it's horrible to see, Suzanne.

"...Mack once spoke to me about looking at you and how hard it is for him some days, because you can't hide anything from anyone with your eyes. They are just so expressive and so beautifully heartbreaking. Some days when you talk to me about little, nothing things I see this look in your eyes that tells me you are fighting your nightmares and your past so hard, and I just want to hug you so badly to make those demons in your eyes go away."

I can't help but choke up at her words. I thought I was hiding everything. I thought I had them fooled. I thought I looked like I was all better now.

"So all I can do is support your decision regarding this situation because you think it is best, even though I DO think you're wrong about this. I *know* you would make an excellent mother, but you don't think you will, so I'm supporting your decision, whether I agree with you or not." Ex-hale...

"Thank you, Kayla. I've been so alone with this and it's been killing me. I know I must seem a horrible person, and I know everyone feels so badly for Z, and I get it. I understand how hard this is for him, I really do. But I just don't want this at all. So hurting him for now is all I can do. But he gets the baby when this is all over. So maybe he'll forgive me for all this upset and pain afterward when he has the baby."

"Probably. He loves you Suzanne very much and he's never hated you, so he probably will forgive you once he has his child. It's just so hard on him, and on you, I know. This whole thing just sucks. And Mack and I wish there was a way to make this work but since you don't think there is, I support you one hundred percent in this decision you've made."

Breathing a 'thanks' I just look at this stunning woman and thank god she's here. Wiping my eyes again, I don't know what I would do without her and Mack in my life.

"I love you so much, Kayla. And I'm so grateful you're here," I whisper.

"I love you too, Suzanne. And it's okay to love him and it's okay to miss him. I love Z. He is truly amazing. And if he ever does move on or if *you* ever move on, I think you two will have a very special love for each other always. You've been through too much to not have a special love for each other. Also, you will always be his baby's mother, which Z will know every time he looks at the baby, so that's pretty special too. That makes YOU pretty special to Z."

"I hope so..." and that's it. I have nothing else to give her. I have no more words because I've said them all. This situation does suck, but it's the best thing for us right now. I'm sure of it.

Feeling exhaustion settle in, I glance over Kayla's shoulder and see its 4:11am.

"Go back to sleep. But I'm gonna sleep here, okay?"

"Yes, please," I breathe.

Suddenly flipping over, Kayla shakes her ass rather dramatically bouncing the whole bed, making me giggle as she fakes stretching out to get comfortable.

God, I love her Kayla-ness.

"Oh, and you owe me a huge breakfast in the morning for my awesomeness," she says with her best smile-voice. "*And* I'm eating in my new PURPLE chair."

"Okay..." I smile right back.

CHAPTER 31

AUGUST 20

Hearing the knock and looking thought the peep-hole I see Marcus. What the hell? Um, should I? Shouldn't I? There's a restraining order against him but I owe him, I think.
 Opening the door, I pull in a big breath, place a fake Suzanne-smile on my ugly face and wait.
 While smiling back at me, seconds pass in silence.
 "Hi. Can I come in for a minute?" He asks timidly, like maybe he's not allowed to be here, which he isn't actually. Duh.
 "Um, sure. How are you?"
 "I'm good. Wow. Look at you. You're huge, Suzanne."
 "I know. I'm a house, and I have 2 months to go." Do we talk about this? Do we not? This seems like a major awkward between us. Waiting, I don't know what else to say.
 "Well, you make a lovely 'house', Suzanne. And the scars are barely noticeable now, which is good." Huh. Nobody brings up the scars, so why did he? I feel annoyed already and he's said, like, 3 sentences so far. *Awesome.*
 "How can I help you, Marcus?" I ask slightly clipped.
 "You can't... I just wanted to see how you were. I have to testify later at your mother's trial, you know, about things she said and did to you when we were together. So I wanted to talk to you about it first." Shit.
 "I don't really want to talk about that stuff, Marcus. I'm not comfortable talking about it, and I don't think we're really supposed to anyway. Legally."
 When Marcus walks past me into my living room, I'm suddenly very uncomfortable.
 "Mack should be here soon. Would you like to see Mack when he gets here?"

"Not really, why? Do I *seem* like I should see Mack?" Um...

"No, of course not. I'm just not sure why you're here," I say keeping a slight distance between us.

Walking to the end table, I start rearranging the magazines, and pick up my iPhone while casually hiding it with a magazine. Trying to slide open the face without him noticing, I feel like I *need* Mack. I don't know why, but I feel nervous and uncomfortable... and just scared.

"Suzanne, what's wrong? You're not even looking at me. You always looked at me before but you're not now. Are we okay?" Nope. Not really.

"We're fine, Marcus," I lie while smiling at him. Making eye contact is hard, but I hold it. "Mack's going to be here any minute and we're going to the movies, so I have to finish getting ready, but it was nice seeing you again. Why don't you give me a call once in a while and let me know what's going on with you. I'd like to keep in touch."

"Good, Suzanne," he replies staring at me. Good, *what?*

Oh god, something's wrong. I can feel it all over my skin. This is not right.

Grasping for anything I ask, "Would you like some coffee?" as I turn for my kitchen.

With my back to him, I quickly look at my phone, pull up the contacts list and scroll for Mack. Please! Scrolling while trying not to look, I hit Mack and make a connection.

"Suzanne, what's wrong? You seem so uncomfortable, like you're afraid of me? I wouldn't hurt you. You *know* that, don't you?"

"Of course, MARCUS," I smile. "I'm not uncomfortable, I'm just surprised to see you at. my. apartment. MARCUS. Would you like some coffee?" Jesus... could I be any *more* obvious.

"No, and you shouldn't be drinking coffee either. Caffeine isn't good for the baby, Suzanne, and I'm surprised you would do something so detrimental to its health. That's very irresponsible of you," he says shaking his head at me. What the hell?

"I know. I don't! I just have decaf when I want the taste, but I don't drink regular coffee anymore." Christ! This is weird. A lecture about coffee?

"That's good. I wouldn't want to be disappointed in you again." *Again?!*

"Well, I'm going to make some for myself, I'll just be a minute-"

"Do you like my shoes, Suzanne?"

Spinning around, I look at Marcus' shoes. What the FUCK?! Converse? I swear to god, everything is getting really weird. *Converse?!*

"Um, cute. I never took you as the Converse-type, Marcus. Cole Haans yes, but Converse?"

I suddenly burst out laughing. Okay, totally weird. But Marcus is laughing with me so I think he knows how weird this is.

Looking at him still laughing I remember how sweet he used to be to me. The memories of early Marcus are so kind and gentle. He was such a gentleman and I always knew he would be good for me back then. Suddenly remembering the kindness we had in the beginning, I find it so sad that we really weren't good for each other in the end.

But Converse? What the hell? This is so strange, and breathing slowly I realize I'm very afraid.

Suddenly, my stomach is in knots and the world is spinning around me. There is a darkness that wants to consume me, but I can't give into it. I'm too afraid this time to give into the darkness. This isn't my body anymore. This isn't Marcus' body anymore. I can't close my eyes this time because I have to protect this body for now. For Z.

Why is he here?

"Do you remember me, Honey?"

Gagging, I hold my stomach trying desperately not to throw up. Staring at Marcus shoes, gagging even harder I can't hold it in. Vomiting all over the floor near the kitchen doorway, I think I remember this.

"Do you remember me, HONEY?" Argh... Stop *saying* that.

Looking closely, Marcus is so still while waiting and watching me. He's so still watching me watching him. What's happening? As the room tilts, I reach out slowly for the kitchen doorframe. In slow motion I'm watching myself fall as Marcus rushes and grabs for me. Holding me as I crumble, I remember him.

Whispering in my ear as he holds me tightly on the floor he asks, "Do you remember me, Honey?" Oh, no...

"I remember you-"

"*Honey...* Do. you. remember. me?" Fuck! Stop *asking* me that! Oh god. This is all wrong. Looking at Marcus' shoes, I remember. Marcus was at Simmons hospital. Oh god, it was Marcus!

Sickness, spinning, screams... then silence. I remember. I saw his face. That's why I wasn't afraid of him. That's why I let him clean up my legs all those times I cut myself. That's why I let him touch me when I was young- because he did it before.

I remember him cleaning between my legs now. I remember him untying my ankles before he cleaned Dr. Simmons' saliva from between my legs. Oh. My. God.

Suddenly gasping and spinning and throwing up again at our sides, Marcus squeezes me tighter, holding both my wrists in one of his hands, while his other hand finger combs my hair. But I don't want this.

I remember.

Marcus' eyes were staring as the sickness washed over me. Dr. Simmons going down on me, licking and sucking, and pushing my thighs as far as they could go with the restraints. I was crying out but unable to move. I was tied down, restrained through the madness and chaos in my mind. I was a broken deadened body that could not move. And did not feel.

I remember Marcus watching from the bathroom doorway. Oh, I see me. Throughout the many sexual tortures, as tears spilled from my eyes, I lay frozen hearing Simmons moaning and lapping up my young body. And turning my head I see Marcus and his red converse so still in the doorway, watching as Simmons abuses me.

Moaning, "Marcus..."

Whooosh. I can't inhale. My breath is quick little hitches and broken gasps as my lungs burn for air.

I remember his eyes on me, always. He always watched and waited. Oh god... This sickness is overwhelming me. Unable to move and unable to breathe, the darkness is all around me.

Holding me tight, Marcus turns my ugly puke-covered face toward him and kisses my lips. I'm restrained by him and I. Can. Not. Move.

Oh god, it's going to happen again.

Whispering, "I didn't know what to do then so I took care of you after. He was your Doctor and I was in my second year of college. It was an accounting placement I got because of my association with the Country Club. My uncle Langdon was a member, remember? Anyway, I was only in the office but then I saw you crying once in the hall and I instantly recognized you. I knew you were Suzanne Beaumont and I had to see you again. So I watched out for you when I was there, and I cared for you after."

As Marcus whispers his confession I'm still trapped by his hands, but I couldn't move even if I wanted to. My world is spinning and the darkness is trying to swallow me whole. There is nothing I can do but let Marcus confess his part in this.

"Um, I watched what he did to you and I liked it. I'm sorry, but I did. It was gross and rude and completely inappropriate, but I honestly like watching. I'm sorry to admit that Honey, but I did like it."

I have no words. I have no voice in this moment.

Continuing, he kisses my lips again, and seems to breathe his filthy confession into my body.

"I only saw what he did 6 times but I have to tell them about it today, because your mother's defense team is trying to push Simmons as the main abuser in all this. I think with your mother's past, she's trying to say Simmons made her insane as well. It's going to come out today what I saw and what I knew, but I've been given immunity from any prosecution from the D.A. for my statement. I guess I just wanted you to know my side first. When I told her I knew about Simmons, she said I could have you, too. She knew I knew all along and that's why she gave you to me to love." Flinch. "But now she's going to tell everyone what I knew, so I wanted to tell you first."

I still have nothing but my silence in this nightmare.

"I'm very sorry I didn't stop Simmons. And I'm very sorry that I liked watching it, but I took care of you afterward. I did. So it's all okay. I went to the Club every chance I got to care for you, and I told your mother that I loved you and would care for you always. And I did care for you, until you threw it all away. I cared for you, doing everything you wanted and giving anything you needed when we were together. But I never performed cunnilingus on you like Simmons did. Did I, Honey?" FLINCH!

Shaking his head, Marcus seems to wake up to this situation suddenly. His voice is strong again and his words are no longer whispered. He sounds like the old Marcus I remember.

"Let me help you up. You shouldn't be on the floor, Suzanne. I'm sure it's not good for you in your condition."

When I stay silent and still, Marcus lets go of my arms, turns from me, rises, and slowly picks me up in his arms again. Grunting from my weight, he begins taking me toward my room.

In this moment I'm so scared, I want to scream and fight, but my muscles won't move and I have no breath to scream.

This is the end of me.

Laying me on the guest-room bed, Marcus lifts the blanket at the end and surrounds me in warmth. Brushing my hair out of my face and bending down low, he kisses my lips again.

"I love you, Honey. Forever. But I took care of you so I did nothing wrong. You can't be mad at me, and you can't blame ME for any of this. This was all Simmons and your mother and the other men, okay?"

Nodding my agreement, I'm too afraid to do anything else. Actually, I CAN'T do anything else. My tears won't even fall from my eyes, and my breath is barely a wheeze.

I am nothing in this moment.

As Marcus climbs onto the bed, my whole body shakes with the terror. My teeth are chattering and my eyes are wide. My breathing is slow and almost a hiccup in my lungs. My world is turning dark all around me.

Fighting to find my voice, my head threatens to explode. This is the end.

When I feel Marcus grab my breast, my body flinches in pain. When I feel him begin tugging at my waistband, I know...

Dying, I finally find a little voice and whisper, "please don't r-rape me..."

Pause.

"Jesus, Suzanne! It's not RAPE! We're married, okay? You don't understand. You *never* understand. I love you, that's why we should make love. That should be MY baby inside you because we love each other, and because we're MARRIED!" He roars in my face.

Suddenly, Marcus jumps up from the bed and glares down at me. Grabbing my hair hard on both sides of my face, Marcus pins me to the pillow and growls in my face as I stare into his dark eyes.

"I took care of you because I've always loved you."

Marcus suddenly pushes off my face with his hands while moving away from the bed. When he turns to me shaking and angry, we stare at each other yet there is nothing but agony in this moment between us. I feel the agony inside my soul, and I see the agony in Marcus' eyes.

This is the end.

When Marcus moves away from me, I turn my head to look at him. Marcus is still staring at me as the darkness washes over me. I am crying out but unable to move. I am tied down and restrained by the madness and chaos in my mind. I am a broken, shaking body that can. not. move, and Does. Not. Feel.

Turning my head I don't want to see Marcus and his red converse so still, watching me again from another doorway.

Moaning, and shaking my head no, I look back and watch his red shoes leave the guest-room as my world collapses around me.

Darkness.

I am gone...

*****

Waking to the chaos of Police and EMT's, I'm taken to the hospital again.
I don't know how they found me and I don't care. I never want to be in that guest-room again.
Opening my eyes in the ambulance, I look at the female as she continues touching me and the machines.
"Welcome back. You're doing much better. Can you tell me your name?" She questions.
Moving my hand slowly to my stomach, I ask without words.
"Your heart rate has stabilized, and your breathing is under control. Your baby's heart rate is a little low but they'll monitor it closely at the hospital. Otherwise, you're stable."
Exhaling, I nod. The mask on my face is really annoying but I think I need it still to breathe.
"How did you find me?" I groan.
"Your husband called 911 and said you were in distress but he wasn't there with you to help you. So the police entered first, followed by us. We found you unconscious on the floor in the hallway. Can you tell me what happened?"
No. I don't think I can ever tell anyone way happened. I don't think I'll ever understand what happened. What happened to the Marcus I knew?
"Are you okay? Your heart rate is increasing again. Are you in distress?"
Nodding frantically, I *am* in distress. And I am so tired again.
God, I need a rest from my nightmares.

CHAPTER 32

9 hours later, I finally let Mack enter my hospital room to take me home. I know Mack, Chicago Kayla and Z have been waiting because the Doctors told me, but I wasn't ready for them. I just couldn't face them and all this insanity, again.

No more tests are needed and I'm fine to leave. The baby is fine, but a follow up appointment was already made with my OBGYN for tomorrow, just in case.

The panic-attack is long gone. And the shock of today is buried deep within me right now, so I'm free to leave.

The police have been and left twice but we're through with each other, at least for tonight they said. There may be more follow-up questions tomorrow, however.

Watching as Mack throws open the door rushing to me, I feel dead inside.

Before he can even speak, I raise my hand in the classic Mack/Suzanne fashion of 'Do NOT speak. This is MY turn' and I beg, "Can you please take me home and stay with me tonight? Just for tonight, I promise."

Nodding, Mack chokes up and hugs me silently. I see his upset and I feel his shaking body, but I feel nothing inside me for either of us in this moment.

"And I'm not talking tonight to you or anyone else. Not in the car and not at home. Just not tonight, Mack," I cry.

"Okay, Suzanne," he gives in with a tighter hug.

Walking quietly into my apartment I smell the vomit at once. Huh. I think I'm surprised no one has cleaned it up yet. Then again, who would've? Gagging again as I cover my face, I turn from the room and walk toward the balcony. Shit. Where can I go?

"I need to lie down, Mack. Can you please close the guest-room door."

"Okay. Can I get you anything else? Are you hungry? Do you need a-"

"I need nothing. Just give me a minute alone, and then I'm going to sleep this nightmare away. That's what I want."

And turning, I give Mack no chance to talk and no chance to corner me with his 'talk to me' face. I'm done today. *This* has been another horrible day.

Once I'm ready, I change into my favorite black maternity yoga pants and a huge T-shirt and I slowly make my way to bed. I've never felt this tired in my life. This is an exhaustion living within every single cell of my body. This is full, complete, mind-numbing exhaustion.

When I feel the bed dip beside me I don't even look over. I'm never afraid of Mack and I know there's no one else here anymore to hurt me.

So whispering, I give all I can in this exhaustion. "Thanks, Mack. I'll talk tomorrow. But not now, okay?"

"Just sleep, Suzanne. And I'll be here when you need me."

"Thank you. Good night, Mack."

And feeling Mack lean in, OVER the covers, he kisses the back of my head briefly and then I feel him move away slowly.

The end. Today is over.

I would cry if I could, but I can't. And I would talk if I could, but I have no words. The sense of betrayal and pain is too heavy on my chest to be spoken of just yet.

Getting comfortable, my last image as sleep claims me is of Red. Fucking. Converse.

*****

So Marty received the call I made because apparently I scrolled one too many on my phone. What a shock for him to come home late yesterday afternoon to hearing me talk on his machine. I've never called Marty before, and I only had his number because Mack programmed my iPhone. And though my words were mumbled and too quiet to actually hear clearly, Marty did pick up the name Marcus. Once he eventually figured it out with a call back to my number, he called Z and Mack.

After calling Mack, Mack called the Police as he was rushing to my apartment. But by then everything was over anyway. Marcus, *my husband* had already called 911 to help me with my 'distress'.

The Police have heard the message Marty received which abruptly stops around the time I landed on the floor with Marcus. Maybe I landed ON my phone with my huge ass and that's why they can't hear anything else. Maybe my huge ass smothered the phone. Giggle. Shit.

Marcus is dead.

Marcus is dead from an apparent self-inflicted gunshot wound to his right temple. And he left a note for me.

In my warped mind, I think I'm more surprised Marcus had a gun, then the fact that he actually killed himself with it.

After he testified yesterday Marcus left the courtroom normally, agreeing to be recalled to the stand should either the Defense or the D.A. need clarification of his statements.

Hours later, the Police waited to question him about what happened between us after they found out about the incident in my apartment. I guess he was in trouble for breaching the restraining order between us.

And that's when he was found. The front door to my old house was left wide open and the note to me was taped right on the opened door. The envelope even had 'come in' written on it. And so they entered.

Hearing they found Marcus in the shower was kind of funny to me. It's like he was so intent on not making a mess, he blew his brains out in the shower so it could be easily cleaned. Or at least knowing how anal-retentive the old Marcus was, that's what I have to assume.

In a weird way, I find it comforting that he was just as anal in the end as he had always been about cleanliness in life. I think I like to believe he was still the same as before in the end, and not so totally screwed up that he wasn't the old Marcus anymore. Or maybe I just hope that's the case so I can be angry at him instead of sad for him, which I really, *really* am right now. Actually, I'm devastated that a man who loved me killed himself because of anything to do with me.

So, Marcus is dead from an apparent self-inflicted gunshot wound to his right temple. And he left a note for me.

I am now 'Marcus Anderson's pregnant by another man, scarred, sexually abused, emotionally unstable, teetering back into the depths of insanity, *WIDOW'*. Well, at least according to the news I watched on TV this morning.

Bursting out laughing again, I know Mack is listening for me in the hallway. I know he's still awesome. I know he's waiting for me to need him, and I know I *will* need him. Just not yet. Right now I'm totally in shock which is making me laugh and giggle at all this insanity.

I wonder if my mother cares Marcus is dead? She always did love him more- almost like a *real* child of her own. I bet if she was capable of feeling love for anyone but herself she would care Marcus is dead. I bet she wishes it was me instead. Giggle. Ugh... I'm still warped.

I still have the photocopy of the note from Marcus to read, which I don't want to do.

I still have a funeral to plan for Marcus, which I don't want to do.

I still have a baby inside me I have to care for, which is getting harder to do. But I will.

THIS is me...

Leaning over, I flick on the lamp, drink a sip of orange juice, eat another Saltine, pick up the note, and sit up against my pillows preparing for this.

Unfolding the photocopied version the Police gave me with remarkably steady hands, I'm ready.

I have no tears still and I feel calm. I mean really, what else could he possibly say to me that he hasn't already confessed?

Suzanne,

I'm sorry it came to this. I didn't mean to hurt you, and I know lying to you all these years hurt you, but I didn't know what else to do. If I hadn't lied to you, your parents were going to keep you away from me- they said they would take you away from me. So I didn't tell you what I knew, even though you didn't know I knew anyway.

I do want you to know I'm not mad at you anymore, and I'm sorry if I ever hurt you. But I'd be lying if I said I didn't like you having a hard life before. I liked when you were messed up because it meant you needed me, and I always liked you needing me. I took care of you for so long that I didn't know how to live without you needing me all the time once you became better.

So I'm doing this because I'm too embarrassed by you and our relationship to keep going. My co-workers all think I'm a pervert. They all wonder why I didn't know about the abuse over the years, and they all question me and accuse me behind my back all the time. Everyone thinks I'm a man who may have contributed to his wife's decline and I don't like that. So admitting now in court that I did know about some of the events will make this so much worse for me.

I love you, even if you don't believe me, but I do. I'm sorry if my death will upset you, but I'm just too embarrassed by all my involvement with you and your past to continue like this.

Marcus Anderson xo

Okay. Wow. Marcus *Anderson*? Like there was ever any doubt. What an idiot!

Huh. At least I don't feel so bad anymore about his death. Well, I mean I *do*, but not as much. What a *fucking* asshole! Even in his suicide letter he talks about HIS appearance and HIS embarrassment? Christ! His suicide note reads like a break-up with some woman who hurt and embarrassed *him*? Well... Fuck. HIM!

He knew about it all! He told me he knew! He knew and he played along and lied to ME so he could keep me, and I'VE embarrassed him? What a FUCKING ASSHOLE!

Bursting out laughing, Mack suddenly opens my door. Looking at him, I just laugh and shake my head.

"Well, Marcus was still a prick, Mack. Even in death. Read this crap!"

Walking to me, Mack sits on the side of my bed and takes the note from my shaking hand. Reading it, I actually see his breathing becoming harder, and I watch him flinch once. Ha! Mack sees it.

Refolding the note, Mack's about to speak but I cut him off.

"I'm not going to the funeral. I'm not even *preparing* the funeral. Could you please call his mother for me and tell her to take care of the arrangements. She can have his money and the house, and everything else she wants, because I really don't care about any of this anymore. I don't want anything to do with this."

"Are you sure? Maybe you need a little closure?" He asks gently.

"I'm sure. I have my closure. That note is all the closure I will EVER need. I'm done. The Marcus/Suzanne facade is finally over. I feel nothing but disgust, and I'm okay with that. I'm sorry he's dead, but I don't care for him, or miss him, or love him or anything else. He's just gone to me. Would you please call his mother?"

"Of course, but-"

"Nothing Mack. There is nothing to say, and I want nothing from this. He knew! When this all came out last year he knew but he still didn't tell me. He let me think I was a sexual Psycho to him, which I guess I still was- but he knew *why* all along! He knew forever! He could have come forward then about Simmons but he didn't. He could've stopped Simmons years ago, but he didn't. He let me go back to him and he let me believe he was the wonderful man I thought he was. He knew..."

"Marcus was desperate Suzanne and he made mis-"

"If you defend anything he did I'm going to absolutely lose it!"

"I would NEVER, Suzanne! I was just trying to explain that Marcus needed you to be weak so badly that he maintained the lie so you would continue to need him."

"It doesn't matter why anymore, Mack. Please just make the call to his mother and leave me alone for a while. I have to go see the Doctor in 2 hours and I want to be alone until then. Please Mack?"

Sighing, he begs, "Would you please see or call Z? He's beside himself with worry for-"

"The baby is fine-"

"Worry for YOU, Suzanne. Do you understand what I'm saying? In this moment Z is worried about you and he wants to talk to YOU. He wants to help in any way he can. He is stunned by what happened, and he is dying to reach out to YOU. This is about you Suzanne, and nothing else."

"No, thanks. Just tell him I'm fine and his baby is fine, and everything else is fine. But I need some time Mack."

"Suzanne, I just want to sit with you and be here to comfort you when-"

"No. I appreciate it, but I'm fine. Please leave me alone until the appointment. That's what I need."

Exhaling a hard breath, I can see Mack is completely frustrated with me. I can see he's trying, but I just don't want it. Not about this. This is mine, and mine alone.

"Just give me a little time, Mack," I whisper.

Muttering an 'okay', he rises from my bed as I reach out for his hand. I owe him *something,* I know I do.

"I love you forever, Mack, and I really am fine this time. I

promise I'll talk to you later, okay?"
"Whenever you're ready, Suzanne," he exhales. And with that, he smiles his beautiful Mack smile and leaves me alone in my room.

And I am fine. I'm angry and hurt, and betrayed and sad for Marcus, but I'm going to be okay.
Marcus is an asshole, and I'm glad I know the truth so I don't mourn him unnecessarily. I will mourn the man I thought he was, and I'll mourn the man who thought he had no choice but to do this. I'll mourn a man who was so ridiculous he thought his appearance as less than perfect was reason enough to put a gun to his temple, but I won't mourn my dead husband.
My husband was dead to me the minute he told me he knew about my past and didn't tell me, whether he was actually dead hours later or not.

CHAPTER 33

SEPTEMBER 2

During the 2 months I've been living here alone, a few Reporters found me and my apartment and even made their way *somehow* past the Doorman to approach me. So when I hear the knock on my front door, I'm still a little frightened because I know Mack isn't expected here for another hour or so.
The last time someone found me, I was absolutely stunned when I opened the door expecting to see Mack. So like a moron, I stood dead still as the Reporter took photos of my face quickly before I could slam the door in HIS face just as quickly.
I remember being shocked by the encounter because I didn't know anyone kept tabs on me anymore. And though my mother's trial was still happening, and Marcus had just committed suicide I probably should have known I would become an interest for the papers again, I just didn't. Mack was pretty pissed at himself as well for not thinking about it beforehand.
Afterward, when I calmed down and called Mack to help me, he went a little postal, and told me even Z went completely mental at the Police station. The Doorman was fired from the building, and security was put in place for me again for whenever I leave my apartment for Physio, or any other Doctors' appointments. The whole thing is super dramatic, but Mack and Z both insisted.
And after that last confrontation, there I was on the front page of the Chicago Tribune again, and from what I understood the 4th page of the New York Times as well, because of the New York connection between me and Z, and Z's piece of shit father.
The Reporter told of my pregnancy, mentioned I was *apparently* single, and implied I was having difficulties adapting to my post-nuthouse life due to post-traumatic stress disorder. He told of my hideous burns from the crash, mentioned my nervous breakdown,

and highlighted my suicide attempt because of all I had had to endure at the hands of my mother, Dr. Simmons and the men. He basically painted a picture of the most whacked-out, knocked-up, pathetic PTSD victim ever. What an asshole!

I remember just staring at the newspaper crying my eyes out because I was pretty gross in the picture, too. Seeing myself WITHOUT make-up was damaging to my mental health, for sure. I looked like the gross little victim the paper made me out to be. I became the young girl whose horrible life was a series of unfortunate events of trauma, looking like a traumatized unfortunate victim of the horrible events.

Later that night, Z and I spoke on the phone for the first time since the hospital. It was such a strange, sad conversation I had to have with Z- so strange I found myself just desperate to be with him again. God, in that moment the weight of my sadness and the want for him was so heavy I felt suffocated by it. And missing him, I was almost desperate enough to beg him to come get me... *Almost.*

When Z called me, he begged me for my sake and for his baby's sake to accept the security again for his peace of mind. And when he worded his request with such desperation and with such sadness in his voice, I absolutely couldn't argue further or refuse him. It was done.

And so Security is in place when I call them to go out, which honestly isn't that often anyway. But it's there waiting, for Z's peace of mind.

Looking through the peephole, I see Mack first, and whooosh... my grandfather. Oh shit! This is going to be bad, *obviously*. I mean, come on! I've spoken to him half a dozen horribly uncomfortable times in the last year, and though he lives in D.C. which really isn't that far from Chicago, I haven't seen him even once since I've been conscious. But he's suddenly here?

Opening the door, Mack walks in with his reassuring smile, my grandfather walks in slowly with a nod, and then suddenly Z follows behind.

Mother *FUCKER!* I didn't see Z through the peephole. Holy shit! This just went from totally sucking to CATASTROPHIC in seconds. Why are they HERE?

"Um..."

"Breathe, Suzanne. Come sit in the living room and talk with me for a minute. Z, could you and Edward wait in the kitchen for a minute?"

Looking behind Mack to my grandfather and Z, I'm beyond nervous. Nothing! Absolutely *nothing* good is going to come from this.

"What's wrong? Is this about Marcus?" I ask confused.

"No. Z and your grandfather are both scheduled to testify, and-"

"Why Z again?" Seriously?

"Because of what you told us in his apartment. The names and people involved."

"But you've already told them everything."

"I did. But now the Prosecutors are trying to set up Z as a second witness to all you said. They don't want my testimony being disputed by the Defense as mere hearsay. Plus, Z found the schoolbook and he needs to explain how he did that before he went to the Police, so the Defense can't claim any entrapment."

"But what about us?" I ask pointing to my stomach. "Everyone will know about me and Z, and they'll know we're not together, and they'll know I'm a terrible person, and they'll know I'm alone and that I made Z lonely, and that I'm pregnant and a terrible person... and Z's so sad and-" I cry.

"Suzanne, I'm okay. I can handle it," I jump when Z suddenly speaks.

"Why are you here?" I beg through my upset.

"Your grandfather has to talk to you before we go to the Courthouse. I was with him when he told me a few things you need to know, so I asked Mack to meet us here."

"But why are YOU here?" Shit, he just flinched a little. "I'm not trying to be mean, but I'm just so confused."

Z and I don't talk, and we never see each other. We have spoken once on the phone, ever. We don't see each other which is good, because honestly, seeing him right now makes me want to beg him to love me anyway, even with this kid I don't want growing inside me.

"I just came as a friend, in case you needed some extra support. That's all, Suzanne. But I can leave if you'd be more comfortable."

Um...

"Thank you for your support. But you should... No, you can stay I guess. It's just hard seeing you and *him* actually," I motion to the kitchen.

Nodding, Z walks back into the kitchen. Returning seconds later with my grandfather, Z takes a seat far from me on a dining room chair, while my grandfather stands awkwardly a few feet away from me.

Huh. Mack WAS right. I hate having a man standing above me like that.

"Hi..." Grandfather? Edward? Mr. Montgomery? Ugh...

"Hello Suzanne, you look lovely." O-Kay. Does he have selective seeing or something? "How are you feeling? I was awfully surprised to hear months ago that you're expecting."

"I'm good. And it was an awful surprise to me as well." Suddenly looking at Z, I feel bad for that one. Ooops... that one slipped.

Nodding, "You have a lovely apartment." Jesus! Can we just do this?

"Thanks. What's wrong? What do you have to tell me?"

"Do you have any refreshments to offer your guests?" He asks with disapproval in his voice. Seriously?! I hate his tone- It's just like I remember from childhood.

"Yes, I do. And Mack and Z can help themselves if they'd like. And so can you. Why are you here?"

"Suzanne, that's not a polite response to-"

"Oh, cut the shit *grandfather!* What do you want? Why. Are.

You. Here?"

Looking, I see Z cover his grin casually with his hand as Mack suddenly squeezes my hand tighter. This is good. Neither is disappointed in me. I can totally do this.

"Just say it. Whatever it is."

"Alright," he says uncomfortably sitting in a chair across from me and Mack. "I'm being subpoenaed today by the Defense to tell the facts surrounding your mother's rape as a child." WHAT?!

Huh. Here's that awesome shock-thing again. Shock is good because it stops me from freaking out *outwardly*, and it makes me stay still while I'm in a nightmare. Nobody really sees me Losing. My. Shit. when I'm in shock.

"I'm sorry...?" I whisper on a gasp.

"When your mother was thirteen, we had some maintenance done on the grounds of our home, and tragically, she was raped by 4 men in the process. Your grandmother and I weren't there at the time, and though we had staff on the grounds they apparently didn't know what was occurring to Elizabeth. Regardless, I fired them all anyway after making them sign a contract to never disclose the events we're discussing." A contract? What the hell? Why does he sound so business-like?

"How is this relevant to me?" God, I sound awesome strong right now but I'm totally faking it.

"After your grandmother and I returned home and found Elizabeth, we tried to help her. We did try, but things were different then. One didn't discuss things like this and a scandal of this nature would have followed your mother forever, so I essentially made it go away."

"Really?" Feeling Mack's sweaty hand in my own is gross, but it's fine. I'm just trying not to barf right now.

"Yes. Your mother was badly abused and we took care of her physically with the aid of a close personal friend who was a Physician, but emotionally we may have failed her."

"Jesus Christ... *Ya think?!*"

"Suzanne!"

"Piss off, *Edward*. Continue."
Shaking his head with disapproval again, he continues.
"When I learned the graphic details of your abuse..." FLINCH! "I knew why she did what she did to you. I knew exactly why she did those things to you in the manner in which she did them, because tragically that's what the men did to her. But your grandmother and I didn't know what to do back then because there weren't many options at the time. It's not like today where there is rape counseling, or therapists readily available..." Pause.
"So we acted as we thought best, which was fairly poorly in hindsight. After bathing and cleaning her wounds, we sent Elizabeth to her bedroom to recover, bringing her food and gifts and anything else she could've ever dreamed of. We did our best, albeit, our best was not very good at all. I know we made mistakes, and I know our mistakes may have hurt you, but that was never our intention at the time. We couldn't have known how terrible she would become to you."
With no more words, Edward looks exhausted, but somehow kind of proud of himself for telling me. It's like he feels he should be applauded for his confession or something. Seriously?
"You made mistakes that *may* have hurt me? Are you kidding me?! You knew! You *always* knew! That's why grandma Tommy was so good to me, and that's why you always tried to step in when I was starving or terribly sick and weak because of her. You fucking *knew* she was crazy. You ALWAYS knew she was fucked up, and NOW you're telling me?! Why are you telling me now? Oh, I know! Only because it's going to get out today and you didn't want to look bad! But you never would have told me today if you weren't going to get caught, RIGHT?!"
"Suzanne-" Mack tugs at me.
"Get the hell out of my apartment. And stay the hell away from me! I hope you DIE, like *I* wanted to every fucking day of my life!"
Grabbing at me, Mack holds tight. Seeing Z stand, he begins walking toward me until I shake my head no.
"Do you have any idea how hard my life was? Did you know

then? Do you know NOW?! You may know the details, but you don't know how awful my life *really* was. My mother had one experience- ONE rape. I had ENDLESS! And she was fucked up for it happening to her *ONCE?!* Well FUCK HER! And FUCK YOU! She did this to me over and over again, *grandfather,*" I sneer. "You saw the damage to her body ONCE. I had it almost weekly for 2 years! TWO FUCKING YEARS OF RAPE AFTER RAPE AFTER RAPE!!"

Lunging for him, I just make contact when Z and Mack get to me. Slapping and kicking and biting my grandfather, and ooops maybe even Mack, I don't care! My grandfather deserves everything I can do to him! All of it! Everything I can possibly do to him he deserves!

"YOU HELPED DO THIS TO ME!" I scream in his face.

"Elizabeth and Simmons did this to you and your father played along," he yells while protecting his face. "I NEVER hurt you! EVER! And Tommy adored you! You were the daughter she lost after Elizabeth was hurt." **WHAT?!**

Wow. Everything suddenly became completely still and silent. Now I remember.

My grandma bathing me and brushing my hair dry, and my mother bathing me and brushing my hair dry. It's the same. They're both the same but totally different. Grandma Tommy loved me because I *was* the substitute, and my mother hated me so I *could be* the substitute. Wow. That's fucked up. Giggle.

Staring at my grandfather, he actually has a bloody scratch down his cheek. Good! The FUCKER! Z is beside me making little soothing sounds while his hand eases down my head and neck again and again. And Mack is holding me tightly from behind with his body flush against me and his arms wrapped tightly around me. One hand rests on my stomach, Oh! And actually his other hand is across my breast, though I'm absolutely sure copping a feel is NOT his intention right now.

"Mack, you're holding my boob," I giggle in the madness, as all three before me flinch.

Abruptly letting go and standing deathly still behind me, Mack breathes into my hair an 'I'm sorry' and I KNOW he is. Mack

would NEVER touch me like they did.
Glaring at my grandfather's stunned face I yell, "Get out of my apartment and never contact me again. I hate you almost as much as I hate her. For all the times I wanted to die, and for all the life I've never had, I hope you have a terrible life and a painful death.
"You know what? I always thought I just had the worst luck, ever. I thought I lived in a ShitStorm because I did something bad- because *I* was bad. But, it's not me! It was never me! I was born into this shit! You're all so screwed up that you screwed me up, too. So take back your inheritance and go fuck yourself. I'm done with you people. I'm done with all you Hampton-Montgomery-Beaumonts, forever! Go. Fuck. Yourself."

Before I even exhale, the headache that hits me so suddenly feels like what I read a burst aneurism feels like. I know the chances are slim, but with me, who knows? Slapping Z's hands away from my hair and pushing off Mack, I limp my way out of the living room for my bedroom.
When my eyesight gets all blotchy and a light starts flashing in my peripheral vision, I'm relieved to know it's just a migraine. A painful, debilitating, barf-inducing migraine. But thankfully, I'll take it.
Throwing open my door, I make my way to my bed and just collapse on it halfway across the middle and partly off the side. But I don't care where I land, I just need to lie down. Trying to calm my shaking body, I reach for the warm blanket at the end of my bed until Z suddenly flips it over my body.
"Thanks. I'm okay. I just have a migraine. Your baby is fine though, I think."
Sitting on the edge of my bed, Z strokes my hair out of my face. "I'm so sorry you had to learn all that. But you were right. No matter what she went through- her *one* experience- it doesn't change anything that was done to you. Your mother chose to be an evil bitch to you over and over again, and I'm very proud of you

for seeing it like that."
"Thanks-"
"I'm serious, Suzanne. I was worried you would take this newest information internally and make it somehow about you, or feel it was your fault, or your problem to deal with. I was so scared you would somehow feel badly for her."
"I can't feel bad anymore. Um... Z? I'm going to throw up. Could you please hurry and get me a bowl?" Before I can even exhale, I hear him running through my apartment.
Returning seconds later, the bowl is placed beside my head as Z continues stroking my hair. Oh, god, I miss him.
"Z, could you please go."
"I don't mind. Go ahead and throw up if you have to, I've seen much worse. I *was* in a fraternity, you know?"
"Ha! I'm sure you have. But this is about YOU being here. I can't have you with me right now."
"I'm fine, Suzanne," he pushes.
"But I'm not. I *need* you to leave, Z."
"I'll just stay here until you fall asleep, okay?"
"Oh, god... You don't get it. You *never* get it. If you stay I'm going to beg you to never leave. I still love you and I think of you every single day but I can't change me, and I can't change this situation for us. So please, before I beg you for things we can't possibly have, please just go. I'm sure Mack is here to help me, so I really need you to leave me before I selfishly beg you to stay..." I choke on a sob.
Crying, my head is pounding so hard now I have to grab and hold onto my hair for relief. Pulling, the nausea reaches its limits and I can't hold back anymore.
"Please, Z. I'm going to throw-up, and I'm going to beg you to stay with me forever."
"Okay, love," he whispers. And rising from the bed, I feel him leave me again. Again.

Sobbing, I finally start barfing up the migraine. The pain is so consuming, it doesn't even let me think of my mother or the past. I am just here in this moment in pain and sick, and pregnant and lonely.

When Mack crawls onto the bed, he pulls my back up against his chest on my side, and rests us against the headboard together.
Snuggling in, I close my eyes again and wait for sleep to take me.

"I am so sorry about today, Suzanne. That was horrible for you I'm sure, but you handled yourself remarkably well. *And* you got to beat the shit out of your grandfather which was pretty cool, too," I hear him grinning.
"AND you touched my boob," I say faking anger.
"Suzanne, I would never touch you like that intentionally. I-"
"I'm kidding Mack. It's been a long time for me though, so I kinda liked it," I giggle.
"You're such an ass, Suzanne," he laughs and holds me tighter.

Within seconds, the headache has sucked all the life right out of me. There is no more thinking and no more fighting it. I have to sleep this horrible day away. With another awful day gone, I know there are endless bullshit days to go. God, I really have lived an absolute ShitStorm of life and it just keeps getting worse.
Though honestly, I think that's it for me now. Now I know why my mother was evil. Now I know why Marcus played along. Now I know *why* grandma Tommy loved me. And it was never me. This was never my shit. This was just a life of agony for me in a place of insanity.
This is good. I have my answers finally. I know why I've had this terrible life. Maybe now I can finally exhale my past and move on.

CHAPTER 34

SEPTEMBER 12

Yesterday was the day of my closed testimony in the Judge's chambers and it went reasonably well. I was good, strong, emotionless and pretty tough, actually. Neither the Prosecutors, nor the Defense team asked too many in-depth questions, and neither side made me recount the actual details of events.

Mack said the Prosecutors have already painted the picture for the Jurors, and the Defense team doesn't want me to relive the events on camera, so as to *sway* the Jurors into feeling sorry for me, effectively convicting my mother before necessary.

My mother's trial is pretty much over, with both sides needing only my closed testimony before the closing arguments could begin. So it really is almost over for me.

Oh, and from I've heard my mother is toast. There is NO WAY she isn't going to be convicted, and there is NO WAY I'll ever have to fear her again in this lifetime.

I was just so relieved it was only about 3 hours of my life, and that was all that was required of me we think. The judge accepted my testimony, and offered me a transcript of the closed testimony I gave, which I really didn't want or need. But I think Mack kept it anyway, just in case.

When I was finished, Mack and I were whisked out of the back into the waiting 'security' car for home. And that was it. All done.

After we left, I had one request of Mack which he agreed to. I think he understood, though this is kind of a female thing, almost exclusively, but he seemed to get it. So when I asked, he took me. And now I feel very different. I'm less secure with what I chose to maintain for years, but I'm secure in the knowledge that it was time to let go of *everything* from my past.

Afterward, walking with my new short, pointed blunt haircut was shocking, but awesome too. The pointy front ends still cover my face nicely, landing at the top of my chest, but the back of my hair reaches only to above my shoulders now.

Finally, my super long hair is chopped off and gone. Grandma Tommy is gone. My mother is gone. And I am once again, another new Suzanne.

So today I'm pretty well. Mack stayed with me last night, which was good because I had tons of nightmares throughout the night. He even stayed in my bed with me ON the covers, but beside me to keep waking me when I started freaking out. And though he looks terrible this morning, we have a huge day ahead of us, so he better wake the hell up soon and get with the program.

In 3 hours we're leaving for New York for his 'surprise' birthday bash Kayla is throwing- The surprise being only that she doesn't know he knows about it.

Regardless, we're both leaving my place, driving to his place so he can get his bags, then we're hopping on a plane for New York. When we arrive at 4:35 in New York I'm supposed to convince him to go shopping with me before we arrive at Kayla's apartment for his party at 8:00.

It's pretty lame, and Mack knew I was full of shit within minutes of trying to convince him I still wanted to go to New York so soon after my testimony yesterday. But when I tried to keep lying he talked me into the truth, and promised to play along- admitting he knew anyway the last 3 weeks because of Kayla's insistence he be at her apartment right at 8:00 Friday night *sharp*. Too funny.

From what I've been told, the party isn't going to be too big, and I'll have Kayla and Mack to help me should I need a minute, but I'm going to try to NOT need a minute. This party is for Mack, and I'm going to keep all the Suzanne-shit out of it. Period.

THIS is me...

*****

Arriving at 8:10, we're late and totally weighed down with bags. Coincidentally, Kayla's suggestion to go shopping was exactly what we did. Okay, it's what I did... with Mack's help.

Mack was a trooper once again though, and I was in my glory, and now we have so much crap between us with Mack taking almost all the burden from me, I feel a little bad for him, and extra limpy myself, actually.

I may have overdone it. Between my limp and the huge 7 1/2 months pregnant belly I'm carrying, I think 3 and a half solid hours of manic shopping was a bit much. Oh well. At least I've kept him from arriving to his 'surprise' party early, so Kayla should be thrilled.

Opening the door with a major flourish, we're hit with the massive shout 'SURPRISE' like a friggin' wall of sound. And though we knew it was coming, both Mack and I actually jump a little like idiots, fueling the 'Mack had no idea' facade for Kayla.

Looking at all the bags in mostly Mack's hands, Kayla raises an eyebrow and says, "Nice work, Suzanne," while pulling us both in for a huge combined hug. After removing myself from her death grip, Kayla stays hugging poor Mack, whose arms appear to be getting longer by the second. Staring at me and my hair, she mouths, 'you look gorgeous, and totally sexy,' as I blush.

When I turn toward the room, I can see it's filled with people, only 2 of whom I actually know. And of course, there's Z. Smiling, he makes his way to me as I feel my body light up with happiness.

God, I love looking at his smile and I love these few little extra moments we have between us so I can stockpile them into my memory vault for later.

Joining us, Z takes my bags, and starts taking all my other bags from Mack.

"Let me help you to the bedroom, Suzanne. You must be exhausted."

"I am. Three and a half hours of power shopping after a flight will do that to you," I grin.

"I'm sure it will. Do you feel okay?" He questions.

"The baby is fine Z," I answer defensively.

Shaking his head slightly he responds, "I asked how YOU are feeling, Suzanne."

"Oh, sorry. I'm good," I mumble.

And that's it. With the sudden discomfort between us, I have nothing more to say, and I'm sure Z doesn't know what he can say to me without me becoming defensive. And once again, Z and I are sadly awkward together, which I never believed could happen to us.

Walking together, we head for the back bedroom behind Kayla's strangely laid out kitchen/living room, past all the people I don't know, at the party I didn't really want to attend, for the man I absolutely adore.

"You wore your hair down and the style looks amazing."

When Z smiles his charming smile at me, I suddenly feel the desperate need to just reach out and kiss him. A hard kiss- smack on the lips. And if there's a little tongue- I want that too. Jesus, this is hard.

"I wear my hair down now when I want to hide from people." Seriously?! Did I just admit that? Dammit.

When Z stops dead, I feel so uncomfortable again I want to get the hell out of this room and away from him.

"Well, it's not necessary to hide," he says turning toward me. "With those beautiful eyes, and those come kiss me lips, and that amazing new haircut, I guarantee no one is seeing your scarred cheek, Suzanne. Trust me."

Blushing, I whisper a quiet 'thanks' as I struggle to take off my coat.

Suddenly Z inhales quickly and before I know it his hands are on my stomach as he towers over me with his eyes closed. Flinching, I just try to breathe in my stillness. Z's hands on me are an absolute NO. I can't handle his hands on me. I can't handle the visual of Z's hands on me. And just as suddenly as he touched me, there is no air in the room between us.

When he opens his eyes to mine, I'm instantly reminded of a time when I could kiss him whenever I wanted to. A time when he was ALL I ever wanted. He is so beautiful, and his eyes are so expressive, and this thing between us is so big that I feel nothing but its tragic loss, as the pain lashes through me.

Lifting his hands away, Z seems to make a groaning noise as he turns and walks from the room quickly. Thank god.

Looking in the mirror I don't see what he sees. I'm dressed beautifully in a classic wrap around dress in black, which highlights my growing chest and my swollen stomach nicely, and my heels are 3 inch black suede wedges for stability.

But I just don't see the Suzanne he sees anymore, not that I ever really did. But when I was with him before, I found myself believing him when he told me I was beautiful to him.

Plopping on the bed, I just try to breathe. This night is going to be very long and I need to keep myself together. I need to be the best Suzanne I can be- Mack and Kayla deserve it.

Lifting my huge ass off the bed, I see Chicago Kayla watching me from the doorway.

"Z looks as gutted as you do," she states deadpan.

"I'm fine. It's lovely to see you Kayla."

"So formal, Suzanne?" What?

"I'm sorry, that wasn't my intention."

"Yup, here we go. Uncomfortable scared Suzanne equals formal, verbally repressed Suzanne," she scoffs at me. Oh *really?*

"Well then... Fuck off, Kayla. Is that better?"

"Moderately, yes. Why don't you start by calling me a bitch, and work your way up to fuck off. I deserve it."

Exhaling the tension I moan, "I can't. I miss you."

"I miss you too. I'm sorry I've been such an asshole..." I laugh. "But you really hurt my feelings back then, and I was too much of a pansy to get back into your life in case you lashed out at me again which was pretty wimpy and very *un*Kayla-like, I know."

"It's okay. But I really didn't mean those things I said to you. I was all messed up, and scared, and twisted up with reality and my past and you just got the brunt of it, as you know. I've never thought you were a whore, or slutty, or anything else I called you that day. Honestly, I've always been so jealous of the way you can do what you do-"

"Whore around?"

"No! God, no. If you were a man, you would be a sexy stud who every woman wants to be with. I think of you the same way. I love that you can just have sex because you want to. I envy that about you. I *always* envied that about you, even back before. You were just so cool, and sexy, and awesome with men, when I couldn't even talk to them. I even used to think I wanted to be just like you, but I wasn't. I couldn't be. And really, probably never will be. That's how I feel about you. There's nothing bad, I swear."

"Okay. I'll stop being a douche then. I was just upset, but I'll get over it now. And obviously we have a lot to talk about. Starting with Holy shit! Look how big you are!"

"I know, and I have a month and a half to go. Seriously. This kid is huge."

"How's Z been? The few times we've spoken he seemed so quiet, or like reserved about you that I didn't ask too much."

"I don't know. I've only seen him 2 times since you know, we ended, I guess. But I know Mack gives him constant updates on the baby."

"No offense, but this situation seems totally unfair to Z. If I was you I'd think about giving him an in, or letting him be a bigger part of all this. I know you don't want the kid but he does, and it is HIS kid growing in you. And I think you're being really unfair letting Mack be the surrogate father during this pregnancy." Wow! *'Surrogate father?!'*

"That's not at all what I'm doing. And you have no clue what's been going on or how I feel, because you haven't been around. So don't try to have an opinion now, Kayla!"

"Okay, fine. I just hate seeing Z sad like he is, and I hate seeing you so sad you can't even leave this room for the party. I was just trying to help."

"Well, don't! This is *my* life and I'm doing the best I can with what I have. Z will have his baby soon, and he can finally be happy and move on."

"And when do you feel happy? When do you move on?"

"I have no idea, but it's not now. And it's not with this huge *thing* between Z and I. Look, I don't want to talk about this with you, okay? I'm tired and I need to get to this party. It was lovely seeing you. Have fun, Kayla," I gasp while turning away.

"I'll call you!" She yells at my back as I practically run from the room.

In Kayla's living room I spot Mack immediately and make my way to him. Trying to breathe, I want to be strong- I do. I just feel so messed up right now but I absolutely won't show it. Screw Kayla and her opinions. Screw Z for touching me. Screw everyone. Tonight I'm strong for Mack and Kayla.

"How's it going?" I ask my constant, steady, wonderful Mack, with a smile plastered on my face.

"Good. You?" He asks while looking at me closely.

"Fine. There are tons of people here. Who are they?"

"Doctors and Nurses I've worked with, and even a few friends from college."

"See, you ARE the greatest, most awesome man ever," I say while side-hugging him. "This isn't even a monumental birthday or anything- just your 38th. But everyone wants to celebrate you anyway. Told ya' you were awesome." By way of response Mack kisses the top of my head and pulls me tighter to him.

Okay, so I'm babbling, but I'm just trying to get through this. Looking around I see Chicago Kayla talking to Z, whose shaking his head looking back at me. Okay, that feels shitty, like they have something against me. *Together.* I don't like that much.

Pulling away from Mack, I see New York Kayla with another drink in her hand, laughing her ass off with a bunch of woman, and I'm instantly jealous. I want to tell *them* to screw off because she's

mine! Yikes. I'm getting loopy... I can feel it.
Walking away from Mack and his friends, I stop near the fully stocked makeshift bar. A drink would be amazing right now. Sometimes a little liquid-courage goes a loooong way. But of course, I wouldn't dream of it in my condition. I'll just yearn for it desperately.

Listening to the music, I suddenly hear Leonard Cohen's 'Suzanne'. Oh, NO! Who plays Leonard Cohen at a party for a bunch of thirty or forty something's? *Who?!*
Oh god... I love this song and I love the memories I have of Z with this song. I don't think he would remember making love with me in his apartment to this song quietly playing in the background. But I remember.
For me it was an amazing moment- making love with Z with one of my favorite songs suddenly playing quietly in the background. It was a moment we had, which I'm sure he's unaware of, but a moment between us which plays out in my memory, time and time again.
It was a beautiful moment filled with promise in a time when I thought we might have a forever.
Standing still, the song washes over me as everything slows to a stop. I feel everything and I feel nothing. I know my tears are falling down my face slowly and I know I look too still in the busy of the room. I know I look odd standing so still when a party continues all around me. I know it, but I'm unable to move.
I have always loved this song even before Z. Mr. Cohen used to sing me to sleep when I was young and when my horrible sadness overwhelmed me.
Singing quietly to myself, "... And you know that's she's half crazy... But that's why you want to be there..." I weep.
Listening to Mr. Cohen's voice sing in the background of my pain, I'm reminded of everything Z has ever said to me. All the beautiful words and loving confessions. I remember the way he touched me and I remember the way only he could reach inside

me.

This moment is a sea of memories washing over me. This is a tragic moment of loss wrapped up in a beautiful song of loving memories.

I love this song and I love Z. I wish for nothing in this moment but a life less dramatic; a life less crushing in its brutality. In my silence, I cry tears for the life I've always wanted with Z, but will sadly never have.

Looking across the room at him, I see he sees me. With absolute dread, I force myself to turn away and walk back to my temporary bedroom behind the strangely shaped kitchen/dining room combo. Turning off the lights, I am engulfed in the darkness that is me.

When the door quietly opens seconds later, I cry harder. These moments are just too debilitating in their despair.

"Suzanne... What is it, love?"
"Please don't call me that," I moan.
"Sorry. Are you alright? Can I help you at all?"
"No. With this, YOU can't help me. I'm okay. But I just need to rest for a few minutes. I must've overdone it today because I'm absolutely exhausted, but I'm fine, Z."
"Tell me what it is, Suzanne. *Please...* I need to know."
"It's everything and it's nothing. It's Leonard Cohen, and memories, and nightmares, and a life not lived," I confess.
Silence.
"We made love to that song in my apartment once. Do you remember that?" Oh! He remembers.
"Yes, I remember. Why do you remember that?" I whisper.
"There is nothing I don't remember about each and every moment we ever had together. Maybe because there are so few memories to hold onto. Or maybe because they were so amazing for me when they happened... I don't know why. But I don't think there's anything about being with you that I don't remember, Suzanne."
Well that was beautiful. Typical Z- love me when I'm down.

"Talk to me, Suzanne. Just tell me what you're feeling."
"Nothing. I feel nothing. Um... next month you can come to the ultrasound if you want. You can be there if you want to be. You *should* be there if you want to be. It's only fair."
"Thank you," he exhales.
"But that's it tonight, Z. Please leave me alone now and have a great time at the party. But please don't tell Mack or Kayla I was upset because I really don't want to ruin this for them."
"Okay, I'll leave you alone. And thank you for letting me be there next month, I really appreciate it. Be well, Suzanne."

Hearing the door open and close to the sounds of music and laughter is numbing. And that's it from Z. Lovely, simple words that stab right through me. This night is already awful but it continues on, just like I will *after* I stop crying again.

CHAPTER 35

OCTOBER 18

Opening the door to Z is hard. I don't know what's expected of me, and I don't know what's expected of him. Because we are complete strangers at this point tied together so intimately, I honestly don't know how we're to function with one another.

"Hi. Um, come in," I mumble.
"Relax, Suzanne. I'm not here for any other reason than to take you to the hospital."
"I can get there on my own. I'm good."
Staring between us, there is only silence as the memories swamp my mind. Why do I suddenly feel like crying? Oh, I know... Because I'm huge, I'm hormonal and I love this man but I just can't *love him*- love him. Duh.
"I'm sure you can get there by yourself, but considering you're as round as you are tall at this point, I thought I'd give you a hand rolling down the hallway." *What?!*
Looking, I see him trying so hard not to laugh- I'm done. Punching his arm, I burst out laughing. What an asshole! Seriously! It's not MY fault I have this monster 6 foot baby growing inside me. But thankfully, the ice is broken and the chill has quickly lifted between us.
"That was totally mean and uncalled for and just really, really mean Z," I stutter through my giggles.
"I know. But Christ! You're huge. Don't get me wrong, you're beautiful still, but man! Your stomach is gigantic. Are you sure there's just one baby in there?" WHAT?!
"YES! They told me there's only one! I asked. I did! And they said there's just one big, healthy kid in here!"

"I'm teasing, Suzanne. Breathe, love. I know there's only one baby. I've seen the reports and ultrasounds."

"Then stop teasing me. I've already got the waddle down, and I can't see my shoes anymore. I know my ass is double the size. My hands and feet are swollen. And look at my boobs! They're huge!" Ooops.

"They *are* huge," he wiggles his eyebrows at me. Dammit. Blush. "But you still look beautiful to me."

"Thank you."

"Grab your coat and we'll get going. Mack's meeting us there."

Turning from Z to grab my coat and purse feels easy suddenly. I don't have that heavy, painful weight on my chest that usually accompanies thoughts of Z right now.

Seeing him for the first time since Mack's party last month doesn't hurt this time. Maybe humor is the key. Maybe Z acting like I'm just a friend is the key. I have no idea, but I'm okay right now. I actually feel kind of good.

Helping me put on my tent-sized swing cost, Z leans in and gives me a little hug from behind. Just a little squeeze. Nothing huge or demanding. Nothing with intent or purpose. It feels like he just wanted to give me a little hug with nothing attached to it, so he did.

When he suddenly takes my hand, I pause.

"I'm just helping you walk. That's all, I promise. I would help any woman whose as unbelievably round as you are *waddle* down the hallway." Jerk. Again. Giggle.

"Fine."

When we get down to Z's car, he again helps me when I struggle to get into his Escalade. Seriously? An Escalade? Looking at him, he laughs.

"Um, I thought the biggest car available was best for you, Suzanne."

"Okay… enough Z. I get it, I'm huge, but it's not my fault. I'm not really gaining weight anywhere else, well, except for my boobs

and butt." He's still laughing though. Argh... "I asked the doctor, Z. And she said the distance between the bottom of my rib cage and my hipbone was so close that this huge kid has nowhere to go, except OUT!" But he's still grinning. "Forget it. Jerk!"
Reaching to put on my seatbelt I can barely get it, but manage somehow, only to more laughs from Z when I have to stretch it all the way out so I can put it below and above my stomach. The ASS!
"I'm sorry, I'm trying not to laugh but you look so adorable and huge, and really quite stunning like that."
"It's too late, Z. You've pissed me off."
"Oh... come on, Suzanne. I haven't seen you in a month and you've doubled in size."
"I'm aware," I growl at him.
"I'm really sorry for laughing. Please don't be mad. I promise I'll keep all the laughter in check from now on, okay?" He smirks at me again.
"You better, or I'll punch you again," I smirk right back.

After the relatively quiet ride to the hospital, Z and I experience our first truly awkward moment in reception. When asked our names, and his relation to me and the baby, everything just stops, my breathing included. What do we say?
Z recovers quickly though. "Suzanne and I are the baby's parents, and I've been invited to this ultrasound. Dr. MacDonald should be waiting for us inside." Z speaks so matter-of-factly there's no room for judgments or further questions from the Receptionist. Jesus, I can finally exhale that round of discomfort.

After I'm lead privately to the room, I struggle out of my black moo moo and *thank god* my side-zipper boots, so I can put on the ugly-ass hospital gown.
Sitting and waiting on the bed, eventually there's a knock, and poking his head in, Mack greets me with a huge smile.
"Hey Tubby... How goes it?" Before I can tell him to piss off

though, I hear Z burst out laughing behind him. Jesus! Now there's *two* of them? I wish to god Kayla was here. She'd beat the shit out of both of them for me.

Pouting, I mumble, "Be nice to me. I'm a huge woman on the edge."

Grinning, Mack walks to me and takes me in his arms. Holding tight, I breathe him in. I know he's teasing, just like Z did, and I'm not really angry or sad, but I just want his comfort a minute longer. Some days I'm so lonely and scared, Mack's hugs are all I have in this world to ease me.

"Dr. Cobb will be in any minute. How was your night?"

"Good. I slept pretty well, though I did pee like 10 times in the night which sucks. Otherwise, I was fine."

Looking over, I see Z standing to the side of the room. He seems so uncomfortable; almost like he knows he's intruding on me and Mack. I feel so bad for him in these moments because he's such an integral part of this equation, and yet he's always on the sideline just watching.

This event is his life changing forever, but up to now he's never been a part of it. Except for the little scraps I give him, or from the information Mack shares with him, he's always been outside looking in. Suddenly, I realize Kayla was right and this just seems so unfair to Z.

"Z... I'm very sorry you always have to look at this from the outside. I swear that was never my intention. I never meant to hurt you like that," I whisper.

"I know it wasn't, and I'm okay, Suzanne. You just do what you have to do to get through what you have to get through. I'll have my part soon enough." God, he's an amazing man.

"You WILL have your part soon enough... diapers and all," I grin through my tears

Clapping his hands together loudly, he yells, "I can't wait!"

Suddenly, I have to know. Don't do it! Don't ask it! Ah, I have to.

"What are you going to call it?" *Jesus...* I could actually feel the air leave the room between us. Mack is so tense when I look at him he doesn't even seem to blink. Was that really bad? Shit.

"'Glass of'," Z replies deadpan. WHAT?! Cracking up in a fit of laughter, I'm stunned by his playfulness. "With the last name Zinfandel, what other options did I have?" He says again with a total lack of emotion like he's serious.

I'm dying here, laughing so hard, I feel almost lightheaded. Looking over, I see Mack has finally exhaled as well.

Grinning at me, Z asks, "What do you think?"

"It's awesome! I once wondered if your name was 'Bottle of', so 'Glass of' is the perfect choice. Is that for a boy or a girl?" I ask, still laughing.

"I think the name applies to either gender, don't you?"

"Yes, it does. 'Glass of Zinfandel'. It's perfect, Z."

When Dr. Cobb walks in and takes in the mood of the room, she instantly smiles. "Something I should know?"

"Z's naming our baby 'Glass of'." Oh! Ooops. Not ours- NOT *ours!* Mack and Z both caught that though, I can tell. They instantly had a little eye contact between them. Dammit.

"That's an excellent choice, Z."

"Thank you," he nods.

"Okay Suzanne, you're up. Lay back, cover up, and lift the gown for me."

Struggling, I lay back and rest my hip on the little cushion so I'm not flat. At this point lying flat on my back causes a pain that is so quick and sudden I feel trapped in my inability to move out of the pain, which I'm told is totally common for hugely pregnant women. Yay! 'Cause pregnancy didn't come with enough side effects.

Once I'm settled, Dr. Cobb squirts the gross jell on me, making me jump as always, and she starts her thing. Looking at Z, I'm struck with such sadness for him again. Reaching out my hand, I motion for him to come closer. So nodding with another smile for me, Z walks the 2 steps until he's right beside Mack on my right.

Looking at the ceiling, I can't do it. I haven't looked yet on purpose and I won't start now. I know Mack bought a picture of

the baby for himself and for Z, and I know they've talked to Kayla about it. But I just can't look. I'm not sure what I think will happen, but looking at it feels like a betrayal or something. It's like I'm afraid I'll give the kid false hope that I actually want to be its mother. Which I still don't.
"Do you want to know what it is yet, Suzanne?" Z asks me softly.
"No, I'm good. But you go ahead if you want to."
"I already know." Really? Huh.
"So 'Glass of' still works?"
"Absolutely," he grins.
Staring back at the ceiling, I feel happy for him. I want him to be happy, and if this is what I can do to make him happy, I'll do it. Plus, I'm almost done my part anyway.

"Suzanne, I need to bring in the Tech for a minute, okay?"
Looking over, I see Dr. Cobb has a fake doctor- try to look reassuring- but something's wrong- smile on her lips, and I don't buy it for a second.
Moaning, "What's wrong?"
Fake smiling again, Dr. Cobb pats my leg, and walks from the room quickly.
Turning to Mack, I know he knows- I can see it. Oh no! Looking at Z quickly, I see his total confusion. Mack knows, but Z doesn't. Holy SHIT! What's wrong?!
"Breathe, Suzanne," Mack says quietly while squeezing my hand.
Looking at Z again, he's statue still. He isn't moving. Or blinking. Or speaking. Or breathing. There is just nothing to him. He is absolutely lifeless in this moment.
Thankfully, Dr. Cobb returns quickly with the Tech and they get right back to my stomach, fake smiles and all.
After forever, with no sound in the room, Dr. Cobb places something on my stomach as the Tech squirts gel on me again, and starts clicking the machine repeatedly, which is quite annoying actually. All I'm hearing is the constant click of the machine and no other sound, which is like a kind of torture

itself. Shit! I need some other sound before I go completely mental.

When the Tech starts typing weird words, like codes or anagrams on the screen, I know. Dr. Cobb doesn't have to say anything. The Tech doesn't have to stop typing. Mack doesn't have to start soothing. Z doesn't have to start breathing. I know.

"What happened?" I whisper.

Turning to me, Dr. Cobb has the grace to dramatically exhale before speaking.

"I don't know yet Suzanne, but the baby no longer has a heartbeat."

Whoooosh.

Nothing moves. No one moves. There is no sound. There is no breath in the room.

"What do you mean?" Z begs in a whisper, as Mack squeezes my hand a little too hard.

"I'm sorry, but I really don't know yet what happened. Two weeks ago your exam was fine. Good even. The heartbeat was strong, and the baby measured just slightly big but otherwise, everything was progressing as it should. Sometimes there is no medical reason for this, and sometimes we find out after the fact that there was a medical reason for these things happening. I'm very sorry Suzanne, but the baby has died."

Turning my head quickly to the monitor I see a flat line and nothing else. The color has faded to grey, and the movement on the screen is static. There is nothing in this moment but death.

And I've got nothing. I really hope this is shock again, otherwise, I just died too. Is that *my* flat line on the monitor?

Looking, I see Mack talking quietly to Z. What's he saying? What's happening? What does this mean for Z?

Oh GOD, Z! **FLINCH!**

"Z, I'm so sorry. I didn't do this on purpose, I swear. Please don't hate me! Please! Um, I did everything I was supposed to do. Ask Mack. I did!"

"Suzanne-"

"Mack tell him! I did, Z. I took the vitamins, and I ate the food, and I took the medication, and I adapted all my Physio to the pregnancy. I swear I did everything right for you!"

Z is still so lifeless while just staring at me in silence. Shit! Does he think I did this on purpose? I didn't! I really didn't do this on purpose.
Begging, "Please believe me. I wanted to give this to you. I did! I didn't want it, but I wanted YOU to have it, and I tried so hard to do everything right. I swear! Please Z, please don't be mad at me. I didn't do this!"
When Dr. Cobb starts trying to explain the significance and the possibilities of the dead baby I don't want to hear her. I can't listen to this. I want to talk to Z. I want him to understand that I didn't do this on purpose to him. I wanted him to have this baby, I really did. I would never hurt him on purpose.
Interrupting Dr. Cobb and Mack, I moan, "Z, I promise I wanted to give this to you. After I stopped hating this, I realized I wanted you to have it, so you had *something* good from me. You wanted this, and I DID want to give it to you. I really did. I'm so sorry. I tried so hard to give this to you. I wanted you to have this, I really did. Please believe me."
"I believe you, Suzanne. Mack told me you hated the baby but you wanted me to have it-"
"I didn't *hate* it, I just didn't want it. That's different."
"Whatever, Suzanne," he shakes his head sadly.
"NO! Not *whatever!* Listen to me, Z. I didn't hate it, I just didn't love it. I wanted it to go away at first, but since I couldn't make it go away, I really wanted you to have it. So I was good for you." Sobbing, I can barely breathe but Z is just so still. "I was good so you would have this. I promise Z. I really was..."
Oh GOD! This pain is just ripping through me. I'm desperate for him to understand. "It was always for you. This time I did everything right. Ask Mack! I did! It was for you to have. I wanted you to have the baby so you had something to love, I

swear. Since we couldn't love each other, I wanted you to have love with your baby."

Closing my eyes, I'm beyond desperate as the sobs wrack my body.

This is the worst feeling I've ever experienced in my life. This sadness is oppressive in its strength. Everything hurts. I can't believe the depth of the despair I feel. This feeling is so powerful, there's nothing left of me that doesn't ache with the intensity of this despair for Z.

When I feel strong arms wrap me up tightly I pray for Z's arms, but I know its Mack holding me tight. I thought for just a moment Z might hug me and believe me and make this all better for us, but Z hasn't moved and Mack is holding me so tightly I'm stuck.

"What happens now?" Z asks in the darkest voice I've ever heard.

"Generally, since the baby is 37 weeks, we can induce the mother into a vaginal birth with medication, which some women prefer so they have a sense of closure. Or we can schedule a C-Section to remove the baby at once. What do you want to do?" Dr. Cobb asks me gently as I pull away from Mack.

"Schedule a C-Section," Z says abruptly. "Suzanne didn't want this from the beginning, so I doubt a vaginal birth will give her any kind of closure." Wait! "Can you do this quickly though. I'd like to bury my son."

And there it is. His son. Little 'Glass of' was going to be Z's son. THIS I feel. *THIS* is unbearable for Z. Oh *god*...

"I'm so sorry, Z," I whisper through my agony.

"Suzanne, are you okay?" Mack leans in close to ask me.

Shaking and barely breathing, I beg. "Z! Please look at me. I'm really, very sorry for your loss."

"Suzanne. You too have suffered a loss," Mack prompts.

"I'm sorry, Z. I never wanted this loss for you, I promise." Crying openly, I can only beg his forgiveness. "Please don't be mad at me, Z. I didn't do this to hurt you. I wanted you to have this baby. I did. I wanted you to have it to love. Please forgive me."

Sobbing, I can't even pretend anymore. There is no tie left between us. We are broken completely. There is just nothing left between us. We are done. We have flat lined...

Z is still so quiet, I don't know if he can even walk or speak anymore. His son died and his son is lying dead inside me, and if I could make him alive for Z, I would.

"Dr. Cobb can you get Z's baby out of me right now? Can you? I really want Z to have him now. Please?"

"Suzanne, I'll schedule the Cesarean for the first available-"

"No! I don't want to wait. Z needs him. Can you get him out of me now? Pretend it's an emergency birth and cut him out of me or something. Dr. Cobb, please give Z his son," I beg.

"Suzanne, we'll get the baby out as soon as possible."

"Mack! Can you do it? You're a doctor. Can you get him out for Z? He needs his son. He needs to hold him and love him. Mack! Hurry up! *Please...*"

"Suzanne... don't do this," Mack moans.

"Oh, *god...* I'm sorry Z. Here! Get him out." When Z turns to me, his expression looks like a mix of agony and disgust. "Z, do it! It's okay. Cut him out of me so you can have him. I won't feel it. I'm okay. But you're not. Oh god... Get him out Z, so you can hold him." I feel so desperate and devastated by this tragedy for him. "Z! Just cut me open and take your baby..." I moan.

"Suzanne! STOP!"

"Mack, I'm fine. This is about Z, not me. Look, I'll be fine! I just want him out so Z can have him! PLEASE! Cut me open! Please get this baby OUT OF ME!"

When Z suddenly lunges at me, I open up my body for his abuse. When he grabs my upper arms hard, I don't fight him. Submitting, I close my eyes and take it all. As Z yells in my face, I take his rage into my body. I deserve all of his hatred. I deserve anything he wants to do to me.

"FUCK, SUZANNE!! Can't you handle anything sanely, for fucking once?! Don't lose it right now, PLEASE! I'm begging you to stay

THIS is me...

sane, just this once. For ME! I can't handle watching you freak out AND deal with this death too. Just stay sane- for ME- just ONCE!"

Exhaling slowly, I know I can do this for Z.

Nodding, I give in. "Okay, Z. Do anything you want. I'll stay sane. I'm sorry to have upset you. I was just trying to give him to you so you had some love from me. That way we both wouldn't be sad and lonely forever."

When Z jumps away from me grabbing hard at his hair, he actually swears and growls out loud in the silence of the room.

Walking toward the door Z shouts, "Mack, take care of her! I've got to leave before I say something unforgivable."

Oh, god. Don't leave me!

Screaming to his back I beg, "I'm so sorry Z. I didn't do this on propose. Please don't hate me!"

Turning toward me quickly, "Oh Christ... Shut UP, Suzanne! I know you didn't do this on purpose, alright?! I know you tried and I DON'T hate you. I'm just heartbroken, okay? This isn't about YOU for once. It's about ME. I'M heartbroken over MY dead son! A son YOU didn't want. So just stop. I have to go, and I hope you're okay. You have Mack to help you, and I have NOTHING anymore. So please stop all your shit for once. This is MY pain, not yours..." And running for the door, he throws it open until it slams against the wall behind him.

Shaking, the upset in the room is so tangible I can see it. There is a grey darkness engulfing the room. Mack has gone running after Z as Dr. Cobb suddenly reaches for me. Slapping her hands away, I close my eyes, and place my hands on my stomach. Lying in the pose of death, I think of Z's little boy.

I wonder what he looked like. I wonder if he was going to be tall like his daddy, or dark like his daddy, or kind and beautiful like his daddy. I wonder if he would have been funny AND intense like his daddy, or if he would have been quiet and self-possessed. I wonder if he would have liked his name. Little 'Glass of'- Z's beautiful boy.

"I'm sorry little baby that I couldn't love you enough to keep you alive. Your daddy would have, and I'm so sorry I didn't let him. Oh, god... I'm so sorry little boy."

Crying for Z's beautiful baby boy, I let the pain of Z's tragedy suffocate me into a numbing darkness while I wait for this nightmare to end. I wish I could cut him out of my body. I wish I could carve out this agony from my body. I wish I could cut myself to release this sorrow for Z.

In this moment of absolute agony, I wish the flat line was my own. I wish I could trade heartbeats with Z's little boy so he had something good from me. I wish I could die so Z's baby boy could live.

THIS is me...

Sarah Ann Walker

THIS is me...

AWAKE

CHAPTER 36

OCTOBER 23

Sitting silently in my living room, I know I'm supposed to get ready, but I can't. Mack will be here any minute, and Kayla has already called to push me into getting ready. And other less friendly Kayla has also called me to say she'd meet me at the cemetery, but I just can't do it. I can't get dressed for this. I can't live for this.

In the last 5 days, I've turned over (another) new leaf. When I had the C-section the day after we learned of the baby, Z waited in the adjacent room for his son. I was in the operating room with Mack, and sadly, Z was totally alone waiting to hold his dead baby in the room beside us.

From what Mack told me, Z was absolutely devastated and broken, and I swore in that moment I would never, EVER hurt him again no matter what it did to me. I swore to never see him again. I swore to let him go once and for all, so he can move past all this Suzanne-SHIT, all the time.

And so I'm stuck. Mack and Kayla have insisted I go to the funeral for my own closure, but I can't do it to Z. I don't want Z to have to see me, or think about me, or take me into account, or worry about my feelings, or have to deal with me at all. I don't want him to have to acknowledge me in the slightest during this devastating day of his.

This is Z's time. This is Z's funeral for his son. This is Z's closure for all the potential he thought he would have for the last 8 months and lost. This is Z's time to mourn. So I'm taking all the Suzanne insanity and drama out of it for him today. This is the absolute least I can do for Z on this horrible day.

Moving slowly through my apartment I make my way to bed. Crawling in, I still flinch and moan at the various pains within my body but I don't care about them. I'm absolutely exhausted from my agony and sadness for Z. I need to simply sleep past this funeral, because this is not my tragedy to mourn. This is Z's tragedy.

Closing my eyes, I can't help but picture Z's son again. It helps that I never actually saw him, so the image changes constantly. It helps that I have no real picture to burn into my mind when I think of his little baby. It also helps that I have only a horrific sense of loss for Z, but no real feeling of loss for myself. I don't feel the loss for me at all, but I feel it straight to my heart for Z.

This is a pain I will never forget. This pain of Z's loss is absolutely unbearable to me. And if I could, I would live the pain of my abusive past forever, to give Z back the life he should be holding in his arms right now.

I will never live past this loss of Z's.

Waking, I suddenly see Z climbing onto my bed. Jumping in fear, then flinching in pain, I try to calm myself for him. I remember his final words to me. I remember him begging me to stay sane for him and for HIS loss.

Slowly, Z lays down next to me on his side. Resting his hand on my still largely swollen stomach, Z doesn't speak and I have NO words in this moment. What can I possibly say that I haven't already said? What can I possibly give to him as apology?

"I'm sorry I wasn't there for you, Suzanne. I was just messed up. I was beyond shocked at the news and so devastated by his death, I was a mess. But I didn't mean to leave you to deal with this alone. And please don't apologize for this. I know you didn't do anything wrong, and I really need you to believe me. I know you didn't do this to hurt me. I know you *wouldn't* do this to hurt me. So, no more apologies. I was just so sad and screwed up, and I wasn't thinking clearly when I left you in the room to deal with this without me."

"I know you were sad. And I'm so sorry about your son, Z. My heart is just so broken for your loss."

"What about for your loss?" Oh shit. "It's okay. Just be honest. Do you feel anything for his death?" Um...

"Honestly... I feel it, but not like that. It hasn't hurt me at all as my own. It only hurts when I think about him as *your* loss, and I know that makes me a monster, but it's true. I'm sad that a little baby died, and I'm devastated that *your* little baby died, but I still don't feel anything for myself. I'm so sorry..."

Nodding, Z seems to pause after my confession. Looking at his eyes, Z looks so sad to me. God, this hurts.

"Would we be together if you hadn't been pregnant, Suzanne? I know that's a tough question to answer, but I think about it all the time. Do you think we would have made it?" he whispers.

Whispering in return, "I don't know. I would have tried very hard to be with you, but my very hard is everyone else's easy. I probably would have screwed up, or gone nuts, or did something wrong eventually, and you and I would have had to struggle and struggle until you were just too tired to struggle for us anymore. That's what I think, though I wish it wasn't the case."

When he nods again, I continue.

"Z, you've become a fantasy to me. You are the novel lover. But I think I've built you up too high to not fail in a relationship with you. I think you are just too big for me in this awful little life of mine."

Oh, god... THIS is our final break-up speech and it's ripping me apart.

Has anything ever hurt me like this before? Has there ever been a greater pain in my life? I can feel nothing but this intense agony as I look into his sad eyes. He's finally going to leave me alone, and I'm going to feel only this agony, forever.

"If you had known he wouldn't survive- if you had known you wouldn't have to be a mother in the end, would you have wanted to stay with me? Would you have loved me enough to not push me away again?"

What do I say? The truth? Do I tell him what a selfish bitch I am? Do I tell him how crazy I am? What do I tell him?

"Suzanne...?" he asks moving closer to me.

"I don't know for sure, but I think probably I would have. I wanted you so badly, but I didn't want a child so badly. But I think if I had known this horrible ending would happen, I would have selfishly stayed with you and waited it out. And I'm embarrassed to admit to such a selfish thing. But yes, I would have done anything to have stayed with you then. And I'm really sorry for being like that, but I think it's true."

When I feel him nod against my hair, I stay quiet. One massive, disgusting confession is enough for today, I think. Plus, how much worse could I possibly paint myself to Z? It's not like I have a great track record with rational, intelligent choices that he's ever seen before. God, I'm disgusting.

Breaking the heaviness of our silence he asks, "Would you come with me to the funeral? I would really like you to be there. You are my son's mother, Suzanne. And even if you didn't want to be- To me, you will always be his mother."

"If that's what you want Z."

"It is. I want you with me when I bury him, if that's alright with you."

"Okay. I just have to change, and I'll put my make-up on in the car." Dammit. This is going to be hard. Z looks so broken, and I can't help him with this at all.

"Thank you," he whispers. Exhaling, I nod my consent as I try to get out of bed.

Helping me, Z is so slow and gentle, and though my insides are screaming in pain I feel very strong suddenly. I can't believe how much my skin and body- my brain and emotions have had to endure these last 8 months. And yet my sanity seems so strong right now. What a weird, tragic way to become sane.

Walking beside me to my closet, Z turns on the light inside and just pauses.

"Well, you certainly have the funeral attire down. Any

preference?" he grins. What?!

Laughing, I look at my rows and rows of black. Stacks of black sweaters on top of rows of black slacks, turned to black capris, turned to black skirts, followed by black dresses, and finally a full side row filled with black blouses and shirts. Around 3 full walls, my closet screams for help.

Grinning, "You should see my shoe closet."

Turning toward me, Z wraps his arms around me, kisses my forehead and hugs me. Not too tightly but completely. I am engulfed by him, and I'm okay with this moment between us.

After forever, Z turns, grabs the clothes I point out and helps me dress in my bedroom.

Never acknowledging my gross leg, or my scarred face, or my hugely swollen stomach, Z sees everything as he helps me dress. Strangely, I'm never uncomfortable or embarrassed, and I never feel the familiar need to cover up or flee from him though. I think the circumstance of this intimacy doesn't allow for simple feelings of insecurity or modesty between us.

Eventually, he takes my hand in his and leads me to the living room.

"How did you get in?"

"I took Mack's key and told him that I was coming for you. I told him that this was finally just between me and you."

Taking my coat, he continues dressing me while I stay silent. I don't want to ruin this moment for him by being all Suzanne-like.

Sometimes, my silence is the best gift I can give someone. Sometimes, my silence prevents the stupidity, the crazy, and the sadness from crushing someone else. And so my silence is my gift to Z on the day he buries his son.

When we get to his car I whisper, "What did you really name him?"

"Thomas," he chokes. Oh!

"My name..." I gasp. "How did you know?" Oh. My. God. Now I'm crying. Dammit.

"Suzanne, I know everything about you. I know when you hurt and I know when you need a moment. I see everything, love."

Suddenly sobbing, I can do nothing but stare at him. This man is just too much. He is so much greater than me. He is so much greater than I'll ever be.

"Thank you..." I finally cry in the dark silence between us.

Smiling, Z leans in and kisses me softly on the lips before we drive away.

*****

Walking back into my apartment I am absolutely exhausted. Keeping everything together throughout the funeral was hard, but I did it. For Z; I stood quietly beside him while a priest laid his son to rest.

With so many people in attendance, I was horribly insecure and uncomfortable but I didn't 'Suzanne' the funeral in the slightest. I nodded and smiled, and shook hands and accepted stranger's condolences gracefully. I acknowledged the few people I knew, and stood stoically strong beside Z while he mourned the little boy that left him.

The Kaylas both stood beside and behind me, but neither talked to me much. I think they could tell I was fighting my emotions. I'm sure Kayla could read my silence as the only thing keeping me together. I'm sure she knew any attempt to comfort would set me off, and so my dearest Kayla stood beside me, shoulder to shoulder without speaking a single word to me, while other Kayla stood strong behind me.

And yes I was emotional. I mean, I'm not a monster. But again, almost all my emotion was for Z and Thomas, not for myself. Hearing Thomas' name said with affection and lost potential was devastating. And seeing Z struggle to keep it together was so hard to watch, but I didn't make it about me at all. I didn't weep and wail, or try to make this pain my own. I was totally strong for Z.

Even when I saw Z's best friend Marty walk directly up to him, taking him into a tight embrace while talking quietly to Z, I stayed strong. When Mack joined Marty and Z, I watched as the three men spoke quietly to each other with their heads bent and with a great sadness and loss between them.

Three strong beautiful men stood together as best friends, as they each felt this pain and sorrow together. It was actually an amazingly touching moment to watch. It was beautiful, really. And it was a moment I will never forget for the rest of my days.

*****

Heading for my bedroom to change, I want to sleep so badly I can barely walk. Actually, there is nothing more I want than to sleep away Z's sadness.

After the funeral, I convinced Z, Mack, and the Kaylas that I was fine to be alone. I insisted that they should carry on without me to the little lunch Z provided for the guests. And though I could tell no one believed me, I was so strong and unemotional, eventually they gave in and Mack had a car drop me off at home.

So here I am. Standing in my on suite bathroom running the shower, while desperately trying to block out Z's sadness by looking at my grossness again.

Christ! You would think I'd be used to the scars on my face, which though significantly better are still horribly obvious. You'd think I wouldn't care about my scarred throat and neck, or about the chunk of thigh that seems to be missing because of the angle of the damage. You'd think I'd be used to all this ugly by now. And though I don't cringe and cry, or obsessively touch the texture of scars any longer, I'm still not quite over all this ugly. Then again, I don't think I'll ever be.

Stepping into the hot shower, my muscles finally relax. Sitting on the shower bench I finally exhale. God, this day has been the longest day of my life. This has been the hardest day yet for me. This is the day I wish to erase from my memory forever.
Seeing the little monument and seeing his little name and the date of his death was just so *sad*. I don't even think there's another word for it. Yes, seeing Z's upset was horrible but the little casket and monument was so devastating I barely held on. God, I don't know how Z kept it together throughout.
I really don't know how he stood there without tears, talking and shaking hands with countless people while the little casket was so close to him.
I don't know how he pulled off a funeral with such short notice for a baby he was never allowed to love. I don't understand why so many people even came to a funeral for his little baby boy who never really was. It was just so *sad*.

As the exhaustion and heat creep into my bones, I feel myself starting to cry. I feel myself letting go of the many months of fear and depression I had. I feel myself letting go of all the potential Z thought he had. I feel myself crying for all the potential Z may have had with his son but sadly lost.
For me, this is the greatest tragedy of all. The baby is gone, and Z is broken, and I am still Suzanne- fucking- Anderson. And though another version of myself, stronger and more sane, I am still me. Always.

Crying harder, I just let myself go because there's nothing else I can do.
The script I wanted to write by my own hand is once again not my own. I didn't write this death and I didn't write these awful pages of my life. I never wanted this movie to turn out like this.

God, I don't want to be in this movie anymore. Life-long contract or not, I don't want to have this life anymore. There is just too much pain, always.

Leaning against the corner tiles, I think of Thomas' little life which is buried beneath a little monument. I picture the little monument from his daddy, and realize his only legacy on this earth is the heavy stone weighing him down.
Oh, *god*...

Thomas Zinfandel
"You were held just once,
But you will be loved forever."
-October 18th, 2012-

Saying goodbye, I weep for his little life lost.

CHAPTER 37

"Suzanne... Wake up, love." Huh? Oh, shit!
"I'm fine! I wasn't freaking out, I swear! Why are you here?!" Okay, *that* sounded freaked out. Dammit.
"I needed to see you, and I wanted to make sure you were alright."
"Oh. Um..."
"I don't think you're supposed to have your stitches so wet, and I don't think you're actually supposed to sleep propped up in a shower," he grins.
"I know but I was just so tired. I'll get out now."
Trying to stand, my left leg is all wonky from being still for too long, but Z reaches for me and steadies me as I stand. Looking at him, I'm surprised again that I don't feel nakedly gross by *my* gross nakedness.

"How can you stand to look at my body, Z?" I whisper without eye intact.
"I can't stand it." OH! "Suzanne, breathe. I can't stand to see the scars you have, or the damage from the accident. And I can't stand to see the scar across your abdomen, or the swelling you still have to carry from my baby. But I don't see the scars as you see them. It's more of a dislike for the *actual* scars, not for your body. Honestly Suzanne, I feel such affection for you I don't think there's anything that could make me not love looking at your body. Even ravaged and damaged as it is."
"Oh." Exhale.
"I see you different than you see yourself- I always have. You are Suzanne to me, just as you are. You are not the scarred version of Suzanne that you see. Does that make more sense?"

Z says all these lovely words to me as he helps me from the shower and wraps me in a towel.

"Do you need help bandaging your stomach?"

"No, I can do it."

"I don't mind. I'd like to help you."

Suddenly the exhaustion weighing on me is so great, I can only nod my head yes.

Lifting me gently onto the countertop, Z looks around for the supplies needed by the sink but suddenly drops to his knees in front of me. Jesus!

Placing his hands on my hips, he kisses my huge, ugly, distended belly once through the towel then turns and rests his head against me. Holding me tighter, he inches my legs open wide for his body.

God, I don't know what to do. I don't know what to say. I have nothing to give him in this moment. So raising my hand, I slide my fingers through his hair as he moans a little cry against me.

Touching Z for the first time in forever is so anticlimactic, I'm surprised by the calm of the gesture. I have wanted to touch him always, but I couldn't. And now it seems I *can* touch him and I just feel so sad for all the lost opportunity and tragedy between us.

"I'm sorry I didn't want the baby, Z. But it was NEVER you. I *always* wanted you. I just didn't want a baby. And I know you can't understand the difference, but to me there IS a difference."

"Tell me, Suzanne. Make me understand," he begs while lifting his eyes to me.

"Um..."

Oh god, this is so hard to say. Okay. Trying to breathe, I look at his beautiful eyes begging me, and I just jump off my cliff.

"A baby is something for me to hurt, Z. Something I probably would have hurt eventually. It was going to be an innocent child, and as a person- as its *mother*- I'm not supposed to hurt it. But I just couldn't be sure that I wouldn't. So I felt nothing for it which was easier than being terrified of hurting it-"

"But you-"

"Please, Z. Just listen," I beg as he silences. "If I ever hurt you,

you would fight back. You would tell me to piss off, or you would explain how I hurt you until I understood. But a child couldn't do that because I was its mother. The child would've been trapped like I was by an awful parent who hurt him, and I didn't want that. I didn't want that for you or the baby, but mostly I didn't want that for me. I didn't want to be the kind of monster who hurt their child." Nodding, he seems to just wait for me to continue.

"Could you imagine if we were together with a baby and I was horrible or mean or... *abusive* to it? Could you imagine how much you would hate me? Could you imagine how screwed up your baby would turn out to be? I mean, *look at me*. Look at what's happened to me. Look at all I've done and said and thought because of *my* horrible parents.

"... So I was scared to death of screwing up your child- YOUR child because I love you and I never want you to see me as a monster. And I never want to BE a monster with you, so I couldn't be in its life in case I was that monster. But even that was wrong because the baby would have still been screwed up eventually by me staying away. Your child would have been messed up anyway knowing it had a mother that just didn't want him- a mother who stayed away from him on purpose. So I didn't know what to do. Somehow, I almost feel like I would've handled this better had it been Marcus' child because I really didn't care if he hated me... But with you I care so much, I didn't want a baby giving me the opportunity to screw up so badly that you never loved me again."

Shaking and breathing heavily, I continue.

"I'm not sure I would've handled you hating me very well, and I think I would have become all messed up again, or desperate, or maybe suicidal or something. I don't know. It was just easier to walk away while giving you something you wanted so badly- your baby. It was so much easier to walk away from you than trying to be a part of his life- The part that could screw him up, which would make me lose everything. I think I believed that no matter what happened, if I gave you your baby, no matter how much I

THIS is me...

screwed up *away* from you, you would still love me a little. And I guess I just always needed to know that you would love me a little, no matter what became of me without you." Ex-*hale*.
 And there it is. That's it. All of it. The whole truth. Shit, it seems way more lame in words than it did all wrapped up in my head forever.
 Silence.

 "You really are fucked up, Suzanne," Z laughs sadly as he stands up in front of me. "I would have NEVER let you or anyone else hurt our child, and I would have NEVER let you hurt me or yourself. Did you not think I was prepared for you to struggle? Did you not think I would know *when* you were struggling, or when you needed a moment? If, and I seriously doubt it, but IF you had struggled to the point of ever hurting Thomas, I would have intervened. I would have found you the help you needed, and I would have protected him until you were well again. But again I say a very hypothetical 'IF'.
 "... I truly believe you would have loved him, and you would have fought day and night to be a wonderful mother to him. Not just for him and I, but because you wanted to be a good mother. I believe you would have done everything you could do to love him, just as you love Mack, and the Kaylas, and even me. You have never intentionally hurt us, and I don't believe for one minute that you would have intentionally hurt him."
 "Intentionally-" I state firmly.
 "Yes, *intentionally*. Christ! Your parents were the extreme, Suzanne. And my parents were monsters as well. But lots of other good parents have bad moments. Even Mack's dad, who was a terrific man, lost it once in a while. But Mack always knew it wasn't intentional, and he has no emotional scars from it. Parenting is hard, I'm told. And even the best-intentioned parents make mistakes from time to time."
 "I know, but what if I *really* lost it?"
 "Again, I would have found you the help you needed, and we would have worked through it together, for ourselves and for our

son."

Exhaling a hard breath and shaking his head a little, Z looks back at my face and he seems just so utterly exhausted in this moment. If only I had-
"I really wish you had talked to me months ago. I wish you had told me all this so I could have talked to you and understood your fears better. I wish you had told me this instead of hiding from me so I could've maybe helped you deal with all this crap in your head. I'm not saying you would've changed, but maybe I could've told you this and you would have felt differently about the pregnancy- about the future. Christ, Suzanne. We just always seem to have missed chances between us."

"I know... I'm sorry."

"Do you remember our last morning together before the accident?" Blush. Yup, I remember, I nod. "Do you remember me asking you to always talk to me about all things *us*? Do you remember me saying I had no issue with you needing Mack, and needing to talk to Mack always, every single day- but I asked if you could, to talk to me about all the things 'us'?" Yes I remember, I nod again.

"Well, I can't keep waiting for you to talk to me. I just can't anymore. Actually, I *won't* do it anymore. After I wait, I always learn something new, something I could've handled had I known. But you never talk to me, and you always leave me waiting on the sideline for some tragedy to take you from me time and time again."

"I know, I'm sorry. I just don't know how to talk," I plead.

"You talk with Mack."

"Yes, but that's different. I'm not afraid of him leaving me. We're friends, best friends actually, and best friends put up with all the bad stuff *because* they're friends. And friends don't leave when they hear the bad stuff. Mack hasn't ever left me when I tell him all the bad stuff inside my head. Mack and Kayla almost split up because of me, but somehow he kept my friendship AND he worked it out with her. I trust him... NOT that I don't trust you, but it's just different. If I told you things, you could leave me and break my heart if you didn't understand the bad stuff in my head."

"And what about my heart?" Um... "Do you think loving you is easy, Suzanne?"

"No. I know it isn't," I mumble sadly.

"It *isn't* easy, but not because it's you like you clearly believe. Loving you is hard because you're sad some days and you don't tell me, or you're happy and you don't tell me, or you're okay and you don't tell me. I never know how you feel. And all I get is the fall out of everything you didn't tell me. That's what makes loving you so fucking hard. That's what I hate about all this between us. I feel like I'm alone in this weird, tragic, beautiful, exhausting relationship with you. I feel like I'm the only one who tries."

"I try. I swear I do! Every day I try."

"You try to NOT tell me and everyone else the bad things. And you try to be what you think me and everyone else want you to be. But it's not working. It NEVER worked. I don't even know what I want you to be with me anymore, because for all the love I have for you, I don't have a clue who you are."

"You DO know me, I swear," I yell desperately.

"That's the thing, Suzanne. I really don't know you because covering up and hiding, and being what you think I want, *isn't* what I want at all. Just give it to me- the good, the bad, the ugly and the beautiful. That's all I want from you. That's all I *need* from you so I can actually know you. So I can know *why* I want this love with you so badly. Because honestly Suzanne, I don't know why I want this love anymore. It makes no sense to me, and I don't think I can wait much longer for what we do or don't have to make sense to me. It's too hard and it's just too fucking exhausting all the time."

Reaching for him, he doesn't pull away, but he doesn't lean in closer either. Trying to get closer without falling from the counter, I pull at his arms. Pulling harder, I'm just desperate for him to understand but I have no words.

"Don't pull me closer Suzanne because you're afraid I'll leave. Pull me closer to you because you want me to stay."

"I am. I do!"

"What do you want? Tell me, Suzanne. Just say it."

"I want you in my life again. Yeah... again and again, I know. It's always again with me, but I don't know how to change that. I'll try though. I'll try to keep you this time."

"I don't want to be kept by you. I want to be loved by you because you love me. Not because you're afraid to *not* love me."

"I do! Oh god, Z... I wish I had the words for you. I wish I could explain you to me. I wish so many things, and you're always a part of it. You're always in the dreams and realities. I don't know what to say, and I don't know how to explain what I feel for you because there really aren't words I don't think, or at least I don't have them. Shit! I'm screwing this up again."

Shaking my head to clear it, I pull in a full breath as he waits for me in silence.

"Z, you're just so beautiful, and awesome, and sexy, and *normal*. And you're all I think about, all the time. YOU are who I love and miss. Even when we're not together you're all I think about. When I'm with Mack I'm thinking of you. When I'm having coffee alone in this apartment I'm thinking of you. I have no peace or happiness when I'm alone because my love for you is just always there without you. Z, you are the greatest thing that has ever happened to me. Shit, it's just *always* you. All the time." Ex-hale.

After a rather dramatic pause, we both stare at each other in silence. Holding my breath, I let my hands drop from his arms and simply wait for something from Z. Anything.

"Well, that was a pretty good start," he grins.

"Thank you. It was quite spontaneous," I huff on an exhale.

"I figured as much from the stunning effort, but horrendous execution," he winks.

And after another long pause, I'm sure Z must be thinking in circles. I've probably messed with his head so many times he's not as sharp as he used to be. Ooops. Giggle.

When he cocks an eyebrow at my giggle, I ask, "What happens now? What do you want to do?"

"I want to get out of this bathroom and lie down for a while beside you. I'm emotionally spent and heartbroken, and you look absolutely exhausted. Do you need a minute?"

"Yes. I just want to fix myself up, but I'm not taking a moment, Z. I'm not!"

"That's a start, Suzanne. I'll leave you to it then."

"Thank you."

And watching him leave, I feel kind of okay, like maybe hopeful or something until he suddenly turns to me with tortured, tear-filled eyes.

"Suzanne, this 'moment' of yours has been very long, but it's not our end. I told you I wouldn't let you end us on a moment and I meant it. This is not our end, love. You needed a moment and I gave it to you, but we will NEVER be over because you need a moment."

Oh! Whoooosh... That was so beautiful. And with that, Z smiles his gorgeous *real* smile at me.

"When you join me I'm going to kiss you Suzanne. A heart pounding- Holy SHIT- we can't even catch our breath- Kiss. So prepare yourself, love." Blush. Dammit. *Still?*

Grinning, I nod as he walks out the bathroom door.

Quickly bandaging myself up, brushing my teeth, dressing in my huge yoga pants and gigantic t-shirt, I'm ready for him.

I know there'll be no sex tonight which I'm not ready for anyway- physically or emotionally. But a Holy SHIT Kiss I'm definitely ready for.

Leaving the bathroom, I limp my way to the bed and just take him in. His pants are on but he's removed his shirt. Staring, he looks so calm and really just so perfect lying in my bed waiting for me.

In this silent moment I don't know what's going to happen with us in the future. But right now in THIS moment, I don't need to know what'll happen later because in this moment I'm happy enough to enjoy what I can with Z.

Crawling into my bed, Z moves me to his side and hugs me tightly. Lifting my face with his hand, his lips slowly greet mine. But slowly turns to not so slowly quickly, and he wasn't kidding! His kiss is deep and thorough and amazing at once.
I love, love, *love* kissing Z. I always remembered I loved his kiss, but the memory definitely pales in comparison. He is just so amazing.
Shit! I need to breathe. Gasp!
When Z lifts his head and smiles his charming 'I'm the man' smile with a raised 'told you so' eyebrow, I'm done. Laughing as he pulls me closer to him, I snuggle up and enjoy this tiny moment of humor and peace, in an otherwise tragic day.
Feeling the exhaustion settle in, he whispers, "Go to sleep, love. And I'll be here when you wake up."
"Okay..." And with no other words, I feel myself fall in love again... Again.

CHAPTER 38

FEBRUARY 6

Okay, so Z and I are inseparable now. Every night he sleeps at my decent apartment, or I sleep at his awesome apartment. But wherever we sleep is about locational convenience at this point, and that's about all.

Z and I go out for dinner. We go to the movies. We've been to the ballet (yawn) and to the opera (wow). We've gone shopping together, and we've stayed home and watched good and bad movies together. We went ice skating in New York at Rockefeller Center together, which I survived without landing on my ass. And we've had fun.

I haven't freaked out. I haven't been overcome with sadness or depression. I haven't had a moment of insanity. And I haven't needed a 'moment' from Z, ever.

Obviously, there have been moments of sadness, but the sadness didn't consume me as it did before. I've been truly happy, which is just so weird for me to experience for such an extended period of time. But I love my new happiness and I'm trying really hard to live with the happiness instead of fighting it out of fear.

Z and I seem to just live each day, together. We do *everything* together, and I know he's happy where we are too.

Not only does he tell me often of his happiness, but he shows me with sweet little notes, or private smiles between us when we're entertaining Mack and/or the Kaylas. And he held me tightly for hours when his other best friend Marty visited from New York at Christmas.

We even went to Mack and Kaylas for their huge New Year's Eve bash, and we kissed in the New Year together, beautifully.

We are together, and we're finally making our way slowly but steadily through the haze that was our first year and a half together.

Sometimes, it just seems so effortless between us. Sometimes, it's just so easy to forget all the bad stuff in our background. Sometimes, just a simple gesture like Z taking my hand and lifting my palm to his lips for a gentle kiss still takes my breath away. It's like we're survivors in this tragically beautiful little love of ours.

Z believes because we experienced so much between us at the start, there really are no learning curves, nor stepping stones to navigate around. Due to our awful past, Z believes there are no big new relationship struggles to overcome, because we've already lived them.

I mean really, how much worse could we possibly go through together? Toothpaste in the sink, or dishes on the counter become inconsequential when compared to the struggles of our past with each other.

Amazingly, Thomas is here with us, too. Z visits his grave often, I know. And I've even been a few times with him, but I still don't *feel* feel him as *my* lost child. It's sad, but I still remember the terrible loss as only Z's child, which is all I seem able to feel for Thomas.

And thankfully, Z doesn't resent my lack of maternal feelings toward Thomas. But rather he almost understands my lack of feeling given the time for me in which I was pregnant.

Z acknowledges there was just too much happening at the time for me to feel for the baby, too. But he believes had my life not been filled with mental and emotional upheavals; the trials, Marcus' death and the constant upset and shock I endured throughout my pregnancy, I may have been able to relax a little *about* the pregnancy. He thinks I was unable to embrace the pregnancy because I had to endure so much throughout it.

I'm not sure if that's true, and we'll never know for sure, so I let him believe that of me because I wish that was true of me as well.

Mack seems to think there is a time when the sorrow of the loss will hit me as my own, but I'm not sure of that either. I feel everything for my friends and for Z now, but Mack and I are unsure if these feelings have slowly come back to me, or if they've essentially *re*grown, after my slight personality change from the coma and from the PTA.

So feeling for Thomas may become my loss one day, or Thomas may stay a sympathetic pain for me, that is only lived as Z's pain. I really don't know what will happen.

But there is no pressure for another child between us. Z and I both know I'm not ready, and we both acknowledge I may never *be* ready to have a child, and Z's okay with that. Z admitted that he himself wasn't sure about ever having children in his future, but once I was pregnant, it was then that he wanted Thomas. So again, we'll see what the future holds.

I don't think I'll ever change my opinion on motherhood. I'm pretty sure I'll always be too afraid to bring a child into this world, though I'll admit I am curious as to what a baby between Z and I would be like.

Once, with a smile and a wink, Z once told me he is going to love me so *thoroughly,* I'll believe I'm good enough to do anything, motherhood included. But for now, we're okay with where we are together.

And because we don't know what exactly went wrong with Thomas and the pregnancy yet, the thought of another hypothetical child in the future still scares me to death.

There are theories, and explanations given, but we're waiting for one final chromosome test to give us our final answer. Again, we aren't sure what happened but Z's theory helps me through the wait. Most days I'm convinced there was just too much emotional upheaval for me, and sadly Thomas suffered the most.

I don't know why it happened so I really need to know *what* happened. I think I just need to understand what happened, so I can be one hundred percent sure I didn't do anything wrong to cause Thomas' death. I need to be sure, before I finally let go of my guilt and fear.

And finally, Z and I decided to move back to New York as soon as possible, so we've been apartment hunting together. Together, we're going to find a home that suits us. Together we're going to find the home that fits us, so we can live this complete new start that is our relationship now. After all the sadness and loss and missed opportunities we've experienced in our past, we want to find a home that is for just us.

God, I'm happy, and though admittedly I still get nervous about this happiness, I try to breathe through my fear of it every day. I talk to Z and I tell him the good, the bad, the ugly and the beautiful like he asked me to. I actually talk to him so there are no more surprises, or pieces to pick up after the fact. We talk to each other and we try to *hear* what is and what isn't being said when we listen. And I'm happy with this give and take. I'm very happy here with Z.

So, Z and I are together fully, and we have done everything together... except IT. And quite frankly I may lose my mind (again) if we don't.
We kiss heavily, and we even touch a little, but Christ! We haven't even come close to sex, and honestly, I'm dying here.
If I didn't know he loved me, and if I didn't see the huge 'evidence' of him wanting me when we snuggle up on the couch or lay together in bed, I may have freaked out by now. But I *have* seen it and I *do* know it. So what the hell is the problem?
Anyway, tonight is THE night. This is it. I'm protected again from pregnancy, and nothing should go wrong, well, in theory anyway. Tonight we ARE having sex.
But Z won't approach me for sex, so I have to approach him which is probably his very sweet, albeit, frustrating as hell way of making me tell him what I want and when I'm ready. How very thoughtful and loving and kind of him. He's waiting for me to be ready. He's waiting for me to be sure. He's so sweet. The jerk!

CHAPTER 39

Okay. I'm post-bath, shaved, smoothed, scented and groomed. I'm wearing a beautiful silk and lace floor-length gown in black, naturally. My hair is down and my make-up is light. I feel pretty, well, pretty with facial scars and a warped leg, but whatever. Argh...

Z doesn't seem to care about all my physical imperfections, so I've decided not to care about my physical ugliness tonight either.

Sitting on my bed waiting for Z, I find myself remembering our past. I remember how amazing he was to me. I remember how amazing the sex was between us. I remember everything he did and said to me, and I yearn for that intimacy between us again.

There is no one in this world I could want more, and there is no one in the world who could reach me so intimately and thoroughly as to wipe out my past sexual nightmares, because Z is it for me.

I know he'll be here any second but the wait is killing me. I'm not even anxious about this, rather kind of nervously excited.

I want this. I want to have sex with Z. I want to make love with the most amazing man (tied only to Mack) that I've ever known. I want this between us again because the memories, though lovely, are slowly fading in intensity. The memories are no longer enough to get me through the physical cravings I have for Z all day, every day.

Hurry the hell up!

When I hear him enter my apartment I'm practically bouncing on my bed. I even did the cheesy candle thing all over my apartment, leading him to me in my bedroom.

What the hell is he doing? *Crawling?* Oh my god... It's been forever since he opened the front door and I can't take the wait anymore.

"Z?" I call out anxiously.

When the door slowly opens, I exhale any nervous tension I felt. God, he's just so handsome and beautiful to me. It's still really unnerving at times how handsome he is, but tonight isn't about my insecurity or neurosis. Tonight is about hot and heavy sex with Z. Ooops. Nervous giggle.

"You look gorgeous, Suzanne," he says somewhat guarded.
"Thank you," I grin.
"Are you sure about this, Suzanne? I'm in NO rush."
"Well, *I* AM!" Wow. What a tramp. Ha!
"What do you want?" He seems to breathe into me.
"You," I blush.
Shaking his head he says, "Say the words Suzanne so I know what you want. I need the words, love, so I know you're with me."
"Um, I want to be with you. I want to have sex with you."
"Make love–"
"Yes, fine, make love. Z, I want you, okay? I'm ready, and I'm good. I'm *really* good."
"Last time, Suzanne... Are you sure?" He practically growls.
"Yesss..." I purr back.
Jumping, Z crosses the room to me so quickly I barely saw him move. Bending low and tackling me with a kiss, I'm pulled upwards by my arms until I'm standing in front of him.
Kissing me so hard my lips burn, I moan into his mouth. Jesus Christ! THIS is what I want.
"It's about goddamn time, Suzanne. I've been dying to touch you," he moans into my mouth.
"Then why didn't you?"
"You didn't tell me you were ready. Remember the rule? You tell me all things us, and until you do I'm not making any assumptions with you."

"How could you not see I wanted you?"
"I did see, but you didn't talk to me about it, so I couldn't proceed."

Placing my hands on his chest, I think I have to take the lead with this. Z still seems a little nervous or tentative with me. He seems unsure of this with me, so I'm going to have to take the lead. And I'm good with that until he's sure *I'm* sure.

Unbuttoning Z's shirt while tugging it from his slacks he stands so still, I'm anxious to undress him quickly. Unbuckling his belt and unzipping his pants, I wrap my arms around his waist and push them down to the floor.

Bending, I remove his socks when he raises each foot. Staring at his nearly naked body between us, he is just so dark and beautiful to me. Our contrast of pale and dark is stunning against one another.

When I tug down his boxers, his erection falls from his belly to stand straight out at me. Yup, it's still huge. Gulp.

"Well... hello there, Z. Miss me?" I ask with a stupid grin. What a loser I am, honestly.

Bursting out laughing, Z pulls me in for another kiss. "I've missed you horribly, Suzanne. And it's been so long since I did this I'm sure to go off quickly, but at least round two should be a worthwhile performance," he grins.

"Really...?"

"Of course. You *know* you were my last, Suzanne. And if you didn't know that, you're a moron."

Yes! God, I had hoped he hadn't slept with other women after me, but I never knew for sure.

Grinning, I tease, "Such sexy bedroom talk, Z. Is calling the girl a moron your usual way of seduction?"

"Nope. You get my really sexy lines. Are they working?"

By way of answer, I take him into my hand and begin a slow easy glide back and forth. When I touch and fondle him like I remember he likes, his sounds against my mouth are exactly what I like to remember.

When Z begins reaching for my breasts I push myself even closer to him. God, I want him to touch me anywhere. Everywhere. I have NEVER needed him as badly as I do right now.

"Please..." I beg against his lips.

Kissing me again, Z's hands start inching up my gown against my thighs. Lifting the dress, he pulls away from our kiss quickly to undress me.

Once I'm naked as well, Z kisses me again so slowly, teasing me with little nips on my lips and the wet glide of his tongue. But I don't want the slowness of his kiss. I need more. So throwing my arms around his neck I pull him closer to me, forcing the harder kiss I crave.

Moving me backward with a hand against my spine, Z lowers me to the bed while lifting me further into the middle of it. Following me on his knees, Z moves up my body until he's kissing my lips while settling in between my legs.

God, I've missed him. I've missed this. I've missed this thing only Z can give me- sex and love without brutality or fear.

"If I start to cry, it's not because I'm weirded-out, Z. It's because I'm happy, okay?"

"Okay," he smiles down at me with a nod. Huh. Talking isn't so bad. "What do you want, Suzanne? Tell me." Okay, well *this* talking is bad. Shit.

"Um... everything. All of it. The things you do with me that make me forget everything but us. The things you do to me that are everything I need from you."

"Okay," he whispers with a kiss.

And moving slowly, Z begins touching my breast as he kisses down my neck to the top of my chest. Moving down my body he finally takes my nipple into his mouth as his hand fondles me.

Sucking my nipple hard, I jump and moan. God, this feels good. Turning to my other nipple, Z's hand moves, tugging my nipple while sucking the other in deep. Moving against him, I find my legs widening further and my mind and body anxious for more.

When he moves lower, I dread him near my gross jiggly post-baby belly, but then he extends his tongue and licks me along the scar line, kissing me gently in the center of the scar. I don't actually feel his kiss but it's such a beautiful acknowledgement of what we both know happened to cause it, I'm suddenly okay with my newest scar.

Moving lower still, kissing down my torso, past my hips, past... *Argh...* where I wish he would stop, Z moves to my nasty left leg and kisses me slowly.

With a kind of reverence, his eyes are closed and he seems to be feeling all the damage on my leg but without any repulsion on his face. It's such a loving gesture from Z, I find myself exhaling any embarrassment and insecurity.

Lifting my leg behind my knee, he begins kissing up the inside of my thigh slowly. Oh, god! Here we go. This is what I'm dying for. This is what I want from ONLY Z.

"Please..." I moan as my hands clench the sheets.

Instantly my body jumps and my hips buck against his mouth when he takes me. Oh *god...*

When he places my left leg over his shoulder and palms my right thigh wider, I'm engulfed in the pleasure. Writhing, I can't even control my body. My body reacts all on its own as my mind blanks.

I hear myself moaning and I even hear myself begging. But I don't care and I can't stop. My body is taking what it needs from Z.

After forever, when everything inside me changes to that tight, hard, suspended feeling, I look down my body at Z and- Oh my GOD...

Looking up from what he's doing to me with his mouth and fingers still working me, everything between us pauses in a rush.

Z's eyes are open and intense, surrounded by eyelashes so dark and long just staring at my eyes. And suddenly this becomes the sexiest, most beautiful moment I've ever had in my life.

With my pale legs against his dark skin, and his beautiful dark eyes watching me, I exhale and give into the pleasure he's given me.

As my body arches and contorts, Z holds my thighs tightly against him as he continues to stare in my eyes while I scream out for him. Unable to break away, I feel Z's tongue still working me in my madness. Gasping and reaching for him, I scream again as the intensity becomes too much.

Stopping with his mouth still against me, we stare at each other in silence.

This is the greatest moment of intimacy I have ever known in my life. There is nothing between us in this moment. There is no past and no pain. There are no absences, nor moments taken. There is no embarrassment or fear. There is no one here but us. This is *by far* the greatest moment of my life.

So naturally, I start crying.

Crawling up my body with sweet kisses and little nips on my skin Z continues advancing until he takes my lips once again. And even as I taste myself on him, I don't care. I need his kiss so badly, I'm pulling and tugging him, wrapping my legs tightly around him while trying to consume him into me. I need him, forever. I need this beautiful tenderness and stunning affection with him, always.

When everything just stops I look up at Z. Holding my face in both his hands he is so silent and still. Looking at his eyes, I am reminded of the time when I didn't think I could ever have this again. Staring at his eyes I realize he is everything to me in every moment.

"I love you, Z," I whisper. "This is the Suzanne I want to be. This is who I want to be with you. THIS is me..."

With his eyes shining, he nods and kisses me slowly once again. So slow and thoroughly, Z kisses our past from us. It really is amazing how a good, deep kiss can make you forget... *everything*.

Resting his forearms on the bed on both sides of my body, we don't speak. Kissing, we begin the familiar move and retreat, back and forth motion as he slowly enters me.

When finally he enters me fully, we again seem to exhale into each other mouths. He may be large, and I may be damaged, but

our bodies fit together beautifully. *We* fit together beautifully.
  Moving, we take our time and enjoy the slow intimacy without pain or reservation. We move slow and deep, calm and intense. Together we each give and take in turn. Together we come back to each other through movement and love.
  And I can see it.
  This life we share is real and tangible. It fills the room with love but it makes no demands and it takes no effort. This love is open and free from all the struggle it took to get here. It doesn't hurt me and it doesn't intimidate me anymore. It's amazing to me in this place between us that we ever found our way to this moment together.

  After forever, Z moves backward to a kneeling position and lifts my body onto his thighs. Remembering the past, I smile as I see his eyes look between our bodies again. Staring, Z looks mesmerised by my body taking his into my own.
  Z's body is incredible in this moment. Seeing his stomach move and flex in rhythm with his thighs is simply amazing to watch. There is nothing damaged about him. His body is gorgeous, and his intensity shows all over his face as he alternates between staring at my eyes and at where our bodies join.
  Pulling me harder against him, I close my eyes and finally feel everything he can give me.
  After endless moments of my building pleasure, Z seems to beg, "I'm going to come, Suzanne. I'm sorry..."
  Teasing him, I open my eyes and smile. "Go ahead, Z. You said round 2 would be a worthwhile performance anyway, so I'm waiting for it," I grin.
  Laughing, Z leans over my body and kisses me again, pinching my butt underneath me, as he slowly slides his hand between us and does that touch-thing to me again.
  Instantly, I gasp and move desperately. My body starts moving on its own again, grinding against his hand while my fingers claw at the sheets. Pushing up against his body, I seem to find a desperate, pounding rhythm against him. Panting, I feel like I'm

losing my mind. But in a good way. The best way.

"Z...?"

"Come on, love. You're killing me," he groans against my mouth again. Ummmm...

And here it is. Ahhh... I'm gonna lose it. When my body locks down tight, I know I'm almost there. Come ON! Ahhh...

With a final touch- that amazing thing he does to me- it's over. My body releases on a gasp as my brain shuts down. Moving desperately, I seem to spasm and contort in his arms. Moving desperately, everything snaps tight around him inside me.

My body is weak, my heart is pounding, my throat is raw, but I'm so unbelievably happy I care about nothing but us in the moment.

Watching Z release inside me is still beautiful. I remembered it was, but the memories are never as stunning as the reality. With his eyes open, he stares at me as he releases everything he can inside me. Closing my eyes, I feel him moving fully inside me. His is inside me, completely.

Holding me close, I open my eyes again to Z staring down at me. Kissing my swollen lips softly, he exhales into my mouth as I breathe him in. And lifting my limp arms around his back, I pull him on top of me heavily. I want his weight on me. I want his body to surround me.

Exhaling, he asks, "Ready for round 2 to *really* blow your mind?" As he grins his 'I'm the man' smile.

Giggling, "Not a chance, Z. I know I'm going to need more Physio after that particular performance, and lots of rest and recovery."

"Fine... But when you wake up I'm going to show you what I can *really* do," he smirks.

"Okay..." I mumble in my near-unconsciousness with a kiss. Sighing my happiness into him, I'm going to remember this moment for eternity.

Feeling Z slide out of my body, he moves to my side and turns me into his chest. I know I'm sweaty and gross and I even smell like sex, but I don't care in this moment. I care about nothing but this moment between us.

This is where I want to be. Right here. Satiated and limp from pleasure with Z. Beautiful and whole from love with Z. I'm happy here.

"I love you, Suzanne," he whispers against my hair.

"I know..." I mumble.

Smiling as he pulls me tighter to him, I kiss his chest and finally exhale our past completely.

CHAPTER 40

APRIL 10

Last month, Z and I finally bought and moved into our new apartment in Manhattan, and I couldn't be happier. New York has been amazing and freeing, and just wonderful again. I'm glad we moved, and I'm glad living in New York makes everything feel easier for me, and for Z.

However, at this moment I'm back in Chicago. Subpoenaed to testify at my father's trial, sadly.

Exiting the bathroom of our hotel room, I'm dressed and as presentable as possible. My black slacks and blouse look lovely paired with a little jacket. My hair is left down, and my make-up is thick for coverage but natural looking. Covering up the reddish coloring on my scarred cheek is easier for me now. And though the texture remains, from a distance with enough make-up the scars are *barely* noticeable, even to me.

Looking at Z, I pause and just take him in. I think the novelty of having such a wonderful loving man has finally wore off, but the intensity of my love for him hasn't faded in the slightest. I can still look at him and picture first; all we went through to get here. Then second; forgive that horrendous journey while embracing this life of ours now.

Z and I are growing so comfortable with each other it's hard to believe we haven't been this way for years. We laugh and love, have crazy *off the charts sex,* and we talk about everything, always.

Z doesn't put up with my neurotic, crazy, insecure, Suzanne-shit, and he doesn't let me close down. And experiencing our real and honest loving relationship makes me not want to ever close down again. I love him too much to ever close myself off from him and our relationship, and I've promised us both, no matter what happens, I won't ever do it again.

Exhaling, I take Z in and thank whoever was gracing me the day I met him. I thank all the things that conspired against me early on because eventually they brought me to this place in my life with Z.

Sometimes when the darkness washes over me, Z still seems like too much light in my little world, but the moments we share of unfettered laughter and happiness make me hold onto him as best I can. And thankfully, he lets me hold onto him tightly.

Holding onto Z has gotten me through my mother's conviction of 46 different counts ranging from the horrendous to the mundane in contrast to what I actually went through as a child. And Z's love even helped me put to rest Marcus and his contribution to the lying nightmare that was our marriage of nearly 7 years.

With Z's help, I am not HER anymore.

"Are you ready, love?" Z asks in the hallway.

"Not at all, so let's go before I change my mind again," I pout.

Taking my hand, Z kisses me softly which effectively stops me from fleeing him. Backing me against the wall and bending down low, he forces eye contact with him. Giving me The Look he learned from Mack is totally unfair, but he waits for me to speak anyway.

"I'm okay. I'm just scared of seeing him. But I'm not scared he'll hurt me. I know he can't. Um, I'm just scared it's going to screw me up and I don't want to be screwed up because I've been so great for a while now. And I don't want to be screwed up right now. Well, ever again actually, because I feel really happy now Z." There. I spoke.

"You've been *amazing* for a while now. And we'll all be there with you, and nothing and no *one* is going to hurt you today. Only you can hurt yourself today with the dark memories, Suzanne. Just remember, if you need a moment look for me or Mack or

Glenn, and we'll get you your moment. But please let us know *before* any pain or panic sets in, okay?"

"Okay..." I nod, as I pull away from him and walk toward the hotel door.

*****

This is going to suck today. My father's trial has been going on forever, but strangely it was his Defense team who called me to testify first, not the Prosecution. So today is the shitty day.

After speaking with Mack about what will probably happen, he seems to think my father's team is going to get me to admit that my mother was the true monster throughout the abuse instead of my father. Their angle is going to be establishing that my father never *really* hurt me, which he didn't- *physically*.

The problem his team is going to have is when I tell the Jurors and courtroom how badly he did actually hurt me by obeying my mother, and by preparing me for the abuses. And mostly, for never protecting me when I was young *from* all the abuse my mother and the men inflicted on me, as most fathers would or should have.

I'm lucky my mother's trial was many months ago when I was still too screwed up to go to court, because it allowed me the opportunity for the closed testimony I gave. But this testimony will be in the open courtroom, in front of all the people, and Reporters, and my friends who are waiting for me to finish this. And though both Defense and Prosecuting teams are likely to go easy on me, I know some questions will still rip me apart.

It's inevitable.
Gratefully, the Prosecution team and D.A. Rose have promised to make the Defense toe the line, if you will. They said actual, horrific details aren't necessary from me because those have already been established, though not by them rather by my father and his Defense Attorneys.
It's strange, but my father has admitted to everything- ALL of it. I know he only did it to set up the angle of the abuse and depravity as instigated by my mother. I know he's only trying to show how brutal SHE was so he doesn't look so bad or guilty to the Jurors. I know he wants to look rather like a victim of hers as well, instead of the perpetrator of the violence against me. I know that's his angle, but as the real true victim in my sadly horrific childhood it totally pisses me off.
Regardless of what they claim, he was a monster too. He knows it, I know it. Every single person who has ever heard or reported my case knows it. I guess he's just hoping for a little sentencing leniency by playing the secondary abuser in my horrific childhood.

When we arrive at the courthouse a few Reporters take pictures of me again. Flanked by Z and Mack I'm used to the picture taking now but I still hate it. Though I was a minor at the time of the abuse, and though the Prosecution team and D.A. Rose have never released my name publicly, early on my mother told everyone who I was- lying through her teeth about her poor, insane, whacked-out daughter who was a liar. By trying to protect herself, she outed me to the public.
And so she got her final punishment toward me after all. Everyone knows who I am, and everyone knows what happened to me. I have no secrets anymore which is painfully embarrassing to me, but again, not something I can fight or control. This reality of mine just is, and so I continue to breathe my way through it.

Inside, the Kaylas are waiting by the side conference room for me. Taking them in, I smile and breathe through all the crap in my head. Seeing my father is going to be hard, but with these two Kaylas in the courtroom I know I can do it. Actually, they'd probably kick my ass if I didn't do it, so I greet them with a smile as I hug them tight.

"Thanks for-"

"Don't start your shit, Suzanne. We're here because we love you and this is going to be a shit day, so we're here for you. The end. No tears. No drama. Marty, Dr. Cobb, and Dr. Robinson are here as well. There is no one else here today who counts in your life, but us. Okay?"

"Okay," I smile at her words. Chicago Kayla is still a right to the point, cut you off at the knees, sexy as hell, awesome woman. And though we're getting closer by the day, I find I still miss her constant in-my-faceness terribly.

"You have a little group of seven to cheer you on, okay? Just look at us if it gets bad, and Kayla and I will kick some ass for you afterward." Looking at Kayla I believe she and her New York tough will actually do it too. "Plus, we're all hooking up at Kayla's tonight and we're gonna get shit-faced." Grinning, I nod again.

When the door opens to one of the Prosecuting Aides, I'm told I'm to be called in the next 15 minutes. Suddenly sitting on a bench hard, Mack and Z instantly sit beside me, each taking a hand, though neither says the lame platitudes that would probably drive me mental right now.

I'm scared and nauseous, and my head wants to fill with all the horrors of my past, but I'm fighting my way through it.

When Mack abruptly rises from the bench, he tugs at my hand and mumbles to Z, "Just give us a minute."

When Mack and I walk to the back of the conference room, he stops me and kind of eases me against the wall as he stands in front of me.

Looking at Mack my stomach is suddenly in knots. Mack doesn't look good. Actually, he looks upset or maybe sad, I'm not sure which.

"Mack, what's wrong?" I whisper as I grab for his shirt. Not speaking, Mack hold my hands in his own against his chest.

"Sorry I'm scaring you, I'm not trying to. Ah, I just wanted to talk to you for a second before you testify."

"What's wrong, Mack?" I beg.

"Nothing at all. I want you to know I absolutely adore you. I think everything about you is wonderful, and I love you very much."

"*Okay... But?*"

"There's no but. Today is going to be hard, and I want you to know how much I love you, and how *proud* I am of you. Your strength is undeniable this time. And though I've said it before, I think you need to hear how amazing you are to me, Suzanne. You and I have gone through so much together, and I wanted to remind you how special you are to me, in case things become very dark today and you forget later how much you mean to me, and how wonderful you really are. That's all, Suzanne. There's nothing bad, I promise."

When Mack pauses, I glance around him to Z and Kayla sitting on the bench together. Smiling at me, Kayla is holding Z's hand, nodding at me. I think she can hear Mack and she must agree with him. Thank god. I really needed to hear that because I'm absolutely terrified of today.

Exhaling, I wrap my arms around Mack as tight as I can.

"Thank you Mack for saying that. Thank you again, for everything, always. I love you so, so much," I say as I try to let go of all the bad in my head for a minute.

Pulling away from me, Mack bends down low, kisses my forehead, and wipes the tears from my cheeks. Watching me closely as always, he hugs me again, tugs me to his side and walks us back to Z.

But before I can sit back down, Mack whispers, "You're such a doll, Suzanne," into my ear, making me smile again.

*****

Show time.
Walking down the aisle to the front bench, I just can't look at my father. I thought I wanted to see him, but now I know I can't. I'm not ready to see if he's still the handsome, distinguished-looking man of my past. I'm not ready to see him as the dad I always begged to love me. I don't want to instantly become the young Suzanne who begged for his love, and cried for his affection.
 I am not HER anymore. And I don't need his love anymore. I have this life and this love now. This is who I turned out to
be. This is me now; good, bad, ugly and beautiful.

"Please state your name for the record," comes a distant voice.
 Shaking my head and clearing my throat, I lean in *way* too close to the microphone like an idiot, as I look at Z. Grinning, he nods his head 'go for it'.
 "Um... I'm Suzanne Zinfandel."
 And when I see the identical look of shock on the Kaylas faces as their heads whip toward Z, I start giggling like a Crazy.

Ooops... Z and I are in deep shit tonight.

THIS is me...

ABOUT THE AUTHOR

Sarah Walker lives in Canada with her American husband and their son.

After attending McMaster University as an English major, Sarah began her career as an Office Administrator, polar-opposite to her studies, until the summer of 2011.
Suddenly finding herself able, Sarah picked up her iPad and a dark, beautiful story was born.

Sarah Ann Walker can be found on Facebook, Goodreads.com, and Twitter.

Made in the USA
Charleston, SC
05 October 2013